PERIL ENVISIONED

F.C. Wayne

First and most important, I humbly thank my Lord and Savior Jesus Christ. To Him, all I owe! May He be greatly honored and glorified by the story told here. Danny, you were an early spiritual leader in my life, and I thank you for helping me to not stray too far off the path that God has intended for my life. Brother Bob, you were my mentor in ministry. Please know that words cannot express the thanks I have for all the wisdom and knowledge you have shared with me, yet I try. Thanks so much, my dear brother in Christ.

To the local church that built me, I express great appreciation to you. I will always have a soft spot in my heart for those who stood behind me as I grew in Christ and in my call to ministry. Your love for me and the challenges you gave me made me the minister and man of God I am today. Thank you all and may you be richly blessed. I owe a special thanks to Linda and Jan, sisters in Christ. Thanks so much for lending me your eyes. Mountain Man, you helped bring a key element to this story. Thanks. I owe my mother a special thanks. You listened to me on numerous occasions as I ranted about the difficulties facing me as I wrote this story. Thanks, Mama. I love you. Finally, much thanks to my wife for having patience with me as I pursued ministry. I love you very much, more than you can know.

"I've written speeches, sermons and poetry but nothing longer than a short story. I'm, by no means, a professional writer, but this story was so incredible; it had to be told...now"

F.C. WAYNE

CONTENTS

CHAPTER 1

John, Liz and Nathan

"So, tell me again why you don't believe in God," said Nathan as he took a seat in his friend's classroom.

"Are we really gonna have this conversation again?" John asked. "You know, you're not the most devout person on Earth either. Besides, I don't know how many times I can give you the same answer. I don't believe in anything smarter than I am."

"Give me a break, John! For goodness' sake, you teach in a high school. This isn't Harvard or Yale, and there's quite a few who are smarter than you. I've had dogs that were smarter than you."

Nathan and John had known each other for as long as they could remember. Their ages were within days of each other, and both believed their long-time friendship started in the hospital nursery. They shared a true friendship, one that lasted through the trials of time. They were in kindergarten together, first grade together, second grade together, and on and on. When they got to high school, though there was a greater chance of separation, they always found some way to be in the same classes. This same pattern of togetherness lasted through college as well.

John was the son of a doctor, so naturally, his parents wanted him to follow in dad's footsteps. Nathan, on the other hand, was the son of parents who were both teachers. Nathan's passion to be a teacher was far greater than John's passion to be a doctor. As both approached decisions about college, each knew they might have to part ways, but the bonds of friendship would keep them together. John and Nathan enrolled in the same education program at the same university. Except for just a few semesters, they, again, managed to stay in the same classes.

Despite the fact they were a troublesome pair, being the pranksters they were, they both excelled in the academic arena. Their gift for learning was so special that their teachers often overlooked the trickery just to have them in their classes. Yes, they were a handful, and if there was a joke to be played, they did it ten times better than anyone else could. Over the years, they shared many hours of detention together. They were inseparable!

Their paths led them to teach in the same school just minutes from their hometown, first as elementary education teachers, then as high school teachers. John, having an analytical mind, went into teaching science and math. Nathan, on the other hand, liked everything history, so he went that route as a teacher.

Their assigned classrooms were in different wings of the school, but they usually found time to see the other at some point in the day. As always, their favorite time was right after the last bell, dismissal of all students.

Nathan fought his way up the hall, going against a steady stream of students whose only passion was to get out of school. He, after all, knew what it was like to be a student in those very hallways. He and John had roamed those same corridors not so long ago. He couldn't help but to think about days past when his own priority at the end of the day was getting home. To be honest, he knew things hadn't changed that much. He still wanted to get home, but this time, as an employee of the school.

He and John had figured out within the first few days of their teaching experience exactly what kind of toll they had on their former teachers. Being educators themselves, they were now on the receiving end of much of the same student melodrama they once caused. They were getting a taste of their own medicine, but still, they loved where they were in life.

Being in the hallways and classrooms served as a constant reminder to them of where they had been and where they still were. It was a sensory delight for them to be in the school of their youth. The smell of the hallways was the same, a smell of school with a hint of lunchroom, Friday pizza, to be exact. The walls were white, with brightly colored stripes, with an occasional Freddy Falcon splashed up on the wall.

Freddy Falcon, the school mascot, hadn't changed that much over the years. Although during winning seasons, Nathan thought for sure the bird had a sneer on his beak. Joining Freddy on the wall, were obligatory posters for anti-drug campaigns, anti-bully campaigns and a few campaigns he had never heard of before. Sometimes it seemed the amount of policy and goings on he and John had to keep up with were mind-numbing. It was all part of being a teacher; he knew and accepted it.

As he approached John's classroom, students were still filing out. He had forgotten John's last period of the day was an Algebra I class. How lucky, Nathan thoughtfully celebrated, his own last period of the day was a study hall which allowed him great flexibility in end-of-the-day scheduling. He noticed someone, probably a student, had placed a small smiling face sticker on the nameplate mounted on the right side of John's classroom door frame. How odd, he considered, that their names were affixed next to the very classrooms in which they were educated.

Standing by the door waiting for all the students to depart, he noticed a new poster on the wall, one for student council elections. The smile on his face quickly disappeared as he remembered he was voluntold to be the faculty chair for this year's council. He wanted to serve the school but not necessarily in the capacity of a student council faculty representative.

It was a well-known fact the students hated the idea of having a faculty member on the council, but he had only himself and John to blame. Years ago, the two of them had started a smear campaign to do away with a faculty member being on the council. The stench of that long-ago smear campaign was still alive and well, but none of the students knew who started it. Some of the older teachers from Nathan and John's school days remembered very clearly who started it, and they wouldn't let either of them live it down. Nathan speculated his not-so-voluntary service was punishment for a bad deed from long ago. Now, the smiles and snickers during the faculty staff meeting, where he was forced into servitude, made total sense.

"Man, I totally forgot about that," he said as his eyes locked onto the poster.

Maybe, he could trick, or better yet, blackmail John into filling the council seat for him. Surely there was some skeleton in his friend's closet that he could weaponize. An excuse wouldn't get him off the Council seat, but a blackmailed friend could.

"Way to go, Mr. Seabolt," someone yelled behind him.

He turned around to see one of his own students placing books into her locker, more than likely ones she needed for homework that night. For just an instant, he thought about how students over the years had not changed. Homework was a curse and something students preferred to avoid if possible. Nathan remembered ditching homework books in his locker at the end of the day in hopes of getting the work done in morning study hall. The practice caught up to him several times and earned him numerous hours in detention for failure to complete assignments. If he could go back, he would still procrastinate with his work, perhaps just do it a little smarter.

"What are you talking about, Sarah?"

She shut her locker, snapped the lock in place with a click, swung around and gazed at him with a cocked head. For all Nathan knew, she may have been reading his mind with the piercing intelligence most of the students claimed they had.

"You volunteered to be the faculty chair for the new

student council. We look forward to working with you and running our ideas by you."

Of course, she literally meant "running their ideas by him." They would mention the idea as they passed the voting cards in front of his face. Nathan knew he was just an unwilling participant in the student body government, merely a formality that kept the seat warm. As much of the student council saw it, the faculty chair was just a road block for progress.

Sarah was a well-known, vocal leader for the student body over the last three years of her brilliant high school career. Now, as a senior, she felt it was her time to be student body president. In fact, many of her peers and teachers felt if anyone could go on to be an attorney or even a US President, Sarah would be that person. Like those before her, she just knew there was so much she could change. She also knew the faculty chair was there to advise against really "great" student ideas.

"Oh, glad I can be on the council this year," said Nathan as he tapped the poster on the wall.

Sarah grinned, chuckled and ran off down the hallway to catch her bus. Nathan wondered if she knew how the principal snared him into membership on the council. Did she just catch him in a lie? Was the cat out of the bag? Was there a traitor and spy among the senior teachers? He scratched his head, shrugged his shoulders and headed into John's classroom.

"I heard that whole conversation," John said. "Don't even think about trying to put this off on me. I'm sure I'll get my due punishment next year."

"I don't really know what you're talking about, John."

"Whatever!"

◆ ◆ ◆

On a spiritual level, John and Nathan were nearly in the same boat. John's father was a doctor and a man of science, and by his own reasoning, a man who did not believe in God. If John's father couldn't see it, hear it, smell it, feel it or test it, then there's no way it could be real for him. John had never heard his father refer to himself as an atheist but guessed that's what he was. There were many conversations in the Reidy household, from family and friends alike, about whether God was real, but science always came into play as the answer-all for religious concerns. John suspected his mother may have had a heart for God but could possibly see how his father suppressed her thoughts on the matter. John, although at times questioning the existence of God, sided with his father on the reality of a supreme being. If John was not going to be a doctor, his dad thought, then his son would at least be a man of science and math. Because of the influences of his father and his education, John shied away from any belief in any kind of god.

Nathan, on the other hand, admitted he was an agnostic, that he didn't know if God existed. He didn't know, but he also didn't make any real attempts to determine if God was real either. Nathan's parents were both Christians, and they tried to raise him to be the same, but he continued to drift away from things of a spiritual nature, especially after he went off to college. He had not totally closed his mind to the idea of a supreme and almighty God, but he just needed proof. Every time he went home to see his parents, they would shove the family Bible in his face and say, "there's all the proof you need." Those visits usually ended in arguments where he headed out the door to go find his comforting friend, John.

Continuing his playful attack on John's unbelief, Nathan boldly stated, "I'll tell you what, John, if there's a Heaven, I'm closer to it than you are."

"What do you mean by that?" asked John with a hint of sarcasm.

Nathan shifted in the desk/chair combo and leaned forward on his forearms. He sat in these same seats as a student and saw they weren't any more comfortable for an adult. He was almost positive one of the seats in John's classroom had "NATE" written on the bottom of the desktop in large, bold permanent ink. John had dared him to commit the act of school graffiti while the teacher was in the classroom and while he sat on the front row in plain view. It was difficult, but he did it and the teacher never caught him. In those days, dares didn't go unanswered because they were a matter of pride among school age males.

John sat down behind his teacher's desk with crossed arms. Strangely, both felt the awkwardness of the seating arrangement. John, the "teacher," seated in front of Nathan, the "student." They both got up at the same time and sat back down on top of their desks, a more rebellious thing for them to do together.

"Well, think about it. If there is a God, then I'm closer to Him. You flat out don't believe in God, but I, on the other hand, can at least acknowledge there may be a God. Therefore, I'm closer to Heaven than you are."

"First of all, there is no God. Second, there is no Heaven. Third, you either believe or you don't. Fourth, this is a stupid conversation."

"I guess we're just brothers in unbelief, aren't we?" asked Nathan with a smirk.

"Whatever," retorted John in annoyance.

The two of them really liked annoying each other, especially if the act somehow made one look better than the other. Public annoyance was even more fun for them and the more embarrassing the better. Both John and Nathan had lost girlfriends to these kinds of hijinks. One good joke against the other in public and their girlfriend would take off, usually to the waiting arms of the one playing the gag. Conversations about God were particularly annoying for John, so naturally, they were a great topic for Nathan. Neither of them realized just how serious these conversations were.

"No, really, man, what if the Christians are right? John, what if there really is a God? What if there really is a Jesus? What if there really is a Savior? What if there really is a Heaven and a Hell?"

John came to his feet and walked over to the whiteboard and erased some math formulas he had written earlier that day. After he erased them, he remembered how he would need them for his next class. He concluded the reason for erasing the formulas was to escape the conversation he and Nathan were having, to take his attention off the nonsense spewing from his friend's overactive mouth. The problem was that lately, John couldn't tell if Nathan was sincere about religious talk or merely joking around. Maybe a change in subject was in order.

"Nate, how's your student council thing going?" He tried to hide his annoyance but knew his friend could see right through him.

Returning to his seat, Nathan said, "Oh, it's going

great! Wonderful relationship with the students! They all love me."

John turned around with a grin stretching ear to ear and replied, "That's totally what I got from your conversation with Sarah. Good luck with that."

Just then, the final bell of the day rang. It was the last call for all students to get on a bus or get in a car to leave. Fortunately, it also meant teachers could prepare to go home, a great benefit of employment with the schoolboard. Sometimes the upper echelon of school management made days longer by having staff meetings. The current regime was especially bad about calling assemblies, often to discuss the need for additional meetings.

Several years ago, the school changed leadership in the vice principal position, a move not popular among the staff at all. It seemed very convenient for the schoolboard to make the change. Some of the staff surmised the change was to allow better flow of new standards and rules from the schoolboard, some of which would make their jobs as teachers much harder. Things were rapidly changing in schools, things which seemed to make it more difficult to give the students a quality education. Sometimes, to some of the educators, the constant flow of changes seemed like a behind-the-scenes attempt to dumb down the students of America.

Suddenly, John and Nathan shifted their attention to a figure darkening the doorway of the classroom. Their eyes, like radar-guided missiles, locked onto her at the same time. Nothing short of a natural disaster could have pulled their eyes from her.

There she was, Elizabeth Prater, quite possibly an angel from the Heavens above. She was beautiful, having a petite, slender frame covered with pale alabaster skin. Her shoulder-length, gorgeous red hair, envied by those who longed for perfectly red hair, framed her baby-like face. Tiny little freckles dotted the tops of her cheeks adjacent to beautiful blue eyes. As she normally did, she wore an ankle length floral dress which accentuated the curves of her body.

Elizabeth was a target for every living, breathing, unmarried male in the school, including faculty and students alike. If there were an award for most gorgeous, cutest or best all-around good-looking female, she would have won it repeatedly. Male students flocked to her during registration just so they could be in one of her classes.

Some of the most unlikely student candidates took Art Appreciation to be near her. She would quickly figure out which students had little interest in the subject when grades started suddenly dropping. Some of them hung in to the end, but others she dismissed from the class simply because it was a waste of their time and hers. She didn't enjoy being the object of affection for so many and never played into it.

Elizabeth was not a local as John and Nathan like to call them. She was born and raised out of state. She also went to school and college in another state. She was hundreds of miles from a part of small-town America she called home. Her only hope of getting out of that tiny town to make something of herself was to attend college on a full scholarship designed to build teachers. Upon graduation from the teaching program, managers would place people like Elizabeth where needed, a draw back for a free ride to college. Unfortunately, she had very little choice where the administrators of the program would send her. At best, she could pick only a geographical region, but it was a small price to pay for getting out of small-town America.

Nevertheless, she was now teaching in the same school as John and Nathan, which she didn't mind at all. Often, she would think about the places she could have landed, conceivably some run-down school in a big city. Here, she was near the country lifestyle she grew up with, not far from some of the most beautiful mountains in the world, and best of all, she was away from the congestions of an asphalt jungle. Thankfully, her assignment was a lot like home.

Small-town America was home for her. As she saw it, home was truly where she hung her hat, if, of course, home had a population under 30,000 people. When she left for college, the population of her town was still under 800 people with no growth in site. Large companies or corporations were not beating down mile markers to get into her area.

It was a small town with a small grocery, a small hardware store, a small school and a reputation for absolutely nothing. The nearest superstore was about 20 miles away, so people learned to use what was in the local mom and pop store. To support themselves, most residents grew food in their own fields and back yards. If they needed something built, they had carpenters. If they needed something welded, they had welders. If they needed something sewn, the town had seamstresses but certainly not one producing New York or Milan fashion. If they needed a doctor, they had one of those too, one who would occasionally make house calls.

The small population had, for the most part,

learned to be self-sustaining. The small-town life her community enjoyed brought about familiarity among all the residents, so much so there were no strangers among them.

Each person in the town drew together by one common thread, church. While amenities were few for residents to enjoy or to occupy their time, they did have two very loving churches, both of which were on the same street. Since the vast amount of the population couldn't fit into just one church on Sunday mornings, the congregation decided to build another to better accommodate the crowds. Seemingly, that was the only expansion the town ever needed.

The townies had two churches and two Sunday morning services, each linked together by a common love for Christ. Fellowship meals, mission fundraisers, prayer meetings: almost every social event in the town was somehow related to the church. If Elizabeth was going to miss anything after leaving her community, she knew it would be her church and the fellowship she shared with nearly an entire town of believers.

Most of the children in the town grew up to do factory work several miles away, or they continued a tradition of farming. In her small municipality, a new job seeker entering the dog-eat-dog labor force had little else to choose from.

Elizabeth would often sit in her upstairs room gazing into the night sky at all the stars, thinking the town might become well-known because she came from there. It was a childish fantasy, but she knew she didn't want to be a farmer or a factory worker. Instead, she wanted something more for her life. Sadly, she also knew that "something more" would take her away from home, but she was prepared for that eventuality. Still, she was secure enough in her relationship with Christ that she knew wherever she ended up, He would be there with her. Currently, "wherever" was standing in the doorway of John's classroom, watching both he and Nathan gaze at her.

"Hey, boys, are you awake or do I need to come back later?" she asked as they continued to stare at her.

John and Nathan painfully broke their eyes away from Elizabeth and gave each other that look that said, "she is so pretty." John, however, broke into a grin that said, "Yep, and she's all mine." Nathan's gawk faded as he sat up and crossed his arms on the desktop.

John remembered the first time he saw her. To ease her transition, the principal appointed John as Elizabeth's sponsor before she arrived. A sponsor, the program managers thought, would be a great way to help a teacher shift into a new school and community. Honestly, when John heard he was to be a sponsor, his immediate thought was one of disinterest and disappointment. Why did he have to be a baby sitter for some stuffy art teacher who would be more at home in a museum with other stuffy art teachers? His appointment as sponsor was supposed to be totally random, but he felt the truth of the matter was that it was about revenge for his early days in the school. Payback was a definite possibility.

John had driven nearly 50 miles to the nearest airport to pick up Elizabeth. He forgot to ask for a description and daydreamed about what she looked like. He remembered every art teacher he ever had and pictured some weird combination of all of them but quickly shook off the image before it burned into his head. He was hoping to be pleasantly surprised but counted on being dreadfully disappointed.

The two had never talked before and had certainly never seen each other. John only had a name, a flight number and a time of arrival. He didn't want to be one of those people standing in the airport holding up a sign with a name on it because he felt that was a bit cheesy. He could stand at the gate repeating her name to every single female passenger getting off the plane but realized that would be annoying.

In hindsight, he wished he had made the effort to get in touch with her to at least find out what she was wearing or to get a general description. Surely someone had her phone number, e-mail address or snail mail address. He wasn't sure people still sent letters as a form of communication. There was nothing he could do about it now except to deal with it and figure out which passenger was her.

John stood outside the gate with others awaiting arrivals. Passengers slowly started to file off the plane. No stuffy art teachers so far. But wait, who was that? A beautiful redhead, wearing a flowing, floral-pattern dress was walking toward the gate. He was mesmerized. She was so stunning, gliding toward the crowded gate like an angel. He watched as she walked through the gate past the waiting crowd. She didn't look like a stuffy art teacher at all. There was no way she could be the one he was looking for. Did he have time to go get her phone number before identifying and retrieving his school's new teacher from the plane?

Ignoring the rest of the passengers deboarding the

aircraft, John began to follow the redhead. Tracking. Tracking. Target acquired. Locked in! He pushed his way past onlookers, all the while, trying not to lose sight of her. Quickening his pace, he managed to get ahead of her a little. *Time to make your move, Romeo.* John popped through the throng of humanity just in front of the redhead, gently bumping into her, causing her to drop her carry-on. She let out a gasp of surprise.

Reaching down to pick up the bag, John said, "I'm so sorry…didn't mean to run into you like that." For just a moment, the two of them locked eyes as if some secret romantic fire burned within them.

Of course, the small collision was no accident. It was a tactic John and Nathan had used before with limited success. Winning the girl was somewhat of a game to them, and there was no way John was going to let this one get away. She was just too pretty.

As he gingerly placed the bag strap back on her shoulder, he looked directly into her hypnotic blue eyes. He hoped she wasn't on to his dating trickery.

"I should really be more careful, shouldn't I?" asked John awkwardly.

She grinned as if she could tell where the conversation was going. "It's okay," she said, "there's a lot of people around here. It would be hard not to have an occasional accident."

"Can I ask you a question?" John chirped, grinning back.

He could smell her, but interestingly, she smelled like apples and not perfume. He didn't mind it at all, and it just made him want to get to know her even more. He was absolutely captivated by her.

"Do I have to give you an answer?" She sounded

playfully sarcastic, as if this weren't her first rodeo either.

"I'm sorry. You're just so pretty. It's gonna take dynamite to blast my eyes off you."

John wasn't kidding, and he felt himself going beyond the playful girl hunt he and Nathan frequently participated in. To be honest, he felt like asking for her hand in marriage–right then and there in the middle of the airport.

"Let me guess, Sport. You want my phone number?"

"You are an absolute angel!"

"So, you believe in angels?"

"Not really, but if you were an angel, you must have fallen straight out of Heaven."

John felt something he hadn't in a long time, something like love at first sight. He knew, however, he wouldn't be able to convince her this was anything other than an attempt to get a date.

"Not only is that corny," she said, "but it's really old."

She paused for a moment, then switched her bag to the other shoulder. She might need to use it as a weapon to get away from this guy. Still, she would play his game a little longer.

"Can I have your phone number?" he begged.

He laid on his best puppy dog eyes and gave her his cutest "poor little boy" voice. It had to work. He was relying on his nonverbal, girl-getting communication skills now more than ever. She couldn't get away.

"Are you a stalker or something?" she asked with scrunched eyebrows.

John couldn't tell if she was serious or just being playful. He was never that great at reading women, especially smart ones. Nathan, on the other hand, was a master at this little game and the verbal and nonverbal jousts that came with it. If Nathan had been there, they would already be married and have children by now. *Don't blow this, John!* he thought.

"Could I at least have your name?" He winced at his overplayed hand. *Way to go, John! Every woman loves a man who shows desperation.*

"Wow! You're not good at this at all," she said, slightly shaking her head.

She took the bag off her shoulder and let it drop at her feet, maybe a silent signal for John to take it easy. She put her hand out for John and said, "I'm Elizabeth, Elizabeth Prater. My friends call me Liz."

This beautiful specimen of a woman was the stuffy art teacher? Ignoring the fact that he had been wooing his future coworker, John lightly grasped her hand and shook it. He was unable to break the gaze he had on her beautiful face and opened his mouth to say something, but no words emerged. No woman had ever had this kind of effect on him. The awkwardness of the situation shifted into overdrive.

She pulled his hand close and inched her face closer to his. "Hey, you in there somewhere, Sport?"

"I'm sorry. I'm John, John Reidy," he said clenching his teeth in embarrassment. "You wouldn't happen to be an art teacher, would you?"

"Yes, I would be an art teacher, waiting to be picked up by a fella with the same name as yours," she said smiling.

The cat was out of the bag. John's face confessed to both disappointment and embarrassment at once. He shifted on his feet and scratched his head thinking about what to say next. It was shaky ground and he knew it. *Oh, my goodness,* he thought, *I'm gonna be working with this person.* He may have inadvertently set the stage for a forever tense working relationship. He may have to seek another job. He had to find a way out of the situation.

Elizabeth, clasped her other hand on top of John's, recognizing his obvious predicament. He was acting like a fumbling high school freshman who had managed to lock in a date with the senior prom queen.

"John," she said, "I knew it was you. I was able to get in touch with Mr. Henry, your principal. He told me you would be the one picking me up today. He told me what you looked like, although I'm pleasantly surprised you look better than he described. He also warned me about you and your little friend. What's his name? Nathan?"

A ray of hope! John thought. *Maybe this wasn't quite so embarrassing. Wait a minute! She said the principal had warned her about Nathan and I! What other juicy bits of info does she know about me? What exaggerated falsehoods and malicious rumors has she heard?* He sensed she was extending an olive branch to him by taking the edge off his self-inflicted embarrassment. He gently let go of her soft-skinned hand. To prove chivalry wasn't dead and regain critical brownie points, he reached down and picked up her carry-on.

"Mr. Henry knows me all too well. He was my principal when I went to that very same high school. I thought I almost drove him away several times, but I think the school board keeps him there to watch or torment me. I haven't figured out which. Anyway, did he have anything positive to say about me?"

They began walking toward the baggage claim. What kind of conversation could they have that would even approach normalcy? They could talk about the weather. Then again, he thought a discussion of the climate might be too cheesy and make his humiliation painfully obvious.

"I don't recall him saying anything positive, but that doesn't matter because I prefer sizing up people for myself," she said, chuckling a bit, still seeing John's tension.

"Well, what do you think so far? Have I redeemed myself?"

Maybe he was playing his cards too fast again. Perhaps he should just let it go for now and pick up the pieces later. *Drop it? Yes? No?*

"Believe it or not, I kind of like you. You're a little socially inept, but even that's cute," she said.

"Would your significant other approve of your saying that to me?" John blurted out without thinking.

After he said it, he realized what he had done. *John, could you be a bigger idiot?* He couldn't have made his interest in her more obvious. He had played the "do you have a boyfriend card" much too early. He certainly wasn't helping himself in developing any kind of long-term relationship with this woman who quite possibly could be his soulmate.

"Would your significant other approve of your hitting on me?"

It was a counter attack. What did she mean and how should he answer her? Maybe she was trying to probe into his life to figure out if he was single. John was not very good with these kinds of dating games. If he were being totally honest with himself, he was horrible at it.

They both stopped their walk toward the baggage claim and looked at each other with a suspicious gaze.

Perhaps they were both playing the same complicated game and didn't realize it. John had to say something to break the silence. *Think fast,* thought John, *and don't blow it with another dumb comment.*

"If I didn't know better," said John, "I might think we were already on our first date."

"Do you normally pick up your dates at the airport?" Elizabeth started walking again, and John quickly ran after her like a lost puppy.

"So, this is a date?" asked John as he caught up to her.

She glanced at him with a smile. John liked where this little adventure was going, and little did he know, she liked it too. Both were feeling a rare, instantaneous, and altogether, hard to explain attraction. They stopped at the baggage carousel, looking at each other, speaking in wordless messages of reassuring gestures. He noticed her normally pale cheeks had turned a cool red and wondered if he was also blushing. A bell rang and a warning light flashed as the baggage carousel sprang to life, spewing out luggage from some unseen holding area.

"I've got two red suitcases coming off this contraption. Good thing you're here because I'm about to make you useful."

John smiled. Her first suitcase came spinning around. They both locked eyes on it and grabbed for the handle at the same time. They giggled and lifted the suitcase off the conveyor, hand in hand. It was the beginning of a beautiful relationship. Despite his misgivings about sponsorship, John and Elizabeth hit it off from the start.

◆ ◆ ◆

After reminiscing, John turned to look Elizabeth right in the face, not realizing he was still wearing the triumphant grin he had just given Nathan. She leaned against the door frame and crossed her arms defiantly, tilting her head and raising her eyebrows as if to tell John she knew exactly what that grin was all about.

She had known them for a while now and had begun to figure out their child-like games. Sometimes she thought their antics were cute, but other times, she simply grew tired of them. When she was alone with John, he seemed perfectly fine, a wonderful example of a gentlemen. He had come so far since their initial blunder of a meeting at the airport. She noticed, unfortunately, when John and Nathan were together, they acted like a couple of children. She completely understood why their former teachers still talked about them as a pair of hooligans.

"What? I didn't do anything," said John as he crossed his arms in equal defiance, realizing he had been caught in one of his childish competitions.

Nathan sat there enjoying the show. He wasn't actively trying to break them up, but he was definitely available to console her in the event of the tragic end of her relationship with John. What are friends for, right? Regardless, Nathan loved watching his buddy squirm, especially when it involved a girl. It was John's fault for falling for her anyway. Elizabeth was much too good for John but a perfect fit for himself.

She tilted her head to the opposite side and asked, "We still going out tonight, Sport?"

For some reason or another, the name "Sport" had stuck, but thankfully, Elizabeth was the only one who called him that. It could have been a pet name for a former boyfriend. It could have been what she previously called someone she didn't care for. He had never asked why she called him by that obscure name but figured someday, when she was ready, she would tell him. He chalked it up as a Lizism.

"I wouldn't miss it for the world, Liz," he said as he stepped in front of Nathan, blocking his view of her.

Nathan peeked around John. This, he knew, was part of the game. Nathan knew John was concerned he might say something that would embarrass him in front of his beautiful girlfriend.

"Hi Liz," he said, throwing a short wave into the air, as he peeked around John.

"Hi, Nathan."

She leaned over enough to see him behind John. She assumed John's blocking tactic was to prevent Nathan from making a pass at her. Realistically, Nathan had already made an advance toward her. He did it the day John brought her home from the airport, and incredibly, right in front of him! However, just as the principal had warned her about John, he had also warned her about Nathan.

She could sense something mischievous about them when they were together, an unusual sensation of not knowing what in the world was going on. Funny, she didn't feel it when she and John were alone, just when the three of them were in the same room together. The fact was that Elizabeth was nothing like John or Nathan.

She was the perfect teacher that administration often dreamed of. As a student, she was punctual, always getting assignments in, always getting good grades and was never in trouble. These qualities carried forward into her adult teaching career. However, after the senior staff of the school learned she and John were dating, she would occasionally draw stares from those who knew John and Nathan all too well.

She couldn't help but to think they thought she was wasting her time with him. As she saw it, maybe if they would take the time to get to know John like she had, they would have a different opinion of him. Then again, they might not. Perhaps they were thinking the same thing about her. But she was a strong, independent woman, and no person on earth was going to make up her mind for her.

She gave the two prank-happy men a critical look, spun around quickly with a slight lofting of her dress and then started to walk away. John, entranced by her movement, watched with a pleasant smile on his face. She seemed to float out the door, as light as a feather caught in a gentle breeze.

"See you later, gentlemen," she yelled back as she walked down the hall.

John followed her out the door and watched her glide down the polished tile hallway. *Man, she is so beautiful,* he thought. If he only had a girl like her in high school, he would have been the envy of every other guy. He snapped around to see Nathan leaning forward, peeking around the door frame, straining to watch Elizabeth walk down the hall. Oh, yeah, she was gorgeous.

John reentered the classroom and pushed Nathan back into the chair while saying, "Can I help you with something?"

It was a game to them, but sometimes the play went too far. John knew there was an outside chance his buddy would someday end up with Liz, but he certainly wasn't going to let that happen if he had anything to do with it. Nathan could sense the anger welling up in his friend, so he brought his eyes back to him and away from Liz.

"Sorry, man, but she's amazingly beautiful," said Nathan as he put his hands up in front of his chest, an act of submission.

John glanced back into the now empty hallway and said dreamily, "She is, isn't she?"

"Hey, Sport, you know she's a Christian, right?" Nathan asked as John continued to stare into the hallway.

Nathan snapped a finger, bringing John back to reality.

"What? Were you saying something useful?" John asked.

"I said, you know she's a Christian, right?"

"Yeah, I know. So what?"

Nathan hit a raw nerve. In the time John and Elizabeth had been dating, religion had come up several times. Right off the bat, Elizabeth had made very clear to John she was a Christian and that his being an atheist made her uncomfortable. When she brought up the subject, usually triggered by some seemingly unrelated topic, John was quick to shut her down. Of course, he changed the conversation politely and tactfully, but he knew someday they were going to need to have that discussion. He was dreading it too, even though she seemed very willing and happy to talk about all aspects of her Christianity.

"So what?" Nathan repeated. "Christians have this thing they call 'unequally yoked' and they're pretty serious about it."

Nathan was agnostic, but he had studied portions of various religions on occasion which, he knew, contributed to his own lack of faith in any one deity. He realized he had no call to talk to John about religion of any sort but enjoyed the challenge of getting on his friend's nerves.

"What does that mean?" John asked as he walked back to his chair behind the desk.

He quickly sat down in case he needed the desk as a barrier between his clenched fists and Nathan's head. They would never hit each other, but having a barrier between them during tense moments was a safeguard.

"It means, my little atheist friend, a Christian will not partner themselves with a nonbeliever. I'm surprised she's even dating you. As I understand it, she would never marry you."

John unclenched his fists long enough to grab the chair arms tightly, as if grabbing an anchor to keep him in the chair. He was getting angry, but he liked his friend too much to assault him. He released his grip and replied the only way he knew how.

"Well, my little agnostic friend, I guess that rules you out too."

Unlike John, Nathan had considered that fact, but he wanted to keep hope alive. To have Elizabeth Prater meant that John wouldn't have her, but what was a little friendly competition for a woman between two friends?

"But you know what?"

"What, Nathan?"

Nathan eased himself out of the desk and walked over to the classroom door, peering down the hallway as if Elizabeth were still there. The whole conversation was suddenly making him feel very uneasy, but he knew John was giving him an out. He was trying to end the talk peacefully.

"I," Nathan said proudly, "would convert just to marry her."

"Well," said John crossing his arms across his chest, "lucky for me she doesn't date idiots. Besides, she has a copy of my house key. That sounds pretty permanent to me."

Nathan fell back against the door frame and clenched his fist over his chest. "Oh, that hurts right to the heart, Sport."

Great, John thought, *there was someone else calling him "Sport."* Maybe if he could get Liz to stop calling him by that name, it wouldn't go any further with Nathan. *Whatever!* He liked Elizabeth too much to even ask her to desist. He couldn't risk an argument that might cause a rift to develop between them. A pet name was a small sacrifice for a wonderful relationship with a magnificent woman.

John stood and started gathering books and folders off the top of his desk. The day was over and it was time for him to go home. Nathan, on the other hand, was stuck at school.

"Nathan, don't you have a meeting to get to?" he asked as he stuffed the day's work into his satchel.

"What are you talking about? It's time to go home, you jerk."

John grabbed the keys out of his pocket, being sure to jingle them for Nathan to hear. Smiling, he casually walked up to Nathan who was still standing against the door frame.

Before walking out the door, he jabbed an index

finger at Nathan's chest and said, "You're late for your student council meeting, Mister Faculty Chairman."

Nathan snapped back at John. "What?"

"Yeah, your meeting started about 10 minutes ago, but lucky for you, it's just a long hop across campus to Hazelwood's classroom. I don't know if you remember Hazelwood or not, but he's a stickler for being on time. It sure would be embarrassing for the faculty chair to be shut out of the classroom."

Nathan tipped his head back against the door frame and closed his eyes in disbelief. *That stupid meeting!* He had forgotten all about it! Yes, his conversation about Liz made him late, but the thrill was totally worth it.

After an agonizing sigh, Nathan snapped his head back forward, shot a reciprocal finger into John's chest and growled, "You knew about that meeting the whole time! Why didn't you say something?"

"Well, I didn't want to interrupt Liz. You know, just being polite."

Nathan pushed John out of the way and took off running down the hallway. He knew as he was frantically running toward the meeting, John was getting a great deal of satisfaction out of his predicament. Somehow, he almost always seemed to end up on the losing side of a joke. *Stupid student council meeting!*

"Hey," John yelled after him, "you know you shouldn't be running in the halls!"

Shouting back as he ran, Nathan responded sarcastically, "I hope you have a wonderful date with Liz. Tell her I'm sorry I couldn't be there."

John stood there listening for a moment as the running footsteps trailed off in the distance. He kind of wished he could be sitting in Hazelwood's class as Nathan came beating on the door to get in. How sweet it would be to hear Hazelwood scold a fellow teacher for being late.

The two of them would never shake the fact that the older teachers still thought of them as students. *Maybe Hazelwood will send Nathan to the principal's office to get a hall pass or something. That would be wonderful,* thought John with glaring satisfaction. However fun and hilarious the thought of torturing his friend might be, he had something much better to do. It was time to go home and get ready for his date with Liz.

CHAPTER 2

The Storm

As John walked across the nearly empty faculty parking lot, he could see the glimmering shine from his cherry, lifted, 1990 Chevy S-10. The flame red paint made it stand out in the low evening sun which was peeking through dark ominous clouds in the distance.

He had worked for years doing odd jobs around town to pay for his sweet ride and the modifications thereof. He remembered the conversation with his father about getting the truck. Like many other kids that age, John hinted to his father that he buy, or at least, help him buy the truck.

When his dad said, "Johnny, I have no problem buying that truck for you," his excitement level shot through the roof.

"Really?" John asked, salivating at the idea of vehicle ownership, wondering if his father was actually going to buy this chariot for him.

Then his father said, "You got it. Just give me the money, and I'll go right over and buy that truck for you."

John was crushed and humiliated, but his dad's joke was motivation enough to work the several jobs needed to pay for the truck outright. When he was finally able to make the purchase, he could say he did it without his father's help. He knew that made him a man!

The S-10 he so affectionately called "Little Red" was his very first vehicle. In his student days, the truck was his high school and college transportation. As a teacher, it now served as his adult ride. He could easily remember, in the not-so-distant past, his truck sitting just two lots over in the student parking section.

His Chevy wasn't a girl magnet by any stretch of the imagination. It was his girl substitute and his real love, but he would never tell Liz that. The hours and dollars spent rebuilding the engine, transmission and dented body panels were too numerous to count, but as a bragging point, he wished he had tracked all the time and money invested.

The exterior of the truck turned out nice, but the interior left much to be desired. He remembered picking Liz up at the airport in his old truck. As she walked up to it, she mentioned how nice it looked for its age. Unfortunately, the second John opened the door for her, nice turned to disappointment.

Several times he had asked himself how he could have such a sweet looking truck on the outside but still have such a ratty interior. He had every intention of restoring the interior too but had to divert money from the S-10 fund to the "place to live" fund. Someday he would finish it for sure. For now, Liz would have to keep sitting on the camo blanket John had lovingly placed on the tattered seat just for her.

John hopped up into the lifted truck, closed the door

and rolled down the window. The lack of power options on the truck didn't bother him at all, but instead, added to the character of Little Red.

A warm wind blew through the open window and drew his attention to the skies just beyond the school. The clouds were growing darker as they began to cover the sun that once illuminated the paint on his truck. A storm was coming. Thunder cracked in the distance as he slid the key into the ignition and turned it, causing the truck to roar to life.

The sound of Little Red's powerful engine covered the claps of thunder from the approaching storm. It was amazing how a good set of exhaust pipes and a retrofit V8 engine sounded. He wiggled the worn shift lever into first gear and made sure to lay down on the gas as he pulled out of the lot. It was important for Nathan to hear him leaving, even in the neighboring building. The act of powering out of the lot was John's way of saying he was going home and to remind Nathan he was stuck in a meeting.

The school was situated between John's small cottage home, town and Nathan's larger, two-bedroom bachelor pad. Turning left out of the school gates would take him home, while turning right would lead toward town and eventually Nathan's house. As the crow flew, John's house was close to the school, certainly within walking distance on a good day, that is, if he wanted to walk through Indian Forest.

John roared down State Road 9 trying to beat the oncoming rain. He often thought how silly it was that he had to drive several miles out of the way, around a protected forest, to get to his house. If he could just cut through the forest, he could be to work, Nathan's house or town in no time at all. The trip around the forest added ten minutes to what could be a two-minute drive. However, John understood the protected nature of Indian Forest and the ancient burial grounds in its midst. Thus, he was willing to forgo the shorter trip.

As John drove down State Road 9, commonly called the Runway because of its long stretches without curves, he noticed ahead of him a hard rain was rapidly replacing the mirage-like heat rising off the pavement. The road, already darkened by trees on both sides, was growing more ominous as the foul weather moved closer. The storm he was trying to beat was swiftly converging into his path. Very quickly the rain began beating down on Little Red and blowing into the truck's open window. Intermingled in the rain were small hail stones which pelted John's arm with hundreds of needle-like stings.

"Dang! That hurts," he said as he started rolling up the window.

Knowing he was driving through a rain and hail mix, he let off what some would call his lead foot. Truly, if gone unchecked, John tended to go a little faster than he needed to. But, driving through the hail, he knew he had better slow down drastically. To be perfectly honest, safety in a storm had nothing to do with his reduction in speed. He, without regard to his own wellbeing, simply had to save his truck's paint from the bombardment of damaging hail stones.

The rain and hail were causing a loud roar inside the confined cab of Little Red and slowing down didn't seem to be making much of a difference. The sheer volume of rain he was suddenly emersed in was unlike anything he had ever seen before. Even on high, his overtaxed windshield wipers were unable to keep up with the large volume of water and hail. Except for speeding, John was a good driver, but nobody was good enough to drive in near zero visibility.

He eased off the accelerator and slowly pulled Little Red off the road onto the wide shoulders of the Runway. No other cars were on the road, probably because their drivers were smart enough to stay home or at work until the storm passed. After making sure he was completely off the road, John wiggled the shift lever into neutral, set the parking brake but left the engine running.

John and his insurance premiums certainly didn't need a collision, so getting off the road made perfect sense. He did think it was a little odd that no other cars were out. Surely the storm caught others by surprise too; but as far as he could see, the roads were empty. It was as if he were suddenly alone in the world.

He felt rather spooked because the road was growing darker as the clouds rolled over him. He was also a bit surprised at how fast the storm came up. Dusk seemed to be coming early that day, even though the fading of the sun was still a few hours away.

Though on high, his wipers could only clear the windshield for about a second. He tried to take quick peeks between wiper swipes but saw little. With every pass of the wiper blades, he could see his headlights shine out in front of the truck, illuminating the hail that now looked like a light snow on the ground.

Unfortunately, the windows were starting to fog up which further reduced his view and added to the eeriness and ferocity of his surroundings. He was starting to feel like the main character in a horror movie and expected a blood-soaked hand to slap up against his window at any moment. His prevailing thought was that the storm needed to hurry and pass so he could safely get back on the road and headed home. He had a date to get ready for, if he survived. Though he would never admit it to any living soul, he was scared.

The storm rapidly grew more bizarre than any other weather he could remember in all his years on Earth. Lightning began to flash across the sky in colors of bright green and brilliant purple. He hadn't seen lightning like that since riding out a hurricane with Nathan in a South Carolina beach bungalow. Still, this lightning, with its brilliantly wicked flashes, was far worse. Thinking back, riding out a hurricane was a stupid decision, but this vicious meteorological anomaly left him no choice but to wait. The thunder cracked wildly, like a million whips in the hands of their masters.

Suddenly, something caught his eye. He wasn't sure at first, but he thought he saw something in front of the truck. John frantically started wiping the fog off the windshield with his shirtsleeve. *There it was again!* He knew he saw something, but what was it? He concentrated, timing his own eye blinks with the wiper swipes, hoping to see it again.

"What in the world was that?" he whispered to himself.

John remembered he didn't have power locks. He had left his doors unlocked for the convenience of any ax murderer who happened to be around. With split-second timing he bolted across the cab and locked the passenger door. Then like a retracting spring, he shot back across to lock the driver side door. He knew he should have done that earlier, but what did he care? After the quick distraction of unsecure doors and potential murder, he again focused his attention between the quick oscillations of the wiper blades, trying to see whatever was in front of his truck.

Again, he saw it! But were his eyes just playing tricks on him or was it some natural pixilation caused by the water on the glass? He inched closer to the windshield trying to reduce the distance between his eyes and the object he thought he was seeing. John didn't want to get too close, as the windshield was probably the only thing between life and death.

The thought of this thing suddenly being right in front of his face reminded him of several horror movies he had seen, but now, he was living a nightmare in his own film. He feared the unknown and this object or being, whatever it was, ranked high on the list of terrifying, unidentified things. His forehead hit the glass next to the rear-view mirror. The rapid swaying from the wipers was starting to make him feel nauseous, further distracting his ability to identify the oddity standing in front of his truck.

John backed away from the glass, closed his eyes and took a couple deep breaths, hoping to calm his nerves and stomach. He eased forward to the glass, covering his mouth so as not to fog the glass again. *There!* He saw it! John jumped back in the seat, left hand gripping the steering wheel, as his mind raced to process what he had just seen.

A figure of some kind? Like a man? A man covered in white? A man, maybe, standing in front of Little Red with something in his hand? A weapon, possibly a machete? It was closer now as evidenced by the headlights causing its white covering to glow through the water covered glass. What could he do? He began to frantically look around the cab for anything he could use as a weapon.

He remembered a hunting knife kept under the driver's seat. Trying to keep his eyes on the white glow, he quickly reached down to grab for the knife. It wasn't there! Nathan had it! Why did he let Nathan borrow that knife? He ripped the glove box open and began tearing through its contents, looking for something he could use as a weapon.

There had to be something. Owner's manual, no! Registration, no! Salt packets, no! Restaurant napkins, no! Ah, a screwdriver, yes! Now what? Where were the cops when he needed them? His rapid breathing was, once again, causing the windshield to fog, but he could see it was still there, glowing white.

Is this how it's really gonna end, he wondered, *murdered on a state road just miles from my house?* The adrenaline flowing in his body was now giving him surges of energy and the fight instinct to survive. For a moment, John sat there holding the screwdriver in his tightly clenched fist, looking at the white glow through the water-flooded windshield.

If this thing wanted him, it was going to get a fight. Surely the adrenaline driving through his body could teach him how to fight for survival in the next few seconds. He had gotten into squabbles in school but nothing in which his very life was on the line. If only he could have taken Karate or some other combative sport when he was younger. Whatever he was going to do, he felt he needed to do it fast. Maybe the chemicals rushing through his body were now beginning to make decisions for him. *Just don't do something stupid, John!*

Decision made! Growling like a wild animal, John jumped in his seat, nearly bumping his head on Little Red's roof. Almost without thought, he unlocked the driver side door and threw the door open, nearly ripping the handle off in the process. The situation reminded him of one of those stories he had seen on television, where someone had barely beaten deadly and overwhelming odds. This was going to be his survival story! Yes, he would live another day! Seemingly, instantly, he was outside his truck, standing behind the door, pelted by heavy rain and freezing hail.

Automatically, his eyes targeted the area in front of the truck where the thing was standing and he instinctively yelled as loud as he could. "Come and get it, you..."

It was gone! No wait, it was behind him now! He spun around stabbing with the screwdriver in case something was there. No, not there either. John looked to the front again. Still, nothing there. Keeping the screwdriver at the ready in his right hand, he wiped the rain off his face quickly, making sure not to keep his eyes covered too long. Suddenly he remembered urban legends from long ago of people hiding under vehicles, slicing ankles with knives. John jumped back from Little Red, landing in the road but keeping the screwdriver pointed forward. Quickly, he peeked under the truck. Nothing there! Where was this thing? His mind searched through infinite possibilities. He looked to the front of the truck and then to the back where the taillights created an ominous red glow on the hail. Nothing! John eased around the back of the truck in hopes of catching the thing hiding on the other side of

Little Red. Nothing!

"What's going on here?" he asked.

The tension in his right hand eased, but his mind wanted to remain alert. He moved cautiously back around to the driver side of the truck, letting the screwdriver drop down to his thigh. Whatever the thing was, it was gone now. He stood there in the road looking at the headlight bathed area in front of his truck, listening to the ocean wave-like roar the rain and hail created around him. The rain was drenching him and the hail was stinging his skin like thousands of needles, but strangely, it was the farthermost thing from his mind.

"Hey, buddy, you okay?"

John whipped around to see an old man sitting in another truck on the other side of the road, staring through a half-down window. *Real observant, John. How could you let this guy sneak up on you like that?* He stood there in the road for what seemed like minutes, feeling the chill of the rain and hail, not paying any attention to the motorist who was obviously concerned for him.

What should he do? Should he act like nothing happened? Should he ask if the guy saw it too? Should he even mention it? What if he was just seeing things? Would this guy think he was crazy? He had a screwdriver in his hand, so maybe this helpful, curious motorist would believe he was having mechanical problems. John's mind was still recovering from the adrenaline rush, and he was finding it difficult to answer, to even talk at all.

The man asked again, "You okay?"

"Oh, uh, I thought I heard something come loose on my truck. Just checking to make sure something didn't fall off. Say, did you see, uh, that, uh…"

John's voice trailed off and his body began to shake as the adrenaline high faded. Biting cold shrouded his trembling body, worsening as the rain penetrated his clothing. If possible, he had to carefully check his words.

"See what?"

The man looked puzzled and started to ease his window back up as if he, himself, thought he might be looking into the eyes of a crazed lunatic. If John had been in his right mind, he probably would have taken offense to the stranger's defensive posture.

"Oh, nothing. Uh, thanks for checking on me. I appreciate it."

"Better get in out of the rain, friend. You're gonna get sick," the man said as he started to pull away slowly, looking around as if suspicious of John's intentions.

"I know. Thanks again," he said as he waved off the concerned driver.

Great, he thought, *now someone in town is gonna think I'm crazy.* John didn't recognize the man driving the truck, but that didn't mean the kind fellow didn't know him. John quickly jumped back into Little Red, closed the door and locked up.

For a moment, thoughts of craziness worked their way through his head, maybe trying to make sense of what just happened. It was still a mystery, a darn scary one too. As he was wiping the haze off the windshield, he half expected the white thing to show up again, but it didn't. The rain, hail, lightning and thunder quickly stopped, just as fast as it had started. *Weird,* he thought.

He sat there in Little Red, watching the sunlight melt its way back through the clouds, creating beams of light on the road ahead. The wet pavement immediately began to dry as the cool rains drifted away, forming an eerie fog gliding just above the ground. John watched as a car approached him, slicing through the mist like a knife. One of the sunbeams rested on Little Red, causing a steamy apparition to drift up and off the custom painted hood to the sky.

He couldn't help but to think about this experience being one of the most unusual occurrences of his life. He had seen some weird things, but nothing like what had just happened. He could try to tell Nathan. No, just to be mean, Nathan would say he was screaming for attention. Liz was a good listener. He could tell her. No, she would find some way to put a religious spin on it, maybe that the Lord was trying to tell him something. He knew he probably shouldn't say anything to anyone.

He sat there for a moment with his hands resting on the bottom of the steering wheel, unable to process what had just happened. The vibration of Little Red's engine through the wheel suddenly reminded him he was in a running vehicle on the side of the road going nowhere. It was time to get going again, especially before another motorist stopped and asked if he was okay.

John put his truck in gear, checked the mirror again and eased back out onto the road. Again, he almost expected to see the figure in white in one of his mirrors, but there was nothing. It was time to get on home. He wasn't going to say anything about what just happened to anyone, ever!

The rest of his trip home was uneventful. He noticed, however, adding to the unusual nature of his trek, that it had not rained at all on or near his street.

Perhaps only he was meant to experience the storm. Was it possible that there really was no storm? *No, don't be ridiculous,* he thought. He caught himself thinking about the idea repeatedly but knew he had to stop doing so.

John pulled on to Liberty Street where his home was located a few blocks away. This time more than any other, he felt so good driving down his street. He was among familiar houses, cars and people. He felt like a soldier returning from a hard-fought battle where life and limb were at risk. Again, he just couldn't shake what he had just gone through. Thankfully, he was almost home.

The houses on John's street were all similar, built as parts of a cookie cutter expansion neighborhood of the 1950s. Most of them, but not his, were two-story cottage style homes with large front porches and decorative woodwork. His house lacked the second story, a feature he didn't miss. Most of the houses were white, the result of a long-forgotten neighborhood covenant from years past. John's house, however, was green, favored by Liz because the difference in color made it easy to find.

Most of the highly manicured lawns were small, giving way to sidewalks cutting through the neighborhood, possibly a design to give it that "small-town America" feel. All the driveways were narrow, and very few of the properties had garages, so most of the cars sat parked next to the home. John didn't mind the absence of a garage because he enjoyed showing off his truck.

Home was just a couple hundred comforting feet away. *Home sweet home,* he thought. Thank goodness because what should have been a simple trip had just about worn him out. If he didn't have a date with Liz that evening, he would probably stay home and unwind by binge watching something on the idiot box.

Thinking about the extraordinarily bad experience that lingered in his mind, he suddenly realized he was going to have to go back down the Runway to get to Liz's house. He knew she was totally worth it. He knew he might be afraid–actually, very afraid. That could be, but Liz was the prize. As he eased Little Red into the driveway, he noticed his neighbors, the Atchleys, were sitting out on their front porch.

This was one of those times when he wished his driveway was on the opposite side of his house, away from the Atchley's front porch. Instead, his driveway sat awkwardly close to their porch, a place where they spent much of their time. Only a short hedge and their driveway separated John from his neighbors. He knew the Atchleys were very good people, about as nice as they could be. He knew they were the kind of people who would give to someone the shirt off their backs. The problem, at least for him, was that they were devout Christians with this crazy idea that he needed salvation from something.

He knew they were Christians when he bought the house a couple years before but really didn't give it that much thought. Sure, he knew. Their Faith was evident from the large white cross in their yard just weeks before Easter when he was driving through looking for a place to live. Later, John shrugged off their putting a large sign on their front lawn at Christmas which read, "Jesus is the Reason for the Season." All he had to do was maintain separation, which could be difficult at times.

They could stay on their side of the hedge, and he would stay on his. John's big worry was they, knowing he was an atheist, would try to somehow convert him to Christianity. There were times during awkward conversations when they seemed to want to talk about their Faith with him, but he would always change the subject or make up something that suddenly required his immediate attention.

Liz, on the other hand, got along with the Atchleys from the first time she met them. It was almost as if their common bond of Christianity tied them together somehow. John thought it was weird how Liz, seemingly with no introductions at all, hit it off with the Atchleys as though they were family. Now, this relationship between his neighbors and his girlfriend made things even more awkward at times. Perhaps it was just a matter of time before they ganged up to convert him. For that reason, when he was with Liz, John would quickly usher her into and out of the house. He had a feeling Liz knew exactly what he was doing, that he was trying to isolate her from the Atchleys. To be completely honest, John tried his best to avoid having Liz at his house at all, simply because he wanted to avoid a Christian confrontation between him and his girlfriend or him and his neighbors.

For a moment, contemplating excuses, John sat there in Little Red trying to look busy, as if answering texts on his phone. There were no texts, but instead, just a whole lot of anxiety over potential conflict with his neighbors. He knew he needed to get it over with. Enough of wasting precious time he could spend with Liz later!

He unlatched the door and pushed it open, listening

to the loud squeal the hinges made as they resisted opening. He knew he needed to fix the obnoxious noise, but he always put it off. The simple act of opening a door on the truck announced his presence to every neighbor within a hundred-foot radius, including the Atchleys.

As he slithered out of the truck, John attempted to avoid direct eye contact with the Atchleys, who were sitting on their porch drinking lemonade. *They were probably waiting on me,* he thought. He could see them in his peripheral vision and they were, in fact, watching his every move.

"Come on. Sip your lemonade. Don't say anything," he muttered to himself.

So far so good. No, wait! The trashcan was still out. Yes, that stupid trashcan was still out! With eyes on target, he walked quickly to the end of the driveway to retrieve the container.

As he walked the obnoxiously odorous waste receptacle back to the side of the house, Mr. Atchley yelled out to him, "Hey neighbor, want to come over for dinner tonight?"

They got me. He failed and they succeeded. *Wait a minute,* he thought; *what's the big deal? Of course, I've got a date with Liz later this evening. Ah, the perfect excuse.* Anticipating, he knew he had to deflect the next request, which was going to be to bring her over for dinner as well. *Oh,* he agonized, *that would be the perfect storm of Christian annoyance. John, think!* He gave no thought to the inappropriate act of using the girl he loved as an excuse.

"Oh, I can't Mr. Atchley. I'm meeting Liz in town tonight for dinner, but I appreciate the offer."

Quick, change the subject before he comes up with

something else. Hurry, move the conversation to another topic, before he thinks of another way to invade your life.

"What did ya'll think of that big storm that rolled through?" he said pointing in the direction of State Road 9 and the school where he worked.

"No storm here, John."

"But, did you not...?" John's words faded away.

Mr. Atchley turned to his wife sitting in the rocking chair next to him and asked, "Mother, did you see a storm today?"

"No, dear, it's been clear and sunny all day," she said as she and Mr. Atchley sipped homemade lemonade.

John, feeling a bit confused, turned to look in the direction he was pointing and asked, "How could it not have stormed? Look at those dark clouds over..."

Again, his words trailed off as he took notice of the clear blue skies in the direction of the school and State Road 9. There was no evidence of rain or storm clouds anywhere. It was just a few minutes ago that he had experienced the storm of the century and the thing on the road. *What in the world is going on?* he thought. The storm was moving toward town so he should, at least, be able to see dark clouds there, but no, nothing but clear blue skies. At the minimum, his neighbors should have been able to hear the thunder.

"Didn't you hear the thunder?"

They looked at one another, shook their heads and she said, "No thunder, John. You feeling okay?"

"Uh, I'm, uh gonna be late for my date with Liz, if I don't get ready. I'll, uh, see ya'll later."

Still in disbelief, he grabbed the trashcan and began pulling it back to the side of the house. Did the Atchleys think he was crazy, maybe under the influence of Satan or something? John kept his head down until he got out of eyesight of the neighbors, not seeing the couple wave at him as he pulled the noisy can by them.

He arrived at the side of his house next to the kitchen door where the trashcan normally sat, then spun the container around so that the lid opened toward the house. As he maneuvered the filthy can into place, the wide top brushed up against his shirt, leaving a large stain. Unfortunately, it was the same shirt he had planned on wearing on his date with Liz. *Great,* he thought, *I've got garbage slime on the shirt I was gonna wear.* John attempted to brush off the dark tinge of grime left by the lid but only made it worse, spreading it into a larger, more visible spot.

Something isn't right, he thought, touching his shirt. As he brushed at the soiled fabric, he noticed it was bone dry. Oddly, his slacks were also dry. Not more than a few minutes ago, the rain and hail from a crazy storm had soaked every inch of his clothing. He rubbed his chest, gazing at the dry material of his shirt and pants. His once-sopping-wet shoes and socks were dry too. He ran his hand through his sandy blond, but dry, hair. Pulling his hand in front of his face, he detected no moisture at all. He knew in his heart something unusual was happening. He playfully considered going over to ask the Atchleys to wake him up but knew that would only contribute to the madness. *That's it! For sure, it's just temporary insanity.*

He turned to walk back around to the front entrance of the house but quickly veered back toward the kitchen door to maneuver away from the Atchleys. *Can't go that way!* After unlocking the door, he stepped back out into the driveway to take one last look at the skies over town.

He didn't see any dark clouds at all. John felt his dry slacks and shirt one more time and shrugged.

"Whatever," he said in denial, walking through the door into the house, "Liz is waiting."

CHAPTER 3

The Road to Liz

T hough he didn't need to, John had a shower in advance of his date with Liz. It was his original intention of meeting her wearing the same clothes he had worn to school that day, but the garbage can changed his plans. Hopefully, blue jeans and a dress shirt were enough for the date at hand. The change of clothes was for the better anyway because he had been feeling that he was possibly getting too lackadaisical toward dates with Liz, that he wasn't putting his best efforts toward her.

Maybe he felt that since he had already won the prize, there was no need to try to impress her any longer. That was the wrong attitude and he knew it, yet it was working its way into his dating life. Would Liz go home, shower and change into another dress for him? Odds said she would. It wasn't that he was lazy toward dating her, but instead, just increasingly comfortable with her as each date passed. However, he didn't want to get to the point where he was taking their relationship for granted. John knew plenty of other guys out there,

Nathan included, were willing to step in to date her.

There was some amount of strain on their relationship in the last few weeks, mainly from Liz who continued to look for opportunities to talk about her Faith. John knew he wouldn't be able to keep shutting her down for much longer, so it was good for him to be on his best behavior.

What was he going to do if she brought it up again tonight? He could simply tell her he didn't want to talk about it, but that was the rude way to avoid the situation. He could creatively deflect the topic of conversation to something a heck of a lot easier to talk about and far less invasive. He could also go out with Liz in hopes of her not bringing it up at all, but the chances of that working out were slim to none. He might be able to think of another countermeasure on the way to pick her up for dinner.

John walked out of his bedroom into the hallway where he stopped to check himself out in the mirror. *Hair? Check! Teeth? Check! Shirt? Check! Jeans? Check!* He continued down the hall, stopping in the spacious living room. *One last thing to check*, he thought. John cupped his hands in front of his face and breathed into them. *Breath? Horrible!* Fanning the air in front of his contorted face, he stepped into the dining area through an open and intricately decorated arched doorway, his favorite part of the house.

The doorway was Liz's favorite part of the home's interior too, followed closely by the bright, shining hardwood floors. During her first visit to John's house, she quickly noted the woodwork in the doorway, at which point, he joked that the archway was eighty percent of his mortgage costs.

John emptied a candy jar out onto the dining table and began to pick through the treats looking for something to use as a breath freshener. Although the candy was mostly chocolate, he did find a small peppermint chew hiding in the bottom of the jar. Since he wasn't a huge fan of peppermint, he knew the piece of candy was probably for use as a minty date saver. After popping the candy into his mouth, he did the breath test again. *Breath? Not great but better!*

John grabbed his keys off a small living room table and headed for the door. He flipped on the porch light for later, grabbed the doorknob, partially opened the door but then quickly closed it back. He had to check something first. He walked over to a large window behind the dining table. From that window he had a clear view of the Atchley's front porch. Lifting slightly on the miniblind, he peered through the tiny crack to see if his neighbors were still sitting on their porch. *No, nobody there.* He knew they must be in the house eating dinner, praying or doing whatever Christians did.

Spying on his neighbors was something he was starting to do almost every time he walked out of the house. Sometimes the practice seemed a bit pathetic, in that he had to spy on the people next door to avoid talking to them. Looking first gave him an opportunity to quickly think of an excuse, a waiting priority or to get in his truck and just go. Yes, it had occurred to John that his neighbors had potentially caught on to his antics long ago, but that wasn't going to stop them from trying to convert him.

Dropping the blind back down, he hopped around the dining table, not completely clearing the chair which banged into his knee. In protest to his pain and clumsiness, he shouted, "Son of a…"

He limped around the table as pain rang through his leg. At least he did it now and not in front of Liz. Her presence would have added embarrassment to the pain. For a fleeting moment, he thought how funny it would be if maybe the Lord was getting back at him for not being nice to the Atchleys. *Stay in the real world, John!*

He headed for the door, knowing for certain he had cleared the battleground. Of course, Ma and Pa Atchley could see him heading to the truck and then step out for a quick question, but he felt they probably weren't motivated enough to do that.

John also wondered if they had noticed how he quickly bolts from the front door of the house out to Little Red. To them, it may have looked like an oddly repetitive exercise. Perhaps they noticed a lot more than he gave them credit for.

He opened the squeaky truck door, slipped in behind the steering wheel and quickly closed the door as a barrier to proselytization. He really needed to fix that squeak but also knew it was kind of an alarm for the truck. If someone got into his baby, he would know it. In his own mind, Little Red was a prime target for thieves.

John wasted no time at all getting the truck started and backing down the driveway. *Get going,* he thought. Mr. Atchley was standing at his living room window watching as John backed out into the street. *Was he watching me the whole time? Should I wave to him?*

"Better to keep the peace than to start a war with the neighbors," he muttered to himself.

Quickly, he put his hand up in a half-hearted wave, then took off down the street. Mr. Atchley's gaze was burning holes into the back of John's head, and he could feel the stare all the way to the end of the street. Maybe he should just get it over with and have a heart-to-heart chat with them, but even that wouldn't guarantee freedom from further attacks.

He practiced to himself as he steered around the corner heading toward State Road 9, "Mr. and Mrs. Atchley, you guys are nice and all, but I'm not a Christian and I never will be. I would appreciate it if you would just let it go."

That might work, but he didn't have the guts or proper motivation to tell them. Then again, the current situation wasn't working either. John questioned if he could have the same conversation with Liz. No, he couldn't! He loved her and knew theirs was a relationship he didn't want to risk losing.

After a few minutes, John made his way onto the Runway, quickly remembering what he had gone through less than two hours before. As he drove, a tingling sensation worked its way up his spine, causing him to shiver slightly. *This is ridiculous,* he thought. *I can't be afraid to drive down this road every time I need to go to town or to work.*

He had a few choices which would allow him to avoid driving the Runway. He could quit his job, for one. No, that would be stupid, and he liked getting paid. He could ask Nathan and Liz to move to his community and hope they understood why without a lengthy explanation. *I'm a big chicken. Could ya'll move closer?* No, that would be just as stupid. He could drive well out of his way, adding numerous miles and minutes to his trip. No, that would be a dumb idea also. He had to stop thinking about it, suck it up and drive the road for goodness' sake! More than likely, it was all just his imagination anyway. Well, no, it was probably just his imagination.

Things were looking familiar now as he approached the exact spot where the crazy event occurred. Funny, though, nothing looked at all wet. John checked for cars behind him, saw none and slowed Little Red to a crawl on the road. He quickly rolled down the window and peered outside at the road. It didn't look the slightest bit wet.

He eased the truck off the road at about the same spot he was when the event intruded on his life. Little Red lurched to a stop on the side of the road, after which John put the truck in neutral, set the parking brake and cracked open the door. He was still on the paved shoulder, so he shut off the engine, unlatched the seat belt and hopped out of the vehicle.

Talking to himself, he said, "It's hot and there's no humidity. It should be humid and soaking wet around here. What in the world is going on?"

He looked around to see if anyone was watching him or if any cars were coming down the road. No, he was all alone, it seemed. Maybe someone in the wooded area lining the roadway was playing a joke on him.

"Hey, come out!" he shouted into the woods on both sides of the road. "Anybody hear me? Come on out!"

There was no response, just dead silence. He couldn't even hear the wind moving through the trees, just quiet. If someone were pranking him earlier, they were most certainly long gone. He walked to the front of Little Red, bent down inquisitively and rubbed the ground with the tips of his fingers. The ground was desert dry.

Again, talking to himself, he said, "What? This

should be soaking wet."

He knew, not more than a couple hours before, at this very spot in the road, a hard rain and heavy hail pelted the ground which now seemed parched. The skin between his eyes wrinkled as he looked at his dry fingers, attempting to make sense of what he was seeing and experiencing. For a moment, he remained bent over, concentrating on his fingers which he rubbed with his thumb, as if sifting through an invisible material. John stood again, straightening his body to his full height, as if showing his mass to a predator.

Looking into the woods, nearly seething, he yelled, "This ain't funny! Come on out!"

Still no response, just silence. After backing up to prop himself up against the front of Little Red, he stood with arms crossed, staring into a sky of blue, accented by puffy white clouds. Was someone trying to tell him something? Was he imagining all the things that had happened to him in the last few hours? Was he going crazy? He knew what Liz would say for sure.

"John, it sounds like the Lord is trying to get your attention." He shook off the thought.

As he gazed into the fairy tale sky, the sound of tires humming down the road brought him back to his reality. Lowering his head back down to planet Earth, he saw a truck approaching on the other side of the road. *Oh no,* he thought, *it's that same guy–the dude who found me standing on the side of the road, rain-drenched and acting like a total weirdo.*

What was the passerby going to think this time, seeing John standing in front of Little Red at the same spot in the road but headed in the other direction? Maybe this was his chance to get some answers. Well, he could get one answer anyway. He could ask the guy what he thought of the rain earlier, that is, if he stopped again. What if it really didn't rain? Then he would be asking the man a crazy question, and in the process, making himself look like an even bigger fruitcake.

The truck slowed to a crawl until it stopped next to John, who continued to lean against his own truck with arms crossed. What were the chances of seeing the same person at the same spot in the road? John tried not to look threatening.

"As much as possible, just try to look normal," John whispered to himself, not thinking about the fact that the man pulling up could probably see him talking to himself.

It was the same guy for sure, this time looking at John through his driver door glass, possibly not wanting to roll the window down out of fear. Chances were he wouldn't stop if he thought John was a mental hospital escapee. There was a ray of hope for John's sanity check as the man rolled the window down to speak.

"Hey, buddy, you okay?" *Wow, that sounded familiar.*

"Yep, I'm okay. I was just looking for something. Thanks for checking on me again. I really appreciate it." The man rolled his window up a bit.

"Have I seen you before?" he asked.

John leaned forward off the front of his truck and turned to face the gentleman who stopped again. Did he not remember just a couple hours before, pulling up on John during a fierce rain and hail storm?

"Uh, yeah, don't you, uh..." John couldn't get his mouth to finish the words forming in his mind.

He didn't know what to say to the guy. Maybe he

should mention the rain and hail. Surely driving in that mess would be just as memorable for him as it was for John. Now, however, John was really starting to question who was crazy, the concerned, but forgetful, motorist or himself.

Again, he found himself choosing his next words wisely, so as not to send the man away frightened. For a moment, he considered why he should even care what this person thought. John didn't know the guy and it appeared the guy didn't know John. What if he knew the Atchleys and somehow was able to describe John in enough detail that his neighbors would be able to identify him? That's all he needed, his neighbors getting a traffic report on him from State Road 9.

Then, memories of his neighbors not seeing or hearing anything resembling a storm came flooding back to him. He rubbed his shirt again, remembering earlier it should have been wet when it was dry. Now, right in front of him, there was this guy who should remember stopping to check on his welfare during the storm but seemingly, didn't. What was going on? Who was crazy?

Jolted back to the current reality, John said, "Uh, I thought you were someone else. You know what they say about the world being a small place and all. I see people all the time who look familiar and they don't remember me either. Sometimes I think..."

He was rambling and not making his case any better. *Okay, shut up, John,* he thought. *Just send him on his way.*

"Anyway, thanks for stopping. I'll be okay."

The gentleman slowly rolled up the window and eased the truck forward, keeping his eyes glued to

John, who threw up a sort of half, two-fingered wave. He stood there for a moment watching the concerned, most assuredly frightened, citizen drive down the road away from him. The bottom of his truck seemed to fade away in the mirage-like waves of heat coming off the road. *What a weird day and what a weird interaction that was,* thought John.

As the frustration of the unknown built inside him, John spun around to face Little Red's hood, then he slammed his palms down on his beloved truck and dropped his head in disbelief. He hated the feeling of having no control over the situations presented to him. He hated feeling as if he were just along for the ride, left only to speculate about the rough turns and drops lying ahead. Shaking his head, he said, "God, if you're real, I'd greatly appreciate it if you would just tell me what's going on, or better yet, just leave me alone...Whatever!"

John slapped the hood of the truck again and marched around to the driver door and opened it wide. The squeak of the door seemed to echo throughout the surrounding woods as if yelling back to him. He slid back into the driver seat and slammed the door shut, probably a little harder than he needed to.

Perhaps he was getting mad over his lack of control of the circumstances. He sat there in silence, hands propped up on the top of the steering wheel, hoping whatever he had seen before in the rain and hail would magically show up again. If it did, it would either confirm he was crazy or that he, indeed, had all his wits about him.

John stared beyond the front of the truck, down the road, almost allowing the waves of heat rising into the air to hypnotize him. He listened to the sounds of his breaths and felt the rhythmic beats of his heart deep in his chest, making him feel sleepy. *That's it! Maybe I'm asleep. Someone just needs to wake me,* he thought. No, he was awake. He wondered if dreams could be so vivid that a person might not realize he or she was in a dream. *No, John, you're awake!*

Suddenly, the ridiculously obnoxious sound of artificial laughter filled the cab of Little Red. John nearly jumped out of his skin, with arms and feet jerking back toward his body in instinctual motion. It was the ringtone on his cell phone. Normally the same ring garnered laughs from those around, but on the side of the road, he was alone and in no laughing mood.

"Son of a mother!" he yelled in panic.

With the ringtone blazing loudly and his heart beating rapidly, he scrambled to pull the phone from his pocket. As the device cleared the lip of his jeans pocket, it slipped from the grip of just two fingers and fell to the floorboard of his truck. He awkwardly pressed his face to the steering wheel, trying to reach down to the still ringing phone. *Ah, got it!* Liz's beautiful face was on the screen with large bold letters stating, CALL FROM LIZ.

John flicked the answer button, quickly put the phone to his ear and answered, "Hey, Liz, what's up?"

"What's up?" she repeated. "Do we still have a date tonight, Sport?"

She sounded a bit upset. Liz was able to express what sounded like anger or frustration, but at the same time, be completely polite. Some thought it was tact, but John thought of it as a unique Liz quality, one of which he didn't want to be on the receiving end of. He knew she couldn't be angry. Unfortunately, it sounded like he was going to be the target of her agitation that evening, but what did he do to deserve it?

"Sure, Liz, why wouldn't we?"

"Because you are exactly one hour and seven minutes late. Getting a little worried about you, John."

"What are you talking about? I'm right on time," he said as he looked at his watch.

He tapped his watch, seeing that it was an hour and seven minutes past the time he was supposed to pick her up. Then, he noticed, all around him the sunlight was dim, that the day had transitioned to dusk. *Dusk? It should still be daylight,* he thought. He couldn't begin to imagine where that hour and seven minutes had gone. Now, he was feeling a bit petrified because he was apparently losing time.

Should he mention to Liz how he and Little Red had only been sitting on the side of the road for a few minutes? To make his case, he might add the part about the rain drenched ground being dry. Better yet, maybe he should mention the concerned motorist who had seen him twice, yet, didn't recognize him or his unique little truck. Should he mention the white thing he saw in front of his truck earlier? Would she believe him? What was he going to say to her that wouldn't make matters worse?

"Right on time? Yeah, right on time, Sport. You feeling okay, John? Maybe you should check that ratty old interior of what you call a truck for exhaust leaks."

That was a low blow but one he was more than willing to take from Liz. She knew how much he loved his little truck. However, he also knew she wasn't a big fan of the interior and on numerous occasions, had politely asked him to fix it. John, knowing the condition of the vehicle's cab, also felt her comments were somewhat justified.

"I'm sorry, Liz. I've been a little distracted today and must have lost track of time. I'm on the Runway now, so I'll be there in a few minutes."

As he thought about the words used to describe how he felt about the day, "a little distracted" was a huge understatement. The fact of the matter was, because he had no idea what was going on that day, he was very frightened. His hands were shaking, and he was feeling chills and shivers up and down his spine. John was barely able to hold the phone to his ear and was wondering if he would be able to drive.

"You're forgiven, John. Just hurry up and get over here. I'm hungry."

"On my way, Liz," he said, now realizing he had committed to driving whether he could or not.

"Okay, love you, Sport."

"Love you too, Liz. See you in a few minutes."

He was shaking wildly. He couldn't keep his finger still enough to push the End Call button, so he held the phone semi-steady on his leg and used his other hand to press the button to hang up.

John sat in the stillness of the moment, listening and looking for explanations of the events of that day. His thoughts trailed off to the immediate time, the here and now that didn't seem to be the same here and now he remembered.

The sun was setting fast, and light was quickly giving way to darkness. He looked around, noting the ominous way the fading sunlight silhouetted the trees of the forest to his right, making him fully aware of how scary his environment would be in total darkness. At that moment, someone couldn't pay him enough money to stick around. He wanted to rest his head on the steering wheel for a few minutes, or lie down across the seat, but instinct drove him to keep his eyes open and get away.

Reaching for the ignition, John could see his hand was shaking but not just his hand–his whole body was shaking. Unable to stand the trembling, he slammed his fist down onto the seat next to him, grunting loudly in frustration. He speculated his quaking body was the result of bottled up rage at the lack of control over his life or that he was just scared. It may have been both.

It wasn't getting any lighter outside, and Liz had already been waiting for over an hour. Ready or not, he had to go. He only hoped the quivering would be gone by the time he pulled up to Liz's apartment complex, but right now, things weren't looking very favorable.

John grabbed the key and twisted, hoping his beloved truck would come back to life and not strand him there on the side of the darkening road. The power of Little Red's eight cylinders roared, giving notice to anything and everything around that it was time to go. He revved the engine loudly to, hopefully, scare off anything lurking in the murky shadows of the woods.

Leaning over the steering wheel, looking skyward, he could see the first appearance of stars; but it wasn't the stars he was looking for. *Liz and all her Christian friends couldn't possibly be right.* A Supreme Being, an All Powerful or an Almighty didn't exist. However, it– whoever it was–might know exactly what was going on that day. Part of him wanted to know, but the larger part said to stay on course and not buy into the nonsense.

Still shuddering like a leaf in the wind, he pushed back into the seat, put Little Red in gear and lurched back onto the road. The shaking of his feet caused him to gun the throttle a bit, making the truck spin out on the shoulder. *Oops, didn't mean to do that.* As thankful as he was to be on the move again, he would be even more thankful to get off State Road 9 and headed into town.

Within minutes, John passed by the school, noting security had closed and locked all the gates. For the first time ever, he noticed the illuminated fence line, topped with barbed wire, made the facility appear prison-like. The only thing lacking was manned guard towers. In fact, if he didn't know any better, he would think he was passing by a penitentiary instead of an institute of learning.

A couple more turns brought him into town, which really wasn't much of a town. There were a few businesses, a few restaurants, some convenience stores and gas stations but nothing incredibly notable or outstanding. Everybody in town used one of two banks and drove a few more miles outside town to do their major shopping at the nearest chain store.

The less-than-sprawling metropolis had only one traffic light, and the only lit street was the main drag he was now driving. People were usually out and about, but on that night, they weren't very active. John knew they were probably where he should have been, in a restaurant having dinner. A couple miles from the back side of town was a small suburb and the apartment complex Liz called home.

He and Liz had several conversations about how small the city was, but they always ended with her saying her own hometown was a lot smaller, which, to John, wasn't even conceivable. "How can you get any smaller than this?" he always asked her. She repeatedly reminded him that someday she would take him to see her old stomping grounds.

John knew exactly what she was talking about. It was the obligatory act of going home to meet her mom and dad and seeing the place where she grew up. Regardless of the size, this hole-in-the-wall speck on the map was his home, and he knew Liz and Nathan claimed it as well.

Driving down Broadway, the main drag, John noted, yet again, how dry everything was when it should have been soaking wet. The same storm that had caught him just hours before should have rolled right over town, but apparently, it had not. *Maybe,* he thought, *there was no storm, no rain, no hail and maybe I'm a few cans short of a six-pack. Whatever! John, just get it out of your head.*

Cars lined Broadway on both sides where Little Red should have been over an hour ago. The vehicles sat empty and waiting for their owners to come back from dinner or a night on the "town."

He drove by Grover's Roost, a family friendly sports bar where he and Liz were supposed to have dinner. Bringing Little Red to a crawl, he strained to peer into Grover's tinted windows, attempting to determine how crowded the restaurant was. If it were too packed, then he would have an excuse to ask Liz if she wanted to go someplace else for dinner. He thought the establishment was needlessly family-friendly. How in the world could he enjoy a good football game or dinner without a cold beer in his hand, an adult beverage he wasn't going to get at Grover's?

The place was widely popular in town and throughout the entire county, but John just didn't like it. Liz loved it, so for that reason, John pretended to love it as well. As best as he could tell, the number of patrons in Grover's was minimal and several tables were open for business.

"Too bad," he muttered to himself in disappointment.

An impatient motorist behind him beeped their horn to get John moving down Broadway a little more quickly. Realizing he was slowing traffic, he threw up a wave in recognition of that fact to the driver.

What he really wanted to do was lean out the window and yell back to the irritated driver, "Hey, if you're in that big of a hurry, you should have started out yesterday!"

John wasn't that rude but knew he could whip it out when life called for it. Thank goodness, though, it wasn't that often because he wasn't very good at it. Though Nathan might say differently, John felt there wasn't a mean bone in his entire body.

Little Red crawled to a stop at the only traffic light in town. Going straight went out of town toward the Interstate. A right turn at the light ran through the oldest parts of town, creatively called Old Town. That road then turned into Ferro Drive which cut through a newer housing area and eventually curved back behind the school. A left turn onto Highpoint Road led to more housing, and in particular, Nathan's house and Liz's apartment complex.

Although John seemed to be sitting alone at the red light for no good reason, the intersection saw large amounts of traffic at other times during the day. When school let out, the junction would get crazy with car volume, especially with inexperienced drivers fighting their way home. Because of this, many citizens declared the area dangerous and requested the County Planning Commission add alternate routes around town to alleviate congestion. Following several accidents occurring during peak travel hours, the City Council asked for the installation of a traffic signal.

The light, although annoying in low traffic times, was a cheaper solution and compromise to building new roads. Of course, sitting at the light waiting for nothing, one would never know there was ever a traffic problem, just a slow, agonizing signal.

John threw his hands in the air and blurted out, "Come on! I could have walked there by now!"

Finally, after what seemed like an eternity, the light changed to green, giving permission to hit the gas and go. Just a couple, short miles away Liz was patiently waiting for him. John had almost forgotten she might still be upset at him for his tardiness, but on the bright side, his nerves were calming as he got closer to her.

Liz had that kind of effect on him and probably other people as well. Sure, she could get upset just like anyone else, but those times were so rare for her. As always, there was something different about Liz–an almost supernatural quality of always being happy and joyful.

John often thought about where Liz's peaceful attitude came from but never bothered to ask her for fear of bringing on an unwanted sermon. She often talked about her family dog Heath, speaking of him as if he were a human member of her family. When she mentioned him, a huge smile would always spread across her face.

John remembered one day last year; Liz's mother called her to let her know Heath had passed away. John was there with her when she received the call and watched a cheerful "hello" turn into a tearful "oh no." He didn't know what to do, except hold her hand firmly as she talked to her mother. Then, after Liz ended the call, he saw something he had never seen before. As her tears faded away, she smiled and looked to the sky and said, "I love you."

John, being just a little confused, softly asked her, "Is everything okay?"

She looked at him, still smiling, and said, "Perfect, John."

"What happened?" he asked.

"Heath passed away." She squeezed John's hand and continued to smile.

"Are you okay, Liz? I know how important he was to you," he said looking deeply into her now dry eyes.

"I'm okay, John. Heath's in a better place."

John was now even more confused. Better place? What? What's better than death?

"Who were you saying 'I love you' too?"

"God."

The answer instantly made John feel a sense of warmth, although he had no idea why. Maybe, he considered, the feeling was radiating from Liz. He could feel a calm and peace flowing from her like a river.

"What? God?"

"I had Heath because God allowed me to have him. I had years of enjoyment from him because God allowed him in my life. Someday, if dogs do go to Heaven, God will allow me to see Heath again. I'm thankful, incredibly thankful to God for putting that very special animal in my life."

"It's okay to be sad, Liz."

"I know, John, but I would rather be glad."

He was so fortunate to have a girl like Liz in his life, and the prospect of losing her to religion made his future seem dim. She, dare he say, was really the best friend to ever cross his path. Smart, pretty, funny, sensible and so very soothing–she was all that and more.

Nathan, just a few weeks ago, mentioned that John was blessed to have Liz in his life. Why did he choose the word "blessed" to describe their relationship? John didn't know, but had he been a pious sort of fellow, that certainly would have been the word he would have used also.

In just these few minutes going down the road, the mere thought of being with Liz had calmed his nerves and had nearly made him forget about the unusual happenings of the evening. She made him feel spiritual without the burden of religion. John was getting closer and closer to her; he could feel it inside.

John realized daydreaming about Liz's qualities was dangerous while driving. Somehow, he was moving Little Red right along, possibly by pure muscle memory. Suddenly, he realized he was almost a mile down the road without a recollection of the short trip. *Thank goodness,* he thought, *there aren't any stop signs between Liz's apartment and town.* Otherwise, he knew he would have probably run right through them in the dreamy state he was in.

The route to Liz's apartment would take John by Nathan's house, visible in all its bachelor pad glory from the street. There were only a few houses on the street front, and Nathan's place was one of them. "Land for Sale" signs dotted the roadside opposite Nathan's property. Obviously, developers were trying to build up the area; but Nathan often talked about enjoying the semi-solitude of having only a few neighbors. He feared the day peaceful seclusion would end when bulldozers began to tear into the earth to build new homes.

As John drove by his best friend's house, pangs of jealousy brewed in his mind. Nathan's abode was the larger of their homes and seeing he could barely afford his own residence, he wondered how Nathan could manage this larger girl-magnet type place. He could have been getting help from his parents, or maybe he had another job on the side.

By whatever means Nathan was able to afford his larger home had never come up in conversation, likely because John was too prideful to mention it. How could John point out to his highly competitive friend that his place was bigger and better than his own meager dwelling? When it came to friendly rivalries with Nathan, John didn't see the need to shoot himself in the foot. *Just don't bring it up and maybe Nate won't bring it up either,* he always reminded himself.

As John drove by Nathan's house, he noticed all the lights were off except for a lone porch light whose illumination barely stretched into the front yard. The pride of Nathan's property was a large oak tree standing tall on the lawn as if on guard duty.

It was an old tree for sure, a fact made obvious by the girth of its trunk. Nathan claimed it was an American Civil War era tree but had no way of knowing for sure. John suggested they cut the tree down and count its rings for age verification, but the idea of doing so drew harsh tones from both Nathan and Liz.

"I don't know what in the world would even make

you think about cutting that beautiful old tree down, except that the Devil has a hold of you," spouted Liz.

Nathan, face in a mild snarl, jumped in for good measure and admonishment, "Yeah, what she said!"

In response, perhaps in sarcasm because of Liz's injection of religion, John said, "We could glue it back together once we figured out how old it was."

After saying it, he realized just how ignorant his comments sounded, but he didn't want to apologize to anybody. He knew he was just trying to be humorous, but his words certainly didn't come off that way to Nathan or Liz. In reality, John was trying to deflect the topic of religion.

Bringing his full attention back to the road, John continued into the darkness of the path ahead of him. He was on a portion of Highpoint devoid of houses or street lights, just near darkness. The moon, in full brilliance, began to peak above the tall trees lining the road, creating an eerie, almost made-for-Halloween glow.

The shadows of the trees crept across the road like monsters with limbs outstretched to grab their next victim. John had to keep his attention ahead, but the moonlight passing in and out from behind the trees strained his ability to maintain focus on driving. The lighting effect was hypnotic.

Suddenly his eyes darted back to the road, his hands grasped the steering wheel in a death clench and his feet immediately found the brake pedal. As tires squealed on the pavement under Little Red, John felt himself slam forward toward the steering wheel as the seatbelt locked and secured his body from perilous flight through the windshield.

In an instant of terror and panic, John felt as though he were pushing the brake pedal through the floor of the truck. His foot on the brake said "Stop." Little Red screamed in protest, "When?" Then the brake pedal said, "Now." Smoke from pavement-stressed tires drifted past the cab of Little Red, like ghosts in the moonlight. As he brought the truck to a complete stop, the moon sat still in the trees, no longer providing eerie flashes of light.

He looked forward through his windshield, maintaining the death grip on the steering wheel and muttered, "Not again."

Ahead of him, about twenty feet in front of his truck, stood a stationary wall of rain, stretching to the sky and off to the sides of the road as far as he could see. It wasn't moving, as if a storm cloud or weather system was parked nearly on top of him, pouring rain down upon the Earth.

He remembered rare occasions, especially as a child, seeing rain in the front yard but none in the back yard. In his short number of years on planet Earth, he had seen columns of rain falling from water enriched clouds, dancing across fields while all around, the ground was dry and rain-free. Right there in front of him, this rain was different; it wasn't moving at all. John was fascinated but terrified at the same time.

Again, as thoughts of Liz faded away, memories of the odd events of the day began to flood his memory. Was he really seeing rain or was it merely a figment of his imagination? For that matter, was the entire day merely a product of an overactive mind? Was any of this happening?

John decided right then and there, he wasn't going

to let the opportunity of discovery slip away, no matter how scared he was. He put the transmission in neutral, set the brake but left the engine running in case he needed to make a fast getaway. Still, the wall of rain didn't move.

John unlocked the door, grabbed the handle and eased the door open. There was no rush of wind, no rain over his head, only the waterfall-like roar of the rain beating the ground twenty feet in front of him. The sound was so thunderous he could barely hear the squeal of Red's dry hinges. Looking around, he didn't see any cars coming down the road, or headlights shining on the other side of the rain wall.

Leaving the door of the truck open, John slowly began to walk up to the anomaly. He walked with his right hand out in front of him as if feeling his way around a room in pitch black. However, it wasn't pitch black–far from it. He could see the rain in front of him, with moonlight above and headlights below, sparkling on the downpour to create a disco ball-like effect.

Stopping about five feet from the rain wall, he noticed the absence of runoff at the base of the aquatic structure. He should have seen flooding on the ground all around but saw none. John closed his eyes for a moment and took a deep breath, hoping maybe, he would be somewhere else or that the rain would be gone when he reopened his eyes. *Eyes open, John! Nope, still there!*

Now slowly inching closer, with his hand still out in front of him, he moved toward the rain wall. He looked around one last time to make sure someone or something wasn't watching and then swallowed hard as if taking one last bite of a final death row meal. He

CHAPTER 3 | 73

moved his hand to within an inch of the rain. Being so close, its sound was now deafening.

John worried the column of water would shift suddenly to immerse him, but it stood stationary, like a great fluid statue. There was absolutely no mist coming off the rain, not even on his hand which was just an inch away. John leaned toward the pouring rain trying to see past the downpour, but nothing was visible inside the anomaly or beyond it. *Should I touch it? Should I risk touching whatever this is? Is it just rain?*

"Here goes nothin'," John said, committing to what was ahead.

He would try just the smallest part of his body at first. He knew it was better to lose a fingertip rather than a couple fingers or even a whole hand. He moved the digit ever so slightly toward the water cascading from somewhere above but stopped short and drew back slightly.

Fear swept over him and survival instinct took over. *John, don't do it!* After all, he had no idea what was in the water or what it might do to him. A great white shark could be swimming around in there for all he knew. For just a moment, John tried to imagine a shark trying to swim around in the watery, clouded thing.

Images from all the scary movies he had seen in his life suddenly came rushing back to him. *What if something grabs me and pulls me in?* Adrenaline was surging again, attempting to swim upstream against fear. Adrenaline, not fear, screamed, "Do it, John! Just do it!"

Again, slowly he pushed his finger toward the water. *Almost there. Just a little more. Contact!* He felt the ice-cold water on his skin, but terror surged again, causing him to quickly pull the finger out of the thunderous flow.

Drawing his hand in front of his face, he examined the fingertip to see what damage, if any, the water-like substance had done. His badly needed body part was still there, a small victory against fear. Then he rubbed his thumb and finger together, thoughtfully noting the lack of water on his skin.

"What? You've got to be kidding me!" he blurted, feeling the dryness of his skin.

What he was seeing and feeling wasn't possible. John looked around once more to see if anybody was watching. No, nobody. It was just him and this very odd rain. If it were some kind of practical joke, it was one of the most elaborate acts of trickery ever conceived by man.

Okay, he thought, *let's try something else.* He cautiously moved his right hand toward the rain, but this time, at the last second, plunged his entire hand into the downpour. Fear fought adrenaline, causing him to immediately retract the hand back out of the still ice-cold water. Once more, John examined his hand, carefully turning it front to back, then to front again before his unbelieving eyes. His skin was dry. Not a drop of water was on it.

"If I'm dreaming right now, I sure wish somebody would wake me," he muttered. "This is getting a little too creepy for me."

He was unsure of what to do. Instinct told him to get back in Little Red, turn around and go home. Then again, he couldn't do that because Liz was waiting for him. Would he be thinking about his girlfriend waiting for him if this were a dream?

Looking back at his truck, he thought about driving through the massive barrier of rain but still didn't know what was inside the huge column of raging water. Rolling in his mind was another scenario. His fingertip and hand were okay. Then, without further thought, John jumped into the torrential rainfall, immersing his entire body.

The heavy rain beat John down to his knees, and bright lightning blazed around him. Deafening thunder cracked frequently, timed with each burst of fantastic electricity that remained skyward and ungrounded. The intensity of everything around him grew, forcing John to his hands and knees as if submitting to a deity.

The lightning illuminated his body, allowing him to see how the frigid rain had drenched his skin and clothing. His athletic frame was shaking violently from the cold and stinging pain of the large drops of water bombarding him. He could have been in a giant funhouse where strobe lights flickered constantly to disorientate those brave enough to go in them. Only, he fearfully considered, this was no funhouse. It was the middle of the road on the way to Liz's apartment.

He yelled the only thing he knew. "Help me!"

Lifting himself slightly, bracing his hands on his knees, he thought he might be able to get up and run, but instead, his legs wouldn't budge. He was frozen to the wet pavement, forced to endure the beating rain, wild lightning and cracking thunder. He could feel the water. He could see the water but still couldn't see through it. He could hear the thunder booming all around him. Was it all real? It all felt real, certainly more real than any dream ever concocted within the depths of his mind.

Suddenly, John felt a presence in the rain with him. Using the flashes of electrical doom, he looked to the right and saw nothing but more rain. Shivering uncontrolledly, he crossed his arms over his chest, attempting to contain any warmth left in his body. He looked left, timing his stares with the wild flashes of light but was barely able to keep his eyes open in the hard rain. In front of him, in a brilliant burst of white and purple, he saw it. Then, he saw it again, fading in and out with the lightning.

Wiping his face, John strained to see through the fierce rain. As an attempt to block as much water as possible, he put his hand over his eyes as if saluting some unseen superior. There it was again, lit by the flashing around him. Just a few feet away stood the silhouette, if not the actual structure, of a tall wooden cross.

Each violent pop of lightning brought out new detail. It was wooden, a carved but rugged looking wood, almost tree-like in appearance. Dazzling flashes of light behind the cross caused its shadow to fall across John. He knew he was seeing it. It was real, just as real as the coldness and stinging his whole body was now feeling.

John forced himself to raise his eyes to look up toward the center of the cross but quickly lowered his head in submission to the beating rain. For a moment, he stared at the object's massive shadow falling across him and the ground in front of him. Slowly, he leaned forward with an extended hand to try to touch it.

As he stretched his arm toward the cross, slightly viscous, red drops began falling on and about him. He feared he might be injured and bleeding from the violent phenomena raging around him. No, even the hardest rain couldn't draw blood. The new substance, which seemed to be replacing the rain, looked like blood, but it wasn't coming from any part of his body. There was too much of it.

John was shaking violently, and his heart was pounding deep within his chest as if ready to jump through his rib cage at any moment. He tried to form words, but his lips only tremored at the thought of speech.

Suddenly, John's mind clouded with thoughts of all the bad things he had done in his life. Images, as if on film, rolled through the circuits of his brain, bringing back painful memories of times past. He saw himself as a child, a teenager, then as an adult, moments lasting hours surging through his mind in milliseconds. His goodness, as seen through his own eyes, was on display in all its wretchedness, showing by some unseen standard, he was, in fact, among the lowest beings on Earth.

His teeth began to chatter, and every muscle in his body started to stiffen as if to hold him in position. The heavy rain drops, now the only thing he could hear, echoed internally as they slammed onto his head and ears.

The red drops grew in number and became less like water and more like blood, thick and oozing. Soon, the blood-like substance covered his entire body and began to pool around him, washing over the shadow of the cross on the ground. *What is this stuff? Blood? Real blood?* The substance rolled down his face in wide drops, eventually turning into sheets that enveloped his skin. The gory flow clouded his vision, making anything he tried to view appear as a red haze.

His strength, once drained, returned in furious spasm. Fighting the urge to just lie down and give up, the muscles in his legs sprang into action as if activated by a switch. He was standing, but his feet, seemingly glued in place, would not move. John raised his head to look at the cross silhouetted by the wild flashes of lightning. It appeared once more and then disappeared into nothingness.

Without warning, as if grabbed by an unseen hand, a force pulled John backward out of the downpour in a blur of unnatural motion. He was abruptly back in the world again, standing in front of Little Red with both hands propped against the hood for support. In a split second, the sound of rushing water and the echo of rain beating loudly on the ground were gone. All he could hear was the low rumble of his truck's engine and his heart beating furiously in his chest.

John, still breathing heavily, heart still pounding, body still shaking, looked at his hands as they rested on the hood of the truck. They were dry. He lifted his right hand, expecting to see a red, wet palm print, but there was nothing. Dry again. As if checking his appearance, John looked all about his clothes and felt them. His shirt, pants and everything was dry. Not a drop of water...or blood. He tried to distinguish between what was real and what wasn't. He should have been soaking wet. He should have been covered in the red fluid raining down on him just seconds before.

Bracing his hands back on the hood of the truck, giving support to legs of rubber, he slowly turned his head to look at the column of rain. It was gone. No torrential downpour, no wet pavement, no blood, no cross, nothing…only the road in front of him.

John's eyes began to fill with rare tears, ones that seemed to come out of nowhere, from some hidden source. A single tear slid down his cheek. He shouldn't be crying. They could have been tears of sadness, but he didn't know for sure. He knew it was okay for a grown man to cry, but there was no reason for weeping. Then again, he couldn't think of a reason for any of the things that had happened to him that day. John turned his head back to his truck; back to reality, or so he thought.

He slammed his fists down on the hood of Little Red, looked to the dark night sky and shouted, "What do you want from me!"

He knew an atheist wouldn't yell to the heavens. For just a moment, he thought about what he had just done. An atheist most certainly wouldn't yell to a God he didn't believe in. This was no ordinary day, not by a long shot, but there had to be a logical explanation for everything that had happened to him since leaving work just a few hours earlier. It had to be an explanation outside and apart from anything resembling God. His head dropped as he agonized over his troubles and trials, wondering if he really was going insane.

An ache crept through his tightly clenched fists. His physical actions were now registering as pain among the tumultuous thoughts running through his brain. Something was building deep inside him, possibly emotional turmoil. No, it was stronger than that. It was anger, a deep-seated anger, almost hatred for someone or something, but where was this fiery emotion coming from? He was a nice guy! Sure, he could get angry just like any other person, but this was different. It was rage but not under his control.

John slammed his fists on Little Red's hood yet again and sprang back away from the truck, growling like a rapid dog. Liz! How long had he kept her waiting this time? This thing, whatever it was, was coming between he and Liz.

He stormed over to the open driver door of his beloved truck, feeling heavy footfalls vibrating throughout his body. Recognizing the danger, he knew he couldn't drive in an angered state. His mind and body were out of sorts, unable to operate mentally and physically.

Before jumping into the seat behind the steering wheel, he stopped, leaned his head against the door post and whispered quietly to himself, "This isn't you, John. Calm down, buddy."

He thought of Liz and the incredible peace and calm within her. Somehow, he was able to channel those emotions from her to calm himself. John felt as if he was in a deep dark pit, but now, there was light in the darkness and a rope thrown down to him.

For a moment, he was looking through Liz's eyes. She was sitting in a rocking chair, rocking gently, reading a Bible resting on her thighs and singing words to a song he had never heard before.

John could hear her sweet voice in his head, "...and I'll cling to the old rugged cross and exchange it some day for a crown."

Her words and the vision of her rapidly faded away, but they left in him a peace beyond explanation. He could sense it was only a borrowed peace, one that did not belong to him. John lifted his head off the door frame, looked skyward and wondered if he could have what he was feeling but permanently.

Well, back to reality, he thought. Now, feeling calm and collected, John eased into the cab behind the wheel. Leaning back into the seat, feeling its familiar curves and bumps, he listened to the hum of the engine, still running from the beginning of the bizarre incident he had just experienced. *Liz! Gotta get to Liz!* He pulled the door shut, threw the transmission into gear and stood on the accelerator pedal. The engine roared like a lion waiting to be uncaged, and the rear tires screamed a call for action. Down the road he sped away. His girl was waiting!

CHAPTER 4

Date Night

Barely dropping his speed, John turned off the main road into the parking lot of Liz's apartment building. He sped past a sign posted at the entrance boldly proclaiming a five mile-per-hour speed limit. Liz reported a rumor floating around that many of the residents were circulating a petition to have John and his prized truck banned from entering the premises. He was unsure if it was true or not but knew it was probably because of his heavy accelerator foot and loud engine. Liz wasn't in the habit of lying, so he knew it could very well be true. With that in mind, as of late, John had made every attempt to drive more slowly and not gun his engine near her residence. However, that day, he had already kept her waiting too long and felt the snooty residents and their silly petition would understand.

Liz's apartment complex was the largest of two located near town and was a product of expansion caused by the construction of the school. It was a grand place with four three-story white, aluminum-sided buildings arranged in a square surrounded by parking. Sitting in the middle of the square, essentially the residents' back yards, was a large pavilion and swimming pool. John and Liz had spent many days sitting by the pool or relaxing under the pavilion enjoying each other's company. It was a great place to live, but John preferred the privacy of a single-family home, even if it was costing him an arm and a leg.

He pulled into one of two designated spaces for Liz, both labeled with her apartment number, "3L." Liz's car occupied one of those spots and was easily identified by a white cross and thorned crown pasted on the back window. The cross, unlike other times, seemed to call to John, to almost whisper his name. He shrugged off the sensation as he pulled into "his" space.

Early on in their relationship, John made the seemingly unforgivable mistake of parking in another occupant's space, which resulted in a rather lengthy argument in the breezeway between Liz's door and her neighbor's. Needless to say, John was not a popular visitor among the folks at The Hidden Reserve Apartments, but he didn't care because Liz was totally worth it.

John quickly and frantically shut down Little Red and scrambled to get off the seat and out the door. Catching his foot on the worn-out seat, he nearly tripped to the pavement. Standing tall, he quickly looked around to see if anyone was out and had noticed his blunder. Fortunately, nobody saw him acting like a clumsy fool.

As he slammed the door, the squeal of the hinges fighting closure echoed throughout the complex. If all the residents didn't know he was there, they sure knew now. John ran across the parking lot to Liz's building, up the sidewalk and then up the switchback stairs going to the third floor. Breathing heavily, leaning against black enamel handrails, he paused at the top of the stairs to regroup physically. Looking forward and to the left, he saw her apartment–her glorious apartment, "3L."

Steadying himself, he straightened, took a swipe at his shirt and pants, adjusted his hair and walked over to her door. After one more deep breath, he reached over and pushed the glowing doorbell button. John heard the chime on the other side of the door, then heard footsteps coming toward him from inside the apartment. His angel was coming!

Quickly, he thought about what he was going to say to her. Thoughts and ideas zipped through his mind in mere seconds. Was he going to mention any of the events of the day? Should he just keep his mouth shut? What? What was he going to say?

The door swung open to reveal Liz. Just seeing her made him feel so good inside, but he hoped he didn't appear like a puppy seeing its owner for the first time in a week. She was so gorgeous, this time wearing a white dress with pleats. The only thing missing were fluffy angel wings coming out of her back. She stood holding the door, examining John with curious eyes. *What is she looking at so strangely? Don't just stand there, John, say something.*

"Hi, Liz," he said as he gazed intently into her cool blue eyes.

She tilted her head and wrinkled her forehead. Most certainly the first word out of John's mouth should have been "sorry." Oh well, he couldn't change what he had already said. Why was she staring at him so oddly? For a moment, he thought he had something on his face, maybe the dreaded booger. He quickly wiped his face.

"You okay, John?" she asked, her voice was full of concern.

"What do you mean?"

"Well, you're as white as a sheet. You look like you've seen a ghost or something."

She grabbed his hand, felt his cheek and then put her hand on his forehead as if gauging his temperature. If she weren't a school teacher, she could have easily been a nurse. Her care and concern were evident.

His struggles of the day were probably showing more easily than he thought possible. Perhaps she could see it in his face. He recognized it could be an opening, an invitation to tell her about all the unusual things that had happened to him since leaving school that day. He agonized over the idea of telling her. Shifting nervously on his feet, his eyes darted around as if searching for answers floating in midair.

"Liz, did it rain here today?" She raised her eyebrows in wonder at the odd question.

"Not that I know of, John," she replied, stepping closer to him. "It's been dry here all day."

That wasn't the answer he wanted to hear. If only she had said it had rained and stormed, then some of his day might make sense. His eyes dropped to the ground as she embraced his hand between her own. His body began to tremble slightly at the thought of the day's events, but he had to control it. He couldn't tell her.

"No rain, no storms, not even thunder?" He almost pleaded for the answer he wanted to hear.

"No, the Lord's given me an absolutely beautiful day."

Sighing deeply, John said, "Liz, I'm so sorry for keeping you waiting. I'll just say the last few hours have been really strange and leave it at that, but I do very sincerely apologize."

"Want to talk about it?"

He ran his fingers through his hair, looking side to side, attempting to hide any emotion showing on his face. He didn't like not being open with her. It was pure dishonesty, but he figured it was probably better for him to keep things to himself for a while longer.

"I would rather not. I'm sorry, Liz. Do you forgive me?"

Gently grasping his hands, she met his gaze. She rubbed the tops of his hands with her thumbs, showing an almost natural talent to soothe. She was so good for him.

"John, do I look upset?"

"No," he replied softly.

"I forgave you the minute you didn't show up at my door when you were supposed to. Of course, I was concerned for you but not angry with you. I just wanted to make sure you were okay, that you weren't in danger, maybe unconscious somewhere. What good would getting mad do anyway?"

She caressed his cheek again like a mother comforting a hurting child. What a shame it would be to lose a woman like her. That thought loomed dreadfully in the back of his mind as he remembered Nathan talking about Christians being unequally yoked.

"Liz, I know I don't say this as much as I should, but," he paused, "I'm so thankful to have you in my life. I knew you were something special that first day I saw you at the airport."

His memories flashed back to that awkward meeting at the terminal, a moment he hoped to never forget. The grin on Liz's face, stretching ear to ear, showed she was also thinking about that same moment of social ineptitude.

"You're so sweet, John," she said wiping a tear from her eye.

Their feelings for each other were so very real, but she knew something dark stood between them, painfully tearing at their relationship. Her tears were not of joy but of sadness in a reality she knew she had to face someday soon.

With puppy dog eyes, but trying to hold back tears, John said, "Liz, I sure could use a hug right now."

"Lucky for you they're free."

She stepped in, slightly on her toes and put her arms around his broad chest and back. He reciprocated by placing his arms around her in a warm embrace, gently supporting her slightly shorter frame. Her perfume was like music to his nostrils, and likewise, for her, his cologne spoke volumes to his strength. A warmth grew between them, with hearts fluttering and breaths caught in time which suddenly seemed to stand still. Each of them enjoyed the embrace, the togetherness, the touching of their bodies in simple love.

"I could do this forever, Liz."

He could feel her heart pulsing on his torso, drowning out the sound and feel of his own. In that innocently humble moment, there was one heart beating for two.

She released the embrace first, stepped back and playfully said, "Forever's a long time, John and I'm hungry. Let's go get a bite to eat."

"Of course, Liz, I'm sorry. I've kept you waiting long enough. I hadn't really noticed, but I guess I'm a bit hungry too."

"I know," she said, "I could hear your stomach growling on the other side of the door."

"Is it that obvious?"

"Yeah, let's go, Sport!"

She turned around to lock the door, then quickly spun back around to grab John's hand. She suddenly and forcefully led him down the stairs, nearly yanking him out of his shoes. *She must really be hungry,* he thought.

As they rambled down the stairs, a curious neighbor opened their door to see what the commotion was. For a moment, John engaged in a glaring stare down with Liz's next-door neighbor. John could see the look in the neighbor's eyes that said, "Yeah, get in your loud, little truck and get out of here."

John managed to smile at the nosy man, even as Liz dragged him down to the lower-level breezeway. Was it a crime to have a nice vehicle that just happened to be one of the loudest in the county? He liked it, and who cares if they didn't. If they could just get to know him and look past Little Red, they would see just what a nice guy he was. Oh well, Liz liked him, and that's all that mattered.

Now jogging, Liz zoomed down the sidewalk to the parking lot, continuing through the sea of cars and trucks until she came to Little Red. John was just along for the ride, but he had to show some courtesy to his girlfriend. Breaking against Liz's aggressive pull, John slowed her pace as she approached the passenger door of his truck. He managed to jump in front of her as she was about to reach for the door handle, causing her to nearly collide with him.

Standing in front of John with hands on hips she said, "Hey, what gives?"

Gently grabbing her by the arms, he moved her backwards away from the truck and said, "Please, allow me."

Here's your chance, John. Show her what a gentleman you can be. He opened the squeaky door, took her by the hand and motioned to the passenger seat. She began to step toward the truck, but John quickly stopped her. The blanket covering the seat was a mess. He leaned into the cab and carefully adjusted the covering to protect every inch of Liz's clothing and skin from the shabby interior. *There, the blanket is perfect–sort of, anyway.* He motioned for her to take a seat in the truck.

"Why, John, you're such a gentleman," she said as she grabbed his extended hand to help her into the vehicle.

"Your chariot is ready to take you to dinner." He tapped the top of Little Red's cab.

"Is this what a chariot is supposed to look like? Somehow, the fairy tales from my youth never mentioned anything like this."

Her sarcasm was funny, but John knew she was innocently poking fun at him. Even though she was his princess, Little Red would have to do.

As she slid into the passenger seat, John responded, "Are you kidding me? Snow White rode in a Chevy."

"Sure," she said with a hint of skepticism.

John gently closed the door, making sure all body parts as well as her beautiful dress were safely inside the vehicle. Liz looked at him through the window as he kissed his fingers and touched them to the glass in front of her face. After his princess was safely tucked in, John cruised around to the driver's side. Dreading the sound, he opened the door and cringed at the loud squeal of hinges screaming for lubrication. Liz closed her eyes and put her hands over her ears, hinting at the need for a timely repair.

"Hey, Sport, you know they have this thing called oil, right?" she sarcastically asked in her sweet but well-meaning voice.

John could dish it out as well as he could take it. "Are you kidding me? Oil's expensive! I'm waiting on the price per barrel to drop."

"Well, I'm sure my neighbors would appreciate it too." Ah, there it was–the truth, maybe.

"Are the people living in these apartments really trying to ban my presence here?"

"I can neither confirm nor deny that."

She made a zipping motion across her lips and pretended to throw away a key, then smiled widely. The threat of disbarment from the premises was a cute joke she had to keep going as long as possible, even if John only half-believed it was true.

"Well, that's okay. I love you and your neighbors anyway."

He jabbed the key into the ignition and gave it a twist. The V8 turned and turned but didn't start. *No, not now.* It was date time and his little truck had to start!

"So, is the chariot out of gas?" Liz asked, as she took another opportunity for fun sarcasm.

"No, I think Little Red knows you're sitting in the cab." Retaliation complete!

She patted the dash and said, "Come on, buddy, you can do it."

"Real funny, Liz," he said as he turned the key once more to bring the engine to life.

Delivering an approving thumbs up, John proudly stated, "See, Red likes you. He just needed a little love."

As John pulled out of the parking spot, he glanced over at Liz for nonverbal cues, something that might be telling him to ease off the throttle. He saw nothing, only her beautiful smile. He could gun it to get her attention. He could tear out of the parking lot like a madman; but with Liz in the truck, that sort of reckless abandon wasn't a good idea at all. He gently applied pressure to the accelerator pedal and eased through the parking lot, paying particular attention to engine noise and vehicle speed. Maybe this would appease the neighbors; he would never want them to be mad at his angel.

They exited the apartment complex grounds onto the main road headed into town where a much-needed dinner awaited. Their stomachs were now growling in unison, almost as if singing a duet together. John and Liz were both thinking the same thing. If yawns are potentially contagious, why couldn't stomach growls also be contagious? No, they were just incredibly hungry.

Liz spoke up and said, "It sounds like our tummies are talking to each other."

"I suspect science would object," he replied, "but it sure seems like a conversation. They're probably talking about the ridiculous amount of time I've kept them from food."

They neared the spot in the road where John encountered the wall of rain, the cross and the blood. Unconsciously, his foot eased off the gas, allowing Little Red to slow. Liz looked at him, puzzled. There were no traffic lights or stop signs she could see and certainly nothing blocking the road, so what was he doing? She noticed he had locked his eyes on the road but not in a safe driver kind of way. He appeared to be petrified, as if he expected something to jump out in front of the truck.

"John, are you okay? Why are we slowing down?"

Her voice echoed in his head as if spoken at a distance. He didn't answer. He could hear her, but his lips were closed tightly.

Snapping a finger near his head, she asked again, "John, are you okay?"

He leapt back into reality, shook his head and realized Liz was talking to him. She had noticed his almost trance-like state. *How am I going to explain this to her? That I sometimes liked to slow down for safety? Sure, she would believe that about as much as she would believe I had rabbit ears growing out of my head. Think fast, John.*

"Oh, I saw a bunch of deer cross the road here on the way to pick you up. I figured they could still be around."

He couldn't tell her the truth and felt bad about lying to her. He knew she wouldn't lie to him, which made his falsehood even more difficult to bear.

"Okay, well, it looks pretty clear to me, so..." she said, her voice trailing off, as if she were in disbelief. Had she caught him in a lie?

Looking at her, he then began to accelerate through the questionable area and said, "Nope, no deer now."

John could sense the awkwardness of the moment and felt as if there were a million eyes watching him. Because they weren't speaking, he knew he had to do something. If not, the night might end before it really started. As he and Liz approached Nathan's house, he had an idea to break the silence between them. All Liz had to do was sit back and watch as the event unfolded.

Checking to see there were no cars in the area, John slowed to a crawl and turned his headlights off, leaving only his marker lights on. He eased off the road onto the shoulder in front of Nathan's house. From the street, John inspected the property for signs showing Nathan was home. *Nothing! He must still be out.*

"John, what are we doing? I'm hungry."

She sounded annoyed but he hoped she would be as forgiving as she was earlier. To save face, he was neglecting her and her growling stomach. However, he saw nothing wrong in taking an opportunity to fill the dent in his pride.

"Just sit tight and yell if you see Nathan."

John put the truck in neutral and set the parking brake. Liz noticed the brake lever also squeaked. *He really needs to perform some maintenance on his truck,* she thought. She watched as he reached under his seat and pulled out a roll of toilet paper. Immediately, Liz knew exactly what he was going to do.

Among the endless stream of other pranks, John and Nathan were both experts at applying toilet paper to front yard trees. Using this bathroom staple, the two had been trading blows with each other for as long as Liz had known them. She thought the ritual was stupid and childish but never told either of them. She watched as John jumped out of the truck and ran up Nathan's front yard to that beautiful oak tree, his intended target.

She rolled down the window and yelled out to John, trying not to be too loud. "John, not now! Come on! How old are you? Twelve?"

He heard her and noted she sounded even more

annoyed. Perhaps his toilet paper escapade wasn't the right tension breaker, but there was no turning back now. After taking one final look around, he lofted the roll of toilet paper as close to the top of the tree as he could get it. The roll unwound itself as it gently fell down the branches of the tree, leaving a glorious white streamer in its wake. After the roll dropped to the ground, he picked it up again and threw it back to the top of the tree, then watched it fall as it painted a white paper stripe back down to the yard.

Liz observed headlights in the distance behind them and yelled, "John, get back here! There's someone coming!"

She wanted no part of the ridiculous act and certainly didn't want those passing by to see her anywhere near the childish stunt. Liz's days of child-like abandon were over, but unfortunately for her, John's were still alive and well.

Hearing Liz's calls of warning, John left the partial, but still useful, roll of toilet paper on the ground under the tree. He hated to waste any, but more importantly, he didn't want to get caught. He ran back across the yard, around the front of the truck then jumped back in next to Liz who was sitting, arms defiantly crossed, with a not-so-pleased look on her face. He released the screaming brake lever, popped the truck back in gear and took off like a criminal on escape.

"Was that really necessary?" Liz asked, making the point that she had moved from annoyed to highly agitated.

As she sat quietly, staring him down with arms crossed in protest, John retorted, "Liz, you don't understand the complex relationship I have with

Nathan. It's a relationship that has to be nurtured like that big, old oak tree in his front yard."

As he shifted into the next gear, he wiped the sweat off his forehead with the sleeve of his other arm. Why was he sweating? Was it the thrill of decorating Nathan's tree with toilet paper; or was it Liz's displeasure? Unfortunately, his true thought was of how he could operate the accelerator pedal, clutch, shift gears and wipe the sweat off his head all at nearly the same time. *Pure talent,* he thought.

"What I understand is that you and your little friend can't seem to move past the sixth grade."

Yep, she's highly agitated, but on a positive note; the awkwardness is gone. John knew he had to do some damage control. He couldn't let his mischief drive a wedge between them.

"You're right, Liz. I'm sorry. I guess I'm just a big kid at heart, a big kid who just wants to have fun," he said, dropping the tone in his voice to one of sadness and repentance, something she would totally understand.

"Listen, Sport, you can have fun without it being at the expense of others. If you're sincere, you'll go over there tomorrow and help Nathan clean that mess out of his tree. Saying you're sorry means nothing if you don't do something to fix the problem and make sure it doesn't happen again. John, let's just get to town. Amazingly, I'm still hungry."

He couldn't tell if she was mad or just being sarcastic. He was unable to home in on her exact thoughts, but regardless, she was reading him like a book. She knew he was attempting to get back on her good side. In hind sight, he thought it might have been better to just talk to her rather than to have performed a stupid stunt.

His immature male ego and pride took a direct hit that evening. In that moment, John suddenly felt something he hadn't experienced before. He had put toilet paper in that old tree more times than he could remember and registered nothing resembling guilt, just playful satisfaction. Now, oddly, he was feeling guilt that pierced through his hard exterior deep down to his heart.

Eventually, they made their way into town and found a prime parking spot right in front of Grover's Roost. Liz hadn't said anything since her admonishment of John's childish act. *If she wasn't mad before, then maybe she was now,* he thought. As soon as Little Red came to a stop and John cut off the engine, she unbuckled her seat belt and reached for the door handle.

John shifted in his seat, gently grabbed her arm and said, "Liz, wait."

He hopped out of the truck, ran around to the passenger side and opened the door. He had to show her that his love for her wasn't rattled, that he still cared deeply for her and wanted to take care of her. He extended an inviting hand to brace her.

As she gingerly slid out of the truck, looking into his eyes, she said, "I know there's a gentleman in there somewhere."

She stood outside the truck holding his hand, still looking into his eyes while he returned her gaze. She noticed his eyes were watering up a bit. *Tears? Tears from John?* She would never get him to admit to it.

"John, are you about to cry?" she asked as she moved up to the sidewalk to allow him to close the door.

He stepped up on the sidewalk with her and gently caressed her shoulders saying, "Liz, I'm gonna go over there tomorrow and get that paper out of his tree. You have my promise, my absolute promise, that I won't do it again. I feel bad for what I did, but I feel worse for the way I made you feel. I don't deserve your forgiveness, Liz, but I sure would feel better if you gave it to me, sadly, again."

Stepping into his outstretched arms, she reached around him with a bear hug. John didn't know what to think. Was she hugging him in preparation for the old "get lost pal" or was she going to utter those precious words of forgiveness? Sadly, he knew she might not say anything at all. Slowly, he wrapped his arms around her small frame to return her embrace.

"John, I know there's another side of you in there just screaming to be let out. Of course, you have my forgiveness, and of course, I'm not mad at you."

Pushing away from his embrace, she grabbed his hands and noticed they were trembling. She could sense John was genuinely afraid for the future of their relationship.

"Liz, you're the best." Hopefully, leaving that positive thought in her mind, he motioned to the restaurant and said, "Let's go get dinner, okay?"

"You got it. Let's go. I'm hungry enough to eat the plate my food is served on."

Holding the door for her to enter, he chuckled at the thought of her eating the food off her plate then tearing into the dinnerware. He watched as she walked through the doorway, gliding like an angel on a cloud. He couldn't lose her! No, he simply had to do better.

◆ ◆ ◆

John and Liz sat in the darkened restaurant enjoying one another's company, chatting while their meal settled. Though he wasn't particularly fond of Grover's Roost, he did have a favorite table, a small booth along the wall across from the bar.

On the wall, over their table, hung a picture of the school's baseball team from his days in elementary school. He was in that picture; taken the same year he and his teammates went to their state championship. They had lost the tournament, but the picture, as well as the memories behind it, were always a good conversation piece for whoever was there with him.

On their first date at Grover's, John specifically asked the waitress to seat them next to his photo, hoping Liz would notice he was in the group of youth baseball players. She didn't notice. He figured it was because of her lack of interest in sports. He knew he could never depend on baseball or football for conversation.

John's lone signature stood out on the picture, scribbled across the chest of his blue and white uniform bearing the number 8. He assumed, at least, Liz would see the photo and ask why only one player had signed it. No, she didn't. He was, however, still prepared to give her the answer; he was the only one left from that long-ago team still in town to sign it.

Waitresses and waiters sped about delivering food and drinks, occasionally checking on customers. Because John and Liz had gotten there later than expected, the Roost was more crowded than they would have liked. They didn't mind the crowds, but it did make conversation a little more difficult. People were even eating at the bar, enjoying a meal with an ice-cold soda. John always felt the bar looked a little odd without beer taps, but the atmosphere in Grover's was warm, cozy and inviting. Sometimes he wondered why he didn't like the place, but maybe it was starting to grow on him.

Flat screen TVs were mounted on the wall behind the bar and other locations throughout the dining area, but most of the time management kept the sound low because folks couldn't have heard them anyway. Gathered around the other end of the bar was a large crowd watching a football game. Their shouts and whistles rang throughout Grover's, revealing the progress of their teams. "No!" they shouted. "Yeah!" they shouted. Their cheers and jeers were frequently accompanied by "oh's" and "ah's" rising and falling in rhythm to the drama in the game. Sometimes the crowds would get a little exuberant or rowdy, but nobody seemed to mind.

Typically, a sportscast of some kind was on each of the TVs, but on John and Liz's TV, the national news was on. Usually, the manager would change channels if anyone asked, but the people sitting at the bar were obviously watching the news. Liz wasn't into sports, and the folks at the bar seemed interested in what they were watching. The news was fine, especially since neither John nor Liz was watching it anyway.

The two of them always managed to have great conversations, mostly about what each other liked and disliked. They never really discussed the future because both seemed happy in their teaching positions.

Another topic, though it sometimes seemed far away and untouchable, was their future relationship. John fully expected they would one day have a very serious conversation about it. Liz was generally okay with talking about their status as a couple, but John tried to avoid in depth discussions about their pairing because he knew exactly where they would lead.

As he sat across from her, hanging on every syllable, Nathan's words rang in his head. "Unequally yoked," he had said. He could ask Liz about its meaning, but that might quicken the "talk" he didn't want to have. It was coming; he could feel it. Oh, how he dreaded it.

A man at the bar next to them yelled, "Hey, Grove!"

Liz, sipping from a straw, was startled and jumped in her seat at the sudden outburst from the bar. She nearly dropped her drink and may have been slightly embarrassed. John smiled and laid a comforting hand on her arm.

Grover left the game he was watching to tend to the needs of his customer, asking, "What's up, Bill?"

"Hey, man, can you turn that up a little," he said motioning to the TV bearing the news.

"Sure," he said grabbing a remote from under the bar.

"Thanks. I think their gonna talk about the Impasse again. Pretty important stuff," said Bill as he sipped his soda and grabbed a handful of popcorn out of a small basket on the bar.

"More power to you, Bill," replied Grover. "It's so common these days, I get tired of hearing about it."

Bill, gulping down popcorn, cleared his throat to answer. He said, "I know, but it seems to be getting worse and worse."

"Oh, I agree. You know good and well what happens when you elect clowns to office, don't you?" As Bill nodded in agreement, though not really knowing the answer, Grover continued, "You get a circus."

"Right, right," Bill said as he stuffed more popcorn

into his mouth.

Grover and Bill were talking about government events which became known simply as the Impasse, a general lack of cooperation between the Republicans and Democrats. It was a term used by all major news networks to describe what many people had seen among politicians in the last several years. Most Americans saw it as the general breakdown of lawmaker function due to partisan politics.

John sat quietly listening to Liz, trying to hear over the noise of the rowdy game watchers and the now louder TV. He was hoping to tune it all out and focus on her, staring intensely, into her beautiful blue eyes. She could see he was struggling to hear her because he was leaning closer to her, possibly trying to catch key words.

"It's a bit loud in here tonight, isn't it?" she said, motioning to the crowd watching their game at the end of the bar.

"Yeah, just a little. If I had remembered that game was gonna be on, I would have suggested someplace else."

He could have tried to use the game and loud fans as an excuse to go somewhere that was a little more party friendly, but he knew Liz wouldn't buy into it. It wouldn't have been a great idea to take Liz to a place where people all around her were drinking, maybe to excess. Out of respect, John had never consumed alcohol in front of her. That was a definite no-no, although he suspected she had seen the beer in his refrigerator.

"It's okay. They're just enjoying the game and enjoying each other's company," she said, smiling, as if shaking off the problems of the world.

They directed their attention to the TV news program playing behind the bar. A catchy tune played as images of elected officials flashed on the screen while an anchor woman introduced the next story.

"Up next, after commercial break," she stated, "our elected officials can't seem to agree on anything. As we face yet another government shutdown, lawmakers appear to be chasing their own agendas. Also, up next: rioting and looting continue as civil unrest rages across the country and around the world. These stories and more coming up after the break."

John and Liz turned away simultaneously as a local car dealership commercial appeared on the screen. The salesman had been using the same annoying sales pitch for years. Why would he ever think screaming at potential customers from inside a costume would sell cars? Well, at least, the tactic hadn't worked on John or Liz.

"Isn't that something, Liz?"

"What? That ridiculous commercial?" she asked pointing to the ad now playing loudly on the TV.

"No, all this government junk and national disunity that's going on."

"What do you mean?" she asked, crossing her arms on the table as if preparing a defense or wanting desperately to hear what he was saying.

"I'm talking about the way politicians have been acting...the way they've been acting for years now. They can't get anything done for arguing with each other. Sometimes, well actually, most of the time, it feels like they're ignoring the needs of the American public. It gives new meaning to the phrase 'gotta be a government operation.' I'll tell you, Liz, it makes me mad to know that the legislators of the greatest nation on the planet are so damn selfish."

He realized he had cursed in front of Liz, who sat listening, unphased by John's rant. "Sorry, Liz, I let that one slip out, but it just makes me mad," he said apologizing.

John rarely let a four-letter-word slip out of his mouth, one of his self-proclaimed good qualities. Liz didn't see it that way, so John worked even harder to guard the contents of his speech in front of her.

In the early days of their relationship, he and Liz were at her apartment making a cake. Liz was the one making the cake while John was fiddling with a broken remote, trying to fix it. As he struggled to pull the cover off the remote, his finger slipped, causing the nail of his index finger to bend backward. In pain, he loudly shrieked the "s" word, as Liz called it, for all the apartment complex to hear.

"I won't have that kind of language in my home, John, or near me, for that matter," she said, scolding him with hands on hips.

"It's just a word, Liz. One little word isn't going to hurt anything," he said, defending his actions.

She turned back to the cake and slowly started to mix it again. "John, there's a cow pasture out behind the apartments, so how 'bout I put a little manure in this cake I'm making for you? It's just a little, right? You would still eat it, wouldn't you?"

She again turned away from the cake, gauging his response, but he only sat there in silence. John would never admit it, of course, but Liz had taught him a small lesson, maybe even humbled him a bit.

She continued, "If the Lord doesn't want us to say it,

then we should make every effort to not say it."

"Sorry I can't be perfect, Liz." He said it but knew he probably shouldn't have.

Liz turned back to the cake and calmly replied, "I'm not perfect, John. I'm not even close to perfect. Sin is a struggle, and I have to ask the Lord to help me steer away from it every single day. I fail a lot, and I ask Him to forgive me. Most important, I recognize the bad behavior and ask Him to help me not do it again."

Now, after reminiscing of the cow patty cake, he gave her a second or two to respond to his political rant. The image of her making that cake and putting a little excrement in it traveled around in his head. She just sat there, quietly, as if waiting for more of the story. *What? No acceptance of my apology? No "thanks" for saying I'm sorry?*

Seeing she had no reply, he enquired, "Doesn't the Impasse bother you, Liz? Doesn't the lack of national unity eat at you? Doesn't it all make you just a bit angry?"

He found her lack of response a tad unnerving, but that was nothing compared to how he would feel in the next few minutes. Liz dropped her head as if looking at something on the table. She was contemplating what to say.

She lifted her head, face tense with sincerity and asked, "John, what if it was meant to happen? What if this was a planned disruption of the government?"

Slightly shaking his head, he said, "I'm not sure what you mean, Liz. Do you mean terrorists or something? Government infiltrators?"

"No, John. How do we know this isn't the beginning of God's plans to bring a morally corrupt country to its knees?"

He twisted in his seat as if recovering from a slap in the face and said, "Liz, come on! Are you serious?"

"You said, yourself, they seemed to be ignoring the American public and that they were selfish. It's not getting better. It's getting worse. Look at all the issues put on the backburner while the American people suffer. I can't remember the last time they voted on a real issue. Costs are up. Unemployment is way up and getting worse. I mean, for goodness' sake, every process that involves the government now takes two, three or four times longer. Businesses are going under left and right. People are going without healthcare. Infrastructure across the country is falling apart. The list goes on and on, John."

"And I suppose the civil unrest, the rioting, the looting and the protests are all part of this plan?" There was no hiding–or taking back–the sarcasm in his voice.

Liz, though rattling off all these negative things, seemed amazingly calm. John, on the other hand, squirmed in the booth, as if unable to find comfort in the seat or the unbelievable words of his girlfriend. He couldn't believe what he was hearing. It sounded like she was talking about a conspiracy theory involving a God he didn't even acknowledge. He had started to believe the weirdness of his day was over but now this. He didn't want it to be real. *Please, somebody wake me up,* he thought.

"Liz, think about what you're saying. Does it really seem possible?" he asked, putting his hands up as if to show disbelief.

"Look around, John. Take a long look at the direction in which this country is going. It's not Godly in any way, shape or form. It's not just the country, John. It's the whole world. As to whether I think it's possible, I believe, with God, all things are possible."

She noted John's frustration level rising like a tsunami, but she remained perfectly calm. Suddenly, they were both thrusted into the dreaded conversation neither of them wanted to have.

"I don't believe this," he said, raising his voice. "Why does this have to be about religion?"

At that moment, he knew he had said something bad. There was no going back. He had given her an opening to have that potentially disastrous conversation about their relationship. Instead of pouring water on the fire, he fanned the flames of her witness.

As she reclined back into the seat and sighed, he reached across the table and grasped her hand. He didn't know what else to do but quickly apologize. Unfortunately, he dreaded, the damage was irreversible.

"Liz, I'm sorry. I shouldn't have said that."

He could see she was starting to cry, that the tears were forming in her eyes, making them gleam like the sun on the ocean. One of those tears, breaking the dam of her eyelids, slowly rolled down her cheek. He knew it was coming, the very thing Nathan had warned him about. Inside his head, he heard those words again, now screaming, "unequally yoked."

He leaned across the table and gently wiped the tear from her cheek but saw that more were coming. "Liz, please, don't do this."

Their waitress saw Liz crying and rushed to their table and asked, "Is everything okay?"

John swatted her away like a fly and said, "We're

fine. Just give us a minute."

The waitress backed away slowly and cautiously, wondering whether she should step in or not. Liz flashed a hand at the server and nodded to put her at ease, as if to say everything was under control. She wiped away her tears and collected her thoughts so that she might have the dreaded talk with John. She sandwiched his hand between her own and felt his nervous shaking. He had to know what she was about to say. He just had to know.

"John," she said choking back tears, "I've grown to love you more than just a friend. A part of me can see growing old with you, spending our lives together."

He cut in on her. "Liz, please, please don't do this."

She squeezed his hand. "When I met you in the airport that day, I knew you could be the one for me. I could see through the awkwardness of the moment to that tender heart beating in your chest. John, I know you feel the same for me, that you love me, but..."

Cutting her off again, he pleaded, "Liz, please, no."

He brushed at his eyes with his free hand, recognizing, he too, was starting to cry. No, his horrible day wasn't over.

"John, there's a huge barrier between you and me. I can't spend my life with someone who doesn't share my Faith. I love you, John, but I love Jesus more."

At that, John pulled his hand from her grasp and buried his face in his palms, trying to hold back the tears but failing to do so. The moment crushed his heart, but as he failed to consider, it had crushed her heart as well.

Neither of them had noticed, but curious eyes had started watching them from all over the Roost. A cloud of thoughts floated throughout the place, hovering in the air like a bad storm. *Did he just break up with her? Did she just break up with him? What are they talking about? Why are they crying? What's going on?*

Liz slipped out of the booth and gently placed her hand on John's shoulder as he sobbed into his hands. She felt the weight of a hundred eyes locked onto them in curiosity.

"John, I need you to take me home, please."

Her voice, now not so comforting, echoed in his troubled head. He grabbed napkins off the table and frantically rubbed the tears out of his eyes so that he didn't have to walk out of the restaurant looking like a bawling mess.

Quickly, he pulled a handful of cash out of his pocket and threw it on the table as he slid out of his seat. He also noticed people staring him down, some showing displeasure as if he were the offender that night. However, truthfully, they both did the wounding, each to the other.

Liz walked quickly to the door, immediately followed by John who was still wiping tears and sniffling as if he had a cold. As they walked out the door, Grover's Roost patrons, realizing the scene was over, went back to their talks, food, news and games.

John was still a gentleman, silently holding Little Red's door open for Liz and holding her hand as she entered the truck. With no further words to exchange, Liz quietly said, "Thank you."

He gently closed the door, caring little for the squeaking. There was an eerie silence on the street, a silence that even covered the rambunctious fellowship sounds of Grover's. John walked through the hush, head held low, bracing for the tense trip back to Liz's apartment. *What a day,* he painfully thought. The climax of an already horrible day was the loss of his girlfriend. *Surely,* he agonized, *things couldn't possibly get any worse.*

John slid into the driver's seat of his old, faithful truck. At least he still had Little Red. After fumbling with the keys in the darkened cab, he was finally able to find the ignition and give it a turn. The engine rolled over but didn't start. *So much for my faithful truck,* he thought. He muttered, "come on," as if his mechanical friend had ears to hear and a mind to obey. After a couple more tries, the cold engine finally started, breaking the silence on the street.

John pulled out of his street-side parking and made a gentle, but illegal, U-turn to get going in the other direction. He assumed Liz might say something; instead, she sat next to him silently, not even indicating disapproval. He knew, though, her silence was not consent. Honestly, he felt as if he didn't have anything to lose at that point.

Rolling down the street, he again found himself sitting at the town's ridiculously long traffic light, making matters worse. Silence, nothing but silence. He considered running the light but agonizingly endured the wait. Then, finally, the green light gave its seal of approval to proceed. The lack of talk between them was torture for John. Not knowing what was running through her head chomped at him like a psychological beast.

He hoped they would find words again. Working side-by-side would most assuredly be awkward and tense. They would probably have to talk at some point, and maybe that moment would work itself out. John tried to concentrate on the hum of the truck's engine or the sound of the tires on the pavement. Little did he know the same thoughts were rolling through Liz's mind, but deep down, it didn't worry her like it did her former boyfriend. She was at peace with her decision, but for John, not so much. He was hurting inside and still fighting back tears.

Going back toward the apartments, they passed by Nathan's house again. He still wasn't home and had not yet noticed the toilet paper streamers hanging from his tree and blowing in the wind like party décor. John and Liz looked at the mess at the same time. He said he would fix it, and he would. He would make it right.

John brought his eyes back to the road, noticing out of the corner of his eye, Liz was staring at him. *What's she thinking?* Was she regretting her decision to end the relationship? He didn't realize it, but she still wanted to be with him badly, but they would have to overcome the Faith barrier. She caught his peek and faced forward again, then dropped her head as if to pray.

Just past Nathan's house, the rain began once again. It was a heavy rain, making its presence known on Little Red's cab with thousands of loud bangs and pops, like multitudes of fingers drumming on metal. It was much like the rain on the Runway from earlier that day, just slightly less heavy and lacking hail.

Again, he found himself questioning the reality of the rain. He could be imagining this too. Liz was there with him. She could certainly confirm whether or not it was raining, but he would have to break the silence. He had to ask her in a way that wouldn't make him sound like an idiot. He had already done so much damage to their relationship in the last few hours and hated the idea of her thinking even less of him. *Whatever*–he just went for it.

"Liz, do you see the rain?"

She lifted her head momentarily, noted the rain and dropped her head back down in what John assumed was prayer. After a few seconds, she replied, "Yes, John, it's raining."

That's all she said. There was no sarcasm, no concern for his mental health. Not a thing. She said nothing further and expressed no emotion at all. She was just cool, calm and collected Liz. *Doesn't she think it's a bit odd that I'm asking if she can see something all around us?*

Maybe it wasn't the same kind of rain as before, or could it be that earlier it wasn't raining at all? What proof did he have that it had rained? The only shred of evidence was in his mind, but perhaps that meant absolutely nothing because he might really be going crazy.

He didn't know what was going on, and it was making him feel sick inside. He just wanted to end the day, get home and go to bed. What if he was already in bed, having a nightmare and just needed someone to wake him? But he silently asked himself, *do people know when they're dreaming?* His sanity was lost in total confusion.

Then, he saw it, about a mile from Liz's apartment, on the side of the road. At first, the headlights reflected off it, a white figure in the distance, seemingly illuminated by its own light. The form blurred in the rain pounding on the windshield. John increased the wiper speed up to high to better see whatever this thing was. He slowed Little Red slightly to reduce the rate of closure on the object standing on the side of the road. Yes, it was standing like a person. Closer and closer they got.

Liz wasn't seeing it because her head was still down. He could ask her to look, to confirm this being, whatever it was, was there on the side of the road. She could potentially verify it was real. She might say no and think he was crazy. Then there would be no chance of getting her back. Maybe she would say yes and would surely understand what he was going through and take him back out of pure sympathy. No, she had no frame of reference for the things happening to him that day. There was no use. No, he couldn't bother her with it.

If Liz did have her head down in prayer, John thought, *could she be praying for me? Maybe she's praying for a healed relationship between us. After all the day's torments, I need all the help I can get. But wait, John, what in the world are you thinking? There is no God to pray to. Don't you believe she's just wasting her time with something as foolish as prayer?*

What did Liz mean when she said, "I know there's another side of you in there just screaming to get out"? Was her Faith real? Did he need her Faith? No, he had to keep his mind on the road and what was ahead.

The downpour began to let up, possibly to allow a more thorough inspection. John drove closer and closer to it, enough to make out details in form. It was an old man, dressed in a long, white robe with a head covering. One hand was at his side while the other grasped a wood staff that was nearly as tall as he was. His face was wrinkled and frozen in sincerity. He gazed back at John with piercing eyes, and for a moment, he and John were locked in a stare down.

The distance between them closed so that John could tell the old man's glowing, pure white robe was dry. It should have been clinging to the curves of his aged body, drenched in rainwater, but no, it was perfectly dry. John slowed more but didn't want to stop. It was right there! Surely, Liz would be able to see it! Her head was still down in prayer or sleep. Was it possible she wasn't there either? John rubbed his eyes, perhaps hoping to clear out of his mind the image of this old man standing on the side of the road. No, still there!

John was passing by him now, looking squarely into the old man's face. How could he believe what he was seeing? How could he wrap his mind around what was going on in his life? As John passed the well-aged man, he quickly glanced backward through the rear glass, noting how the man's head tracked him as he drove by. He was still there, brilliantly lit but now fading away in the distance, shrouded in rain that seemed to bounce off him.

John suddenly felt a sense of attachment to this stranger, this weirdly placed and oddly dressed visitor on the side of the road. This was the same figure he saw on the Runway; it had to be. He questioned if he should stop to talk with him. The mysterious character could have answers. If he drove on, he might not see the old man again. John needed to know who he was.

Whipping his head forward again, looking down the road ahead, John wiped at his eyes once more. He peered into the rear-view mirror to notice the man on the side of the road was no longer there. *Mirror tricks?* Quickly, he turned back to the rear glass. The man in white was gone, not a trace of him anywhere. Little Red's tail lights should have been reflecting on the brilliant white robe, but no, he was gone. John tapped the brakes slightly to illuminate everything to the rear of the truck with eerie red taillights–still nothing.

As suddenly as it started, the pounding rain went away, no longer beating the metal skin of the truck. Rain sound gave way to engine and tire sound. An unexpected and unexplained calm fell on John's mind and body. The events of the day were still making their rounds in his head, but they were oddly calming, like a sudden awareness of safety and security. He glanced at Liz, still sitting by his side with her head down. *Is this,* he thought, *the calming she feels from her Faith? Is she praying for me right here, right now?*

A little further down the road, realizing her home was near, Liz finally lifted her head. She said nothing at all but just stared straight ahead as if John wasn't even there. Little Red slowed to make the turn into the apartment complex. It all now seemed eerie for John as the comfort he felt just moments ago began to slip away. In his mind, the sad finality of the evening was beginning to dig in. Liz would get out of the truck and that would be it for them, the end of what he thought was a beautiful relationship.

The lights in the parking lot created sad glares that danced across the windshield. John looked at her as he slowed the truck to a stop. A single tear, glistening in the light filtering into the cab, fell down her cheek. He so desperately wanted to reach over to her and wipe the tear away, to hold her and comfort her but knew he couldn't.

"John, I can let myself out," she said.

There was no need for a gentleman to open the door

and hold her hand as she exited the truck. *There,* John thought, *was no need for me. Is this how it ends?*

Liz unlatched the door and pushed it open, giving no notice to the squeal of the truck's dry hinges. As the sound reverberated through the complex, nosey neighbors pulled back curtains to peek at the cause of the awful noise. John couldn't stand the verbal silence, and he had to know where Liz's mind was. As she lifted her legs over the door frame to get out of the truck, John gently grabbed her left shoulder, stopping her exit.

"Liz, what did you mean when you said, 'I know there's another side of you in there just screaming to get out'?"

Maybe, he thought, *I can get at least one answer tonight, although I know it probably won't be anything I want to hear.* He hoped, but knew otherwise, the answer she gave might help him salvage their relationship.

She sat on the edge of the seat; legs hanging out of the truck and her back to John. She sat there for a moment, wiping painful tears from her cheeks, thinking about what to say. John removed his hand from her shoulder, feeling as if he were just prolonging any grief she may be going through. But, what about his own sadness and his need for answers, possibly even closure? Was it too early for closure?

Through tears and sniffles, not looking at John but talking away from him, she said, "John, right now, you don't understand. I know you hurt. It's hurting me too because I know we have a special relationship, just not a spiritual connection.

"In the heart of every man and woman is the desire to walk their own way, to walk away from God. John, you've gone that way, but I've gone another. There's a part of you, just like in me, that wants to go God's Way, but this world is trying to hold you back. John, I pray you are at the start of a journey to find God's Way for yourself. Hopefully, someday, John, when you find that Way, I'll be there waiting for you."

She hopped down off the seat to the pavement, still not looking back at him. He wanted to say something that would convince her to not walk away. Maybe he could agree to learn, to sample her Faith, that in time, they would be together again. He knew this wasn't like some silly trial period with a piece of furniture from a store. No, he knew it was much more. *I could tell her I would try it, that I would try her Faith. No, don't say that, you fool. You're going back on everything you believe.* Obviously, anyway, Liz didn't want him to try it, but instead, wanted him to do it.

"Liz, please…" She cut him off.

"Goodbye, John. I'll be praying for you."

She eased the door closed behind her and walked up the sidewalk to the stairs in the breezeway. John watched her go all the way up to her apartment door, noticing that, not once did she look back at him. There were no waves, no gestures of any kind, just the end of something he thought would last forever.

He sat there in Little Red for a few minutes after she disappeared into her apartment, maybe hoping she would pop back out and come running to him. It never happened. He wondered if the breakup was easier for her than it was for him. Could she be sitting up in that living room of hers going on with life as usual? In desperation, he considered parking and chasing her up to the apartment. No, John knew that wouldn't be a good idea.

John had to go home, to get away from the day, to bring a new day about through that wonderful portal called sleep. Slowly, he drove forward, then circled around the parking lot to the exit. He knew eyes were peeking at him through barely shut curtains, watching his every move. There was no way he was going to leave Liz with angry neighbors beating on her door, complaining about how some idiot she knew tore through their quiet parking lot.

He rolled up to the stop sign marking the exit of the Hidden Reserve Apartments. He could go left back the way he came or right to take the long way around to his own home. John knew if he went left, he would have to drive by where he saw the old man. He may or may not be there again. He would have to drive by the place where the rain beat him to the ground. He might have to go through that terror again. He would have to drive by Grover's where Liz broke up with him. He would have to drive the Runway again, that awful place where the whole horrible day began.

In all honesty, he didn't know if he would see any of it again, no matter which direction he went. Perhaps, if he did make it home without incident, it would still storm and rain on him in the comfort of his own living room. *Wouldn't that be great,* he sarcastically thought.

Well, he had to get home, so right he would go. It was a much longer trip, giving him several more minutes to think about what had happened that day. John attempted, hoping to take his mind off the day's events, to concentrate on the future. What was he going to say to Liz the first time he saw her at work? How could he avoid the awkwardness of working together? How was he going to counter Nathan when the inevitable "I told you so" came up? Should he let Liz keep a copy of his house key? Hundreds of scenarios rolled through his head, and he had answers for none of them. Like many aspects of his life, he thought he could just wing it.

John's drive home was uneventful. There were no rains, storms, crosses or creepy old men on the side of the road. As he pulled into his driveway, it occurred to him that he didn't remember many details of the drive back. Maybe his mind was so busy with the weird stuff, he made it home purely on muscle memory. Lately, he was making such reckless driving a habit. How many stop signs did he run through, because goodness knows, he didn't remember stopping for any of them? Luck or something was on his side, ensuring his safe arrival home.

After shutting Little Red down for the day, John simply sat there with his hands propped up on the bottom of the steering wheel. He was home but couldn't motivate himself to get out of the truck. Suddenly, all the emotion of the day came rushing back into his mind, as if a great dam had burst. He sobbed uncontrolledly and pounded his fists on the steering wheel and seat next to him. There were no words or thoughts to comfort him. John was lost but far more lost than he could possibly imagine.

After several tear-filled minutes, John said to himself, "Get over it. You're stronger than this."

It was as if there was a tiny drill instructor inside him, a voice from deep within him, urging him on. The voice was supportive but dark. He had listened to it before but never realized its seemingly bad intention.

"Pick yourself up, John," it said.

"You don't need her," the voice whispered in his head. But that wasn't true because he did need her. He loved her and she loved him.

"She doesn't love you, John," it said. No, he knew, that's a lie!

He grabbed the steering wheel in a death grip, then slammed his head into it, growling at the new pain in his body. He quickly yanked the keys out of the ignition, unlatched the door with a loud pop and kicked the door open. *Oh,* he thought, *the Atchleys are gonna hear that for sure.* There was too much to talk about, too much ammo they could use in spiritual warfare. He slammed Little Red's door and headed for the soft glow of light coming through a window behind the front porch. Home! He was almost there!

John ran up the walk, up the stairs and onto the porch to the front door. He remembered turning the porch light on, but it was off. *Stupid blown bulb!* He stole light from the window to search for the correct entry key.

"Come on!" he yelled, scolding himself for his inability to see in the dark. Finally, he located the right key, then, like reading brail, slid the key into the lock.

As he opened the door, a blast of cool air flowed across his body. His house was freezing, as if he had apparently forgotten to turn the air down before he left. In that moment, he could care less. After slamming the door behind him and engaging the deadbolt lock, he walked into his living room, chucking his keys through that beautiful arch onto the table in the dining area. The keys slid across the table and over the edge onto the floor.

"Perfect!" he said, knowing he would leave them

lying on the floor, just another casualty of the day.

His eyes locked onto the couch in the corner of the room, sitting there bathed in the same lamp light that spilled out of the window onto the front porch. He grabbed the curtains mounted over the window and yanked them shut, as if cutting himself off from the world outside his house. John quickly sidestepped from the window, turned around and plunged back first into the cool comfort of the couch. Rather than turn the table lamp off behind his head, he shaded his eyes with his arm. Good enough for a welcome sleep.

He had a bedroom with a comfortable king-sized bed, but the living room couch had been his favorite place to sleep for many nights. John found the rhythmic lighting of the TV across the room completely soothing, filling the room with light and dark shadows that seemed to dance across the floor and walls. However, on this night, there would be no TV to put him to sleep, only a tired mind and body, too wiped out to do anything else.

As memories of the day faded away, trading their time with restless slumber, John's arm fell from his eyes to his chest. His pupils darted about behind eyelids in their socket homes, chasing away final events of the day, giving way to sleep and dreams. The worst day of his life was over, or so it seemed.

CHAPTER 5

Times Past

John slept, stretched out on the couch as dreams rolled like film clips in his tired but active mind. His dreamscape was a refuge from the world outside but not an escape from his troubles and trials. Occasionally, his body twitched in reaction to the dreams and his mouth uttered incomprehensible mutterings that faded away in the silence of his home. His dreams revealed themselves in trend, over and over, again and again. Liz and God, then Liz and God, then again, Liz and God.

If he were awake, perhaps he could change his thoughts, but now, seemingly unconscious, programming was out of his control. Dreams were rare for John, but on this night, incredibly vivid visions were the only product of increasingly restless sleep. Hours in the world passed as images of Liz rolled through one after the other. One dream, or nightmare really, was causing much distress in his sleep. *End this, John! Wake up!* There would be no relief.

◆ ◆ ◆

He stood on a large rolling hill covered in tall green grass, wind gently blowing through the blades of grass creating ocean-like waves. Trees off in the distance swayed to the breeze as if dancing in place. Liz stood in front of him in one of her beautiful floral-print dresses. Her eyes and smile sparkled as she reached out to grasp John's hand.

The wind picked up, brushing her hair and dress to the side, then back behind her. The gusts grew stronger and stronger, and their sound rushed past John's ears in a piercing whisper. He reached for her, attempting to grab her hand, but she was too far away. As if lifted by an unseen force, she began to slide backwards, fading away from John. Liz's smile washed away as John tried to scream her name. His mouth moved, but there were no words or sounds. Maybe she couldn't hear him.

She continued to slip away, hands outstretched, grasping for John. He too began to slide away, pulled backwards by invisible claws.

Through the screaming wind, he heard a booming voice that said, "Elizabeth, come to me!"

Oh no, Liz heard the call too. John was screaming now but still with silent words. He watched, to his horror, as Liz stopped, turned around and looked skyward.

"No, Liz, don't go!" he pleaded silently.

Could anyone hear his screams, his urgent pleas for the love of his life, now slipping away to who knows where? The air moved with fury around him as lightning began to flash and thunder blasted across the undulating landscape.

"Liz, no!" he desperately yelled.

He watched as she zipped into the air, like a rocket seeking a target. In a split second, she was gone, blasting through bright clouds backlit by the sun. John stretched his hand to the sky as if trying to pull her back. His voice returned, but wild cracks of thunder covered his screams for her.

Then there was silence and stillness. The wind, thunder and lightning were suddenly absent. The skies darkened, covering the light of the sun where Liz had just passed through. John could feel it to his bones. Something very bad was about to happen, something far worse than anything he had ever experienced before.

He fell to his knees, stretched his arms to the dark, ominous skies and screamed, "No!"

The same voice that called for Liz rumbled around him, "I never knew you!"

The loud words of steel drove through to John's very soul, snapping the breath out of him and knocking him off his knees flat on his back. The wind, lightning, thunder and now rain, broke out around him in painful hysteria. The earth under him began to shake.

No, he wasn't crazy. His mind screamed, *John, this is real! This is really happening!*

As he stabilized his body, getting back to at least being on hands and knees, the ground around him began to open. Gaping holes in the terrain replaced vast stretches of beautiful green pasture. A crevasse opened underneath him, and gravity from deep within the Earth began to pull his feet and legs into an abyss. Scorching heat fed up through the fissure to burn his tender skin.

What have I done? he thought. *What's going on? Can't someone save me?* Painfully, John slipped over the edge, grasping at grass and dirt, anything to keep him from falling. *Wait! Liz! She tried to warn me,* he frantically thought. She tried to pull him off the road to perdition and out of the clutches of the world, but he didn't listen.

Her Faith was all nonsense to him, but now nonsense was eating him alive. An unending chain of thousands of images ran through his mind, things he had done over the course of his life. Tears burned down his cheeks, as he suddenly felt lawless, low and empty of life.

John's grasp failed and he began to fall, screaming unheard words at the top of his lungs. As he descended into the bowels of terror, the blackened clouds above gave way to darkness all around, and the air grew hotter and hotter. He closed his eyes, not wanting to see what was coming, though he had an idea of the horror awaiting him.

His ears were now open to the painful and chaotic screams from all around him. They grew louder, to the point where it was the only thing he could hear. Thousands upon thousands of people were screaming in different languages; the anguished voices deeply penetrating him, pounding on him like hundreds of sledge hammers.

He was feeling pain and agony as he had never felt before, and quickly, his screams were among the others, a testament to his torment. Finally, the only light he could see through burning eyes, was the fire all around him. John's fall ended abruptly, as he found himself lying on black sand riddled with coals and flaming embers. Painfully, he stood, screaming among the damned, looking at the unquenchable flames dancing around on his body.

Before him was something like a lake of fire, like molten lava bubbling inside a massive volcano. An invisible being compelled him to walk toward the fiery cauldron. All the while, he was screaming his heart out, completely cognizant of his surroundings and everlasting pain. Slowly, he walked, as if pushed, into the lake of fire. His body dissolved in flames. Every pain known to man surged through his body. He knew he should be dead, but he wasn't. John felt the pain all the time, like never-ending torture.

Something or someone forced his eyes open to look up and far away, past the flames, darkness and throngs of screaming humanity to a bright and glowing place. He saw her. It was Liz, dressed in pure white, standing in the sky, held up by a heavenly floor. She was smiling, face shining in expressions of bliss.

Between John and Liz was a vast expanse through which no one could travel. She was in Heaven and he was in Hell. *No, it can't be! It's all just a fairy tale, a myth.* Yet, he was there, burning forever and ever–alive and aware! He was immersed in an eternal blaze of agony and tormented by the life he chose not to live.

It was this dream of Hell John experienced repeatedly that night. He could not escape its terror, as it finished like a movie then started again for another punishing round. His tired body twitched and convulsed during the worst parts of the frightening visions. His restless legs had run a marathon right there in the living room. Sweat covered his body, drenching his clothes and the now not-so-comfortable couch he was lying on.

If only he could awaken. If only he could come back to the woken world to leave these nightmares behind. Was he sleeping? Maybe these were not really dreams. If he were dreaming, how could he ever get back to snoozing blissfully? He couldn't stay awake for the rest of his life in fear of the things he might see as he slumbered. Hours in the world passed as the tragic scenes ran like a horror movie repeatedly for what seemed like days. Vivid terror consumed John's mind.

"John?" called an unfamiliar voice outside the dream.

It was a male voice of age and wisdom that spoke to him through the harsh images rampaging through his head and body. *It may not be real,* he thought. It may be part of the hellish visions tearing his conscious thoughts apart. Maybe a new nightmare was getting ready to start. Someone was calling for him, perhaps trying to pull him out of one terrifying world for entrance into another.

Something was tugging at him, bending the light and space all around him, pulling him away from his nightmarish sequence. Suddenly, John felt as if he were levitating away from the cracked green fields and away from the earth that was about to swallow him like a hungry man gulping down a choice steak. The sound of earthquake, thunder and rain faded away to stone cold silence. His pain and agony were gone. *That's it, John! You're waking up! Don't stop now! Keep going!*

"John, wake up." Yes, it was the voice again, calling to him from outside the dream.

John's presence in the world slowly started to

return. He began to feel the couch under his body. It and his clothing seemed to be wet. His damp skin, touched by the cold air of the living room, caused him to shiver slightly. He was sweating profusely, a product of the horrible images running through his head. Yes, normal thoughts were coming back. *Thank goodness,* he thought, *no more being dragged along like a puppet in a terrible story.* Familiar light from the table lamp behind his head started to break through closed eyelids. Yes, yes, he was coming back to the world and the dream–the nightmare–was fading away. *Welcome back, John! Enough is enough!*

"John, you must awaken now."

The voice spoke to him again! *Wait a minute, who's in my house besides me? Who's this intruder waking me from these ridiculous nightmares? Maybe I should thank them. Somebody's in my house!*

John's eyes fluttered open, blurred by sleep, to see a white figure standing in the middle of his living room. *What was that?* he thought. As he attempted to open his eyes wide to see who or what was before him, stinging sweat from hours of torment flooded from around his eyes to touch the delicate corneas of his eyeballs. Frantically, he rubbed at his face trying to remove the painful fluid hindering his sight. His eyes burned as he rubbed and blinked repeatedly to gain a clear picture. Finally, success, as he could see.

Standing in front of him was the man in white. He was the same man standing alongside the road to Liz's apartment, and surely, the same man or figure John had seen on the runway earlier that day. The old man stood before John, wearing a bright white robe with a hood. The fabric of the garment reached down all the way to the tops of his feet, shod in what looked like leather sandals. The unusual clothing covered all but the old man's feet, hands and face. Like before, he was holding a twisted, but carved, wooden staff which stood almost as tall as he was. The man's face was wrinkled, aged and solemn in appearance. His cold, dark eyes locked onto John.

Now seeing clearly, knowing someone else was in his house, John scrambled and kicked his feet to push himself down the couch further away from the intruder. Surely, he wasn't afraid of a frail, old man. After the day John had just gone through, the old man could be the Angel of Death descending on him like a bird of prey. Yes, he was scared senseless. Old man nothing–he knew this guy could be a killer.

John couldn't seem to right himself into a sitting position on the couch or stand to confront the trespasser. His heart pounded explosively. His eyes darted about, looking at the space around him, trying to select something he could use in a defensive fight. *Nothing weapon-like! Wait, behind me, there's a lamp!* John swiftly stretched his right hand back behind and beyond his head, grasping for the tall slender body of the lamp lighting the room. He didn't dare take his eyes off the old man but quickly felt for the pseudo-weapon. *Got it!* John grasped the lamp body tightly and pulled it off the table to the side of his head, wielding it like a sword. As he yanked the lamp from its home on the end table, the light in the room changed wildly.

John managed to sit up on the couch, putting his arm out to the old man as if to say, "stay back." He shook the lamp in his hand, like a batter getting ready to hit a baseball. He wanted to say something or shout a threat to the man, but his mouth and tongue were unable to form any words. John sat, lamp at the ready, trying not to appear frightened but knew he probably exuded terror.

It was a strange standoff, each of them looking at one another, but John could tell the advantage went to the old man who stood there calmly leaning on his wooden staff. In mere moments of fleeting thoughts, John tried to remember what to do if attacked by something, maybe a bear. *Don't show fear! Make yourself look bigger! Make a lot of noise!* He wasn't doing any of those things and didn't know if he could. *How hard would it be to defend myself?* he thought. It's an old man for goodness' sake!

After a few terrifying seconds, the old man in white finally spoke. "You won't be needing that," he said, motioning to the lamp in John's hand.

Instantly, John felt the iron grip he had on the lamp's body collapse, as if someone had taken it from him. Incredibly, the stand-in weapon was no longer in his hand but immediately back on the end table behind him. He snapped his head around to look at the lamp sitting on the table as if undisturbed. *What? Did that really just happen? Am I still dreaming?* Suddenly remembering his eyes were off target, John snapped his head back around to the old man who simply stood there watching.

"This is not a dream, John. I am just as real as you are. Are you real, John?"

The intruder grinned slightly and motioned to John, who clenched and unclenched his fist, to see if he was, indeed, real. Without taking his eyes off the man before him, John thumped his sternum, listening to the hollow sound of reality within his chest.

John considered the repercussions of answering the man's question. He could be admitting to seeing this guy. Worse, he might be confessing to a state of insanity. His reactions could lead to his understanding of everything that had happened that day being real. He didn't know and only mumbled meager sounds. He was unsure of what to do.

"John, you are not insane, and yes, everything you have experienced is real."

John was puzzled about how this stranger standing in his living room was able to know the very thoughts running through his mind. Good or bad, he knew he had to say something.

"Who are you?" asked John as he eased back against the couch arm, cornered in the room.

"John, I mean you no harm. I am a friend," said the old man as he placed both hands on the staff, as if tired.

A gentle calm swept over John's body, as if a giant weight fell from him. His heartbeat began to slow and his breathing returned to normal. Yes, he was afraid, but strangely, felt invincible. The man's voice was calming, as he sounded wise beyond his apparent ancient years.

As skepticism crept back in, though, John couldn't help but wonder if the calm was just a mind trick of some kind, that possibly, the visitor was luring him into a horrible trap. He measured the consequences of engaging in a verbal defensive.

"Friend? What kind of friend scares the hell out of the people he calls friends?"

Oops! Maybe he overplayed his hand. He knew he had to be careful with his answers so as not to draw retribution from the stranger. However, the man seemed calm and not violent at all.

"John, when you were eight years old and you hid in Nathan's locker at school to scare him, and we both know you succeeded, were you being a friend?"

John's jaw dropped open and his eyes bulged in surprise. How in the world did the old man know that? John had all but forgotten about that incident that earned him detention for two days. It was the only time in all his shenanigans he had ever made Nathan cry. In fact, despite his friend's reaction, John had done it more than once. He had even done it as an adult, hiding in a trashcan at Nathan's house, waiting to spring out at him when he came home. Did the stranger know about that too?

John shot back, asking, "How did you know that?"

"That is not important," said the old man.

"Well, then, who are you? What's your name?" John asked, as he braced himself against the couch's arm in case he had to bolt forward in defense or escape.

"That, too, is not important. You must calm down, John. I mean you no harm."

While keeping his eye on the stranger, John relaxed his grip on the couch and settled back into the cushion. His body continued to unwind from the stress of the moment. Now was his chance to get some badly needed answers. The man stood staring at John, as if waiting for the next round of questions.

"Did I see you out on State Road 9 earlier? Was it you standing in front of my truck?"

"Yes," said the man plainly.

John was a bit unnerved by the simplicity of the man's answer. Where was the apology? Hey, sorry if I scared you. Hey, sorry if I made you think you were about to die at the hand of an ax murderer. Let me buy you a cup of coffee and make up for it. Okay then, on to the next question.

"Was it you standing on the side of the road when I was taking Liz home?" John raised his eyebrows as if begging for an answer.

"Yes." Again, a simple answer containing absolutely no details.

"John," he spoke again, "what details would you like?"

John knew things were getting well beyond bizarre. However, it motivated him to get answers for the tough questions that were most prominent in his mind. *Go for it, John! Ask away!*

"Earlier, did you make it storm and rain out on State Road 9? Was that real? Did you make the weird wall of rain on the way to pick up Liz? Was that real?"

Now, he was getting somewhere. *Let the answers come forth,* he thought. His questions gave him the boldness to take command of the conversation.

"No, John, I did not, and yes; it was all real, as real as you here in your home."

"Well, then who did?"

John's agitation grew and his growing lack of patience was on display. However, he knew he might not want an answer to his question. The next words spoken could potentially bring to him an answer he had denied his entire life. For that reason, he was afraid for what he would hear.

"Fear not, John. Can the Creator not manipulate the created?"

The man's face remained firm and void of any kind

of emotion John would be able to read. There were no nonverbal signals he could easily interpret. The man was like a machine standing in the living room, steady and unmovable in word or action.

John contemplated the answer for a few seconds, letting it sink into his head. Maybe he shouldn't have asked. *Wait a minute! Was the old man implying he was...? No, it can't be! The man admitted he didn't create the rain and storms. What did that answer mean?*

John sat in silence for several seconds thinking about the words just spoken by the stranger in his living room. *Okay, John, think this through. The old man asked if the Creator can manipulate the created. Yeah, probably, so what? Did he mean Creator as in God the Creator?*

John didn't believe in any of that stuff. He thought it was all just a fairy tale of moral teachings man created over the years. His brain was saying the visitor and all the weird events of the day were just illusions, yet, it all felt so real.

John slowly stood to face the old man whose eyes followed every movement he made. John looked him over once more. Long, pure white robe, head covered, uses a staff and seems to do supernatural things. He begged to know if the person in front of him was doing those things. John could only begin to imagine who or what in the world the guy was. Then, it suddenly occurred to him, however ridiculous it sounded, that this robed oddity might not be of this world.

Then John's mouth fell open once more in incredible amazement. Was the God of the Christians standing right there in front of him, right there in his very own living room? It couldn't be because there was no God as far as John was concerned. On the other hand, what if He were? Should he drop to his knees and beg for forgiveness?

John lifted a hand and slightly extended finger to the intruder and uttered in a broken voice, "Wait, uh, you aren't, uh...How do I put this?"

"No, John, I am not the Being you think me to be," the man stated while remaining perfectly tranquil.

"Then who are you?"

"John, I am merely a messenger. I am not the One whose name I am not worthy to speak."

"By the 'One,' do you mean God?"

Maybe that was another question he shouldn't have asked. Really, it was another question he didn't want answered, a truth he wanted to walk away from and a fact he wanted to ignore.

"You will see, John."

Fear gave way to confusion and doubt. John shook his head slightly and then carefully stepped forward toward the man. When he got within touching distance, he stopped, contemplating what he was about to do. He would try to touch the man in white, knowing it could be the worst decision he could make in a life full of bad choices.

John swallowed, shook his head and breathed what could be one last breath. Slowly, he extended his hand out toward the man's sleeve. *He's letting me do this,* John thought. It was go or no go at that point.

With great hesitation, he touched the fabric of the sleeve, rubbing its rough texture between his fingers. *Okay, the robe is real, at least, but what about the body inside it?* He squeezed slightly on the sleeve until he felt the man's arm inside. *Yep, that's real too!* He jerked his hand back to the safety of his own body.

"John, we are wasting precious time."

"Precious time for what?"

John sensed things were about to change, that a new phase of his extraordinary day was about to begin. He didn't want to trust the old man but felt compelled to do so. There were answers out there somewhere and he had to find them, even if it meant trusting someone or something he didn't know. It appeared to him that knowledge would begin right there in his living room at the direction of someone he had never met.

"John, you must see the things to come. You must warn those who deny the Way, the Truth and the Life," said the old man whose eyes burned a clear path straight to John, a mere man feeling the weight of the gaze.

The Way, the Truth and the Life sounded vaguely familiar to John. He had heard that somewhere before but was unsure where. Maybe the words were from a television show, a book, or some other person. The man spoke those words with such reverence and respect, John felt they had to be important, but at that moment, they were just words to him.

All of it, the thought of a God and Heavenly messengers, seemed utterly ridiculous to him. Seeing things to come seemed purely outlandish. As crazy as the idea seemed, perhaps he was going to see the future now.

"Okay, I'll bite," said John with an expression of sarcasm.

The old man slightly nodded his head in acknowledgement. He slowly extended the staff toward John, letting it rest on the floor between them. It was a beautiful, almost artistic piece of wood, lacking any kind of unnatural ornamentation. It was aged, but preserved, slightly curved in the middle and narrowed to a point at the bottom. On top of the staff was what appeared to be a knot in the wood, obviously something to take hold of if necessary.

The man said nothing, but John sensed he needed to touch the staff. *What harm could that cause?* he thought. Cautiously, he again put his hand out, this time to touch the staff. Quickly, he tapped the wood and pulled his hand back, checking to make sure his fingers were all there and that there were no injuries. *No digits missing—good to go!* He had tested the waters and now it was time to jump in for a swim.

Still, he hesitated for a few seconds, mere seconds that seemed more like minutes. Suddenly, standing there in the living room in the presence of the visitor, time and space felt distorted, as if they were moving in unnatural ways. John's body felt painlessly twisted, turned and pulled in multiple directions, all the while moving in rhythm with the altered state of a now hazy environment.

Dizziness invaded his body, giving rise for the need to stabilize on something. He knew the staff was there as a tool to steady against at a time like this. He only needed to reach out for it. With one more deep breath and one huge leap of faith in something, but not sure what, he stretched out to the staff and grabbed it just below the old man's hand.

John's physical environment changed rapidly. After grasping the staff, a cool tingling sensation enveloped his hand, then began moving up his arm, eventually taking hold of his entire body. Suddenly, a bone-chilling darkness surrounded him. He was standing, maybe, in nothingness above, below and all around. A blast, something like a shock wave, rocketed past him. John gripped the staff, as it seemed to be stable and immovable, but not for long.

He felt the piece of wood suddenly pulling him somewhere into the darkness. Forward? Backward? Sideways? Up? Down? In the emptiness, there was no way to tell or pinpoint direction. John pulled closer to the staff as it propelled him further into the dark. In the distance, or a false sense of what might be distance, light appeared. John and the light were converging on each other. The light may have been moving. He didn't know.

Then a most unsettling thought wedged its way into John's head. *I could be dead.* Yes, he had heard stories of people seeing the light at the end of the tunnel. He didn't know if he was in a tunnel or not, but there was light, for sure. To go toward or to go away from the light was not in his power, as the staff was pulling him along like a dog on a leash. He didn't want to let go of the strange wooden device, his apparent ride to somewhere.

The old man was gone! The staff was still there, but its owner was gone. John turned his head in all directions looking for the stranger, who just minutes before, had invaded his space. It could have been minutes, but he wasn't sure. *Where did that guy go? Did he disappear and leave me for dead?* The light was closer now, growing brighter and brighter.

Out of the darkness, something like headlights were zipping toward him. He assumed cars might exist where he was going. If there were vehicles of any kind, he could be standing in the middle of the road and their path of travel. Closer! Closer! He wondered if being hit by a car would cause instantaneous death so that he wouldn't suffer. John held his arm in front of his face to shield himself against the rapidly approaching lights. He yelled in defiance, or possibly fear, hoping to escape what was about to happen.

A cool rush of wind raced over his body as he seemed to float in the darkness, held in place by something invisible. Suddenly, millions of life moments flashed all around him in an awesome strobe effect. It was his life on spiritual film at super high speed. John could see each of the thousands upon thousands of moments as they passed by and then faded into the darkness behind him.

Accompanying the kaleidoscope of life moments on display were thousands of different voices, all talking at the same time. He could hear his parents, Liz, Nathan, Nathan's parents, friends from long ago, teachers going all the way back to his grade school days and a host of other people. Their voices, in concert, sounded like someone zipping through multiple radio frequencies without stopping. Their garbled words were in tune for just fractions of a second, but he knew exactly who they were.

With all the sights and sounds, John's mind should have been in sensory overload, but it wasn't. He knew he was, very quickly, taking a journey through his own life, witnessing things far removed from present time. He saw himself, as clips of life passed by like a speeding train. Yes, he was seeing himself from the perspective of another set of eyes. Then, there were other times, perhaps memories relived in spirit, where the view was from his own eyes. It was all crazy, yet, it was happening.

Again, the idea of death pierced the moment. Stories of people seeing their lives flash before their eyes invaded his blurring thoughts. Was he seeing his own life flash before his very eyes? Was this it, his demise on display?

In an instant, the light, the memories, the people and their voices were gone. The wind rush over his body and the sensation of movement ended abruptly. John simply existed there in the dark nothingness, floating with the staff in hand. He looked around but couldn't even see his hand in front of his face, nor could he see the staff clenched in his fist.

Is this Heaven? he thought. Then, he remembered the vivid dreams from before of what he assumed was Hell. He recalled there were "things" in Hell–very bad, very scary things. Surely there would be "things" in Heaven too, unlike the dead and empty space he seemed to be floating in. He guessed he could be in a holding cell, a momentary stopover in a continuing journey. He closed his eyes, not wanting to be witness to the next stages of the odyssey.

Light slowly began to penetrate through John's eyelids, as if someone was turning the dimmer up in a dark room. Heat, possibly warm rays of sunlight, danced about on his skin. His feet, once again, began to feel body weight and sweet terra firma underneath. With eyes still closed, he now listened to the sounds emerging from the silence. He heard men and women talking, happy children playing, exuberant yelling, joyful applause and cheerful laughing. This wasn't Heaven, and it surely wasn't Hell either.

With eyes still closed, probably afraid of the

unknown, he continued to listen intently to his new surroundings. He heard the familiar "ping" of an aluminum bat smashing a baseball. The sweet, familiar sound reverberated around him. The ensuing crowd noise of cheers and jeers was deafening. A booming voice rang out, "Base hit and bases loaded. Injury time out called on the field."

Slowly, John opened his eyes to see a baseball stadium, a bright sunny day and thousands of people enjoying the game at play. He knew exactly where he was, Howard J. Lamade Stadium, a wonderful venue in which he once had the pleasure of playing. As he stood gazing at the field and stadium from beyond the outfield fence, a wide smile broke out across his face in remembrance of yesteryears.

In the moment, John hadn't considered how he was able to be there at the stadium hundreds of miles from his house. But, to be honest, he was caught up in the bliss of the sensation and didn't much care. He was suddenly transported to times past through those playing on the field–wonderful times and memories without all the worries of being an adult.

However, after soaking in a few seconds of his surroundings, reality–maybe–set in. How did he get there? Looking around, he didn't see the old man, and he no longer clutched the staff in his hand. The gears and cogs of thought turned in his head. *If everything is real, as it appears to be, then the old man and/or the staff has somehow gotten me to this stadium. How am I going to get home, or do I even need to concern myself with that?*

A familiar voice spoke softly behind him, saying, "John, do you recognize this place."

The man in white, stepping up beside John, was

back. The bright sun reflected off his pure white garment, almost blinding and surely obvious to those around. He leaned on the top of the staff as if he had just walked a thousand miles. Though John wouldn't admit it, he was somewhat happy to see the old man, who in the last several minutes, had strangely become normalcy in his out-of-whack life.

"This is Howard J. Lamade Stadium. I played in a baseball tournament here when I was about twelve," said John smiling.

John noticed the people all around didn't seem to be paying any attention to the weird guy in a white robe standing next to him, giving birth to the idea that nothing around him was real. Blurred reality said he might be dreaming again or hallucinating. It could be that he was still sitting on his comfy, little couch in his home.

"John," said the old man, "you are wondering if this is real."

"I don't know what's crazier–wondering if this is all real or wondering how in the world you know what I'm thinking."

John scratched and rubbed his head as he looked about. The sights, sounds and feelings sure seemed authentic enough. The light from the sun was bright and he could sense its warmth on his skin. The people looked real enough, moving about and doing seemingly real things.

"John, you are in the way."

"What? What do you mean?"

"In a few seconds, a young, red-headed girl will ask you to move."

John wasn't at all sure what the old man was talking

about. How could he know about anything or anyone?

As if right on cue, John felt a tug on his left arm, accompanied by the nearly inaudible voice of a child. He turned around to see a red-headed girl standing behind him, holding a sheet of cardboard as big as she was. She was wearing red shorts and a white t-shirt with the words "I LOVE SOFTBALL" spelled out in the shape of a heart. She looked up to John's face, shielding her eyes from the sun with her empty hand.

"What did you say?" John asked her.

"If you keep standing here, you're gonna get hit, mister."

She pointed back behind her up to the top of a tall, grassy hill on which her friends were waiting. John saw that rambunctious kids were standing at the crest of the hill ready to race down on their cardboard sleds.

Of course, now he understood. Afterall, he had done the same thing in his day. When he and his teammates weren't playing baseball on the field, having meetings, practicing or sitting in the stands watching, they were riding pieces of cardboard down that same grass hill. It was a time-honored tradition. He smiled widely.

"I gotcha," he replied to the youth. John motioned for the old man to follow and said, "These kids are trying to have fun. Let's get out of the way."

As he began to walk away, he turned to notice the little girl was staring at him with curiosity painted across her face, looking around as if trying to find something or someone. She eventually shrugged her small shoulders and started to run back to her friends at the top of the hill.

"Time to race, losers," she yelled back up to the group of carboard-happy kids.

"She couldn't see you, could she?" John covered his mouth as he talked, not wanting anyone to think he may have been talking to himself.

Very calmly, and again, without explanation or detail, the man spoke. "No, John, she could not see me."

"Can any of these thousands of people see you?"

"Only you can see me, John."

The two of them continued to walk around the outfield fence until they were behind the shortstop position on the field. Of course, John knew this place, after having played several of the most important baseball games of his life there. However, there was something even more familiar with the surroundings, or maybe the time. From a distance, the coach looked like someone he knew from long ago. The player's uniforms stood out. Even the players seemed memorable.

John noticed the old man was watching the activities on the field. Why? Why should he care about a baseball game? He didn't look like the sporting type. They both watched as the medical staff tended to the first baseman, having been involved in a serious collision with the last baserunner. The crowd cheered as the injured player, assisted by the coach, stood and limped back toward the dugout. A replacement player met him by the pitcher's mound and tagged him with a gloved hand as if to say, "I got this."

"I love good sportsmanship like this," John said, motioning to the crowd. "All the fans are standing, clapping and cheering for this hurt kid. Even the fans and players for the other team are cheering this little guy on. I hope he'll be alright."

"The boy will come back into the game in the fifth

inning."

"How do you know that?" asked John, perplexed.

John thought about the futility of his query. Who was he to challenge anything happening to him? How was it that any of these things were occurring? They were. How was it the old man ended up in his living room? He was there and John physically touched him to be sure. How did he know the little, red-headed girl would speak? She did. How in the world did he know, though still unseen, the injured player would be back in the game later that day? John was growing tired of the questions and wanted hard answers.

"That is not important, John." The old man was still calm and emotionless.

"What do you mean it's not important? It may not be important to you, but it is to me."

John realized he had not been covering his mouth and that some of the people around him were staring. Parents clutched their kids tightly, as if to protect them from the crazy guy talking to himself.

"Again, John, we are wasting time."

The man shifted on his feet, possibly from exertion, or maybe from his first display of frustration with an unbelieving John. Perhaps he was growing tired of the questions.

Covering his mouth, obviously annoyed, John said, "There you go again, talking about wasting time. Whose time are we wasting by standing here watching a baseball game?"

The man kept his eyes on the field of play. "John, you know this looks familiar."

"Of course, it looks familiar. I told you I played here when I was a kid," replied John as his agitation grew and his fond memories began to fade away.

"Look closer, John. Tell me what you see."

"A bunch of kids playing baseball," said John as he motioned to the field.

The old man closed his eyes and sighed deeply. "On the next pitch, the batter will hit the ball toward the shortstop who will catch the ball for out one. Then, he will tag the base runner off second base for out two. Finally, he will throw the ball to first base for the last out of the inning."

"What? Do you know how rare a triple play is?"

The man lifted off the staff to let it lean toward the shortstop on the field. "John, please watch."

John watched the batter take his stance in the batter's box, digging his feet in and preparing to hit the ball thrown to him. The batter swirled his aluminum bat in the air overhead as if to say, "bring it on."

Part of John wanted the kid to swing and miss, to prove the old man was wrong, that maybe this was all a dream. The catcher signaled and the pitcher nodded in return. *Here it comes,* thought John, *the moment of truth.* He had seen it so many times–the wind up, the pitch, the miscalculated slash at the ball and the loud smack as the ball slammed into the catcher's glove.

A loud "ping" echoed through the stadium as the batter laid aluminum on leather, hitting a perfect line drive to the shortstop for the out. With smooth, precise, almost mechanical motion, the shortstop tagged the runner caught off second base. Then, seemingly without thought, probably perfection made by hours of practice, the young player threw the ball across the field to first base. There, the baseman tagged the runner as he attempted a returning slide to safety.

The exuberant fans erupted in commotion, some cheering wildly and some yelling in disbelief. Every baseball enthusiast in attendance that day knew how rare the triple play was, yet they had just seen one from players who were years away from calling themselves professional athletes.

The PA announcer boomed to the stadium of onlookers, as if they didn't know, "Triple play! No runs batted in! That's the end of the third, folks."

The old man slowly turned his head toward John, who stood in amazement of what he had just witnessed. John's mouth hung open in disbelief. What he had just seen, especially from kids, was amazing and suddenly very familiar.

With a slight grin, the old man said, "It was the best play..."

John cut him off saying, "...of my life."

Why they were there at that moment in time, at that place, now made sense to John. He now understood why everything was familiar. The players, the coaches, the experience on the field all rang bells of familiarity in his head. He was watching himself play in a baseball tournament from years ago.

Of course, the player who had just made the spectacular play was wearing good old number eight, John's number from his early baseball days. His judgement was so clouded he couldn't see the moment. The kid playing shortstop on the field was himself from years ago. *Amazing!*

Number eight, the shortstop, his younger self, turned around momentarily as his fellow players congratulated him with hugs, pats and verbal accolades. For a few fleeting seconds, kid John locked eyes with adult John, who smiled back in recognition of the truth—that everything he was now experiencing was very real.

He wanted so much to run down to kid John, now sitting in the dugout. He wanted to look closely into his young face, to see the life of youth once again. He wanted to shake hands with his fledgling self, maybe give him a hug of congratulations but knew it could never happen. He wanted to tell young John how great life would turn out. He desperately wanted to tell him about Liz and what he needed to do to keep her.

Liz surged back into his thoughts. John knew what he needed to do to keep her, but seemingly, that time had passed. Perhaps he could change his entire known life to spend the rest of it with the woman he loved so deeply. For a moment, the way ahead looked promising.

He longed to march down to young John and boldly tell him, "You're gonna grow up to be an atheist, but it's gonna cost you the woman you love."

But there was an even greater truth that eluded him—being an atheist was going to cost him so much more. How could he make things right? Did he even want to make things right?

"John, do you understand why we are here?" said the man as he motioned to the area around them.

Again, covering his mouth, John said, "I think you're trying to prove something."

"Correct, John."

Okay, he thought, *here they come. I'm finally going to get some answers. Give them to me; I can take it. Oh yeah, time to find out what was really happening.*

The man in white gave no immediate answers. Disappointed, John felt he needed to ask a probing question, but what? Okay, the old man was trying to prove something, but what?

"What is it that you want me to understand?"

Great question, John! He was so proud of himself. In a self-fulfilled, sarcastic kind of way, he had finally figured something out. He knew, though, he was only scratching the surface of something big.

"Soon you will see things of a time to come. But to understand, you had to see the things of a time past."

With great satisfaction, smiling, John answered, "Oh, I get it. You showed me this so that I would believe something else later."

"Correct, John," said the man as he pulled the staff close and leaned on it with both hands clasped over the knot at the top. "Are you ready?"

John now knew he was moving through time. He wasn't sure how it was working, but it was, indeed, happening. The man in white had something to do with it for sure, but John sensed there was a greater power at work. Though he didn't want to admit it, somehow intertwined in his whole adventure, there was something exceedingly greater causing things to occur. For the first time in his life, John was beginning to doubt every motivation he ever had to be an atheist.

Feeling somewhat sad at the idea of leaving familiar territory of days gone by, John side-stepped closer to the man in white, maybe his vessel of travel. A single tear trickled down his cheek, but he quickly wiped it away with his palm. He strained to hold back any further display of emotion.

Through trembling lips, John spoke softly, "Let's go."

The old man eased off the staff and lifted it from the ground in front of him. As John watched, the man moved the staff over and lightly jabbed it into the ground between them. Without any words spoken, John knew exactly what he had to do; grab the staff. He hesitated, considering where the two of them would go next. Would it be a good place? A bad place? Peaceful? Dangerous? The anxiety of not knowing was eating at him like acid.

Closing his eyes, the man in white said, "You know what to do, John. We must go."

With a deep, cleansing breath, John closed his eyes and grasped the staff below the old man's shriveled hand. Instantly, a frigid darkness enveloped his body and, without pain, he felt as though he was being stretched about like a toy with rubber limbs.

He clenched the staff tighter as it pulled him along into the black nothingness. There was a sensation of movement, but his internal gyroscope was unable to determine direction or placement in space. He was at the mercy of the staff, or perhaps, a greater, imperceptible authority.

John opened his eyes to see a visible, but hazy, light bending and twisting all around him. The man in white was gone again, giving way to a gentle feeling of loneliness. Suddenly, images of his life returned, rapidly zipping through his field of vision. Voices from a lifetime lived penetrated deep into his auditory senses, garbled together like listening to a thousand distant radios. Although the visions and voices rocketed by him at the speed of light, he was able to see and hear many of them clearly.

He saw the day he met Nathan and the way he, in his toddler voice, asked, "Do you wanna be my friend?" He saw his dad running along beside him as he learned to ride a bike without training wheels. He heard his dad say, "You're okay, John. I've got you." He saw his mom, standing with hands on hips, asking, "Why did you have to do that to Nathan? Isn't he your friend?" He saw himself as a child kneeling at the foot of his bed, hands clasped, as if to pray. He saw his father walking into the room saying, "Stop that foolishness!"

The visions and voices became too fast to see or interpret, and he began to experience sensory overload. His head began to throb and his stomach began to churn. He remembered his mom telling him to close his eyes and relax during bouts of car sickness. *I hope it works here too,* he thought. John closed his eyes, trying to put away the film reel that was his life, but he could do nothing about the voices that raged all around him. Maybe he could let go of the staff and cover his ears. No, he couldn't.

At the pinnacle of his emotional response, nearly all sense of motion in his body stopped. For a moment, he floated in the nothingness with his eyes closed, not wanting to see what was around him. John was suspended in the middle of something but had no idea what. His mind was unable to determine if he was upside down, facing left or facing right. He just couldn't tell. He thought to himself that the floating sensation he was experiencing must be like what astronauts feel in space. He wasn't in space as far as he knew. Honestly, he had no idea where he was.

Courage and curiosity forced his eyes open to see waves of light slowly moving around him, like smoke moving through the light of a projector. The sensation of movement was completely gone, but the overlapping voices still blasted through his ear canals. Looking around, John saw only the hazy light twirling about like spectral lifeforms. Yes, the visions of his life were gone, but the voices were still there.

Was he now stuck there–wherever there happened to be? Was he supposed to do something to get himself moving again? Was he ever really moving? Was there something more he needed to figure out? Nothing came to mind except to trust in something he had not yet seen.

The voices slowly faded away as he floated there in space in sort of a suspended animation. Away the voices went until the waves of light, apart from the cold, were the only sensory input for his entire body. Trying to think, he closed his eyes again to hide the distraction of light, but he could do nothing about the cold biting into his skin.

A familiar voice broke through the silence, that of the man in white, saying, "John, you must now see the things to come. In time, you must warn those who deny the Way, the Truth and the Life. You must not fail."

There were those words again–Way, Truth and Life. He hoped someone was going to tell him what those words meant. How could he warn people if he didn't even know what warning he was supposed to give? He opened his eyes again but saw nothing but the light. John attempted to yell out to the old man, but his mouth moved without speech. He yelled again, but in futility, as there were still no words.

Suddenly, John's body felt compressed, as if a giant shockwave blasted by him in the void. The clouds of light rapidly transformed into bright white all around. *It's brighter than the sun,* he thought, closing his eyes once again. He heard a loud boom, like a single crack of thunder on a stormy day. Quickly, the frigid cold eating away at the sensitive nerves in his skin, gave way to merely being cold. His sense of motion returned, but this time, in an obvious direction–down.

John remembered the dreams he had while sleeping on the couch in the living room, trying to snooze away the ridiculously bad day he had. He remembered falling through the earth in the nightmare. *Down is bad!* Anxiety grew as he thought about going back to that horrible place to see something else. Surely that wasn't what the old man wanted him to see because he had already been there and didn't ever want to go back.

In an instant, John's body achieved stillness. Without opening his eyes, he could tell he was on his back with arms and hands at his sides. Fortunately, he was also back at the mercy of gravity. Movement ceased and he heard no sounds. He wondered what he would see when he opened his eyes. More importantly, he feared for where and when he would be.

He told himself, "I should be used to this by now."

Slowly he opened his eyes, allowing them to adjust from the intense brightness to which they had just been exposed. His vision became clearer and clearer until everything was in focus and sharp. Before him was a textured ceiling, a familiar one. He thought, then quickly laughed off the idea that if he were in Hell, it had a textured ceiling. *That's silliness,* he thought. The things he was now seeing were all very familiar.

Keeping his body firmly planted and still, John rolled his head to the left. It was his living room, his walls, his pictures and his hallway. Then, he rolled his head to the right. It was his rug, his couch, his end table and his lamp. He imagined his tired eyes might be looking at an incredibly detailed facsimile of his home. He rolled his head back to the ceiling and rubbed the chilled skin of his arms, noting his raised hairs. His place was cold, just as he had left it.

Grimacing in pain, John slowly sat up and propped himself up with aching arms. He looked around. *It's my house! Was all that a dream? Did I experience everything I thought I had? Why am I so tired? Why am I on the floor?*

John searched for answers. Maybe he had stopped for some beer on the way home, gotten drunk and was now just waking up from a stupor that put him on his living room floor. He had heard of people blacking out from drinking binges, but the problem was that he had never been drunk in his entire life. There were no beer bottles around, so if he had gotten hammered, the alcohol must have been in stealth mode. He reasoned that a state of intoxication wasn't a plausible explanation.

John remembered everything clearly, as if he were an active participant in the events of the last several hours. No, he didn't get drunk. The saga must have been real–maybe. His head was hurting and his body was tired and aching, the opposite impacts of a regenerating sleep.

The couch looked as if it were calling his name, "Hey, John, come and take a nap." Yes, that's what he needed, a nice long nap. Then, he could wake up refreshed and figure everything out tomorrow, that is, if there was anything to figure out. Oh, how good his beloved couch would feel! He could only hope for a dreamless slumber.

John reached for the couch arm and pulled his legs under him to self-right off the floor. Every movement brought a new pain, it seemed. He felt like someone had beaten the living daylights out of him while asleep, if what he had been doing was actual sleeping. He ached as if he had travelled in a cramped, little car for thousands of miles without a break. *Boy,* he thought, *does it hurt!*

He huffed and puffed until he was able to get to his knees, then used the couch to propel his body upward into a standing position. John put his hands on his sore hips, then slowly leaned forward, backward and then side to side to stretch. *Little movements, John! Little movements!* With almost military precision, John did an about face but immediately recoiled backward to the couch, clutching his chest in surprise.

Standing there in front of him, alone and not held by human hands was the staff the man in white had been using. The wooden stick just stood there, perfectly balanced like a pencil propped up on its own eraser. John quickly rubbed his eyes, thinking he might be seeing things. However, clear eyes verified the staff was positioned upright in front of him with no strings attached. He was seeing it for sure but this time without the owner. The old man was nowhere to be seen. John hastily looked around, knowing the man could be hiding somewhere, watching every moment unfold.

John yelled out. "Okay, you can come out now! This isn't funny!"

There was no response, only the sound of his own heart rapidly beating deep within his chest. Locking eyes on the staff, he knew a new phase of his adventure was about to begin.

CHAPTER 6

To the School

Time wasn't standing still, and the clock on the wall over the couch continued to run, ticking off second after second. It was dark outside, very late, but tomorrow had not yet come. John was still experiencing the worst day of his life. Perhaps time, in a relative sense, had stood still while he was away. Yes, he recognized he was truly away, somehow traveling to that moment of his baseball youth from long ago. It was all very real, and the biggest proof of authenticity was standing in his living room.

John paced rapidly back and forth in front of the staff which continued to stand on its own, possibly held in place by invisible hands. He couldn't take his eyes off it, for fear of what it might be able to do on its own. He didn't know the object's capabilities. As he paced aimlessly in the living room, he began to gnaw on his fingernails, a habit he had not practiced until that point. His hands fidgeted nervously from mouth to hips, then to his head and then back to his mouth, over and over.

His mind was racing, considering all the

possibilities and outcomes of any and every action he could take. As well as he could, he had to consider the facts. Fact one: he was having one incredible kind of a day. Fact two: the man in white was as real as he could be. Fact three: the old man said John would have to see something more in the future. Fact four: the staff, now standing intrusively in his home, could somehow take him to see those future things.

Then, his thinking switched gears. What if he didn't want to see whatever he was supposed to see in the future? What if he didn't want to go on any more adventures? Where was his choice in all this? Why should he care about anything that happens in the future? He stopped his pacing to face the staff, as if he were about to address it like a person.

"What if I don't want to do this? Why me?" he asked loudly.

No answer! He might as well have been asking himself.

If it were possible to have a stare down with an inanimate object, John was doing it. Maybe he could just walk away, and the staff would just fade away or disappear. He might be able to go out for a short drive, and when he came back, it would be gone. If he weren't afraid to touch it, he could just grab it and hide it somewhere. From experience, he knew touching it would probably initiate his next trip through time to who knows where.

Okay, he would go back to his bedroom and lie down. *Good decision!* If he went to bed and had a nap, it might be gone when he got up. Maybe whatever entity was making this thing appear would also give up on John, take the staff away and find someone else.

Suddenly, he was thinking of himself as an unwilling participant in the things going on that day or the next.

Carefully, John sidestepped past the staff, headed for the hallway where his bedroom was located. He didn't dare take his eyes off the mysterious piece of wood, until it disappeared behind the wall as he moved further away. He felt his way along the wall until he found the door frame to the bedroom. *Almost there,* he thought.

John eased into the dark room, quickly fumbling for the light switch on the wall. He never liked being in dark rooms. In all honesty, his fear was from old childhood stories about monsters lurking under and inside things. Finally, his fingers danced across the switch to turn the light on.

"What the..." he shouted, jumping back out of the room into the hallway.

In front of him, next to his bed, stood the staff just as it had been standing in the living room. Quickly, John ran back into the living room, sliding on the floor to a halt, barely avoiding collision with the staff that was now back where it started. "No Way!" he shouted.

He snapped around and ran with breakneck speed back to the bedroom, stopping himself by slamming his body against the doorframe. The staff was back in the bedroom. As he stared at the apparently magical wooden stick, he considered it couldn't possibly be in two places at once.

Staying in the doorway, within eyeshot of the staff in the bedroom, he peeked around the door frame, down the hallway, past the corner to see if the staff was in the living room. It wasn't. John snapped his head back to the bedroom to make sure the dreaded device was still there. It was. As if playing a game of cat and mouse, John took off for the living room, yet again, stopping short of a collision.

"Incredible," John muttered between gasps for air.

John was breathing heavily with eyes locked onto the traveling menace. Okay, he knew it was following him. He assumed the two of them could now be one–inseparable man and staff. Whatever was meant to happen was apparently going to happen, and there was nothing he could do about it.

He remembered times in school, as a child, sitting in class with his hands down while the teacher asked for volunteers. One didn't dare raise their hand in submission to a request. John knew it was usually smarter to not offer services, a practice still in use for him as an adult. He remembered how the teachers picked he and Nathan as "volunteers," usually because of some trickery they had done. Rarely, was the chore for which they were "voluntold" beneficial to them in any way.

For the task at hand, whatever it was, John knew it somehow involved him and that there would be no escape from it. Everything that had happened that day led to this moment. He walked around the staff to stand between it and the couch, figuring if he touched it and fell unconscious, he would fall on the couch. His body was still hurting, and he had to take precautions to prevent further injury. The measure made perfect since to prevent a painful collapse on his hardwood floor and thin rug. Something was about to happen...something very big.

John checked the distance behind him to ensure he wouldn't miss the couch if he fell backward. Logically, he knew he could fall forward or sideways too. He peered down the hallway toward the bedroom and contemplated dragging the mattress into the living room as added padding on the floor. Then again, he may not fall at all, and he was just wasting time. Deep down, he knew he was just stalling and postponing the inevitable. *Just reach out and touch it, John!*

Slowly and carefully, while maintaining eye contact with the staff, he extended his hand out toward the device. He stopped short, clenching his outstretched fingers into a tight fist. Then, as tension and anxiety in his body grew, he pulled his hand back and vigorously rubbed his face. *One last chance to wake up,* he thought. He wasn't asleep.

One more time, he extended his hand out to touch the staff, again stopping short of gripping its smooth wooden surface. John couldn't bring himself to do it. He just couldn't wrap his mind around the consequences of putting a hand on it and trusting. The old man told him he couldn't fail, yet, he was failing already and hadn't even seen or done anything.

John, once again, pulled his hand back, dropping it to his side. He lowered his head with a deep sigh and closed his eyes. Maybe someone or something could help him.

Almost in half-hearted prayer he said, "I don't know if I can do this. I don't know if I'm supposed to do this. Please help me."

Who am I talking to? John knew exactly who but didn't want to believe he was doing it. There was no God. *I'm talking to myself. Yeah, that's it. I'm just talking to myself.*

He lifted his head and opened his eyes. The staff had moved closer to him, closing the gap between them to just several inches. There, in the movement of the staff, was the answer to a petition he wasn't yet ready to call prayer. It, the time navigating marvel, was closer, so yes, he could do it. He was supposed to do it. It was closer, so yes, the touch would be easier–it was just inches away. *Just do it, John! Trust!*

This time, without hesitation, he wrapped his hand around the staff just below the knot at the top. Instantly, his strength drained and his legs began to collapse beneath him. Holding the staff, he tipped forward then pivoted his body around and backward as he fell to the floor. *So much for falling on the couch!*

John's vision grew dark and his bodily senses seemed to shut down. Was he fainting? Worse, was he dying? He wasn't sure. He wasn't certain of anything lately.

His mind was still working, processing thoughts and potential actions without the benefit of sight or any other sensation. His eyes were open, but there was nothing but dead blackness to see–if his vision was working. He couldn't even see or feel his own body. Unlike the other movement through time, there were no lights, no images of his life lived or voices of those who crossed his path. He was fully aware of his thoughts, possibly indicating the presence of mind and brain. However, it seemed his physical body didn't exist. *What an odd feeling,* he thought.

He felt his present condition might be what others called an "out of body experience." No, it couldn't be that. In those cases, people often said they could see themselves. Though it seemed his mind was present, his body was absent. He was fairly sure that those "out of body" crazies were dead or dying, but at that particular moment, he felt very much alive.

As his mind continued to process thought, he contrasted the difference in this and his last travel through time. Before, there were images and sounds of a past life lived. Now, perhaps moving forward, there were no life moments or people talking. John was moving through uncharted territory, a time yet to come. He was advancing through an era for which there was no record.

He remembered the man in white very clearly saying, "John, you must now see the things to come."

That's where he had to be going, to see future events or things that had not yet transpired. *How can I see something that hasn't happened? If it hasn't happened yet, then how can it exist? Does time have a rewind and fast forward button?* John was driving himself crazy thinking about the possibilities.

Maybe this time the reason there were no images and sounds from his life was that, at some point–past, future or whatever–his life had stopped. It was possible the blackness all around him was the vision of death or his absence from the world, an idea he painfully measured.

He slipped into a dream state, no longer concerned for the past, present or future. His brain was at rest, without visions or thought. For several minutes, John's mind and body regained critically needed strength in the solace of sleep, totally unaware of his current surroundings and upcoming trials.

"John, you must now see the things to come."

John, on his back, although asleep and seemingly

dead to the world, heard the words of the man in white. The words rang about like a wakeup call, piercing through the process of sleep to awaken his mind and body.

Once again, his senses were coming to life. He could smell. A horrible odor invaded his nostrils. He could feel. The floor under him was very damp. His eyes rolled around behind closed eyelids, trying to find light. John lifted a hand to his face to clean away the remnants of a sleepy world, wiping and rubbing his eyes, forehead, cheeks and mouth.

Without opening his eyes, he rolled over onto his stomach and slowly came up to his hands and knees. Moisture from the soft, mushy, sopping wet floor saturated his clothing, making them uncomfortable. The last time he checked, he had hardwood flooring in the living room covered only by a thin area rug. He couldn't think of a valid reason why his floors felt the way they did.

He opened his eyes as he propped himself up on hands and knees. His floor was wet, but it didn't look or feel like his floor. Under his palms was a plush rug he didn't own, an ugly one too. He would never put something that hideous in his house. The rug was soaking wet. John pulled away from the carpet to a kneeling position and took a short sniff of his hand. *Mildew!* He also noticed, as best as he could tell in the dim light, the presence of broken and shattered lumber, soggy insulation and roofing shingles scattered about on the floor around him.

"What in the world," he said with confusion and uncertainty.

His eyes began to adjust to the darkness in the room,

soaking in available moonlight coming through the windows. Like night vision goggles, his eyes began to adjust for clarity and detail. It was his living room, but it wasn't his exact living room.

He slid a foot forward and up to rest on the floor. Using his knee to push up, he slowly attempted to stand on both feet. As he rose, his head hit something hard and metallic overhead, causing him to fall back to a kneeling position. He immediately grabbed the top of his head as pain from the impact danced across his scalp. He didn't remember his ceilings being so low that he couldn't even stand up.

"What the..." His words trailed off as he rubbed the top of his head feeling for blood. *No blood!*

Still on his knees, John tilted his head back to see what he had just hit, knowing it couldn't possibly have been the living room ceiling. As he looked up, his mouth dropped open in utter amazement. There, in the ceiling, protruded the front of a small aircraft. He literally had an airplane sticking through his living room ceiling.

He couldn't believe what he was seeing. It was a small red and white plane, poking through the ceiling almost up to its wings. The craft was relatively intact but damaged nonetheless. Impact had dented and bruised its metal skin. Collision with his home's roof had severely dented the chrome nose cone over the hub which held bent propellers to the engine. The crash had also cracked and broken the plane's windscreen. Its front landing gear jutted out, seemingly with little damage at all, except for a tire barely clinging to the wheel rim. *I have a plane in my house! What in the world is a plane doing in my house?*

Yet more startling, was his vision of the night sky as

he peered past the plane through the gaping hole in his roof. Beyond the hanging insulation, broken roof joists and structural supports jutting out around the plane, he could see a nearly clear, star-filled sky with light whisps of clouds moving overhead. *Why is there a plane sticking through a hole in my roof?*

John carefully pushed himself up again until he was standing next to the wreckage. Immediately, he noticed there was nobody in the plane–not even a dead or injured pilot. As the mystery grew, he touched the cold metal skin of the tiny aircraft now occupying his living space. *Yep, it's there alright. I'm not imagining this.* Stronger light filtered into the room as if a cloud had just moved out of the way of the moon. Suddenly, John could see his living room in the fullest.

It was his living room, but it wasn't. Maybe, physically, by size and shape, it was his living room and, therefore, his house. It was different. He stepped back from the plane to get a better look around. Something had broken out his front windows, allowing tattered curtains to blow in the breeze; but they weren't his curtains. His beloved couch was gone, replaced by a ratty recliner and end table, both of which were toppled over on their sides. The walls, though covered in mold and mildew, were a totally different color. Faded pictures of people he didn't recognize barely clung to the wall in frames with shattered glass. He was looking at a Halloween funhouse, not a residence.

Something peculiar was going on. It looked like his house but with someone else's belongings in it. John walked around the plane for a better look. His television, his furniture, his knickknacks and his pictures of Liz and family were gone. They were all gone! As he made his way around the plane, he noticed all too well, the intricately decorated archway leading into the dining area. He walked up to it and touched its smooth carvings. This was his house but not the way he left it.

Is this what the man in white wanted him to see: a moldy, ransacked shell of a house that used to be a comforting home? John continued to look around at what he could only think of as remnants.

He was feeling uneasy and a terrible sensation of lostness and dread began to well up within him. He didn't know why he was seeing these things or why any of the events of the last several hours had happened. Then a most unsettling thought burst into his mind. *I could be stuck here!* He had to find the staff, quite possibly his only way back to his own time and place.

John began to frantically look for the staff. He rummaged all around the room until he found it on the floor against a baseboard near the overturned recliner. He knelt next to it and just looked at it for a moment, contemplating how he would use this tool of travel. *Maybe,* he thought, *if I touch it again, it might take me back where I belong. But what if it takes me to some place and time that's far worse?* Throwing caution to the wind, without hesitation, John closed his eyes and grabbed the staff. *Nothing!* He was still there in his house which was currently masquerading as a war zone.

He let go of the staff, then grabbed it once more. Still, nothing happened. There would be no teleportation or whatever it was called. He was stuck there until a higher authority deemed it necessary for him to leave.

What was he supposed to do? The uncertainty of the situation was making him feel extremely apprehensive.

If he had a comfort zone before, anxiety was now pushing him out of it. Obviously, if he were meant to leave, then the staff would have worked as advertised. John couldn't help but to think that his adventure was about to get a whole lot worse. Perhaps this was the beginning of his look into the future. So far, in what little he had seen, the world appeared to be a dismal nightmare.

As he knelt there in front of the staff, tears began to flow from his eyes. His thoughts returned to Liz and the way they had parted. What had been a near perfect world in his own eyes was now in shambles, maybe a fragment of the distant past. Was Liz in this world somewhere? Was she out there waiting for him? For several painful minutes, John simply knelt there sobbing like a lost child. However, he knew mom and dad wouldn't be coming to save him this time.

As drops of sadness fell from his tired eyes, he remembered times of old when he knelt at his bed with hands clasped, attempting to pray. He felt a sudden, bright hope in all that was going on. It worked for Liz, so it might work for him too. He could pray! It undoubtedly couldn't hurt anything. He was almost certain his dad wouldn't interrupt, scolding him and telling him to stop. John thought about what he would say as he spoke to God, but nothing leapt to mind. Praying was something he simply didn't know how to do. He tried to remember the times he had seen Liz pray, but meaningful words escaped him.

John raised his head toward the dirty ceiling and wiped away tears with the back of his hand. He put his hands together at his waist, just under his stomach, still not sure of essential prayer posture. He could only hope the attempt was good enough. *Now,* he thought, *comes the hard part–trying to figure out what words to speak.*

"If you're up there," he said quietly, "I sure could use your help."

Great, John! "If you're up there;" that's what you start with! He paused, trying to gather his thoughts. He had to make this work.

"I'm trusting, sort of, that you really are there. Honestly, I'm not exactly sure how to do this. I think I'm here where you want me to be, but I don't know what to do. Is this what you wanted me to see? I feel so stupid doing this," he said wiping away tears which continued to gush from his eyes.

"I feel terrible and confused right now, but I guess you probably already know that. I need help. I need direction. Please, tell me what to do. I don't know what else to say or ask or whatever. Please, help me."

That was it! He felt foolish talking out loud to something or someone he didn't know existed, yet his raging nerves were calming and losing momentum. For sure, incredibly, he was feeling better.

John spun around off his knees to sit against the soggy wall. The staff was behind him, simply resting there with seemingly no more power. He looked about the room, the ugly room, bathed in moonlight and said sadly, "What a terrible mess."

Suddenly, a stout wind blew in from outside, causing the tattered curtains to dance around in the windows. A cool breeze filled the room and brought along with it a foul stench, forcing John to cover his nose and mouth. As John watched the graceful movements of the curtains in the windows, he heard a slow creaking sound, as if the wind had opened a door.

He stood and slowly walked around the living room's protruding plane to notice the wind had blown the front door open.

For a moment, he stood there peering out the door, over the threshold, beyond the apparent safety of his decrepit home. John sensed there was something waiting for him out there, through the door and out into the world. He had asked for help and maybe this was it. Perhaps someone or something was telling him to leave the house and go somewhere else. He dropped his hand from his face as a new reality set in. *That's it! The house is just a starting point, but a starting point to where?* He didn't know what was next and wasn't sure he wanted to see or experience any of the coming attractions.

He walked up to and through the doorway to stand on his front porch, only what he saw was nothing of what he remembered. Liberty Street was dark, absent of electricity and bathed only in moonlight from above. There were no lights on the street or in any of the homes, or at least, what were remnants of the homes. Many of them were in bad shape, battered, bruised, torn and broken. Some of the once habitable structures stood only as burnt-out shells.

Trash and debris littered the streets and overgrown lawns. Abandoned cars and trucks, some of them burned and ruined hunks of metal, lined the street or sat idle in some of the driveways. In his own drive, he noticed a dirty, white Volvo with flattened tires, dented panels, broken glass and a passenger door nearly torn off its hinges. *That's not my car! Little Red's missing!*

Where was his yard? Within the overgrown mess, John could see the remains of a flower garden he never planted. He wasn't into beautifying his property, but someone had apparently done it for him, quite possibly the owner of the destroyed Volvo. In the center of what he imagined was a once vibrant flower garden, stood a dead oak tree he had also not planted. Looking around, John noticed many of the trees on his street appeared to be dead or dying. The entire neighborhood was lifeless, as if shattered by the harshness of some apocalyptic event.

He walked down the steps leading to the sidewalk running to the driveway, paused, then turned to look at the exterior of his house. Instead of the recognizable green, someone had painted every inch of his home white. He didn't like white on any kind of structure and certainly wouldn't have put that color on a house he had to live in. *My green house is no longer green!* John backed up into the yard for a better view. He saw the tail of the small red and white plane poking out of the roof like a giant mail box flag.

John listened as the breeze blew dead and dry leaves down the street, creating a scraping sound that added to the eeriness of the moment. The fallen leaves sounded like hundreds of little feet running to escape some impending horror. Riding in with the breeze was the ever-worsening smell that had been invading his senses since his arrival in that time and place. His face wrinkled as the rotten odor permeated the air. He made a futile attempt at burying his nose in the inside of his elbow and shirt sleeve, but the smell was so rancid he couldn't escape it.

He was alone, it seemed. There was not a soul around or even evidence that anyone had been there recently. His neighborhood no longer appeared to host birds, dogs, cats, or any other signs of life. The place, Liberty Street, once his home, was just a shell of what it used to be. John remembered seeing news footage on TV of once flourishing residential areas turned into war zones. However, he knew this area–*home*–was supposed to be within the confines of the United States of America. As far as he knew, the ravages of war had not yet reached inside his nation's secure and powerful borders.

Cold, hard reality flooded in, as he realized something very drastic had changed in his community– maybe even his country or the entire planet, for that matter. The looted, broken and lifeless place he was now seeing was nothing like what he remembered. He stood there in the high grass of his former yard, bathing his eyes in the vision of doom that had fallen on his world.

Loud cracks off in the distance snapped John out of his trance-like state, causing him to turn his head in the direction of the sound. *That wasn't thunder,* he thought. He and Nathan had often gone on target shooting escapades. The sound of their pistols and rifles would reverberate throughout the surrounding valleys and hills. The loud claps and echoes he was now hearing resembled his target practice days. It was gunfire, for sure. Instinctively, he wanted to run and hide but knew the weapons were well off in the distance. He wasn't completely sure where he would hide anyway. *Did the people once living on my street try to hide? Did it do them any good?*

Quietly, he asked, "What in the world is going on around here? Has this place gone mad or something?"

John knew he was whispering to himself, perhaps as a defense mechanism to soothe his fears. From what he could see, not one soul was around with whom he could communicate.

John looked to his left, noting the dire condition of the Atchley's home. The couple's property fared no better than his own. Something or someone had burned the entire back half of it away. Not one window, that he could see, was intact. He walked rapidly across his overgrown lawn and across the driveway to the hedge that separated his property and theirs.

Terror revealed itself in the moonlight, as he could almost see what appeared to be bullet holes sprayed across the front of the house. Quickly, John walked around the end of the hedge, headed for the Atchley's front porch, or at least what remained of it. The railings were smashed, with parts strewn throughout the tall grass of the forgotten yard. The corner support column was knocked over, allowing the heavy roof to dip slightly over the porch.

He stood at the base of the steps leading up to the porch, contemplating the structural security of the floor and low hanging roof. Wanting a better look, he stepped lightly up the stairs onto the porch which groaned under his weight. He stopped. *Close enough,* he thought.

Upon closer investigation, John could see a clear pattern of bullet holes across the siding of the house. His neighbors may have been victims of some heinous crime. They were Christians, but they were very nice people, much too nice to have enemies.

The front door was knocked in, held in place by a single bottom hinge barely clinging to the door frame. Spray-painted on the door was a large, red letter C. He didn't know what the strange symbology meant but assumed it had something to do with the condition of the house.

John looked to an overturned rocking chair on the porch and noticed underneath it a small wooden plaque. Carved into it were the words "God Bless This Home. The Atchleys." He couldn't help but to think the home was anything but blessed.

He cupped his hands in front of his face and yelled into the house, "Hey, anybody home?"

Hearing no response, he tried again, "Sir, Mister Atchley, it's John. Anybody in there?"

Still, no response. If they had been there at one time, they didn't seem to be there now. For fear of what he might find in the house, John didn't want to enter. The last thing he wanted to see was the dead and rotting corpses of his neighbors, assuming they were still in the house.

Slowly and carefully, John backed down the stairs to the sidewalk and yard. Suddenly, he heard what sounded like a convoy of big rigs coming up the street. He knew this could be an opportunity for help or, based on what he had seen so far, a time to hide. The sound of multiple tires on pavement and roaring engines grew louder and louder. If only he had someone to tell him what to do! Those approaching could be the United States Army coming to save the day. Then again, they could be a foreign army searching for lone survivors to snuff out like a candle. Judging from the appearance of his former neighborhood, a battle may have already taken place there.

Just as the lights from the vehicles came into view, John ungracefully ducked behind two large bushes in front of the porch. He knew he had a mission to perform but wasn't sure of the exact nature of his assignment. The big question of what he was supposed to see loomed heavily in his mind. For the moment, discovery was on hold in favor of safety.

Maybe the brigade of vehicles coming down the road was supposed to rescue him and take him somewhere else to see something more. Then again, the people in the coming convoy might shoot him on site for suspected looting. *Stay put, John,* he thought to himself. *Too many unknowns right now! You're safer hiding like a coward!*

He hoped the bushes completely covered him but wasn't sure. The ground was moist and covered with rotting leaves, making it difficult for him to stay still. John figured, by the time he did finally come across another human being, he would look awful. He also realized the stuff he was lying in could also provide needed camouflage.

He was still wearing his date clothes but saw they weren't very "date worthy" at that moment. The environment had painted his shirt and pants with dirt and grime. His clothing looked more like a soldier's uniform. *Who cares about the way I look?* he thought. This was life or death, right here, right now.

John, with as little movement as possible, tried his best to peer through the thick cover of the bushes to see what was going down the street. Passing in front of him, he could see they were very large, military-like vehicles, probably armored personnel carriers. He had seen them on the news years before when American troops were in Iraq, except these all-terrain monsters were green instead of tan.

The vehicles were hard to see through the

overgrown bushes, but he could tell the massive pieces of equipment moving down the street in front of him were American. However, he wasn't at all sure if the mammoths of war were American operated.

The small print on the doors of the machines may have read "U.S. ARMY." Even if they were labeled as belonging to the United States military, he knew that didn't necessarily mean they were driven by or filled with American service members. John simply had to stay put as the line of eight huge, ground-shaking vehicles roared through.

Finally, they were gone, but John stayed behind the bushes for a minute to make sure there was no further traffic or that they didn't come back. He wondered if the group of vehicles had anything to do with the gunfire he heard earlier. They were headed in that general direction. He assumed the band of armored personnel carriers might be a suppression force, but what were they suppressing? He speculated the earlier gunfire was potentially a far-off battle, maybe just a small part of a war raging around him.

The thought of accidentally stumbling onto a battlefield brought fearful images for John. Perhaps he should just stay right where he was and hope that whatever he was supposed to see would eventually show itself. Maybe a war had already ravaged his neighborhood and wouldn't be back. He didn't know that for sure.

It all seemed so surreal, like an extraordinarily vivid dream. But at the same time, it was like no dream he had ever had before. He needed to see more of this world, more of the future that was to come and possibly the linchpin that would say everything he was experiencing was so very real.

He pushed himself up and crawled out from behind the bushes on hands and knees to the tall grass of the yard. He sat motionless like a dog on the prowl, listening for any further vehicle traffic. He heard nothing at all. No machines, no birds, no dogs barking, no people...just eerie silence. Slowly and cautiously, he stood up, brushing the leaves and dirt off his filthy clothes.

John walked down the yard to the sidewalk lining the street, making note of all the abandoned houses, many of which were damaged or burnt out. He could spend more time on his street looking through the shells of what used to be homes but somehow felt the effort would be a waste of time. He sensed an investigation would reveal no pertinent clues.

What he needed to see was out there in the world beyond his decimated neighborhood. He had to get to the school where he learned and eventually taught. There, the puzzle of what happened in the world might start coming together. Yes, he needed to go to the school. He felt a mysterious, inner urge to go.

He saw there wasn't a functioning vehicle anywhere. Transportation would have to be the old reliable shoe leather express. He knew the road to the school was several miles of travel, but as the crow flew, it was much closer.

John calculated distance and direction to get to the school by walking. He simply had to cut through the neighbor's yard across the street, hike through Indian Forest, cross State Road 9 and then jump a fence onto the campus. He could be at the school in less than an hour if he kept moving, that is, if it wasn't easier imagined than done.

He headed diagonally left across the street toward what used to be his neighbor's yard and home. Pausing in the middle of the street, he noticed just how much of a ghost town his community had become. It was more than crazy; it was a nightmare. Something evil had been there.

As he stood there in the middle of the street, another gentle wind blew in, bringing with it the low and familiar crackling sound of leaves on pavement, like several clawed animals creeping toward him. Even more familiar from this world was the horrible stench riding in on the waves of air like whitecaps riding onto the beach from the ocean. It was one of the worst odors he had ever experienced.

His eyes had now fully adjusted to the lack of light. The moon above was bright, far brighter than he could ever remember. He knew the moon's illumination was simply a reflection of the sun's light. For this reason, he recognized there still had to be a bright, burning star in the center of the galaxy. The truth of the matter was he didn't really want to see this world in the daylight hours. If it looked this bad at night, how much worse would it be in the daytime?

John had to keep moving if he was going to get to his target destination. He couldn't have any more distractions. He had to travel urgently but with great care to avoid injury on the way to the school. For a moment, he pictured himself writhing in pain in the middle of Indian Forest with a broken leg, screaming for help that would never come. He imagined himself fighting off wild animals nipping at him as if he were their dinner. *Press on, John, but do it safely!*

He quickly walked through old man Avery's front yard, headed toward the back lawn which adjoined a giant area zoned for power lines. If Mr. Avery were still around, John knew he wouldn't mind his passing through his property. Old Man Avery was a kind and gentle widower who kept to himself most of the time but was very cordial during social interactions.

As John passed through the yard, clinging to the perimeter of the house, he noticed another red C painted on the aluminum siding next to where the door used to be. Upon seeing the symbol, he slowed his pace slightly, wondering what it meant. Unfortunately, he knew there was no time to investigate, so he kept moving.

As he moved past the Avery household, he found it to be like most of the other dwellings on the block, wrecked and uninhabitable. Very few windows were still intact, and not one door was left standing, many viciously ripped from their frames. The structure appeared to have been gang-rushed, perhaps trampled by an angry mob. Just like the Atchley home, John soon discovered Old Man Avery's place was also peppered with bullet holes. He had missed something big, maybe a skirmish but hopefully not an all-out war.

John trudged through the overgrown lawn of the Avery property until he came to the even higher grass under the power lines and their massive support towers. He remembered his neighbors having several battles with city and county officials about the responsibility of mowing that area. For good measure, but to no avail, they sought assistance from the power company as well. Seemingly, none of the agencies involved wanted to take responsibility, thus causing a perpetual, almost jungle-like field of tall grass and weeds.

Residents along the power line zone were worried about snakes and other creatures that could have been living in the overly abundant flora. They were really upset about the matter, but for John, it wasn't a big deal because his property didn't border that area. Judging from the nearly chest high field of grass and weeds, property owners were never able to resolve the issue.

Unfortunately, his neighbor's problem was now personal because he had to go through the mess to get to Indian Forest and beyond. Now, John was experiencing what his fellow land owners had felt–deep anxiety over what could be living in the overgrowth. There could be a tiger in there for all he knew, but he had to get through it. In his mind, he calculated the best method of travel. He narrowed his choices to creeping through, walking through or running through.

John looked back at the neighborhood he knew he may never see again, remembering a time when it teamed with happy life. He imagined children still riding up and down the street on their bikes, ignoring the come-to-dinner calls of their parents. In his mind, he pictured neighbors talking, others mowing their lawns and some gardening in flower beds. All those warm times were apparently gone now, having faded away with what looked like a dead world.

Turning his attention back to the chest high vegetation, he sighed deeply and then began to slowly walk through the overgrown field. He had hoped to be able to see where he was stepping, but the moon's light failed to penetrate to the ground. He tried to sweep the thick grass out of the way as he moved forward, but the action was futile.

John was attempting to see, feel and hear his way through the clogs of grass but wasn't performing the task very well. Trudging through it, he found it hard to believe there were people in the armed services who powered through that kind of stuff for a living. Not him! He liked adventure, but this was ridiculous. His hat was off to those brave souls who faced the rigors of the environment for his safety and security.

As he cautiously inched through the field, he noted the clear absence of static popping in the power lines above. He determined electricity was not flowing through the cables overhead. Oddly, the world was devoid of electrical energy, a resource he now realized he had taken for granted almost every day of his life. With all he had witnessed, the lack of power feeding into homes and businesses was now inching toward normal.

About a third of the way across the field, he paused to listen more closely, thinking he had heard something rustling in the grass near him. His spine tingled, and cold shivers spread into his arms and legs. He stood straight and tall, carefully scanning the space above the waves of overgrown meadow.

Yes, he heard the sound again. It was certainly not emanating from his own movements because he was perfectly still. Something was moving through the growth with him, maybe toward him.

John snapped his head around in the direction of the sound and noticed the tops of the tall grass jolting about in the moonlight. Something was moving a short 20 feet away from him. *What is that? What in the world is that? Is it some wild animal on the prowl for dinner? Am*

I about to become an entrée for some ravenous creature? Surely it could smell his fear ringing in the air like a dinner bell.

Suddenly, slow and cautious movement didn't mean jack squat. He had to get out of there quickly. Something was hunting him, and it may well be a hungry tiger or other escaped carnivore from the zoo not too far away.

As he broke into a heart-pounding sprint, he feared the likelihood of zoo escape. Knowing what he had already seen of a disorderly world, the possibility that gates and fences no longer confined dangerous animals was very real. Predators, once locked in safety enclosures, might now be free to roam and prey on humans.

Whether it was a wolf, tiger, leopard or bear, he didn't want to be wild animal food. He ran as hard and as fast as he could, not looking back for fear that it would slow him down. Whatever was chasing him was still there, loudly shuffling through the high grass in pursuit. Warm memories of animals he had seen at the zoo came to mind. *Funny,* he thought, *they seemed harmless enough.* Of course, he knew, at that time, they were behind bar and cage.

The thick grass grabbed at his feet and legs like claws reaching out of the soft earth. It seemed every other step would sink into the marshy ground, slowing his pace even more. *Great! I'm also running through a swamp! Alligators live in swamps!* He had seen videos of these reptilian creatures and knew they were lightning fast on their turf. *No, please, not an alligator!*

John scooted along as fast as he could. His mind raced, conjuring up a horrible death at the lethal paws of an exotic animal or being eaten alive in the thick overgrowth. He didn't want to die that way. He had a mission, and he couldn't accomplish that mission if killed.

With terror, he considered his death was meant to be. *Maybe I'm supposed to see and experience a slow, agonizing demise! Surely not!* He tried to imagine what it would feel like when a tiger bit into him like a side of beef. John knew it wouldn't stop at just a bite. It would gnaw, chew and swallow until he was a bloody, human remnant.

He was almost out of the mess of wet sod and thick grassy weeds. The end of his nightmare run for life was in sight–maybe. He realized this thing, whatever it was, may continue to chase him beyond the grass into Indian Forest. The trees of the forest loomed closer and closer until he finally broke out of the marsh and into the wooded area.

Instantly, John reached footing on solid earth. Pine needles from surrounding trees covered the ground and hid trip hazards. The trees surrounded him like giants on sentry duty, perhaps witnesses of his passing. He struggled to control his forward momentum as he emerged from the run-inhibiting vegetation. In a moment of clumsiness, his shoe caught on a tree root, causing him to tumble violently to the ground.

Following the fall, he quickly rolled off his belly to sit up with hands propping him up from behind. Now, facing the marshland he had just popped out of, he could see a parting of the tall grass headed straight toward him. Death was imminent and approaching rapidly on four flesh-grinding paws.

This is it! Do I fight or run? Keep running! His muscles froze, locked in place under intense fear! Suddenly, he couldn't move at all. Apparently, a wild–and probably rabid–animal tearing him apart in the moonlit forest was his destiny. Seemingly, his incredible journey was about to be over before it had really begun.

He couldn't even lift a hand and arm to shield his throat and face, as if it would do him good anyway. He quickly contemplated whether to close his eyes or watch this thing as it jumped on him like a cat pouncing on a mouse. Would the last thing he saw be powerful jaws clamping down on his neck for the kill? Before he could close his eyes, the creature broke through the grass and weeds but stopped before entering the forest.

John squinted, struggling for a better view. *Why isn't it attacking?* He leaned forward slightly until he saw the terrible beast. *Have mercy,* he thought.

Before him, standing on four short, little legs was a basset hound. *Really,* he thought, *this is the wild animal that chased me and made me fear for my life!* Now strengthened and once again gaining control of tired muscles, he stood, keeping an eye on the dog, understanding it could still be rabid.

He stood, towering high above the hound which backed away slightly. They looked at each other, examining for threat potential. John rubbed the dirt and pine needles off his hands and slowly approached the animal. The little critter appeared to be frightened.

John put both hands out and gently spoke to the dog, saying, "Take it easy, buddy. I won't hurt you, if you don't hurt me."

Clearly, the poor creature was a product of the world in which it was living. Its fur was heavily mud-matted and dirty. The dog looked as if it hadn't eaten anything in weeks, evident from the narrowness of its body and its visible rib cage. John could see the animal was still wearing a collar, albeit dirty and tattered.

Still wary of the dog, not completely sure it wouldn't try to take a bite out of him, John slowly knelt next to it and reached for the collar around its filthy neck.

"Easy fella," he said.

John felt the animal was very trusting or possibly suckering him, the stupid human, in for an attack. Regardless, he rotated the collar to find a small aluminum tag proudly displaying the name "FRED" in huge block letters.

"Well, Fred, maybe you know what's goin' on around here, but you can't tell me, right?"

Talking to the basset hound brought huge comfort for John. It wasn't a ferocious beast, only a lost and weary creature, much like himself. They were both just trying to survive. Looking into the dog's big, sad eyes, John wished he had some food to give to it but could only offer comfort in rubs and pats from empty hands. Come to think about it; he was a bit hungry also.

John knelt next to Fred the predator for several minutes, scratching its head and rubbing its thin, malnourished body. He wished he could see what the dog's eyes had seen. Truthfully, it probably didn't realize what was going on. Its owners might be long gone or even dead. If only he could peer into the basset's mind to catch just a glimpse of why the world seemed broken.

However, did he even want to see, to know what had gone down among fellow humans? Just how long ago did all this happen? John remembered the words of the old man very clearly saying, "You must now see the things to come." *Obviously, I'm seeing something from the future,* he thought. *If it's gonna get worse, I don't know if I wanna see any more of it.*

Where was Liz in this world? Where was Nathan? Where was he in this world? Could he meet himself in this time and place, most likely in great suffering and distress? That wasn't a thought John wanted to entertain for very long.

Still, he had a feeling this was bigger than just his, Liz's or Nathan's lives. There was a bigger picture he needed to see, something out beyond Indian Forest and maybe well beyond the school. He felt led to seek it out.

Suddenly, a series of gunshots rang out, echoing through the stiff air. This time they were much closer to him, possibly as close as his neighborhood. John felt the basset hound slip out from under his comforting hand, bolting away at the ominous sounds. The dog ran as fast as it could along the perimeter of the high grass until it was no longer visible in the moonlight. The poor animal was probably a seasoned survivor and knew enough to run from the blasts. As a testament to his own survival skills, John simply knelt there on the sopping wet pine needles, watching Fred run away. He could follow the dog, but knew that would take him away from his intended destination.

As he stooped there adjacent to the giant trees, wondering where the dog was going, the reality of the nearness of the shots set in. They sounded a little too close for comfort, maybe less than a half mile away. John had to get out of there and fast, or at least, at a pace that would quietly carry him to a safe distance. He didn't know how far to go, just that he had to move.

He had no idea of the dangers ahead or how to best protect himself against the coming perils. Further, he had absolutely no protective equipment and was feeling regretful frustration for leaving the staff back at the house. *Why didn't I bring it with me?* At least he could have swung it like a baseball bat. For sure, he could hit even the smallest of targets with a bat. Perhaps the staff would have worked in a similar manner, like a defensive weapon.

He decided he was going to survive to tell the story. Hunkering down or hiding like a coward wasn't going to get him anywhere, certainly not to see the "things to come" as the old man had stated. John snapped to his feet and headed into the forest, adjusting his course for an intercept of the school campus.

"Quickly, but carefully, John," he muttered to himself.

Walking through the forest was relatively easy compared to the swampy grassland. It wasn't a jungle by any means. The tall pine trees were far enough apart so as not to be obstacles and a hindrance to travel. If anything, they provided convenient handholds for the comfort and safety of the journey. The pine needle-covered forest floor was a little moist and slippery but nothing he couldn't handle if he were cautious.

As he eased through the forest, moving further and further from the grassy area, the moonlight began to dim slightly, an unwanted byproduct of the increased overhead tree cover. He didn't have a flashlight and was depending heavily on the moon's light, which was visibly fading as he walked deeper into the heavily wooded land.

After just a short distance, John stopped, straining to see the way ahead. He had good visibility of things relatively close. However, he knew his travels wouldn't be any easier further away where hazards might be lurking. He looked up through the canopy of the trees trying to find the moon but only saw the soft glow of its presence. *If only,* he thought, *it was just a little brighter.*

Standing there among the tall trees like a stranger among strangers, he wished that silly dog hadn't run away. At least if the hound were still there, he would have someone to talk to while he trekked through the woods. *Why did it have to run away? Stupid dog!* Who was he kidding? Fred couldn't carry on any kind of intelligent conversation. Still, he felt lonely, maybe a bit heartbroken. More light on his path would be good and had potential to brighten his mood, so to speak.

Unexpectedly, the moonlight filtering through the tree tops intensified slightly, extending his visibility by several feet. He attempted to formulate a valid reason for the sudden increase in brightness. The night was fairly clear, with very little cloud cover. There were no clouds over the trees scooting along out of the way to allow more light. Factually, he may have just witnessed the moon grow brighter. *Surely not,* he thought. As far as he knew, what he had just seen wasn't possible. *The moon doesn't grow brighter in a matter of seconds,* he pondered.

John looked skyward, then forward at his now brighter path and whispered, "That's so weird."

He was grateful and a little mystified. Finally, something seemed to go his way, possibly by unusual, supernatural means. Maybe the rest of his journey would be easy, that things would work out to his advantage. Then again, he was in an ugly world. For him, that fact spoke volumes to the things to come.

Before everything he had experienced, John's view of the supernatural was a bit clouded in unbelief. In fact, he didn't want to think his newly brightened trail was anything other than coincidence. However, things were changing in his little part of the world and in his mind. Very suddenly, the supernatural seemed like it could be a real thing.

As he continued his hike through the forest, he occasionally looked up to wonder if God was watching his every step, perhaps even guiding him. Was this the leading he felt? John's spiritual doubts, built over a lifetime of disbelief, were crumbling with every experience. He was changing mentally, but more importantly, he was changing spiritually.

Then, some interesting thoughts popped into John's head. *If I had been a believer, a Jesus-seeking and Jesus-loving person, would I be going through any of this? Is God singling me out because I'm a professing atheist? Is God trying to get my attention?* He couldn't help but to ask himself an even tougher question and could think of no way to brace for the potential answer. *What more would God be willing to do or show to me to get my absolute, full attention?*

At that terrifying thought, John once again heard gunshots afar off, but this time they were different. He stopped, leaned against a tall pine tree and listened for distance and direction. They sounded a little further away than the first ones he had heard and were in the same general direction as the school. However, the multitude of shots seemed to originate from a location beyond the school. Still, the mere fact that he was going to have to march toward the clacks of automatic weapon fire was unnerving. One was supposed to run away from things like that, not go toward them.

The gunfire occurred in distinctly different bursts.

John formulated the variance might be due to the use of a diverse mixture of weapon makes and models. It was a large exchange of fire, like a battle raging somewhere between two enemies. He was frozen in place, listening for the sounds of war to stop.

As he leaned against the tree, listening to the violent trade of bullets, a vastly different sound–almost like a mechanical buzzing–began to emerge behind him above the trees. The ominous sound grew louder and louder until it was nearly on top of him. Out of fear, he was petrified and unable to move a single muscle. It, whatever it was, was extremely close.

It was an unusual sound; one he didn't remember hearing before, but one that resembled thousands of insects loudly flying overhead. They had to be big ones too, maybe something like locusts. He wasn't entirely sure they were actual bugs. They also sounded man-made with undertones of small motors working feverishly to keep them in the air. Unfortunately, they were too high for John to see, soaring well above the crest of the trees.

His mind struggled to separate the intensifying gunfire off in the distance from the sounds directly above. As best as he could tell, the insect, swarm-like sound was flying in the direction of the gunfight, perhaps to the heart of the battlefield. Why? Eventually, the loud buzz of overhead flight faded away until he could no longer hear them. Thankfully, he escaped their attention.

John managed to drop to his knees, afraid to move forward until the distant bangs and booms of weapons ceased. He assumed the fight could take a while or possibly spread closer to the school where he was headed. He contemplated whether to wait or to keep moving and hope for the best. Instinct took over to remind him that running into a buzz saw of bullets would be bad for his health. He would remain there until the barrage stopped.

As he listened to the vicious battle far away, it occurred to him that he had nearly forgotten about the stench which permeated throughout the thick, stale air. The rancid smell had become normal to him in a way that he was no longer paying attention to it. However, at that moment, John began to realize the odor was growing worse as he trudged deeper into the forest. Now that his nose had been reintroduced to the death-like scent, he would have to endure it. The scary thought for him was that anything from that world would start to feel or seem normal.

Then, John began to wonder about the people in that time, living in that world. He knew there were still human beings around. Someone was driving the military vehicles he had seen earlier. Someone was off in the distance firing the weapons now ringing in his ears. Whatever had happened in the world hadn't managed to kill off all of humanity.

Thinking of these apocalyptic survivors, he wondered if the world had become normal to them. Sadly, the destroyed neighborhoods, decimated homes and burnt cars could be as commonplace as breathing. He was terrified of what big cities might be like–once sprawling centers of life, now graveyards of death and devastation. He shuddered at the possibility of wicked firefights being an everyday occurrence. Maybe citizens of the day were accustomed to the awful stench of death. Then he had a most frightening thought–*what if*

190 | PERIL ENVISIONED

death is normal to these people? They could be living as if every single day of their lives was their last.

A chill had settled in the air and a slight breeze began to blow through the trees. He could have been cold the whole time but didn't notice it until he stopped his advance. After several minutes of inactivity, listening to the far away conflict, his body continued to cool, making hypothermia a real possibility.

His movement through the woods had been keeping him warm, so he had to continue the journey. He wasn't entirely sure how cold it had to be for hypothermic symptoms to set in and didn't know how much colder the night would get. Unfortunately, he would have to continue the trip before the gunfire ended, an equally unpleasant a thought as dying of exposure.

Boom! Boom! Boom! Three large explosions rang out through the night air with concussive blows echoing through the forest. John remembered hearing such sounds on television news shows reporting from deadly skirmishes in other parts of the world.

"Well, that's not gunfire," John said as sound waves from the explosions rocketed into his ears. He could feel the blasts on his cold skin and knew they were coming from the general direction of the conflict.

For a moment, he considered if he might not be in the United States. A trickster would want him to think he was stateside, but maybe he wasn't. Someone could be perpetrating the most intricate hoax of all time on him. Of course, that someone would have had to recreate John's house and neighborhood elsewhere, perhaps in a war-ravaged country on the other side of the globe. For all he knew, he wasn't even on the same planet. *Ridiculous,* he thought, *but no more ridiculous than anything else I've experienced in the last several hours.*

Jumping to his feet and ready to run, he continued to listen, but interestingly, there were no further thunderous claps or weapons fire. He was back in eerie silence. He knew the blasts from afar were not guns, which had to mean they were quite possibly bombs. This was a new development in the world–a new horror! Not only were gun battles common in this period, so were bombs. *Bombs!* It sounded as if someone had brought high explosives to a gunfight. He could only speculate about what new terror was next.

Regardless of the dreadful thoughts scrambling through John's mind, the journey to the school had to continue. *Stay? Go? Stay? No, go!* Obviously, the explosions had somehow brought an end to the combat from afar, which meant maybe it was time to move on.

With heavy feet, John began walking again, moving closer and closer to the school. He calculated, based on progress thus far, he was nearly halfway through Indian Forest. The walk really wasn't that bad, except for the occasional stumble on roots hidden by pine needles and shadows. His biggest physical obstacles were the numerous trees and the occasional evergreen bush. Ferns were abundant on the forest floor, but they were no match for his dedicated forward progress. Fear, although he didn't want to admit it, was his greatest obstacle. If only he could ignore fear as he ignored the ferns.

As he steamed on, he remembered some of the ghost stories people had circulated about Indian Forest. He had heard stories of decapitated Civil War soldiers roaming through the trees looking for their heads. He had listened to tales of entire ghost armies seen moving through the forest at night. John had even heard one fable about the forest's own Bigfoot, unimaginatively called the Monster of Indian Forest. The local school kids, trying to outdo one another in tall tales, perpetuated many of these stories as they bounced the untruths around in the hallways between classes.

As far as he could tell, there were no ghosts or monsters weaving trails between the trees. Honestly, an apparitional specter would be the least of his worries. Obviously, much scarier things, beyond the devious imaginations of children, were going on in the world. Amazingly, he was traveling toward those frightening things rather than away from them.

John was guilty of spreading the same tales, even as an adult. He had attempted to inject several of these stories into his relationship with Liz, probably to make her feel vulnerable. The plan was to be there for her and play the part of the hero to comfort and protect her from the potential dangers of the forest. Well, he discovered even best-laid plans didn't quite work out because Liz didn't buy into any of the stories. He suspected her lack of fear was based on her deeply grounded Faith.

He missed Liz so much. If he could stop for a few minutes, he might even cry for her because he longed for her comforting embrace. He agonized over the loss of their relationship.

On his journey, he occasionally thought about skipping the school to head straight for Liz's apartment complex. Even though he felt Liz was not his mission, he still had an urge to find her. Out of love, he wanted to know if she was okay. In the end, it was dread of what he might find at Liz's apartment that kept John on course. Still, he couldn't ignore the curiosity and fear for her safety.

John stopped and leaned against a towering pine tree to catch his breath. The air grew increasingly stale and the bold stink of death was becoming unbearable. He had nothing to cover his mouth and nose. He considered tearing off part of his shirt to make a mask but knew he needed the precious fabric to fend off the wear and tear of his brutal environment.

He noticed ahead of him there appeared to be a strange opening in the trees where the moonlight beamed in from above. Unable to see from his current vantage point, he knew he was going to have to get closer. He pushed off the tree and slowly started walking toward the anomaly. Closer inspection revealed a lengthy, ten-foot-tall mass in what appeared to be a narrow clearing of trees. John had to get even closer to be sure of what it was.

On approach to the object, he noticed that, whatever it was, it was blocking his ability to see further into the forest. As he neared its edge, he could see the dark mass stretched to his left and right as far as the eye could see. Through the choking odor of death, he could barely make out the smell of freshly turned soil. He knew he was looking at an earthen mound, stretching across Indian Forest for an undetermined distance.

The structure was much taller than he was, and it prevented him from seeing across to the other side. However, he knew the mound couldn't be too wide because he could see the trees shooting skyward again on the other side of the obstruction. It was as if someone had built a giant wall of dirt in the middle of the forest, but why?

John spoke softly, as if not wanting to awaken a sleeping dragon, saying, "What in the world is this thing and why is it here...out in the middle of nowhere?"

Whatever it happened to be; it was in his way. Unsure of its nature and origin, he wasn't too keen on the idea of going over it. He could walk around it but didn't know how far it extended. Looking left and right, John could see the massive pile of dirt disappeared into the darkness in both directions. If he wanted to try to navigate around it, he could potentially be walking for several thousand feet, all the while, getting well off course.

Reaching toward the base of the mound, he collected a sample of the soil and crumbled it in his hand. Because he was able to easily dig into the loose dirt without tools, he determined the structure wasn't very old, maybe just a few months. He figured the object blocking his path was some kind of man-made construction. However, its purpose eluded him.

Why was it there in a protected forest? It was just creepy and out of place. There were supposed to be Native American burial mounds in Indian Forest, but this structure was not ancient, and it was not built by Native Americans. What measure of madness would drive humankind to desecrate grounds where the dead were laid to rest?

Regardless of the knoll's identity or intended function, he had to get to the other side of it to continue his expedition to the school. To that point, this thing in front of him was merely another obstacle in his way. Massive piles of excavated earth had never stopped him as a child. This was no different, except he, as an adult, wasn't planning on playing on it.

The foul air around him prevented a deep breath in preparation for scaling the massive pile of dirt. Like an athlete preparing for competition, he stretched his arms and legs to get them ready for the climb. Mentally, he knew he could get up and over the obstruction. Time would tell if he were physically ready.

"Just take it slow, John," he said to himself as he placed a foot into the dirt.

Slowly, he began to climb up Mount Unknown of Indian Forest. His feet sank into the soft earth, much as they did in the swampy area he had traversed earlier. As the unstable ground gave way under his feet, he quickly realized he would have to go up on hands and knees like a baby crawling across a floor.

As John moved up the massive wall of earth, his arms and legs seemed to move in place, as if he were on ice. Rather than going up the embankment foot by foot, he was only gaining inches of forward progress, greatly slowing his advance. Unfortunately, the mound was somewhat steeper than it first appeared. However, there were no thoughts of retreating and walking around because going up and over would surely be much faster than a long march for who knows how far.

With growls and grunts, he pushed harder and harder to get to the top. No pile of dirt was going to beat him. When he was little, he remembered, he was the absolute best dirt climber in the state, possibly even the entire country. Then again, John knew he had a great imagination, one that led to an inordinate amount of pride and a false sense of security. He didn't recall hauling himself as a child, even with construction toys in tow, up a mountain of dirt being this hard. *Maybe everything's easier when you're a kid.* Still, he powered on like a soldier seeking a target.

Finally, he reached the summit of the mound. It seemed to flatten out slightly as if to provide a perch for his feet. Carefully, he stood, holding his arms out like a high wire artist performing a death-defying feat. When he regained balance, he slowly lowered his arms to his sides but still felt uneasy due to his feet sinking into the soft platform. The unstable ground on which he stood felt like quicksand. Of course, he had never actually been in quicksand but guessed the sensation of being in it would be very similar.

From atop the mound, John's view was slightly better. As far as he could see, the structure he was standing on continued off to the left and right like the ridge of a mountain chain until it vanished into the darkness. It appeared to have no visible end, at least one he could see with the available moonlight.

Unknown hands constructed the giant wall of dirt perfectly among the trees, as if done carefully to not leave a large, unnatural footprint in the forest. Clearly, the builders took great care to only remove enough trees to build the mound, leaving indigenous trees still towering along its flanks. The structure created a valley or void which seemed to split the forest in two.

Although John would have liked to stick around and satisfy his growing curiosity with exploration, he knew there was no time for such a thing. He had to get back down the other side of the soil beast and continue his journey. He had to get to the school!

Would going down prove to be as hard as going up? Ascending, gravity was working against him, but on the descent, the same gravitational forces would hopefully be on his side. Still, the soft earth was a huge problem, a tricky element that existed on both sides of the mound. There was nothing to hold onto moving down, nothing at all to prevent a tumble down the hill into the immovable tree trunks below.

I'm overthinking this. In a moment of self-proclaimed brilliance, he remembered how the kids at the baseball game rode the cardboard down the hill on their bottoms. He could do the same thing but without the cardboard. He could slide down the pile of dirt on his tail and land softly on his feet. He couldn't think of a single reason why it wouldn't work. *Ah, a great idea,* he thought.

Still standing, John inched over to what he thought was the edge of the crest. Slowly, bending at the knees, he began to lower himself to a sitting position. *This is totally gonna work,* he thought. Suddenly, the soft soil gave way under his heels, causing his legs to buckle underneath him. As his legs and feet slipped away, his arms flailed, trying to gain balance during the awkward fall. *No use!* His left leg caught on an area of hard, compacted dirt while the right continued down in an avalanche of soil. In a split second, John's body was twisted, turned, tumbling and rolling down the side of the earthen mound.

He was rolling down the hill with no way to stop momentum. With eyes open, his view rapidly changed from dirt, to starry sky, to forest trees and then back to dirt where the vicious vision cycle started again. His body churned the soil around him, throwing it into the air in a cloud of dust and debris.

As John violently rolled down the hill, he knew

exactly what would stop him–the trees lining the bottom of the mound. Unfortunately, they weren't the soft fluffy kind of trees he was hoping for. No, he would collide with very rigid pine tree trunks.

Almost as soon as the fall had started, it was quickly ending. Even if he had time to somehow brace for collision, he couldn't because he had absolutely no control over his thrashing limbs. He knew hitting the trees was going to hurt but hoped the crash wouldn't kill him. *Great*, he thought, *here rests John, an idiot killed by a tree and a whole lotta stupidity.*

Impact! John's body slammed into a couple of the trees at the base of the mound, head into one tree and knees into another. After the bone-rattling crash, he ran a short mental checklist to determine injury status. *Still conscious?* He was aware. *Check. Arms okay?* They were painfully moving but moving. *Okay, I guess. Legs okay?* They were moving too, but his right knee was really hurting but hopefully not broken. *Not okay. Head okay?* He reached to his head, now pounding under intense pain. Carefully, John ran his fingers through his dirty hair, feeling for lumps and cuts. His right temple was profusely wet. Pulling his hand back to his face, he saw his blood-covered digits shining in the moonlight. *Definitely not okay.*

For a moment, before moving any further, John lay there on his back at the base of the mound. The trees towered over him like watchful titans, but they were not able to help him. He put his hand back on his temple, placing pressure on the laceration, unsure if the first aid procedure would work.

He could remember the words of so many people saying, "apply direct pressure to the wound," but couldn't remember if that advice was also for bleeding of the head. *If only I had listened a little more closely.*

If only Liz were here, John thought. She had a knack for fixing things, especially people. She was not a mother, but she had the instinct of one. He had seen her tend to scraped knees and elbows in the school, all the while calming nerves and drying tearful eyes. Many of the girls in the school went to her when they needed a shoulder to cry on or someone to talk to. She wasn't a therapist by any means but could talk through problems and worries with the best of them.

Liz would tell him to stay still for a bit or to keep pressure on the gash. She might also tell him to get to a doctor immediately! Even if he needed the care of a physician, he didn't know if he could find one. For a fleeting moment, John could almost see her there in front of him like a moonlit angel, holding a bandage to his injury and gently kissing his forehead. Sadly, she wasn't there, and he was all alone, now in a worse situation than ever before.

His head throbbed from the concussive impact with the tree. In one humorous moment, John mentally compared his head knocking into the sturdy pine to a wooden bat hitting a homerun baseball.

He grumbled to himself, "This must be how a baseball feels."

As his mental faculties returned, he suddenly realized there was dirt in his mouth. He could taste the disgusting, red clay and feel the sandy dirt mixture grinding under his teeth. He attempted to spit it out to the ground but only ended up splattering it on himself. *No problem. I'm already filthy. Who cares?* Appearance was still the least of his concerns.

Not only was his clothing shrouded in the world's grime on the outside, but he also sensed his shirt and pants were dirty on the inside. John could feel small bits of soil lodged in his clothing between the fabric and his skin, creating an uncomfortable sensation, as if resting on a bed of tiny gravel. He hoped the irritating remnants of his hill climbing venture would fall out of his clothing once he managed to stand up.

However, he feared standing wouldn't be an option. If impact with the mighty pine tree had broken his knee, his travels could be severely hampered, or worse, over. Slowly, John shifted his weight toward the giant mound and used his bloody hand to push off the forest floor and roll himself toward the dirt wall. His knee was hurting terribly, and his head began to throb more as if suddenly locked in a vice. He knew his body was probably speaking to him through the pain, warning him of severe injury. Despite the bodily agony and nausea now starting to set in, he managed to roll over onto his side, facing the structure down which he had just plummeted.

That's when he saw it, or at least, thought he saw it. Things were hard to see, especially at the base of the mound where shadows created optical illusions and made accurate sight difficult. Something odd was sticking out of the dirt at the bottom of the pile.

John closed his eyes, hoping to adjust his night vision to better see into the darkness. The tactic didn't work. Perhaps his head injury was causing more problems than just pain and blood loss. *Maybe,* he pondered as he rubbed his head, *my injury is causing loss of visual acuity.* The thought of impending blindness was unsettling. Another chilling thought bounced through his aching skull–his stumbling through the forest blind and lost.

No, please don't let me go blind. Was he praying again? He just needed to calm down and inch a little closer to this thing poking out of the earthen structure. Painfully, he rolled toward the pile, stretching his neck out as much as possible to see into the shadows.

He saw it! His body recoiled in fear, snapping up and away from the base of the mound, to sit against the tree on which he had hit his knee. Amazingly, in the blurred, adrenaline-rushed movement to get away from what he had seen, there was very little pain. He knew the hurt was there, but that it was simply swimming upstream against a flow of hormones.

John's heart was beating wildly, and he could hear its thumping inside his chest. Still doubting the clarity of what his eyes had just witnessed, he eased back toward the object in the dirt. Did he want to know for sure what it was? On hands and knees, he slowly approached the thing again, thinking he must be stuck in a horror movie.

Upon seeing it again, he slapped his hand across his mouth and nose to avoid vomiting. Nestled in the soil, was a nearly skeletal human hand, exposed at the wrist as if reaching out of the mound to grab something or someone. John knew there had to be a body attached to the hand, a decaying corpse buried inside the pile of dirt.

Suddenly, he was all too aware of what the mound was–a mass grave. The source of the smell of death that made the air uncomfortably stale and unpleasant was right in front of him. He had just scaled up and over a vertical cemetery. He could not fathom the number of people buried within the gigantic earthen walls. He couldn't begin to understand why someone had buried their dead in the middle of Indian Forest.

Feeling the world around him spinning out of control, John could no longer avert the effects of nausea. He barely managed to turn away from the decomposed hand before his body began dry heaving in painful convulsions. On hands and knees, back arching upward in rhythmic undulation, his body reacted to the insanity of the moment.

He had to get up and away, as far away from death as he could. A voice deep within his soul yelled for him to get up and move immediately. Now coughing and gagging, John pushed himself off the ground and broke into a run, like a sprinter off the starting block. As if he couldn't feel the massive headache and battered knee, he ran through the trees like a man possessed. "Get away! Get away fast, John!" the voice said.

John dodged limbs, trees and bushes as he ran through the forest like a mad man. Dead people couldn't hurt him, yet he was running from them as if they were zombies. He ran carelessly, perhaps still on course but not quite sure. As he frantically ran far and away to escape one chilling obstacle, he realized he may encounter many more. The nightmare that entrenched him would probably continue to get worse.

He agonized over the idea of his abandonment in that time and place. How would he ever endure? As he zipped through the trees, his mind began to formulate tentative, alternate plans for survival. But surely whatever or whomever had brought him to that fear-infested world would take him back to where he belonged. Hopefully, he would see what he was supposed to see, and then they or it would magically carry him back home.

In that time of panicked sprinting, John suddenly realized he had been running from something his entire life. Sure, he was running from physical death at that moment, but all his life, he had also been running from a different kind of death. He remembered Liz talking about a second death for people like himself, people who didn't believe or trust in Jesus for salvation.

Much like all the other things Liz had rattled off to him, the idea of a second death or eternal separation from a God he didn't believe in, seemed foolish. Yet, he was running from unimaginable death, having experienced things, which just days before, he would have said were ridiculous. Oh, if only he could stop his rush through the forest to talk to Liz in that moment.

After running for some time, physical pain began to win the fierce battle against his own production of adrenaline. His head was throbbing again, and his knee nearly collapsed in severe pain with every footfall. His pace slowed as his body gave way to agony and labored breathing. Finally, nearly at the end of his physical rope, John stopped and quickly sank to his hands and knees.

For several minutes, he crouched on all fours, attempting to push away his body's aches and regain control of his heavy breathing. As he wheezed from the sour air, John was abruptly overcome with an intense emotional pain like he had never felt before. The weariness of all the events of the past few hours came crashing down on his mental stability. He was crying again, like a lost child in need of his mother.

Choking back tears, still out of breath, John muttered, "What else do you want me to see?"

Partially lifting himself, John rose to a kneeling position with hands grasping the pine needle-covered ground at the sides of his feet. He knew what he wanted to say but was afraid to speak. His mind and body were tired and hurting.

Looking skyward, babbling in tearful sorrow, John said, "I want to go home. Please, just let me go home."

He sat motionless for what seemed like an eternity, perhaps waiting on his harsh environment to change. Nothing changed! He dropped his head and closed his eyes, hoping his whole being would slip into some magical portal that would take him away from everything bad. He opened his eyes...again, nothing changed! He was still there in the moonlit forest, nearly suffocating from the odorous punch of death in the air and the overworking of his delicate lungs.

Will things ever go back to the way they were? Would God, if my misfortunes really are of a divine source, pull me out of this world of misery? Is God even listening to my petitions? Does He care?

As if on cue, the man in white's voice rang out in his throbbing head to say, "You must now see the things to come."

John, very disappointed and slightly angry, sharply whispered, "Okay, I get it."

Feeling dejected and alone, but sensing the need to move on, John slowly and painfully stood to his feet. He wiped his hand on his pants and then placed his palm over his wounded head, now covered in dry, clotted blood. Thankfully, his head was no longer bleeding. *Providence?* he thoughtfully asked.

Unfortunately, however, his knee was still very tender and stinging with pain. He surmised if the fall had broken his knee, then he wouldn't have been able to run through the forest like he had. He knew he had to keep going; otherwise, the terrifying events, still accumulating, would never end.

In a glimmer of hope, John saw what looked like an opening in the forest up ahead, where the dark shadows of the trees gave way to a brighter moonlit setting. He knew the way ahead had to be an intersection with the Runway, the road where all his adventures began.

With haste, but limping from the terrible pain in his knee, John surged toward the opening in the trees. The moonlight grew brighter and brighter as he neared the clearing. Finally, he broke out of the dense foliage onto the grassy shoulder lining State Road 9.

He knew exactly where he was. Going right would take him down the Runway, past where he first saw the old man. Going left would take him to the school, his next objective. He reasoned the facility was situated less than a quarter mile away.

For a moment, he stood there on the side of the road wondering if he should walk the rest of the way along the pavement, or instead, jump back into the forest to travel behind the cover of the trees. There were no vehicles in sight, but he knew that didn't mean they couldn't show up at any time.

Good or bad, he didn't want to encounter anyone out driving the road at night. He would compromise by slipping back toward the tree line of the forest, walking along its edge, ready to jump into the concealment of the trees at a moment's notice. As he progressively limped his way along the road toward the school, he knew the next phase of his journey was about to begin.

CHAPTER 7

The Journey to Nate's House

I f John's overland navigation skills were correct, he would be walking up on the school entrance in just a few minutes, just a short walk around the shallow curve ahead of him. An unusual mixture of fear and curiosity swept over him as he thought about exactly what he was going to find.

Suddenly, he had no recollection as to why he was going to the school. As if suffering from temporary amnesia, he couldn't figure out what he was doing or why he was doing it. He stopped momentarily on the side of the road, looking behind him as if contemplating going back. John was abruptly confused about his actions going forward. Sure, as he stood there on the side of the road, he remembered every event up to that point but was unsure of what drove him there. Something unknown and unseen was pushing him along.

John pictured a drill sergeant yelling at a young basic trainee, loudly urging him on to perform a certain task. However, there was no one shouting in John's ear, just an odd sense of knowing what to do at the moment. *Maybe it's something like instinct,* he thought. He knew where he was going and assumed he would know what to do once there, but he had no idea how that juicy bit of information would come to him.

Still, he looked forward and began walking again, moved by what he could only explain as a deep urge or conviction. "Go to the school, John. Don't wonder why, John. Just go." That's what it was saying but without words. He had never been one to follow mere feelings, but this was different, like being driven by some hidden might.

The pain in his head and knee were easily secondary to the silent leading now spurring him on to get to the school. He could feel the pains but didn't care to give them any attention. No amount of bodily discomfort was going to prevent him from achieving his mission, however mysterious that mission might still be. John couldn't help but to think that Liz would probably call these urges Faith-based.

As John walked around the curve of the road, he noticed a tall chain-link fence behind the trees on the other side of the pavement. He knew it had to be the school, the only property in the county sporting a security perimeter and resembling a prison compound.

He remembered when the school board installed the barrier, just a week after rival team vandals caused several thousand dollars in damage to school grounds. He also remembered being among the small group of kids who made a retaliatory strike on that opposing school. He never told anyone of his antics that night, not even Nathan. It was a painful memory and an action he regretted. Hopefully, the fence would not keep him out that night.

Slowly, the silhouette of the main school building came into view, but it was oddly different and not the shape he remembered. There was something triangular protruding from the roof of the left half of the school, partly Nathan's history and social studies wing. John was still too far away to determine what the object was, but as he walked closer, moonlight began to shed more light on the facilities.

He quickly crossed the road, making sure to check in both directions for oncoming vehicles. He wasn't simply following mom and dad's instructions for a safe crossing. "Always check left and right before crossing the street," they used to say. On this crazy night, he looked both ways three times because he didn't want to be discovered. Basically, he didn't want an armed gang to drive up and beat the living daylights out of him. Safety for life and limb was more important now than ever.

John needed to get to the gate located a short distance down the fence line, and he hoped it would somehow be open. He could scale the eight-foot fence but preferred not to due to the potential for further injury. The chain-link part of the climb wouldn't be much of a problem, but the barbed wire at the top posed a serious laceration risk. He knew the grounds keepers typically locked the gates at the end of each day, so unfortunately, they would probably be secure.

As John walked along the fence, the buildings in the distance, enhanced by available moonlight, began changing from mere shapes to detailed structures. Looking through the chain-link, John could see the main building was not the same one he had left just hours before, and the triangular object protruding from the roof was well out of place.

John's pace along the fence slowed as he became woefully aware of his surroundings. Emerging out of the obscure darkness of the night was a horrific scene of destruction, in a location he once called his childhood haunt and later his adult workplace.

As he slowly moved along, eyes glued to the shell of what used to be a building full of wonderful memories, a break in the fence appeared. Something had smashed the chain-link, barbed wire and support poles to the ground. Someone, for whatever reason, had breached school grounds.

Looking down, he could see he was standing in wheel ruts running deep into the grassy shoulder. A vehicle, or perhaps, several vehicles had crashed through the fence to penetrate the school's security. As far as he could see, the muddy tire tracks continued through the lawn, across the parking lot and then faded into the darkness toward the football stadium behind the main building. Someone apparently wanted onto school grounds badly enough to blast through the fence.

"I guess I don't need to go to the gate," said John sarcastically.

Before infiltrating the school grounds, John looked about and listened carefully for anything that could be a danger to him. For all he knew, there might be someone or something waiting in the shadows ready to pounce on him. He never thought he would deliberate on how hazardous entering the school could be. There were no visible threats, only the dead emptiness of a once flourishing place. Except for the rustle of nearby trees swaying in a slight breeze, silence reigned. He was where he needed to be but sensed there was something more to see inside the facility. He would proceed.

He carefully walked through the broken section of fencing. Much like other areas he had seen, the grass was overgrown as if left abandoned to overtake civilization. John followed one of the wheel ruts to a parking area in front of the school. In one of many passing thoughts, he remembered his parents picking him up from a hard day's education in that very lot. He could almost see his mom waving him down as if he didn't know what the family car looked like. Of course, he was too macho to wave back to his mommy or even acknowledge her presence in front of his friends. As he approached the school's main building, now visible under the moon's light, the true scale of devastation appeared.

John's school, like many of the homes in his neighborhood, was mostly a fire-ravaged shell. Most of the windows were broken, even those on the second floor of the building. Much of the white, textured concrete of the facility's outer walls was blackened, having been scorched by intense flames. Several large, pebble-stone columns along the breezeway running the length of the school had been knocked down, allowing huge sections of the rain cover to fall. Trash and debris were strewn about as if all care had been abandoned.

"I don't believe this," John whispered to himself, shocked at what he was seeing.

Then, he saw a new level of destruction, the identity of the triangle shape he had seen earlier. Jutting up out of the school like a sky scraper was a dark-colored, possibly gray, vertical tail of a large aircraft.

It protruded out of the building like a sail waiting for wind that would never come. Painted on the midsection of the tail was a small American flag. John could also make out writing on the tail, large block letters reading "ANG" and the number 71428 underneath. A plane had crashed into the school, causing devastation on a mass scale.

As John looked upon the ruin of the school, panicked thoughts crept into his mind. He passionately hoped Liz and Nathan were nowhere near the school when the plane crashed. He knew Nathan's classroom is, or was, in the rubble where the aircraft's wreckage now rested. Rubbing the terror out of his eyes, he tried to believe the building was empty when the metal bird dropped out of the sky. He had many questions but so few answers. However, if the school was a grave for his friends, John didn't want to know.

Everything seemed so crazy and surreal, yet he was looking at it all with his very own wide-awake eyes. He was well beyond the point of pinching himself to see if he was sleeping through a nightmare. Then he remembered–*This is the second crashed plane I've seen. What,* he speculated, *happened in the world to make planes fall out of the sky? Are there more of them? Was it a terrorist event?*

John was alive on September 11, 2001, when planes under the control of terrorists smashed into the World Trade Center towers and the Pentagon. He was just a young boy when the events occurred, but he had enough wits about him to be scared and afraid for his own life. He recalled running to his mother's outstretched arms asking her if he would be okay. There were no comforting arms to run to now. He recognized the planes could, once again, be a part of some coordinated mass attack on his American home.

Like his neighborhood, something or someone had laid waste to the school. This unknown entity had battle-tested a harmless and defenseless seat of education. Sadly, much of the facility succumbed, no match for the destructive forces at work.

Small dimples, presumedly bullet strikes, were scattered across the concrete walls of the building's exterior. The damage wasn't merely target practice or random acts of vandalism. Something incredibly bad went down at the school. Still, as distressing as the scene was, he knew it wasn't what he was supposed to see. "Go inside, John." There were those feelings again. "Go inside, John. Go to your classroom."

He made careful observations of the building and grounds around him, paying particular attention to places where someone could be hiding. He was relatively sure there was nobody outside but had no way of knowing who or what was lurking inside.

Slowly, while continuing to monitor his environment, John walked down the cluttered breezeway toward the main entrance of the school. Entry wasn't a problem, as any fractured window could grant access. Still, he would try the door first to reduce the risk of cuts and bruises from climbing through shattered panes of glass. He feared additional wounds would impede his progress. His head and knee were still sending painful reminders of injury to his brain, but he pressed forward.

With stealth movement, like a tiger on the prowl, John headed for the school's main entrance, swaying through debris as if on an obstacle course.

He had walked the same path more times than he could remember, but this time things were vastly and dangerously different. A golf cart used by the maintenance staff was left in front of the doorway on its side, beaten, broken and vandalized. The steel entrance door was torn from its frame and laid against the top of the overturned golf cart. Fate would not deny him an easy entry that night.

Someone had wanted inside the school in the worst way. However, all John could think of was why anyone would want to break into a school, of all places. *Maybe there was a run on text books for their sudden spike in value,* he sarcastically guessed. *Perhaps thieves were after the highly coveted supply of aspirin and bandages stored in the nurse's station.* John almost chuckled at the thoughts, a waning moment of humor amidst the madness all around him.

John eased up to the door and peeked past the lobby and down the dark hallways. Up to that point, he was fortunate enough to have had the moon lighting his path. Regrettably, very little moonlight penetrated the darkness of the school's interior which, much like his neighborhood, lacked electrical power. As he considered how he was going to navigate the halls of the school without light, he wondered if any place he might find would still have voltage coursing through its power carrying innards. Something happened in the world that seemed to make electrical energy a rare commodity.

He definitely needed a light. There were all kinds of dangers around, and he was reasonably afraid of them. His dad once said a person shouldn't be afraid of something they couldn't see. That theory may have worked for the imaginary monsters residing in the closet next to his childhood bed, but his father's spark of wisdom wasn't, at all, applicable to the current situation. If dangerous things lurked in the shadows, he wanted to be able to illuminate them.

There had to be something around he could use for a light. *Maintenance guys use flashlights, don't they?* John looked in and around the disabled golf cart for a tool box but didn't find one. The only item he found was a lone, small screwdriver, oddly stabbed into the seat cushion of the vandalized cart.

Leaning on the side of the golf cart, John whispered, "There's got to be a light around here somewhere. What kind of maintenance guy doesn't have a flashlight?"

Feeling dejected, he continued to look around the cart, finally noticing the vehicle had a glove box. *Maybe there's a flashlight in there.* Excited, like a child reaching for a candy bar, John grabbed the handle on the compartment door and gave it a tug. It was locked!

"For goodness' sake," he whispered, expressing disappointment.

John's eyes returned to the screwdriver he had seen earlier, seemingly jammed into the seat cushion as if for this very moment. The moonlight glistened on its knurled, black handle as if calling for his attention. He knew the screwdriver would serve as the key that would get him into the glovebox.

He pulled the tool from the white, foam-cushioned seat and carefully placed the blade of the slotted screwdriver into the gap between the door and cart frame. Slowly, trying to keep noise down, John attempted to pry the door open.

"Come on...open," he growled.

The door was moving but still not opening. He repositioned the makeshift prybar closer to the locking mechanism on the door and applied pressure once again. Suddenly, the door bounced open, and the contents of the glovebox came crashing out, blasting the attention-getting noise John was trying to avoid. He stopped all movement to cautiously scan his surroundings to see if anything or anyone had come out of the shadows at the racket. Nothing!

Only time would tell if the noise was worth the gain. After all, he didn't know if there was a flashlight among all the junk that fell out of the glovebox. Had he potentially alerted someone to his presence only to not find what he was looking for? He looked to the ground where the contents fell, scanning for that all-important light. Nestled under the owner's manual for the vehicle, was a small yellow flashlight which he quickly retrieved. *Thank goodness*, he thought.

He had the light, but it might not work. Surely it would, after all the trouble he went through to get it! John pulled the light tight to his chest, covered the lens and pushed the power button. It worked! The end of the flashlight body glowed with a soft yellow under his hand. With an odd x-ray effect, his hand illuminated slightly from the brightness penetrating through his skin. He quickly turned the light back off to avoid attention from any eyes that were possibly observing nearby.

John looked skyward and whispered, without hesitation or reservation, "Thank you." His spiritual life was changing.

He slipped around the golf cart and positioned himself at the edge of the entryway, peeking into the dark lobby like a thief on the prowl. Bringing the flashlight up to chest level, John scanned the area once more before activating the light. Satisfied there were no dangers, he aimed the flashlight into the lobby and clicked the power button.

Immediately, the beam of light penetrated through the dark to illuminate, in bright reflection, the eyes of a creature lurking in the night. Before John could react, the glowing eyes bolted forward as if in attack mode. A cat, hissing wildly, zipped through the doorway, scrambling across John's foot on the way out the door.

At the passing of the animal, John clicked the light off and slammed himself back and away from the doorway, coming to rest on the adjacent exit door. He felt as if the creature had just jumped through his chest, leaving a heart that may have skipped a life-giving beat.

The cat ran away, quickly vanishing into the hedges along the breezeway. John put his hand to his chest to feel the hard pulsing of an adrenaline-rushed heart screaming to let him know he was still alive.

"One more scare like that and I'll have to get a pace maker," he muttered through labored breaths.

Wild animal or not, he had to get into the school. John returned to the edge of the door frame for his second attempt. Once again, he scanned the area around him for signs of life other than is own. Nothing. He aimed the flashlight into the darkened lobby and clicked the power button, sending a beam of light into the dead blackness.

John slipped through the doorway behind the light he projected into the lobby. Particles of dust danced in the beam stretched out in front of him, reminding him that the air was not clean. Quickly moving the light through the space around him, he searched for anomalies and hazards to his progress. At first sight, the place was an unbelievable mess, but one he could walk through.

The white cinderblock walls were dirty, soot-covered, sparsely tinged with graffiti and marred by several bullet holes. The office windows directly in front of him were shattered with a multitude of pieces and shards on the ground, glistening in the light. A bulletin board was knocked off the wall and rested on the floor, while another clung to the wall diagonally by a single fastener at its corner. The main trophy cases displaying the school's prowess in everything academic and sports related were smashed, and the awards and accolades were in piles on the dull, once pristine, tile flooring. Papers and books, learning tools of times past, were strewn about as if abandoned in place by their student owners and master teachers. Overhead, acoustic tiles were displaced and broken, some fallen and cluttering the walkway. A short piece of silver ductwork snaked out of the damaged ceiling just in front of one of the smashed trophy cases.

Sneaking through the ever-present odor of mortal demise, was the sour smell of mold and mildew. The smell of something burnt and scorched crept into his nostrils as well, probably the pungent result of the crashed plane. He only hoped it wasn't the revulsion of burnt flesh, but he knew, based on what he had already seen, the possibility was very real. He was in a world of death and destruction.

Remorsefully, and with great hesitation, he pictured the moment the aircraft crashed into the school, suddenly engulfing the building in raging, fuel-fed flames. *How horrible it must have been for anyone in that area, or anywhere else in the school, for that matter,* he thought. He saw young students and their teachers running from an inferno backdrop, down the halls, toward him in slow motion. They were screaming and dragging along tendrils of fire clinging to their bodies, and their faces were twisted in searing agony. The visions caused him to tightly clench his jaws and shut his eyes. John didn't want any part of it but was seeing it clearly in all its horror. It wasn't his imagination. He was painfully viewing it as it happened. He could almost feel the heat from the flames on his skin.

He shook his head, trying to rattle the nightmare out of his mind. For a moment, before reopening his eyes, John listened to the sounds bouncing around in the school. He heard the echo of dripping water and the clanging of metal in a light breeze, both resonating through the broken hallways like bad music. These were the postmortem sounds of a place that was once a memorable part of his life.

Upon reopening his eyes, John shined the light down the hallway to his left, seeing much the same kind of destruction as in the lobby. However, toward the middle of the corridor, he could see rubble, twisted metal and broken cinderblock piled skyward, the physical remnants of the plane crash. He tried to mentally block the thought of anyone being on that end of the school, especially Nathan or Liz.

Switching directions, John pointed the light to the right, illuminating a hallway that led to his classroom. He knew which way to go. Just a hundred or so feet down the hall from the lobby, then left about another hundred feet, then right again into a third hallway would get him where he needed to go. Yes, his classroom was the destination.

"Go to your classroom, John," said the voice, urging from within his head. He needed to follow the leading and the conviction to go.

Leaving the lobby behind, he slowly and quietly began walking down the hallway, chasing the light brightening his path and hopefully revealing anything dangerous as well. As he moved further down the corridor, away from the crash, he noticed the black soot covering almost everything began to diminish. Regardless, other damage to school property was quite extensive.

At the first intersection where he was to go left, a block of lockers had been torn from their mountings on the walls and thrown to the floor. He stopped ahead of the lockers, analyzing them for evidence and meaning. The metal containers rested one on another, bent and bruised, some closed and some open and spilling contents, perhaps telling part of the story John had joined. Looking at the downed lockers, he couldn't help to wonder why anyone would bring such destruction to a school. *Why? Maybe angry students or parents rebelled over some new policy drafted by the school board. No,* he thought logically, *this demolition was post-crash. It's angry, violent vandalism.*

He stepped forward enough to align himself with the hallway on the left, his next path of travel. Tearing his eyes from the mass of metal in front of him, he looked left into the dark corridor. He was distracted by the level of ruin surrounding him. *Snap out of it, John! Shine the light down the hallway! The lockers won't hurt you! They don't need light!* He knew a predator, human or animal, could be hiding in the dark anywhere around him. *Use the light, John!*

He swung the flashlight to the left, allowing its beam to brighten the way ahead. Except for the debris scattered about and the bits of ceiling and ductwork hanging precariously, the hallway was clear, at least of anything that could hurt him. John pivoted on his left heel and began a slow, steady walk down the hall toward the next intersection.

About halfway down the hall, John directed his attention to a giant hole sledge-hammered into the cinderblock wall on the left. He moved toward it, stepping around the bits and pieces of broken block scattered across the floor.

Directing the light through and beyond the hole, he saw what appeared to be the nurse's station. The first aid cabinet was empty and knocked over, toppled onto an examination table. Splattered throughout the room on the walls, floor and furniture, some appearing as smudged handprints, was a brownish, sort of rust-colored substance.

Stepping back from the opening in the wall, John suddenly realized what was before him. The material covering the room was, at one time, red—blood red, in fact. He knew the room was witness to the overwhelming emergency that had occurred in the school some time ago. In a flash, almost like a memory, he saw the school nurse and secretary working feverishly to stop blood from spurting out of the neck of a badly burned teenage boy. John could hear his screaming across the expanse of time.

As an escape from the vision in his head, John tried to imagine someone, possibly a vandal, smashing at the wall, bent on destruction of school property. Upon breaking through and seeing the carnage on the other side, the criminal element recoiled in fear at the sight of what looked like a slaughter. John backed away, stumbling on pieces of block on the floor. He had to walk away before nausea set in and left him on his knees and gagging.

John continued down the hallway, sweeping the light from left to right, making note of damaged, bullet-impacted walls. His thoughts slipped away from navigation. *What happened in my school? A firefight? A student uprising that turned into full rebellion? What could turn a good, well respected, institution of learning into a warzone? A war? Is the United States at war?* He knew post-crash vandal damage made more sense. *What if this is pre-crash damage?* he asked himself. All possible explanations were bad.

He recalled a growing trend of school shootings in the news. Sadly, his school may have fell victim to such rampant evil. Still, that didn't explain the plane now resting in the ruins of the school or the rest of the destruction he had seen thus far.

Yes, the school was an extension of the catastrophe he had seen in his own neighborhood. Horrible questions persisted. What was it like beyond the school? Were things going to get worse? He felt driven to find out but afraid of what he would learn, or worse, experience.

The devastation was all too distracting, *Press on, John. Get to your classroom.* He continued until he reached the end of the hallway, at which point he was supposed to make a right turn. Pausing his march, he directed the flashlight's beam to the left. The light eerily vanished into the darkness toward the middle of the hallway.

He assumed there could be several things residing in that black unlit space, and he didn't want to see any of them. His spine tingled at the thought of something or someone blasting out of the pitch blackness headed toward him in attack mode.

Nathan was the kind of practical joker who would wait in the shadows and spring out at just the right moment. Then again, so was John. Really, they were both awful clowns getting their thrills at the expense of others. The creepiness and constant defensive posture brought to light the torment John had perpetrated on so many people he called friends. He now realized that there was no such thing as an innocent joke. He didn't like the guilt surging through his conscience–a dreadful culpability for causing anyone to experience the same insecurity he was now feeling.

Before proceeding, John twisted around to illuminate the path he had just travelled. He was back! Standing next to the rubble from the cinderblock wall, was the man in white. The light from John's flashlight magnified his glowing appearance. John turned to face the old man. The ancient figure was standing in the hallway with hands clasped at his waist, face void of expression and body completely still.

Would he speak? Why was he there, once again placing himself into this dreadful adventure? John wondered if he should speak to him. If he did, what should he say? For a moment, the two of them stood there within the battered school simply staring at one another.

Without words or even a hint of emotion, the old

man in white slowly raised his right hand and gestured to the right. John immediately knew the man wanted him to proceed to the classroom.

John broke eye contact with the man long enough to look left and shine the flashlight down the hall toward his room. He could see the room's door just up the hall on the left, waiting for entry. He returned his gaze and light back toward the old man, only to see the hole in the wall at the nurse's station and the piles of broken cinderblock on the floor. The man in white was gone again.

Move on, John! He backed into the corridor, looking once again with flashlight in hand, at how the darkness seemed to devour the light. *The other way, John!* Yes, he knew, but he hesitated. Maybe there was an answer in that classroom, one he was uneasy about discovering.

He directed the light toward his class and immediately began to follow the lit path. Amazingly, except for a few papers in the floor and a little graffiti on the walls, that part of the school was relatively untouched. Whatever had happened, hadn't quite made it to his part of the building.

Walking down the hall, sweeping the flashlight to the left, John saw Freddy Falcon painted up on the wall. It was the same Freddy Falcon who had welcomed him to work almost every day. However, this time the mascot wasn't so hospitable. Someone had spray-painted a large red X across the bird's mural and boldly posted the word "DEAD" over his head. John felt saddened, perhaps angered, by the senseless act of vandalism. It was just a portrait of the school mascot, but at the present, it was a simple symbol of hatred in the world.

Within seconds, he was standing in front of the closed, steel door to his classroom. From a few feet away, everything appeared quite normal, as if he could walk into the class and start teaching. John used the flashlight to trace the frame around the door. *So far, so good,* he thought.

He had an idea of taking a quick peek into the room without going in. From a few feet away, John attempted to shine the light through the tiny sliver of a window in the door. Bad idea, he discovered, as the light merely reflected into his eyes. He would have to go inside.

John approached the door and grabbed the handle to prepare for entry. He knew the door would make noise when it opened, so he used the flashlight to look left and right down the hallway for anyone who could hear it. Nobody. As he turned the handle, his light shined up on the nameplate to the right of the door frame. That's when he saw answer number one.

He released tension on the handle, backed away from the door slightly and then shined his light directly on the nameplate. Right there on the wall, next to HIS classroom, and on HIS nameplate, was the name "Mr. Henry," clearly posted for all to see. Just yesterday, or at least he thought it was just yesterday, the nameplate had read "Mr. Reidy," and it proudly displayed a smiling face sticker from one of his many students.

Touching the plastic nameplate to see if it was real, John whispered in disbelief, "What's going on here? Who's this guy? Why is his name on my classroom?"

He was more confused than he had been before. He even considered that maybe he went to the wrong room. He might not be at the right school. *Don't be absurd,* he thought. *You grew up in this place, and you taught here too.* For sure, he could have found his way to his own classroom blindfolded. Of course, this was his school and his classroom but not the same one he had left just hours before. Something crazy was going on, and possibly, another answer was on the other side of the door waiting for him.

John grabbed the door handle again and turned it, hoping the door he had always left unlocked would still be unsecure. He pulled, and the door eased open. *Thank God,* he thought. Pausing with just a small gap between the door and frame, he beamed light into the room to make sure it was empty. His desk sat at the head of the classroom in front of neatly positioned student desks aligned like silent soldiers standing in formation before their commander.

With all-clear confirmed, John eased the door open enough to slip through. He then allowed the door to close quietly behind him, being sure to not let it slap against the frame. He saw his desk but not with his things on it. The student desks were familiar and in nearly the same order he had left them.

The room décor hadn't changed much. There were still familiar posters and learning aids, all declared standard by the school board. John had always resented the fact that he wasn't allowed to decorate his room the way he wanted, but he understood the motives of those in power over him. The room may have been ordinary, but the teaching was cheerful and exciting, a learning experience cherished by his students.

He looked across the classroom to a row of windows lining the wall. Interestingly, not one of the panes was broken. He noticed there wasn't even a single, stray piece of paper on the floor. Not one inch of the learning space was askew or defaced by vandals. He thought it was odd how his room seemed to escape the calamity of what had occurred in the rest of the facility. The condition was too good to be true. The room, seemingly intact, was there amidst all the destruction. *It's almost like it's untouched and waiting for me.* Perhaps, there he could find answers, or at least, partial ones.

The student desks cried for John's attention. He was simply drawn to them. For a moment, he stood there looking at the empty chairs, scanning them with the flashlight, trying to imagine his students sitting in them. Quickly, he dropped to his hands and knees, crawling between the desks, shining the flashlight to the undersides of the writing surfaces. Row after row, he searched the bottom of the desktops until he found what he was looking for.

About half way up the middle row, he paused at one desk, stood and then flipped the piece of furniture over on its side. John backed away through the sea of desks he had just searched, bathing the underside of the flipped desk in light. Written on the bottom of the writing surface in large, black letters was "NATE," the name of his best friend.

He remembered, very clearly, the day years ago when he dared Nathan to secretly emboss the bottom of the desk with his name. John was looking at another answer, and it was written in permanent marker on the underside of the desk. It was there! It was real, and he was seeing it!

A part of him wanted to believe everything that had happened was just a figment of his imagination. A part of him wanted to believe everything he had seen was merely an intricate fabrication designed to enhance the nightmare he might be having. If someone created this world in jest, he knew they did so with great care to input the smallest detail into the environment.

He stared at the name, once hidden on the desk, waiting for him to find it. Nathan's autograph, put in place clandestinely years ago, was a reality not so easily copied by the forces at work in the world. The moniker written on the bottom of the desk was not his imagination. It was genuine! He wasn't in some odd sort of alternate universe. Everything he had experienced up to that moment was sadly real. He fearfully guessed everything afterward would also be real.

"Yes, John, everything is real," said a fatherly voice from near the door.

John spun around to his right, allowing the light to fall on the man in white once again. He was back, standing in front of the door, statue-like, hands clasped at his waist. To John, he seemed cold and unemotional.

He said, "John, this place and these things are just as real as you are. There is more to see and you must go."

Just after speaking his last word, the old man vanished right before John's eyes. Gone again! John moved the light about the room wildly, hoping to find his wise and aged friend. No such luck.

Forgetting protocols to be as quiet as possible, John loudly asked, "See what?"

No answer. He fell to his knees and dropped the flashlight to the floor. He was so very tired, and his knee and head still throbbed from the injuries sustained in Indian Forest. He didn't know how much more of this terrible world he could take or how much further he could go. He could cry a gushing river of tears at that moment, but what purpose would it serve? He was in this predicament until someone chose to remove him from it, if they would be so gracious to do so.

After taking a deep breath, perhaps trying to regain his composure, John scanned the room once more. He hopelessly felt as though he was trying to solve an intricate puzzle without the benefit of clues. Then, like a shining beacon in a sea of black, he saw a bright reflection in the window on the other side of the room. His flashlight, resting on the floor in front of him, was causing something on the wall to his right to reflect on one of the windows.

Curious, John grabbed the flashlight, stood and faced the painted cinder block to his right. Hanging on the middle of the wall, about eyelevel, was a small wooden plaque bearing a bright gold plate, the obvious source of the reflection. It hung solo, and not one poster or piece of ornamentation was near it. *Weird– I don't remember that,* he thought. He aimed his light directly onto the gold plate and stepped closer, noticing a message engraved on the shiny metal.

Stepping closer, he quietly read the words on the gold plate, "THIS ROOM IS DEDICATED TO THE MEMORY OF TEACHER AND FRIEND JOHN REIDY. THOUGH HE IS ABSENT FROM OUR LIVES, HE IS EVER PRESENT IN OUR HEARTS."

What? What did that say? He had to read it again but slower so he didn't miss anything. "THIS ROOM IS DEDICATED TO THE MEMORY OF TEACHER AND FRIEND JOHN REIDY. THOUGH HE IS ABSENT FROM OUR LIVES, HE IS EVER PRESENT IN OUR HEARTS."

No way! Still, he read it again, this time tracing the words with his finger. "THIS ROOM IS DEDICATED TO THE MEMORY OF TEACHER AND FRIEND JOHN REIDY.

THOUGH HE IS ABSENT FROM OUR LIVES, HE IS EVER PRESENT IN OUR HEARTS." His mouth dropped open in utter disbelief.

After reading the inscription several times, John didn't quite know what to think. It was too sick to be somebody's idea of a joke. Someone was possibly trying to convince him that he no longer worked at the school. Was he finally fired as retribution for all his past trickery? First, there was the unfamiliar name adjacent to the door of his classroom. Then, adding insult to injury, there was this insane monument on the wall.

"This is less than funny. This isn't even joke worthy," he said as he rubbed his aching head.

Reaching into the recesses of his mind, he knew people typically didn't dedicate something to someone's memory unless they were... *No! It can't be! I'm not dead! I'm standing right here, reading this unbelievable junk on my wall. Obviously, someone wants me to think I'm dead. That's it! Someone just wants me to think I'm dead.*

Maybe I'm really dead, he thought. *What if I'm dead, and everything I'm going through is my own personal Hell? Does it work that way?* He remembered the recurring dream on the green pasture that quickly turned into a heart-pounding nightmare. He remembered falling through the earth, eventually burning in a lake of fire. He knew that experience was far worse than this one, so no; this world surely couldn't be Hell. *Maybe I was there too,* he thought, recalling his horrific time of slumber. *It could have been more than a hellacious dream.*

"John, you must go," rang the words of the man in white.

The old man was no longer in the room, but the order bolted into John's ears clearly. Yes, he needed to go, but where? Where in this ugly world would he go next?

He spun around, moving the light left and right, sweeping the room for evidence of his next destination. There were no clues jumping out at him to tell him where to go. He had to be missing some important detail. Then, his light came to rest on the overturned desk, highlighting his best friend's name. Something clicked, like a mental switch turning on to bring synapses to life. Clearly, John had to find Nathan. Every part of his being was now saying he had to go find Nathan.

Think this through, John. He knew where his friend lived, just a couple miles from the school. However, did he still live at that last known address, or had he moved on? There was only one way to find out–go there.

To do so, John would have to go back out in the world, a journey he wasn't all too keen on making. Then again, the school was part of that same world, and his presence there had offered no comfort at all. Like ripping off an old bandage, he just needed to do it quickly and deal with the pain as it came. For survival, maybe this wasn't the right attitude to have. After all, death would be far worse than pain, and surely, there were things out there that could kill him. *Just go,* he thought. It was a chance he was going to have to take.

John walked to the door he had used to enter the classroom, thinking about his trip back through the school to the exit. He wasn't crazy about his first journey through the hallways of the dead facility, and prospects of a second made him feel uneasy.

He gently grabbed the door handle and twisted until the door opened just slightly. Before opening it more and exiting, he listened for sounds echoing in the hallways. *Listen, then proceed.* He heard the familiar, already established, sounds of the school, but he also homed in on additional sounds not present during his first walk-through. Trickling down the halls to his waiting ears, he heard shuffling, like multiple feet on the tile floors. Someone was in the building with him! In addition to the sound of traveling feet, he identified voices but was unable to determine what they were saying.

Yes, others were in the building. He had no way of knowing if they were good others or bad others. Maybe he would be able to reason with them. Perhaps he could just simply explain the nightmare he was going through. *Sure, John, they'll want to sit around a campfire and roast marshmallows while you talk about your incredible story!* He had to assume their intentions were less than honorable.

Easing the door closed, John whispered to himself, "There's no way I'm going back through to the main entrance. I've gotta find another way out."

Having spent most of his life there, he knew the school grounds and buildings very well. However, using this knowledge to "go around" the other people in the school wasn't an option. John had no idea where the intruders were and wasn't sure which hallways were still accessible in the aftermath of the plane crash. For all he knew, he would end up cornered somewhere, a less than ideal situation.

He had no way to lock the door from the inside, so waiting it out wasn't a great idea. He could be perfectly quiet and hope these people, whoever they were, wouldn't try to enter the room. No, he couldn't take that chance. He had to get away, but how?

Thinking about how stealthy he could be, John suddenly realized he was advertising his presence with the flashlight. The light was still on and flashing about the room! *John, you idiot,* he silently scolded, *you might as well build a signal fire.* Quickly, he covered the lens on the light and fumbled for the power button, finally turning it off with a click.

He excitedly looked around for solutions. In his moment of fear and panic, John noticed the moonlight filtering through the room's windows. With his flashlight off, his eyes were quickly readjusting to the natural light. He peered through the glass, then across the quad and parking lot to the distant shadow of the football stadium.

"Of course! John, you moron, go out the window," he whispered, quietly reprimanding himself.

He walked around the student desks to the middle window. Recalling he had never really opened it before, he hoped the window would open easily and silently. After putting the flashlight in his back pocket, he reached up with both hands to release the two locks at the top of the window. He tried to twist the latches open, but they wouldn't budge. *More effort, John!* He needed both hands, one hand pushing out on the window to ease friction on the lock's slider and the other hand to spin the locking mechanism. Victory! It worked! With the extra energy, the frozen fastener opened with an audible clacking sound.

He paused to listen for sounds outside the classroom, thinking someone may have heard his work. No footsteps and no voices. *Get going, John.* With a gentler touch, he released the other lock, greatly reducing the noise. With both hands, he slowly lifted the bottom of the window but stopped almost immediately when the weather seals started to squeak.

"Come on. Give me a break," he mumbled, now feeling the rush of frustration amid the panic.

John agonized about how he could have opened the windows long before this critical moment, possibly before class one day when things were normal. If he had noticed how they squeaked, then he could have called maintenance down to take care of the noisy problem.

If I had just been a little more proactive, squeaky window seals wouldn't be a life-threatening issue now. Whatever! How in the world could I have known about the future need for silence in opening a silly window? Could I have predicted any of the crazy things I'm seeing now? No!

He was just going to have to open it. He analyzed the actions of slow or quick opening, calculating which would produce the least noise. He didn't have a clue. He wasn't an expert on windows or the sounds they made. He knew, although it was just raising a window, the decision could have life or death potential. He would pull the window up quickly but only far enough to get out. He counted silently to himself: *one, two, three... open!*

The window went up with a sharp squeal, echoing between the walls of the room but hopefully not blasting into the hallways beyond. Without wasting time, John hopped through the window and took refuge behind the brick at the bottom of the window frame. Did anyone hear the loud cry of the aging seals? Should he try to close the window? Would someone see the open window and know that he had been there?

He didn't want to create even more noise, perhaps the very sound the intruders would need to zero in on his location. Worse yet, they could catch him as he attempted to push the window shut. Then it would be just a matter of a short foot chase across the high grass, then capture. Beyond that, he didn't want to think about what would happen next, knowing full well, it couldn't be pleasant.

John rested in the damp grass under the window for several minutes. He waited for the sound of someone opening the classroom door, but he never heard anything. He could move on, but he would have to do so quickly and quietly. He assumed the intruders could be in any one of the adjacent rooms peering through the windows looking for him. That is, of course, if they knew he was there. *Are they looking for me? What's the difference? I don't want them to see me accidentally either.*

His dad used to tell him, "Fail to plan, then plan to fail." Never would John have considered his own planning could be the difference between life and death. He carefully worked the trip to Nathan's home out in his aching head, calculating the shortest route. Unfortunately, the shortest route wouldn't be easy, as there were several fences he would have to get through or over.

First, he would run across the quad to the parking lot. No big deal. Then, he would run across the parking lot to Falcon Stadium. Not so bad. Next, he would jump a short fence at the stadium, run across the football field and then hop another short fence exiting the field. No problem. He would then have to run another hundred or so feet where he would have to scale the school's perimeter fence. Unfortunately, as he recalled, it was topped with barbed wire. He knew that crossing could be problematic. From there, he would have to run through some nearby yards, then onto and up Ferro Drive into town. Once there, he would cross over Broadway, through the town's one and only traffic light, then head down the road to Nathan's house, probably under a mile from town.

He had a plan. There was, however, something missing. He had no idea what the world had in store for him as he navigated toward Nathan's residence. What good was getting over a fence, if there was some lunatic waiting on the other side with a gun ready to shoot him down like wild game? He was less concerned with the high grass, fences or other obstacles than the unpredictable human element. Of course, he knew there may be some ferocious critters out there too.

Still, something inside him was saying, "go this way." He felt compelled to go a certain direction, as if someone was looking out for him. He wasn't a puppet. The feelings were for his safety and wellbeing. His original plan was to go back through the school, but that changed when he detected the presence of others. He had a hunch that those people roaming the hallways were there to deter him from going back through the school. John was beginning to see a pattern of things happening for his benefit.

First, he sensed the urge or conviction to go to the school. *What's the source of the urge or conviction?* The same feeling was now leading him to Nathan. The moonlight seemed more incredibly bright than he could ever remember. *Why? Was there a scientific explanation?* The fence to the school was knocked over, allowing for an easier entry onto school grounds. *Coincidence?* He needed a flashlight. He found one, thanks to the screwdriver "thoughtfully" placed in the cushion of the golf cart. *Odd? For sure! John, stop thinking and get going!*

He pushed up and away from the moist grass beneath the window and immediately broke into a run across the unmanicured grass of the quad. Instantly, pain began shooting through his nerves into his throbbing head and nearly overloaded brain. His injuries screamed furiously, but they didn't matter because John was commissioned for a yet unknown, important purpose.

While running to the parking lot, he crouched as low as he could. His eyes darted about, constantly checking for hazards. He figured he could drop down into the high grass and almost disappear if the situation suddenly demanded it. However, there was nothing to hide behind and even less concealment in the upcoming parking lot. He felt like a soldier running across the battlefield, except he was no soldier, and he certainly had no weapons. Thank goodness, in that moment, there were no bullets, bombs or scorched earth to worry about.

John quickly made it to the edge of the parking lot where the tall grass and his travel abruptly ended. Looking ahead, except for the occasional concrete base of a light pole, there was nothing to hide him as he moved across the pavement to the football stadium. Because of the intense moonlight, he had lost the cover of darkness. He kneeled low in the high grass and scanned the area all around visually and audibly. Nothing detected. *Go!*

He bolted forward like an athlete breaking out of the blocks for a sprint to the finish line. His knee and head protested in sharp waves of pain, but he had to ignore them. *Run fast, John.* In total concentration, he heard only his heavy breathing and the sound of sand and small stones crunching under every footfall. *Halfway there!* As he neared the stadium, he noticed the sound of each running step echoing off the tall concrete structure. *If I can hear it, so can they!*

Braking painfully hard, John stopped short about three quarters of the way to the stadium. Recognizing the possibility of snooping eyes, he hurriedly dropped down behind the base of a light pole. He strained to see any kind of movement of shadows or shapes back toward the school or around the arena ahead.

The further he traveled from the school, the harder it was to see anything prowling around it. Anyone listening could have easily heard his feet pounding across the asphalt of the parking lot. He woefully realized someone could now be looking for the source of the sounds he inadvertently made. He considered quietly walking the rest of the way to the stadium but knew he had to keep a swift pace.

Leaving the safety of concealment, John resumed his travel but at a much slower pace, an action that greatly reduced the noise of his feet hitting the ground. He stooped low, creeping along while scanning the rear of the massive structure ahead. He also glanced at the fence line protecting the football field, calculating potential escape routes.

As he approached the towering sports facility, he saw the security gate had been torn down and dragged into the parking lot. Normally, it would have blocked pedestrian traffic into and through the bottom of the stadium. He knew, because the barrier was down, he had one less fence to get over, essentially making his journey a little easier.

John stepped through the entryway, being careful to avoid the torn and broken chain-link. Someone had wanted into the stadium badly enough to tear the gate down. He knew, without a doubt, the destruction all around him wasn't random acts of vandalism. He felt robbed of life and saw the world was even beginning to taint his memories. Many times, now recalled in sadness, he and Nathan had walked through this very gate for pep rallies and football games, both as students and teachers.

Every noise he made reverberated off the stepped, concrete slabs rising over his head. The shape of the venue greatly magnified the sounds of his breathing, his steps and even his clothing. At one point, standing perfectly still, he even thought he heard his own heartbeat bouncing around the block walls and alcoves of the facility. The environment was a bit spooky and motivated him to quickly resume his journey.

Suddenly, off in the distance toward the school, John heard glass shattering. He fell to his knees behind a support column, eyes trained on the school building. It was so hard to see anything but shapes across the parking lot and overgrown quad. He could still see the tail of the airplane prominently standing on top of the building, but he strained to see the source of the broken glass.

He heard short yelps, hoots and hollers emanating from the school, bouncing around in his own cavernous surroundings. That's when he saw four shadows moving around the outside of the building, nearly in the same position where he earlier exited his classroom. He questioned if these dark figures were the same people he detected roaming the hallways just minutes ago. More importantly, and with great anxiety, he wanted to know if they were searching for him. He realized they could simply be looters, but he knew they might also be stone-cold killers.

Not wanting to find out, John stretched away from the column, turned around and headed through the tunnel onto the running track circling the football field. He paused before crossing the overgrown turf, taking the opportunity to look back into the bleachers. They were empty and lonely, as if waiting for cheering sports fans to return. The press box, once perched atop the center seating section was now just a pile of rubble, toppled onto the concrete bleachers below. John didn't have time to be sad for his alma mater; he had to move on.

Before continuing, John scanned the area for unfriendlies, possibly the very ones he previously spotted loitering around the school. He didn't know where they were, and he couldn't be sure they weren't tracking him, maybe waiting somewhere to pounce on him. With no indication of their presence, he broke into a jog across the grossly unmaintained turf. Falcon Field, at one time, was one of the best kept football venues in the state. Sadly, it now resembled a field for cattle grazing. If he had to, he could drop and hide in the high grass.

Typically, the grounds keepers took great pride in the appearance of the property, but obviously they were no longer able or available to do so. Something caused their meticulous lawn care efforts to abruptly cease. John assumed the triggering event must have been the same thing that led to the downfall of the school and beyond, but what was it? Unfortunately, the answer was in the world he didn't want to see.

John contemplated using the flashlight in his back pocket, but he knew the light that could lead his way might also identify him has a target. His travel through open terrain was bad enough, and there was no need to make it worse by creating a shining beacon to his location. For the time being, the moonlight would have to suffice.

He quickly arrived at the other side of the field, feeling the grassy turf give way to the synthetic rubber of the running track. Across the track was a short strip of grass, then a small four-foot chain-link fence which he knew he could easily cross.

John crept up to the fence and vaulted over it, ignoring the pain pulsing in his body. Upon landing, he fell to his knees once more and used the opportunity to practice some situational awareness. *Is there anyone or anything around that could hurt or kill me? Nothing–I hope.*

The school was now so far away that its shape began to vanish into the darkness like a fading memory. Leaving the brokenness of once-great facilities behind gave him a momentary sense of relief, but he knew there had to be much of the same, or worse, coming up ahead. *Forget it! Just move on!*

John was tired, especially from the mad dashes he used to get away from the school. A break to catch his breath and to give rest to his aching knee and head would have been nice but not very practical. He understood sitting still too long was unproductive and potentially deadly. *Keep moving,* he had to tell himself. *Go, go, go!* Getting to Nathan was all that ran through his mind.

Leaving the shorter fence that enclosed the football field and track, John knew there would be an even bigger fence coming up shortly, one which would not be so easy to get over. After an upcoming hundred-foot ascent of a gradual incline in terrain, he would then descend about another hundred feet toward the next feared barricade, the school's perimeter fence.

The chain-link wouldn't be an incredibly big issue, but the barbed wire at the top would be exceedingly burdensome. He had nothing to throw over the piercing wire except his own clothing, but even then, the barbs would still puncture the weak cotton in his shirt and pants. *If only,* he thought, *there had been a pair of bolt cutters in that stupid golf cart.*

John walked uphill, lurching forward, trying to maintain his balance. He was breathing harder with each rising step. Oddly, the smell of death was now intermingling with the aroma of fire. Something was burning off in the distance. He theorized the fire may have been started by the people prowling around the school, or worse yet, another unseen group of urban terrorists who wished to do harm to life, limb and property.

As he approached the top of the hill, John once again saw deeply rutted tire tracks in the overgrown grass. The vehicular imprints ran the crest of the hill he was on and then continued down the slope in front of him. Interestingly, they ran toward the perimeter fence he was to cross.

Looking to his left, he saw the soft glow of orange and yellow light filtering through the dense trees. In the distance, he could see a dark column rising into the moonlit sky, maybe thick smoke from the fire he sensed.

As John watched the smoke rise from the flames seen twinkling through the trees, he became aware of the fact that he had stopped on top of the hill. His view was mesmerizing, but it was causing a very hazardous situation. He realized he was in danger of being spotted on the crest of the hill, silhouetted against the night sky without concealment.

John, he thought to himself, *you can't do stuff like that!* Quickly, he resumed his movement, as stealthy as possible, following the tire tracks down the hill, toward a clearing in the trees and the dreaded security fence.

He followed the impressions down the hill as if they were a road. He wondered if the vehicle that made the ruts was the same one that blazed a path through the fence in front of the school. He knew it was probable.

The security fence slowly began to emerge from the darkness and light fog at the bottom of the hill. *I'm almost there, but how am I gonna get over this thing?* John contemplated. Easing up to the fence line, he could hardly believe his eyes. Thrown to the ground and sprawled out before him was the very fence he had to cross.

The tracks he had been following led through the barrier and off school property. As he walked through the downed chain-link and barbed wire, a smile broke across his face. How odd that an entry and exit point had somehow materialized for him. Still smiling, he thought about the grand, seemingly impossible, idea that the flattened fence was meant as help for him.

Thinking back, he knew if he had gone back through the school, he may not have gone the way of Falcon Stadium and the football field, thus never finding the second and third downed fences. Someone, it seemed, was still watching out for him. In his mind, coincidence now seemed less likely than the providence of God.

"I'm not believing what I'm seeing, but it's real," John said as he peeked upward into the night sky.

Continuing his trek, John began to see moonlight shimmering on a small pond that was partially covered by a light fog. The tracks he had been following abruptly ended at the edge of the pond, disappearing into the still, glassy water. He certainly wasn't going to follow the tire gouged earth into the pond but felt it easy enough to go around.

He knew of the pond from as long ago as his youth. The small body of water served as an unofficial recreation area for many of the locals. It was rumored to contain fish, snapping turtles, water moccasins, and for those with vivid imaginations, dead bodies. Nevertheless, he tried, many years ago, to extract fish from the pond, but he only reeled in weed-covered hooks. Some people dared to swim in it, but others strictly avoided it because they felt the water was contaminated and unhealthy.

Walking around the edge of the pond, John could see a shape in the water coming into view through the fog. Clearer and clearer the object became until he was able to determine it to be a vehicle, specifically a pickup truck. The long-forgotten automotive relic rested in the water, submerged about halfway up the windshield. The driver side door was open, as if to allow the operator to escape.

As he continued his walk, alternating attentive glances at the drowned vehicle and his path ahead, John pictured the truck's intrusion on school grounds.

First, for whatever reason, maybe insanity, the driver blasted through the front security fence. Then he took a lawn-damaging joyride through the school's well-manicured property. Finally, the crazed operator made his way through the rear security fence and ironically plunged into the depths of the pond. John could see the driver, frustrated at the misfortune of sinking his truck, stomping out of the pond, spewing four-letter words that could be heard in the next county.

Looking ahead, Ferro Drive was just about a hundred feet away. Besides being a busy thoroughfare between the school and town, people using the pond would often park along Ferro Drive, creating an informal pull-off in the grassy area next to the pavement. At the request of nearby residents, the city put up a "No Parking" sign, but it did little to deter the average pond user. John cautiously noted how dead and dark the road now appeared to be. Unfortunately, this road was part of the path to Nathan.

John walked past the "No Parking" sign to the pull-off. He noticed the grass and weeds were beginning to reclaim the vehicle-worn patch on the side of the road. As he had already noticed in many places, nature seemed to be taking over, attacking with green hands areas once dominated by man.

He quickly turned around to look at the sign prohibiting parking. Perhaps in a fit of rage or antiauthority, someone had sprayed the sign with bullet holes and peppered it with buckshot. The damaged sign was a very small testament to the current world condition. John sighed heavily and turned right to look up Ferro Drive, now lined with the ruins of what used to be homes. Whatever was ahead, John knew he would, unfortunately and unwillingly, become a part of it.

The safest plan, it seemed, was to traverse through the yards rather than using the road. The road was more open, and therefore, riskier in that dangerous elements could effortlessly monitor his movements. Out in the street, the moonlight would more easily announce his presence. However, in the yards, among the trees, bushes and high grass, he might be better concealed.

John knew every step would take him closer and closer to Nathan's house but felt terrible and fearful of the things he would see on the way. As he stepped into the yard of the first house in a series of many, he saw much the same as he had in his own neighborhood. There were houses just beaten and bruised, while other homes were incinerated wrecks. Cars, also battered and burnt, sat in driveways, yards and in the middle of the street. There was so much destruction and no answer to its cause.

John could now clearly see the source of the fire and smoke he first noticed while still on school grounds. Several properties ahead, flames engulfed a home in a sun-like glow. He knew the blaze could potentially be his chance for assistance. He could wait for the fire department or the police to show up and then seek help from them. However, he regressed, they might believe he started the fire. He looked quite the mess, probably not too far off in appearance from the average looter or those who actually started the fire. He reluctantly entertained the notion that rescue services may never show. He would be waiting around for nothing. *No, John, just keep going.*

Crouching low, using whatever concealment he had,

John made his way through the yards, bounding from a tree here, to a bush there and then over to some other object. His travels were inefficient, but he was making progress. About three houses away from the inferno, he hid behind the rear fender of a car that had crashed into a tall oak tree and subsequently burned.

This yard, he thought, *was someone's pride and joy at one time. Now, there's a demolished car sitting in it.* Though he found it to be odd, he was not surprised. The burning house ahead was just as unusual, and it fit perfectly into the world he was trudging through. As scary as the thought was, he seemed more accustomed to his surroundings than he cared to admit.

As he squatted beside the car, stopping to take a breath, he scanned the house attached to the yard he was in. On the home's exterior, he saw something familiar, something he previously saw in his own neighborhood. Spray-painted in red, on the dirty white vinyl adjacent to the beaten down door, was a large C. The markings, whatever they were, weren't localized to his own street. Maybe they were everywhere.

Continuing, John moved low and slow alongside the scorched shell of the car. As he approached the driver's door, the condition of the car incited his curiosity. He had never seen a vehicle ravaged by flame, and he was especially curious about how the delicate features inside fared under the intense heat. He lifted himself enough to investigate the remains of the car's interior. Instantly, he recoiled from the scene like a snake returning from a strike. He tumbled rearward in the high grass until finally coming to rest on his backside.

Inside the burnt ruins, stretched out across the bare springs of both front seats, were the fire-touched skeletal remains of a person. John sat in the grass, covering his mouth, fighting the urge to dry heave. He didn't want to set eyes on the image of death again. He tried to erase the horrid picture from his mind, but it lingered as if permanently imprinted. A question and vision emerged. *Why did the car crash?* Then, as clear as day, he saw the answer.

As if happening right in front of him, he saw the moment the accident occurred. It was during daylight hours, and everything around him was normal. Homes sat intact with pristinely landscaped lawns, on which, he, himself, was sitting. Cars sat, waxed and shiny, in their driveways. The sun was beaming through clear blue skies with just wisps of clouds present above.

John watched as the car came up Ferro Drive, headed toward town. It was a pretty, red car, but it was a model he didn't recognize. Suddenly, there was an intense flash on the passenger side of the car to which the driver reacted wildly. The vehicle jumped the curb and then smashed head on into the tree, immediately bursting into flames with the driver passed out behind the wheel. He could literally hear the fire crackling, feel its heat and smell the toxic fumes from the burn.

Incredibly, John was there helplessly watching as the car burned right in front of him. But then, in an instant, he was back again. He was back to sitting in the high grass under the moonlight, staring at the scorched remains of the same car. He sat next to the vehicle for a moment, thinking about the scene that had just played out. *Was I imagining that or was it real?*

Attempting to understand what just happened, he muttered to himself, saying, "Was I there? Was it all in my head? It seemed just as real as all this other crazy stuff."

John decided it must have been an extremely vivid daydream–maybe. The event wasn't like before when touching the wooden staff physically moved him and carried him away. There were no weird lights, tunnel visions, voices or an old man in white. It was a different experience altogether. Still, he felt as if he was supposed to see it, possibly as part of the giant puzzle he was trying to piece together.

He snapped out of his contemplation and looked past the torched vehicle to notice a sign of life in the house across the street. In a large front window, a darkened figure peeked through a sparsely separated curtain which was slightly backlit by a dim, flickering light. John tilted his head slightly, like a dog trying to understand spoken words. *This could be something, or better, someone who could tell me what's going on.*

Maintaining eye contact on the house across the way, he bolted up off the ground to his feet. Almost instantly, the curtain in the window shut, and the light behind it went out. Answers denied!

In sarcastic sadness, John said, "Well, I guess they don't care to entertain guests right now."

He didn't take the disappearance as a hostile act. Maybe they were as scared of him as he was of the world. Realistically, having an ever-growing situational awareness, John realized that had he pressed his curiosity, he may have ended up with a bullet in the head. By approaching the home, he could have forced the would-be answer person into a protective posture. Was the individual he saw capable of killing in defense? Staring at the house across the street wasn't getting him any closer to Nathan. He had to keep moving.

John faced left with near military precision and then continued his focused, stealthy march on and through the yards. Well ahead of the burning house, he began to feel the heat of intense flames as they writhed all about the structure. As he moved forward, he began inching closer to the street to avoid the suffocating blaze.

Out in the traffic lane, he stopped momentarily to look at the burning house. The fire department or police were apparently not coming. He couldn't even hear the distant approach of sirens. The home had been burning for some time now, certainly long enough for a reasonable response time. Potential existed for the flames to spread, so he thought the person he saw across the street might, at the least, try to extinguish the fire. Surely they were worried about the blaze spreading to their own house. *They aren't even trying!* Among other destructive things, there was an ostensible lack of concern for fire in the world.

John stood facing the house, listening intently to the inferno breathing, sounding much like a great, rushing waterfall. His senses zeroed in on the rhythmic cracks and pops of the fire eating its way through combustibles. The raging beast seemed to be calling his name. Visually, the dancing flames of glowing oranges and yellows were hypnotic, begging for his complete and undivided attention.

Suddenly, every part of his being was locked onto the fire. Every bodily sense was engaged, if not enamored, in the sun-like mass before him. The danger of standing exposed in the street, illuminated by the massive fireball, was far from his mind. His muscles froze in place, unable to carry him away to safety. He didn't want to move away, but why? The flames were alluring, yet he knew they were hazardous, potentially life-threatening. At that moment, he didn't care. Why?

While John watched the burn in a trance-like state, a narrow tendril of flame began to creep like a snake away from the apocalypse toward him. He watched it move through the air, getting closer and closer to his fragile body. He should have been afraid, but he wasn't. Why? He didn't care. John was in the moment, taking part of the experience with no concern for his safety. The long fiery appendage stretched out toward him horizontally until it came to rest just feet from his chest.

He couldn't blink his eyes or even think of looking away. The fire before him was so beautiful, so powerful and so stimulating. It was speaking to him in a pleasurable language without words and appetizing his earthly senses with supernatural, illusional lies. John's inhibitions faded away along with the oxygen consumed by the inferno. He was living for the here and now, however temporary they were.

A light smile broke across John's emotionally void face. He gazed as the end of the long, horizontal tube of fire began to twist and turn as if trying to form itself into something. As he watched, the flames transformed into a burning hand with fingers opening and closing as if stretching tired muscles. Slowly, the hand opened and turned almost palm up as if beckoning for John to participate in a handshake.

He didn't know why, but something deep inside him manifested a desire to reach out and grab the hand of flame. Slowly, driven by an inner, hidden passion, John raised his hand to engage in an act of submission. Just before contact, he stopped abruptly and pulled his hand back slightly.

"Won't this burn?" he whispered.

"No, just do it," the hidden passion whispered back.

John once again began to extend his hand but quickly retracted it to his chest as he snapped out of the treacherous delusion. *This is crazy!* he thought. *A person can't touch fire without suffering a burn. Why am I even considering this?*

Suddenly, he knew something evil was influencing–probably controlling–his thoughts and actions. The power, pleasure and freedom felt invigoratingly good at the time, but an even stronger force told him the acts weren't worth the unseen forever-pain. "Turn away," he heard from deep within his soul.

Then, as if a clouded layer peeled from his eyes, John could see for the first time what was right in front of him. It was a deceptive evil. He felt like a blind man seeing a world he had never seen, viewing clearly the spiritual path in front of him and the unspiritual path behind him. He silently asked himself if there was purpose in his life and who that purpose served. He was abruptly and sadly aware that he had gone the way of the world. *What am I doing with my life?*

He thought about Liz and how she was always so very happy, except for one time. He knew he had hurt her by attacking her Faith and by breaking her heart. *Was it me or was it the atheist in me? John,* he thought, *they're the same. You are the cold-hearted atheist who broke Liz's heart. You, John, shattered her hopes and dreams for a relationship because your eyes have been closed to the truth.* But she wanted to change him into something he didn't want to be. He didn't want her Faith, but he never wanted to hurt her either. What evil would cause him to harm such a sweet woman and compassionate girlfriend?

John clenched his teeth tightly, balled his hands into fists and took a couple reassuring steps back, away from the outstretched flaming hand. He felt torrid sensations of both anger and sadness surging within him. He was angry at himself for living the life he had and sad that he had wounded Liz in the process. His eyes flooded with tears as he continued to back away.

The flames of the burning home twinkled in his tear-glazed eyes. Suddenly, forgetting protocol for silence in a dangerous world, John passionately yelled into the fire, "You're not going to get me! You hear me? You're not going to get me!" At that, the flaming arm and hand quickly retracted back into the fiery bowels of the inferno.

Crying and shattered, John turned and broke into a sprint down the street toward town. He was in the middle of the roadway where surveillance could easily detect him. He didn't care. His head and knee screamed in pain. He didn't care. He was bawling like a baby. He didn't care. His lungs, poisoned by the polluted air, strained to pull in oxygen and expel toxins. He didn't care.

Running with all the speed he could muster, John began to concentrate on his rhythmic footfalls, heavy breathing and pounding heart. For all he knew, in that moment, everything came down to the run. Time seemed to slow, and his heart pulsed in rhythm with every other footstep hitting the pavement. His breathing, though labored, fought furiously to keep up with his body's demand for life-giving oxygen.

With each step, breath and heartbeat, John began

to regain control over his emotions. The run displaced his sobbing, and the wind across his face dried any remaining evidence of tears. There was no more time for crying, just the run. He had wept more in the last several hours than he had in his entire life. *That's enough of that! I've got to get to Nate.*

He ran down the street at a steady pace with near mechanical continuity. He passed burned and assaulted homes on his left and right, merely objects in a world of agony. He easily dodged abandoned cars, trucks and debris left carelessly in the middle of the road to serve as monuments of destruction.

The wind blowing down the street picked up slightly, as if to push John away from town or to slow his quick progress, but he didn't care. *Just run!* The same wind blew leaves, trash and remnants of a forgotten world down the street. The bits and pieces moved along as if carried by the strings of a puppeteer. Gusts, in combination with his forward momentum, roared in his ears, speaking unintelligible natural words.

Riding on the backs of the cool winds, was the renewed stink of rotting death. John barely noticed the putrid smell, possibly a testament to his adaptation to the madness all around. He loathed the thought of becoming one with this time and place or that he was merely a passenger on a long, terrifying journey. He hoped for an end to the heart, mind and body-breaking expedition but couldn't see one coming.

Further and further he ran, with thousands of feet fading in his wake. As he neared the old commercial district of town, the level of devastation in surrounding structures grew tremendously. Just past the homes lining Ferro Drive, over a small bridge-covered stream, were some of the older businesses in town, but many were damaged or even burned to the ground. Debris from the buildings covered the sidewalks and streetside parking. The amount of ruin was nearly unspeakable, but he feared he would soon see worse.

One of his favorite places, a two-story barbershop and general store, sat gutted with only the exterior brick and mortar walls remaining. He had fond childhood memories of buying candy downstairs then rushing upstairs for a haircut and to listen to the town's old men gossip. The building was declared a local historical site and identified by a polished marble marker, which now rested mangled and graffitied on the ground. History was destroyed!

Another building almost directly across the street also provided wonderful recollections. In its long life, it had been a toy store, a fudge shop and finally, a small family-owned bakery. At each stage of its existence, John had partaken of its products.

As a small child, he bought his first toy with his own hard-earned money right there in that old shop. He remembered the toy–a small play set containing a plastic hammer with a wooden handle, a pair of plastic pliers and a plastic screwdriver. *What a dumb toy,* he would later think, but he bought it on his own. The act made the boy feel more like a man. Now, the toy shop, turned fudge shop, turned bakery was all gone, just a shell of what it once was.

Another place, a small eatery called Harmon's Diner, served as a hangout for him and other schoolers back in the day. They had the world's greasiest hamburgers and the most delicious french fries on the planet. Locally, their food was legendary. Sadly, the place closed following the death of one of its owners. It later changed to a coffee shop but remained popular with a new generation of kids from the school. Now it was gone, destroyed by the chaotic forces of the world.

The obliterated remnants of Old Town zoomed by on his left and right as he dodged debris in the street. He swerved and dodged like a football running back bolting between and around defenders. *Am I running through an apocalyptic warzone? How much worse is this gonna get? What's the climax of catastrophe gonna look like, and do I wanna see it? It doesn't matter, John! Just keep moving through this hell on earth, and maybe you'll make it to Nate!* Thoughts faded and instinct carried him along through harsh mental and physical pain.

Suddenly, skidding to an abrupt halt, John popped out of Old Town to find himself standing in the middle of Broadway under the town's one and only traffic light. He quickly turned to face back down Ferro Drive with the odd feeling of not remembering most of his furious run. Everything between the burning house and the point where he emerged onto Broadway was a faded blur. Perhaps his mind was helping him cope. Then again, most likely there were toxins in the air that were eating away at his brain cells. *What's the deal? I've always had a mind like a steel trap.*

Upon realizing he was standing in the middle of Broadway, out in the open for anyone to see, John dropped to a crouch and scanned for a place to hide. There weren't many options. Quickly, he scooted over to take refuge behind the remains of a corner structure that used to be Elton's Lock and Key.

Its storefront was smashed and barely recognizable. For a moment, he leaned against the exterior concrete of the building, trying to regain control of his breathing. Physically, the run was catching up to him, and his lungs were screaming for him to take a short break. He had to breathe slowly for fear of someone hearing his labored respirations.

As he braced against the remains of Elton's Lock and Key, his hands found deep intrusions in the concrete wall. John bent down to his knees to have a look at the pitting but found he was in a shadow and unable to use the moonlight to see the anomalies on the wall. Reaching for the flashlight in his back pocket, he discovered it was no longer there, that it must have slipped out during his furious run into town. He reasoned that it was probably better for him not to have it, as it could have highlighted his location to prowling eyes. With little doubt, he knew he was feeling several bullet holes punched out across the concrete.

He stayed low and peeked around the corner trying to get a good view of Broadway. Because the moonlight was now fading, features were more difficult to visualize. John squinted through the darkness and began to see some of the town emerge out of the shadows.

Diagonally, across from him, he saw what was left of Grover's Roost. A torched car sat in what used to be the dining room where he and Liz had parted ways just hours before. Maybe it was just hours before–he wasn't sure. *I wonder if my team picture's still hanging in there. Can't go look. At this point, it would be a waste of time and an unnecessary risk. Nate! Gotta get to Nate!*

John saw absolutely no evidence of power in town. City lights and even signs once saying "Closed" were dark and lifeless. Swaying in the breeze, the one and only traffic light was unlit and seemingly cut off as if to never shine again. If the town appeared dead to the world before, it was even more so now.

Down the debris-cluttered street from Grover's, John could see what looked like the remains of some type of armored personnel carrier. It was a military vehicle, but it was unlike the ones he had seen rolling down Liberty Street earlier that night. It was a much older model, lightly scorched, having what might possibly be green and brown camouflage. He had seen them before when the local Army Guard performed displays of patriotism during Fourth of July parades through town. At present, the machine sat lifeless and without dignity, smashed into a car up on the sidewalk. He reasoned whatever had happened must have involved the Army Guard. Otherwise, explanations to the presence of one of their vehicles in town were scarce.

From his vantage point, much of the Grover's side of the street seemed pummeled like everything else. Much of that side of Broadway was hardly recognizable; he wasn't all too sure the place he knew as Grover's Roost was actually Grover's. All John could do was identify it by its location on the street, like knowing where a building should be based on an old picture.

The level of destruction was overwhelming, causing his stomach to turn with unpleasant sickness. He knew the cure for such malady was to keep moving and not give his mind the opportunity to contemplate such upheaval. He simply had to keep going. *Go, John! Stop looking at it and move on!*

He stood straight up with his back to the wall, working up the courage to leave his cover and concealment to cross the street. He had to do it. He had to traverse Broadway to get to Highpoint Road, which would eventually lead to Nathan's residence. He scanned the way ahead for places to duck into should the need for stealth arise. There were no hideaways until he arrived on the other side of the street. Unfortunately, he had to take his chances out in the open.

John couldn't help but to think about the possibility of the journey to his best friend's house being a total bust. The assumption was that Nathan still lived there, or for that matter, that the house was still standing and intact. He didn't want to acknowledge the bitter thought that Nathan may not be alive. *No, I'm not even gonna consider that!*

Still, what if he arrived only to find Nathan was long gone or that somebody else was living in the house? If so, what would his next step be? Find Liz? If so, what if she was long gone as well? Find his parents? The possibilities, potential disappointments and prospective futility of his actions were mounting, but the urge to continue burned deep inside of him.

John stepped out and around the corner to the storefront of the former Elton's Lock and Key but held against the cold concrete of the structure. *Baby steps, John! Be careful!* He scanned the visible areas of Broadway and Highpoint, straining to see movement in the shadows all around. *Nothing, go!*

As he began to push off the wall behind him, John heard several voices creeping out of the dark down Broadway to his left. *Whoa! Stop!* With as little movement as possible, he dropped to a crouch, hoping to minimize his target size. He realized keen eyes could conceivably see him squatting in front of the key shop. He also considered slipping back around the corner, but the risk of motion detection was too high.

Not more than a couple hundred feet away, John saw the dim silhouettes of three, maybe four people crossing the street. They weren't trying to conceal themselves at all, and they certainly weren't worried about their voice levels as they hooted and hollered at one another.

In John's eyes, their lack of concern for safe passage probably meant they weren't scared of anything in the world. If they weren't worried for the hazards of the world, they wouldn't be troubled by him either. They were hoodlums out for fun and destruction, likely some of the same people he saw earlier at the school.

These thugs were a threat and presented a seemingly insurmountable challenge as to how John would cross Broadway to Highpoint without them seeing him. Assuming they would beat the living daylights out of him, or worse, he had to hold his ground to see what they did. For all he knew, they would turn and head right up the street toward him. He ran alternate plans in his head, trying to figure out the best way to avoid the potentially bad people and still get to Nathan's house. The fear of sudden and imminent death loomed.

John was prepared to bolt in several alternate directions. He watched patiently and fearfully as the loud group of gangsters made their way across the street and up the sidewalk toward Grover's. Closer and closer they progressed. Anxiety urged him to move away from the danger, but frozen muscles dictated he stay still. *Don't move,* he silently reminded himself.

He could see they were carrying pipes, maybe bats for protection or destruction, but he suspected the latter purpose. Their yelps and shouts grew louder as they strutted up the sidewalk. One of them stopped and swung wildly upon a street sign along the way, beating on it with a metal pipe until it fell to the ground. The metal-on-metal clanging reverberated down Broadway into John's ears. The others laughed at the spectacle, secretly jealous they hadn't attacked the defenseless sign first. The act confirmed John's suspicions of their intent for malevolent behavior.

Upon reaching Grover's, the crew of thugs ducked into the remnants of the once popular family friendly bar. *Crazy thought, John; they're probably going in for a bite to eat. Ridiculous! Now's your chance! They're in the building and won't see you! Make a break for it! Go!*

He jumped up and out from his low squat and sprinted across the street like an Olympic runner going all out for the gold. Any bodily pain he felt was masked by an incredible fear of death. He desperately hoped the vandals, maybe killers, wouldn't see or hear him running for life and limb.

If they were able to see him running across the street, his dash to the opposite corner could turn into a scamper for life. John didn't take his eyes off the prize to watch for crazed gang members bursting out of Grover's in pursuit. *Just gotta get to that corner wall!* Either they were going to see him, or they weren't. *Just run!*

With cheetah-like swiftness, John arrived at the opposite corner, the beginning of Highpoint Road. He stopped, turned and slammed his back into the brick covering of the building on the corner of Broadway and Highpoint. Inching as close to the Broadway facing part of the structure as he dared, John listened carefully for footsteps coming down the sidewalk toward him. He heard nothing at all, not even voices.

Feasibly, he had escaped their surveillance, and they were none the wiser that he had ever been there with them in the remains of the town. He looked to his left to make sure they didn't somehow sneak around him, possibly through a delivery door in the back. Nothing. He fearfully wondered where they were, hoping to somehow pinpoint their exact location. He knew they were close, certainly close enough for him to engage in a losing game of cat and mouse. Undoubtedly, he would have to be even more careful to avoid them, as it was not an encounter he desired.

He needed to take one more look at Broadway before heading to Nathan's. Slowly, John turned his head and body to look around the corner of the building. He also listened for signs of the barbaric thugs he had seen just moments before. For the first time, he was viewing the other side of the street, a mere fifty feet from where he hid next to the dead remains of Elton's Lock and Key. His eyes focused, and his mouth dropped open as he slowly began to back away in awful horror.

The entire side of the street leading up to the building adjacent to Elton's was leveled, simply destroyed. All that remained was rubble, massive piles of brick, wood and steel. There were no standing walls, just the scorched remains of structures collapsed in on themselves.

A section of the sidewalk had been forcefully replaced by a large crater pitted deep within the earth, most likely the result of an explosion. The images filtering into his eyes served as a testament that something very bad had happened in town on Broadway, further proof of a dismantled society.

Sudden chills engulfed John's body as he continued to back away from the horror burned into his brain. Evil was at work in the world, and he was a witness to that fact. He folded his arms across his chest as if in an empty embrace, then turned quickly to look down Highpoint. There was no doubt; the wickedness was widespread, even on the way ahead.

After one last look at what used to be his hometown, John turned back to Highpoint to begin the last stretch to Nathan's house. There was no time to shed tears for things lost, and only the journey ahead mattered. He wouldn't run, but instead, would walk carefully in an expedited manner.

Every part of his body now ached and showed signs of extreme mental and physical fatigue. The world was wearing him down, breaking him under the weight of its destructive power. Surely, he hoped, there was enough energy in his body's fuel reserves to scoot along a little faster should the need arise.

Of course, he didn't want to handle another emergency, certainly not an escape of some kind. He knew the gang roaming through town had to be somewhere, but where? Assuming they were the same crew he had seen at the school, John realized he and they were heading in the same general direction. He knew they could even be ahead of him, hiding in one of several ransacked homes, waiting in ambush.

Now, walking quickly and with purpose along the edge of the road, John knew he had just under a mile to the finish line at Nathan's front door. He could almost picture himself walking across the yard under that huge oak tree, maybe seeing Nathan run out of the house to grab him in a giant bear hug. Such thoughts led to emotional highs rapidly followed by lows as he contemplated the possibility of his best friend no longer being there. It was a chance he was just going to have to take.

About a quarter mile from town, John noticed the presence of new houses on Highpoint Road. In his time, he remembered signs along the road, all the way to Nathan's house and beyond, advertising properties for sale. Completed homes now stood where those signs once proclaimed empty lots on the market for potential new owners.

Highpoint, during the time he remembered, was not a haven for that many homes. In fact, Nathan's bachelor pad was only one of a handful of dwellings stretching all the way from Broadway to Liz's apartment complex. Now, there were several finished homes lining the road to Nathan's. *It would take months, probably years, to put this many houses in,* he thought.

As John walked further from town, he noted the condition of the homes was getting increasingly better. There were fewer damaged structures and more of them that still resembled livable habitats. The yards were still overgrown and in need of care, but many of the houses were quite intact. Oddly, there were metal bars or sheets of warped and rotting plywood covering windows and doors on several residences. Obviously, security was of great concern here, but that's not what he recollected of his peaceful hometown. These homeowners were simply surviving.

As he walked, scanning the homes, John mumbled in wonder at all the new construction, "When did these get here?"

The sun was beginning to rise off in the distance, creating an eerie deep blue to purple glow on the horizon. He needed to get to Nathan's under the cover of darkness, so he picked up his pace slightly. According to his calculations, he was just under a half mile away. *Almost there!*

Walking by one home, John noticed a dim light through the closed curtains and protective metal bars covering the window. He knew someone was in the house. If Nathan were gone, then he might be able to backtrack to that house, knock on the door and potentially find peaceful people inside. Hopefully, though, he wouldn't have to worry about that. Sadly, he questioned if there were still peaceful people in the world.

The very next home, in stark contrast, was in very poor shape. Windows were broken out, and the door was torn off and carelessly placed on the front porch. Large holes were torn into much of the exterior siding. He could also see scorching from obvious attempts to set the home ablaze. Most notably, he saw, was the presence of a large, red C painted next to where the door used to be. At the moment, he couldn't presume to know what the symbol meant.

Then, the next house in line was in relatively good shape. Of course, there were standard coverings on the windows, but the residence was largely intact as if occupied. Why was the house with a large, red C painted on the exterior virtually destroyed, yet the homes to the immediate left and right were nearly unharmed? He began to speculate that the level of destruction had something to do with the marking of the letter on the home. Perhaps Nathan had the answer to that question, among others.

John's walk along Highpoint seemed to be the easiest part of the journey so far, but he didn't want to let his guard down, as the world was still a dangerous place. He had to maintain a consistent pace, mainly because he feared what the daylight would reveal. However, with each house he passed, destroyed or intact, he found himself slowing to study each residence to find meaning as to how it fit into the worldly puzzle. He was, by estimation, just under a quarter mile from Nathan's front door. *Just about there!*

Suddenly, John's senses lit up, and he felt an odd awareness of being watched, or worse, followed. His spine tingled in anticipation. In the darkness behind him, he heard sticks breaking and gravel crunching underfoot. *There's someone behind me! There's someone following me!* Still walking, but a bit faster, John turned to look behind and beyond, straining to see into the night's evil shadows. He couldn't see anything, but the evidence of sound said something or someone was there.

Without hesitation, he broke into a panicked run and immediately heard yelling emerge out of the dark behind him. "Get him!" they shouted.

John was being pursued, the very thing he wanted to avoid. He had a lead on the gang chasing him but knew that advantage would soon begin to fade away because his body was tired and unable to attain top running speed.

As the group of assailants gave chase, they taunted and laughed, shouting promises of physical harm and even death. They were trying to demoralize him, to slow his progress that they might obtain the prize they had been seeking for who knows how long. John knew they had to be the same wolfpack he had seen in town and maybe at the school. They may have been stalking him the whole time. Getting to Nathan's house and finding him there was John's only hope for safe haven and survival.

Run faster, John! No, he couldn't! His body was physically incapable of producing any more velocity beyond what he was already doing. His knee and head exuded searing pain. Adrenaline no longer seemed to be his friend. The gang was getting closer, maybe thirty feet behind him. Their jeers pierced his ear drums like ice picks. This was no game and he was in more danger now than he had ever been in before. Nathan's yard was just a short couple hundred feet away. *Almost there!*

As he ran down the street, he questioned why someone wasn't coming to his aid. They were supposed to be pouring out of their homes to help in his incredible time of distress. Maybe the houses were empty. No, he saw light in the windows. They were just ignoring his flight to safety, undoubtedly afraid for their own lives. That's the world they live in. *There aren't any peaceful people left! There aren't any Good Samaritans. I'm on my own! Just under a hundred feet away!*

The thugs were getting closer and closer. John could almost feel them swatting at his clothing, trying to grab him and take him down like an escapee on the run. Among their scoffs, he heard their breathing and their evil growls, like wild creatures on the hunt. He hoped their presence would suddenly fade away, as if someone came to help him, but he knew that wasn't going to happen. *Fifty feet to Nate's yard! Just fifty feet!*

His body hurt so bad and was quickly draining every ounce of available energy. He hoped to avoid becoming a forgotten statistic in a world that didn't care. *Twenty-five feet!* He suddenly realized he could be bringing the fight to Nathan. He could be bringing these punks to Nathan and they could hurt him, or worse, kill him. *No!*

As John stepped into Nathan's yard, he could feel one of the gang members grab at his collar trying to take him down. He missed but probably wouldn't miss again. Nathan's house looked dark, worn, tattered and had bars over the windows like so many other homes. *There aren't any lights! No! He's not there! The house looks empty! What am I gonna do?* There was no time for alternate plans–this was it.

About halfway through the high grass of Nathan's untrimmed lawn, one of the aggressors lunged at John to grab his arm and shirt collar, taking him down to the ground in a release of pent-up rage. As he fell, John could see that Nathan's beautiful oak tree had been cut down and was toppled dead in the yard. He couldn't help but to think that he would soon be lying lifeless in the weeds and grass just like that old tree.

Nathan would walk out his front door or come home to find his best friend beaten to a pulp, murdered on his front lawn, just short of the goal. There would be no answered questions and no understanding of what had happened in the world. Instead, John would become a byproduct of an evil remnant, merely someone for Nathan to sadly bury.

John fell to the ground with one of the assailants attached to him. In a moment of futility, he struggled to get up and fight back but was held down by his attackers. Immediately, there were four thugs wailing on him out of what seemed like pure joy. They didn't care that they were beating on a living, breathing person. Life meant nothing at all to them.

They were buzzing over him like killer bees on the attack. John felt kicks to the back, stomach, legs, arms and head, each blow adding a new level of agony among existing pains. One of them had a metal pipe but wasn't using it, as if they were trying to make John's torment and agony last as long as possible. *This is the end!* he thought. *I'm not gonna make it!*

This was how his life and the incredible journey of the last several hours was going to conclude. With each blow to his fragile body, he prayed this wasn't what he was supposed to see–his own death at the hand of a cruel world. After all, he wouldn't be able to tell anyone what he had seen if he were dead. All he could do was try to curl up in a fetal position to protect vital organs, but his efforts failed. John felt powerless against their attacks, that he was at death's cruel doorstep.

He remembered Liz trying to talk to him about Jesus and this thing called salvation. Unfortunately, he would always cut her off or quickly end the conversation with a stupid joke or some inappropriate comment. He had never let her talk long enough to explain how to achieve this so-called salvation. *Oh no,* he agonized, *I'm gonna die without salvation! If only I had listened!* But honestly, he didn't want to listen because he enjoyed his life and liked it just the way it was. He was worldly and loved it. He wasn't concerned about life ever after, as if he ever believed there was such a thing.

As John began to slip out of consciousness, he could hear Liz's sweet voice, maybe one last time in his aching head. Her words rang clear as she softly said, "John, without salvation, your only eternal option is Hell."

One of the villains made a striking final blow to John's head. The world began to fade away as his senses let go. As he slipped into unconsciousness, one last audible sound blasted into his ear canals, a loud boom, possibly a gunshot. That was it, his end in this world and the beginning in the next–Hell.

CHAPTER 8

Nate's Revelation

"**H**ey, wake up! Come on, you still in there?"
Those were words. Wait a minute, actual words! Someone's talking to me! Yes, he was thinking and slowly regaining consciousness, and his mental faculties were returning. He was coming back into the world! *Oh,* John thought, *thank the Lord. I'm not dead!* He was still alive. He was in a great amount of pain but living and breathing for sure.

The haggard, male voice calling him back into awareness sounded oddly familiar, but he figured his priority needed to be to determine his location. Was he in a safe place?

Where am I? John was in a sitting position on something soft, maybe a chair or couch. His hands were tied and resting in his lap. He also realized his feet were bound together, as he was unable to separate them. His eyes were open, yet everything was dim. He hoped he wasn't partially blind from his beating. No, there was something over his head, possibly a cloth bag of some kind that prevented his eyes from soaking in new images.

Although still groggy from being out of it, John could sense sunlight on the right side of his body. He could feel its radiating warmth on his skin and was beginning to see particles of the sun's rays penetrating the covering on his head. He might be sitting next to a window.

Sounds of nature were notably absent. He heard no insects chirping, no birds singing and no dogs barking. He had to be inside a building of some kind. Beyond the voice calling on him to wake up, all he could hear was a light rhythmic ticking, certainly much louder than his now calm heartbeat. He assumed the ticking was probably a clock–time still mattered to someone.

"Come on, snap out of it! Wake up," said the owner of the familiar voice, calling to John again, shaking him slightly, trying to jar him awake.

John, now coming into his right mind, was beginning to wonder about his safety. None of his predicament was normal by any means. Then again, up to that point, he hadn't seen anything ordinary. In the last several hours, now possibly days, there was no such thing as normal. Still, he was sitting there with his hands and feet tied and a bag over his head. Any sane person would be worried, so he contemplated the pros and cons of speaking.

"Hey, can you hear me? I need you to say something," his captor said.

John coughed to clear his throat, working up the courage to talk. He didn't know what to say. How does a guy converse with someone who has apparently tied his hands and feet and thrown a bag over his head? *Oh, I'm fine; just peachy. How are you?* John's thoughts were sarcastic, but his concerns were very serious.

"Look, I know you're awake. I can hear you groaning. I'm not gonna hurt you. I just need to make sure you're okay." *Oh, a polite kidnapper,* thought John.

There was a slight amount of desperation in the unidentified voice. *Okay, maybe it would be better if I try to talk.* He would reply to the person who held him bound and captive.

"I hurt, but I'm okay," John said through the fabric covering his throbbing head.

"Good. I need you to answer a question. I don't want to hear anything but the answer to this question. Do you understand?" asked the person whose voice was beginning to crack a bit.

"Okay," John replied.

He thought the situation was getting weirder by the minute, as if he were entangled in a TV spy drama. Strangely, he felt calm and collected.

"The night Liz broke up with you, what did you do to Nathan's tree?"

"What?" John was confused.

Now excited, the familiar voice repeated, "Just answer the question! The night Liz broke up with you, what did you do to Nathan's tree?"

Whoever this is, John thought, *he knows Liz and Nate.* His brain tingled with confusion and excitement. For a moment, he thought someone was pranking him, as if a person might yank the bag off his head and yell, "Surprise!" Forget answering the question because he had inquiries of his own.

"Do you know Liz and..."

Cutting John off, the man with the familiar voice grabbed him by the shoulders and said, "Please, just answer the question. The night Liz broke up with you, what did you do to Nathan's tree?"

John could feel the captor's hands trembling on his shoulders. The guy was either scared or psychotic, but there was no way of knowing which one. John could hear the cracks of excitement in the man's voice. Apparently, this person was emotionally passionate about what John had done to that silly oak tree. Why?

"I put toilet paper in it."

Okay, there, I said it. There's your answer. Now what? He listened behind the fabric as the person with the familiar voice broke into loud sobbing. *Interestingly, my throwing toilet paper into a tree has set this person off emotionally. What's going on?*

John spoke boldly, "You wanna tell me what's going on here?"

Suddenly, he felt a hand grab at the top of the bag on his head. *Uh-oh, I've angered them beyond their limit! This is it! They're pulling the cover off my head so they can look me in the eyes as they kill me!*

The bag slipped up and over John's head. A sudden rush of sunlight flooded into his eyes from a window to his right. He tightly closed his eyes at the intrusion of brightness, then opened and closed them several times to correct for the new intensity. At least twenty seconds passed as his eyes slowly adjusted. He was still alive! They weren't trying to kill him!

Squinting, he began to see a figure emerge out of his hazy vision, right in front of him and nearly face to face. John struggled to get his eyes to adjust to the strong light easily penetrating his partially closed eyelids. Lubricating tears began to stream in, making his ability to focus even more difficult. After several stressful seconds, the image flowing into his pupils was finally clear.

Sitting in a chair, staring right back into John's eyes was Nathan. It was him, but it wasn't him–at least not the best friend he remembered. He had changed. Beyond the tears, John could see Nathan's drawn and worn face hiding behind a close-cut beard. His hair was disheveled and displayed signs of age in light touches of grey. John's best friend had always been thin and athletic, but he now looked skinny and weak, even malnourished.

Without words, just tears bursting forth in emotional relief, Nathan leapt out of his chair and threw his arms around John. They were best friends reunited in a painfully evil world. Oddly, John was not able to cry, though other things had made him do so. He merely sat there, hands and feet tied, absorbing his friend's embrace. There had to be much more to the story than rediscovering his best friend. John mentally searched for ways to start the long conversation he wanted to have with Nathan.

In typical John fashion, without acknowledging his friend's emotional display, John said, "Uh, I'd like to return that hug, but I'm a bit tied up at the moment."

Immediately, Nathan disengaged from the hug and began wiping the tears out of his eyes, maybe remembering who was watching him cry like a baby. They knew each other shed tears, but according to stringent guy code, such behavior was private, not public.

"Of course," Nathan said, "I'm sorry. I had to make sure it was you before I cut you lose. Let me get these off you."

Nathan returned to the chair in front of John and leaned back to reach into his jeans pocket. After struggling momentarily, he pulled out a small pocket knife, frantically opened the blade and began cutting at the rope wrapped around his friend's wrist and ankles.

Seeing Nathan was shaking a bit as he attempted to cut the rope, John said, "Hey, be careful. I don't want to come this far to have my veins slit by my best friend."

Nathan, noting John's words "come this far," silently cut the rope from his friend's wrists and ankles. *What did he mean? How far? From where?* Once cut away, he tossed the bindings to the side to show he no longer needed them and that there should be mutual trust between them. With hands still shaking, he carefully closed the knife, crammed it back into his pocket and then looked deeply into John's eyes. For Nathan, it was like looking at a ghost.

"Nate, why are you staring at me like that? You okay?" John asked as he reached out to put a hand on his friend's shoulder to offer comfort by physical contact.

"I can't believe you're here. I thought I would never see you again."

"What do you mean?" John retracted his hand of comfort and cocked his head slightly.

Nathan tapped John's knee and said, "I feel like I'm looking at a ghost, but you're real. I can touch you. You're right here in my den."

Nathan seemed strangely crazed. He moved around in his chair as if it were on fire. His eyes darted about, scanning John top to bottom several times. He repeatedly touched himself on the arm and leg, then performed the same action on his friend as if verifying they were both there. He looked like an addict needing a fix, but John knew Nathan was, instead, greatly distressed.

"Of course, I'm real. What else would I be?"

John had to control his sarcasm in hopes of not pushing his renewed friendship away. He had to guard his words and speak with tact and purpose.

"Dead, John. You're not dead."

John felt as if a wrecking ball had just slapped him in the face. The skin hiding behind hours of dirt and dried blood suddenly went pale. His body abruptly weakened, so much so that had he been standing, he certainly would have fallen. *Did I hear him correctly? I swear I just heard Nate say I wasn't dead.*

"I thought I was a goner out in your front yard with those creeps beating me to death. When I heard what sounded like a gunshot, I thought that was it."

"That was me and my shotgun. I was up reading and heard them out there having their brand of twisted fun. I grabbed my shotgun, went outside and fired a slug into the air. They took off like scared kittens. They weren't gonna bring a pipe to a gunfight; that's for sure."

"Nate, you saved my life. I'm alive, beaten and bruised but very much alive because of you. I can't thank you enough."

"When I saw you out there," Nathan said, motioning to the lawn through the window, "sprawled out and unconscious, I knew it had to be a miracle you were here."

Nathan would have never used the word miracle to describe anything he had seen. John had never heard him say the word except to associate it with a coincidence. Something had changed in his best friend's life, but that remained to be seen.

"Miracle? What do you mean?" John asked anxiously.

Nathan leaned in closer to John as if he were going to whisper a secret and then asked, "You don't know? Do you?"

"For goodness' sake, Nate; what don't I know?" bellowed John as he tightly grabbed Nathan's arm to reassure him that he was actually sitting there, that he was, in fact, not a ghost.

"John, you never came back."

"Back from where?"

Seemingly, Nathan knew details about John that he, himself, didn't know. Maybe Nathan could shed some light on the subject. After all, that's why John had trudged through what appeared to be a crazy, wicked world to find his best friend. The answers should be forthcoming.

"John, the night you broke up with Liz, you went missing. She felt so bad about how things went that evening, she drove over to your house later that night. When she got there, you were gone. She couldn't find you.

"We went to the police the next day and told them you were missing, but they told us we had to wait another day for your disappearance to be official. For weeks, Liz and I drove streets and roads all over the county looking for you. We made fliers and posted them everywhere for at least a couple hundred miles. The students organized hundreds of search groups but to no avail. You were gone."

Nathan got up out of his chair and walked over to a bookshelf attached to the wall behind him. He grabbed a piece of paper out of one of many books.

John noted how his friend's jeans and t-shirt appeared to be a few sizes too big, as if he had lost an unhealthy amount of weight. Nathan had undergone both physical and mental changes. He returned to the chair in front of John, then handed the worn and slightly wrinkled paper to him.

John accepted the paper and read its simple words very carefully. He couldn't believe what he was seeing. In his hands, he was holding a missing person flier in which he was the subject. The document displayed his vital statistics along with his staff photo from school.

Suddenly, the plaque in his classroom at the school made all the sense in the world. He remembered the words which read, "THOUGH HE IS ABSENT FROM OUR LIVES, HE IS EVER PRESENT IN OUR HEARTS." *For goodness' sake, they thought I was dead!*

"John, where have you been?" Nathan threw his hands outward to punctuate the question with an implied "where in the world."

"Nate, I'll be honest with you and say things have happened which I don't really understand. I can't even begin to describe what has happened to me, and I'm not sure if I should even try."

John gingerly stood, walked over to the window and peered through curtains and metal bars. Should he mention the man in white? Should he mention the staff? Should he mention his apparent movement through time? Should he mention any of it at all?

Nathan said, still sitting, "Try me."

"Nate, I don't think you would get it. How in the world can I expect you to understand something I don't even understand myself?"

"Fair enough."

As John pulled the curtain back to look at the blazing sunrise, he noted the ambient purity a new day provided. He knew it was a false hope in a decaying world in which he had already been a witness.

John motioned to the world outside the window, then faced his friend to say, "I just want to know what's going on. What happened to make things the way they are? Just look outside at this mess. I've seen some of it, and I'm not sure I want to see any more of it. I mean, look at this house; look at you. This is not the house I remember, and you look like death warmed over."

"Really, John? You haven't changed a bit. You obviously haven't seen yourself."

That was true. John hadn't really stopped to take a good look at himself, maybe because he was too busy fearing for his life. His clothing was a mess, so dirty it seemed he was wearing a military camouflage uniform. His skin was covered in dirt and dried blood, evidence of his interaction with the world. From his friend's point of view, he probably looked much worse than death warmed over.

Walking back to the couch to sit down, throwing a thumb back toward the window, John asked, "What happened out there?"

Nathan sat quietly for a moment as if searching for the right words to say. There was so much he needed to tell John but no easy way to get the information into an understandable narrative. He was John's witness to all the global events that had happened. He sighed deeply as he began.

"The world," Nathan explained, "was already a hard place to live in, but after it happened, things reached a whole new level of awful. Believe it or not, it was only the beginning, and what you see out there is gonna get a whole lot worse."

"Okay, but what happened? What is this 'it' you're talking about?" John leaned back in the couch, bracing for a harsh reality to come.

Sighing, Nathan closed his eyes for a moment of clarity. After what seemed like minutes, he reopened his eyes and calmly said, "John, they were right."

"Am I supposed to play twenty questions here, Nate? Who was right?"

"The Christians, especially the conservative ones."

Feeling frustrated at his own apparent lack of knowledge, John shot back by asking, "Right about what, Nate?"

The answers weren't coming fast enough, but he knew Nathan was trying. Perhaps he was having just as much trouble explaining what had happened around the world as John would have had explaining all the unusual things that had occurred with him in the last several hours. Obviously, what had transpired for both wasn't typical chat.

He had to give his friend some leeway in his account of things and not get pushy or agitated. Both men had transformed, and conversation styles of the past were no longer applicable. Considering the gravity of the situation, neither one of them could afford the cold hand of sarcasm and heckling.

"Everything," Nathan replied. "The Christians were right about everything. A little over four years after you disappeared, wicked things really started happening in the world. Well, they were already happening in previous years, but they got a thousand times worse."

Okay, John thought, *I've been missing for at least four*

years. He knew this was the beginning of a timeline that would become a very agonizing story of the world's progress. He wanted to hear everything Nathan had to say, but in another way, he didn't.

Nathan asked, "Do you remember the division in government, the political disruption, the Impasse and the subtle attempts to introduce Socialist principles into our lives?"

"Yeah, it's hard to forget."

"Do you remember the division in the country, the rioting, the looting, the protests and the unchecked rise in crime?"

"That too is also hard to forget."

"Well," explained Nathan, "not only did it continue, but it got worse. There were so many people learning to hate their country. Solidarity in the United States quickly went out the window, and patriotic people were getting harder and harder to find.

"A general lack of respect for law and order began to spread across the country like an infectious disease. Russia, China and North Korea were sitting over across the pond watching the country tear itself apart and loving every minute of it. The people of the United States became their own worst enemy"

"So, this is all isolated to the United States?"

"No, John, democracies all over the world were impacted in much the same way. But this was all leading to something bigger on the horizon, something that would very rapidly change the world forever but in a very bad way."

"What happened?" John leaned forward again, intent on listening and hanging on every word.

"About four years after you disappeared, the

government, under heavy social pressure, started to take a hardline stand against religion. They said it was against all religions, but they quietly directed the brunt of their changes and enforcement to Christianity.

"Christians became targets for persecution within the continental United States. Abroad, especially in countries already hostile to Christians, bad treatment of anyone professing Jesus Christ as Savior got worse, and many foreign governments followed suit with what our own country was doing in enforcement."

"What kind of enforcement?"

"Well, at first, it was a mandate that all crosses be removed from public display, even if it was part of the church's physical structure. There was to be no display of crosses, they ordered. Then, another directive came out stating images of Jesus couldn't be on display outside the walls of the church. Shortly after that, groups began to call for the dismantling of Christian churches all over the country. Some churches were successfully shut down, but the majority remained open. John, they were targeted for their stand on prominent issues. Political correctness groups used any excuse they could find to say churches were not inclusive, and therefore, should be shut down. In effect, Christians were no longer being allowed to practice their Faith."

"So much for religious freedom, right?"

"John, I'm not so sure the Constitution means much of anything anymore. I'm not even sure the United States as a nation still exists. Things are just so messed up right now, and I can't see them getting any better."

John winced at the thought of his More Perfect Union fading into the sunset. Maybe the land of the free and the home of the brave were really gone. From what he had seen, it seemed that way.

Getting back on track, John asked, "Well, what about the other religions? Were they part of this attack on religious freedoms?"

Nathan continued, "There was some enforcement at first, but society quickly realized the Christians were a much bigger and easier target. Christians became victims of vandalism, beatings and even murder. In fact, about five years after you disappeared, the murder of Christians in the United States became a daily occurrence. I couldn't pick up a newspaper or watch the news without seeing stories of attacks on Christians. I remember one headline in a newspaper a few days before everything really changed. It casually said, 'Another Jesus Lover Found Dead.' John, it's interesting how the very people who called Christians intolerant and hateful were the ones doing the beating and murdering."

John noted Nathan's change in attitude toward Christians. Where before, he would often joke about them or taunt their religious practices; he was now talking about them honorably and with reverence, as if appointed to be their historian. He assumed Nathan may have been converted. Obviously, he had seen or heard something that changed his way of thinking.

"So," John asked, "what were Christians right about?"

Nathan continued, "Many Christians saw the world situation as a sign of national downfall, the weakening of predominantly Christian nations all over the world. Particularly hard hit was the United States. Many Christians, including Liz, saw the things happening as a sign of an even greater event."

Nathan brought up Liz. John's memory flashed to that awful night at Grover's and how she mentioned God bringing a morally corrupt nation to its knees. He wanted to consider what she had said but quickly dismissed the thoughts.

He badly wanted to bust in on the conversation to ask about her but felt the time wasn't quite right. Somehow, he sensed all the things they were talking about would explain what, if anything, happened to Liz. He had to let the story play out; otherwise, his understanding of why things were the way they were could become flawed.

"And what event would that be?" John asked as he shifted on the couch, maybe feeling uneasy about something. Out of fear, he thought about retracting the question but knew he was starving for the answer.

Nathan stood, looked down at John and said, "It's easier if I just show you. Just sit tight for a few minutes, and I'll be right back."

John watched as Nathan walked out of the room and disappeared toward the back of the house. He heard locks snapping, a door opening and closing and assumed it must have been his friend going outside. He contemplated sneaking to a window to see what his buddy was doing but decided to trust and let events progress without intervention or snooping.

John took the opportunity to get up and explore the room in which he and his friend had been talking. He could also see the living room and part of the kitchen from the den, but he wouldn't wander off to those areas because he didn't want to give Nathan the impression he was spying.

As he peeked into the living room, he noticed virtually the same house as before the world fell apart. Nathan's bachelor pad had wood floors, hardly any furniture, no wall coverings and apparently zero presence of a woman. There was no evidence he could see that showed his best friend ever tied the knot. His home lacked a woman's touch, as it was very much all about Nathan's nearly minimalist aesthetic.

Spent candles were present throughout the areas John could see, and he assumed there were probably others in the parts of the house he couldn't see. The well-used candles, John knew, served as illumination in the absence of electricity. Power outages were apparently wide spread, and perhaps his conversation with Nathan would indicate why. For now, during daylight hours, the sun brightened the home.

In the den, the furniture was much the same, except for the book shelves which now held far more literature than before. John knew Nathan was never a big fan of reading, which made his decision to become a teacher an odd one. John didn't like to read either, which also made for an unusual decision to pursue a career in education. Before, neither one of them enjoyed burying their faces in a book, but now, according to the packed shelves, that was a trait they no longer shared.

John moved in closer to look at the collection of books on the shelves. He saw several Bible commentaries, each of which had various papers and notes emerging from their pages. He also saw several books dealing with Christian doctrine, all clogged with notes from beginning to end. Jammed between many of the publications were well-used notebooks with ruffled pages. At the end of the middle bookshelf, John noticed a brown, well-worn, leather-bound *New King James Bible.*

He knew Nathan, on rare occasions, browsed through books about Christian doctrine to better understand a God he didn't "know" existed. That's how he defended his reading of such materials, but John speculated the knowledge gained was really for the winning of some girl's heart. However, John never knew him to own any kind of Bible, a shocking revelation about his friend's life.

He picked up the Bible and began flipping through its pages randomly. All throughout the sacred book, especially in the New Testament, Nathan had handwritten tons of notes in the margins and either highlighted or underlined massive amounts of the text. Clearly, a man who swore to never read the Bible was now studying it intensely.

John heard a small engine start up behind the house. It could have been a lawn mower for all he knew but guessed the overgrown yard was the least of concerns. He then heard the back door open and shut again, followed by the rattle of locks, so he quickly put the Bible back on the shelf. Did he care if Nathan saw him looking at it? Not really, but again, he didn't want his friend to think he was snooping. John and Nathan had to build a new kind of relationship based on trust, one that lacked childish behavior and probable suspicion.

Nathan walked back into the room carrying a small metal box covered in speckles of rust. He also dragged in a long, orange extension cord which smacked the hardwood floors with echoing clacks. Before sitting, he went to a cabinet on the back wall of the room and opened its two large doors to reveal a small flat screen television and media player. He then reached behind the cabinet to pull out a power cord which he plugged into the orange extension cord. The lights on the television and media player came on as the electronic equipment came to life.

Nathan motioned for John to sit back down on the couch and said, "Sit down. I need to show you something."

John returned to his seat, wondering what he was about to see. Nathan also returned to his chair, holding the small metal box close to his body in a death grip. Apparently, whatever was in the box was tremendously important. John couldn't decide if he was honored or afraid to see the contents.

Nathan, now calm, said, "Before I show this to you, I need to tell you something."

"Okay," John said approvingly.

"I almost don't want to tell you because I'm worried you may think I'm crazy or something."

"At this point, I don't think anything you say is gonna surprise me, Nate."

With a deep cleansing breath to begin, Nathan said, "A couple nights after you disappeared, I had a dream. It might have been a dream, or at least I think it was a dream. It was so vivid."

"What was it about?"

"Well, I had this dream that this old, Moses-looking man dressed in all white appeared at the foot of my bed. It was weird in that I was asleep but could sense his presence in the room. I remember hearing my name being called and then sitting up in bed to see this guy standing there. I wasn't afraid at all."

John was jumping up and down inside but didn't

want to say anything. *Maybe Nate saw the same man in white I encountered just hours ago. I think it was hours? Whatever! This is incredible! How could two people dream about the same thing?* John knew what Nathan had seen was real and not a figment of an overactive imagination. He knew it wasn't a dream. Rather than enlightening Nathan about the truth of what he had experienced, John chose to listen carefully to the story.

Nathan continued, staring into space as if reliving the moment in his mind. "Then the man spoke to me, and it was as clear as me talking to you right now. I'll never forget what he said." To John's dismay, Nathan paused.

"Well, what did he say?" asked John anxiously as he tapped his friend's knee.

"He said, 'Do not fear. You will see John again. When he appears to you, you must tell him of things past. In time, you will be spared of the greatest of Tribulation.' Then he faded away, and the last thing I remember was waking up the following morning."

John was screaming inside, wondering if he should say something about his own experiences with the man in white. He so very much wanted to reassure Nathan of what he had seen in his "dream" that night, but a deep conviction held back his confession.

"John, you don't think I'm crazy, do you?"

Smiling, John gently patted his friend's arm and said, "Not at all, Nate. Not a bit."

"Anyway, since that night, I've been waiting to talk to you. I knew you would come back. I could feel it. When things started happening in the world about four years later, I knew those were the things I was supposed to tell you. Then, when it happened, I knew for certain everything I told you would revolve around this one event."

"What event?"

"Let me show you. It's much easier if you see it for yourself."

Nathan got up with the small metal box and knelt in front of the television. He then opened the box and pulled out a thin, clear plastic case containing a media disc. As he opened the case to extract the disc, John scooted nearer to the end of the couch for a closer look and better view of the TV screen.

Holding the disc up for John to inspect, Nathan said, "I've had this buried in my backyard for months because I knew you would need to see what's on it. If certain people knew I had this, I could be put away for a very long time, maybe permanently if you know what I mean."

Apparently, whatever was on the disc could lead to imprisonment or death. Was this normal for the current society? John had seen some really bad things thus far, so he imagined the contents of the disc weren't going to surprise him. He was feeling like a character in a spy novel but with actions bearing real-life consequences.

John asked, "Is it bad?"

"Bad for some but good for others. You'll see," said Nathan as he inserted the disk into the media player.

Nathan pushed a button on the side of the TV and watched as the screen came to life. He used a small remote to click through a couple menus on the screen, eventually finding two media files on the disc. After clicking the first file in the menu, the screen lit up with what looked like a newscast. He used the fast forward function to zip through several minutes of the broadcast, finally returning to normal play and then pausing the video. John's curiosity grew as he watched his friend scroll through the video, doing so as if he had done it a couple thousand times before.

Paused on the screen was a typical news anchor desk. Behind the desk was a well-dressed man, and to his left, sat an equally well-dressed woman. He was handsome and well-groomed; she was a blond bombshell and finely accessorized with jewelry. To John, the male anchor looked familiar, while the female anchor did not.

Nathan pointed to the man in the paused image on the screen in front of them and asked, "Do you recognize that guy?"

Knowing who the man was, John replied, "That's Jim 'The News' Story. He's the guy who was fired from Hot10 TV for refusing to cover the same-sex marriage between the two senators."

"That's right, John. He was later picked up by another station, the one recorded right here."

"Okay, Nate, what am I supposed to be seeing?"

"I'm gonna let this play, so watch very carefully. Okay?"

"Sure, go ahead," John said as he leaned closer to the flatscreen.

Nathan used the remote to initiate play on the video once again. The female anchor was talking about a story through which Nathan had apparently fast-forwarded.

She was saying, "Local officials were unavailable for comment. However, we will continue to follow…"

Suddenly, there was an intense flash of light on the screen, a bright flash greater than the strobe on any camera John had ever seen. The anomaly lasted less than a second and was hard to examine for any kind of detail, as the event had started and finished in the blink of an eye. After the powerful light quickly faded, John watched as the male anchor's empty clothing fell limp somewhere behind the news desk.

The female anchor chirped in fright and quickly jumped out of her chair to somewhere off screen, while others off camera were acting in a similar manner and living their own little nightmares. Sudden chaos erupted in the news studio as people scrambled to figure out what was going on. For several seconds, the image on the screen remained void of human presence, but John heard their panicked voices in the background.

A male voice shouted, "Where's Jim?"

There was a scream, then a female voice shouted back, "Christie's gone too!"

Another male voice shouted over the panic, "Stay calm, people!"

The female anchor slowly and cautiously came back into view with her hand over her mouth in horror. As she peered into the chair her colleague was sitting in, another male voice shouted, "Cut the feed! Shut it down, now! Shut it all down!"

The live images changed to a color test pattern and a message which read, "PLEASE STAND BY. THIS BROADCAST IS EXPERIENCING TECHNICAL DIFFICULTIES." Nathan paused the video and examined his friend's reaction. John sat with his eyes glued to the screen and his jaw practically on the floor. *What did I just see?* thought John. The blinding light from the video was very familiar to him. *I've seen that somewhere before, but where?*

John, stunned, turned to Nathan and asked excitedly, "Uh, what was that?"

Nathan put a halting hand up to John and said, "In a few seconds, I'm gonna play this back to you ten times slower. Just watch carefully because it still happens very quickly."

John, still dumbfounded, returned his gaze to the TV screen while Nathan went backwards in the video until both anchors were, once again, sitting behind the news desk. He skillfully used the controls on the remote to find the precise location in the video, as if he had performed the task repeatedly. *Obviously,* thought John, *Nate has this video memorized.*

"Watch closely, John."

Without reply, John watched as the video played at a much slower speed to reveal its secrets. The female anchor's mouth moved slowly but remained silent while the video was in a slower mode. With the images at a greatly decreased pace, John inspected the frames as the bright flash began to show itself.

At first, the brilliant light appeared on the skin of Jim Story's forehead and then quickly spread to other parts of his body. The light seemed to emanate mostly from exposed skin, but it also penetrated through clothing from behind. An explosion of high intensity light rapidly replaced the on-screen picture of the male anchor. Then, in an instant, the bright white light was gone, as was Jim Story.

John continued to watch as the female anchor, in slow motion, began her mad scramble out from behind the news desk. Simultaneously, Jim Story's empty clothing began to fall downward. Nathan paused the video to show the vacant suit coat and tie seemingly hovering in midair.

"Nate, I've seen some crazy stuff today, but that really blows my mind."

"We're not done. I want you to see something else in this video."

Nathan reversed the video back and paused at the point where both anchors were present behind the news desk. In reverse, the bright light faded and gave way to Jim Story as if he were being born from the light itself.

"John, this time, I want you to watch Jim's head and face. Notice what he does."

Nathan started the video again and pointed to the male anchor's head. John watched as, just before the light appeared, Jim tilted his head back as if to look skyward. Nathan paused the video at the precise moment when Jim Story slightly smiled, just as the light began to appear on his forehead.

Pointing upward, John asked, "What's he seeing?"

"He could be hearing something too. I don't know, but he's seeing or hearing something, and he's reacting to it. Obviously, from our point of view, we can't tell what it is. Whatever it is, it's apparently making him happy. The guy's smiling."

John suddenly remembered where he had seen the bright flash of light. He searched the recesses of his mind to take him back to a moment on Ferro Drive, just before his experience at the burning house.

He recalled the vision of the car coming up the street toward him. He recollected seeing the same intense flash on the passenger side of the vehicle and the subsequent, chaotic crash of the vehicle into a tree. John realized he was sitting in Nathan's den watching a similar event, but one captured on video.

294 | PERIL ENVISIONED

John looked squarely at his friend and said, "Nate, pretend I'm totally ignorant here, and tell me what in the world this is."

"You never were very bright, John," Nathan replied with equal sarcasm.

"I know. Thanks for reminding me. What did I just see?"

Nathan sighed and stated rather bluntly, "It was the Rapture, John. The Christians were right. You just witnessed the Rapture, for goodness' sake."

Shaking his head, John said, "Again, Nate, please pretend I'm stupid, and tell me what you're talking about." After speaking so harshly, he remembered the need to control his sarcasm. With hands up, he apologetically said, "Sorry, Nate. I'm just frustrated."

"That's okay. I'm sorry too, and I shouldn't have taken that shot at you. I just need to slow down. Anyway, many Christians believed that they would be taken out of the world prior to an event called the Tribulation, a time of unprecedented peril on the Earth leading to the end of present days and the eventual return of Christ. John, what you're seeing out there," he said motioning to the window, "is the beginning of the Tribulation."

The reality of the situation was just beginning to sink in for John. The world was saturated in evil turmoil, and he was bearing witness to the events as they were–or would be. He was now seeing what the man in white wanted him to see, a forthcoming, dying world. He fell back into the couch, covering his eyes with his hand, feeling nausea welling up from within his beaten and tortured body.

Nathan spoke softly, like a father speaking to his

injured child. "John, I know this is hard for you to see and hear. I know for certain the reason I'm here to tell you about all this is because I was not a saved Christian. I never put my trust in Jesus. I never let Him into my heart. Now, I have to go through this peril just like the rest of the unbelieving world."

John quickly wiped away unwanted tears and dropped his hand down into his lap. He looked at Nathan with swollen eyes and asked, "What about now? Do you trust Him?"

Still speaking softly, but with bold undertones, Nathan said, "I'm not the person I used to be. About a couple years before the Rapture, I began studying the Bible. I didn't just read it; I studied it. I guess I was trying to find comfort among all the junk that was happening in the world."

Nathan, groaning like an old man, pushed himself out of the chair and then walked over to retrieve his Bible from the shelf. Upon returning to his seat, he gently placed the sacred book on the couch next to John.

Nathan continued with his testimony. "Liz gave this Bible to me right after you disappeared. She tried to tell me about things to come and what I needed to do to get into Heaven, but I always cut her off with a stupid joke. For years, this Bible sat in a box in the attic because I didn't want anyone to know I had it. I'm ashamed of that."

Yes, what happened to Liz? John leaned forward, grabbed Nathan's wrist and asked, "What about Liz? Is she okay? What happened to her?"

Nathan placed a comforting hand on his best friend's quivering shoulder and said, "John, she's not here, in this world, I mean. She was raptured with the rest of the Christian Church. I know it sounds weird, and it's hard to understand, but you should feel better knowing she's in Heaven, in the presence of God. She's truly in a much better place. She's not going through this nightmare like you and me."

John leaned back into the couch, feeling an inexpressible joy for Liz, that she was okay–no, better than okay! He felt relieved by the knowledge that she was not experiencing any part of what he had seen in the last several hours or apparently would see in the many days to come. He was also feeling painfully guilty for having not listened to her, for ignoring her Faith.

Brushing away tears, John asked, "Nate, are you a Christian now?"

Without hesitation, Nathan stated firmly, "Yes, John. I am now a Christian. I studied God's Word of the Bible but held out in seeking salvation until after the Rapture. It wasn't until a few months ago that I accepted Christ into my heart. It wasn't until a few months ago that I turned away from my evil ways and sought the salvation of Jesus Christ.

"I prayed for the first time and asked the Lord to help me walk away from all the bad things I do in my life. I was down on my knees in humble prayer asking God to forgive me for walking away from Him and to forgive me of all the ways I've displeased Him.

"I admitted to Him, that in my heart, I recognized His plan and purpose in Jesus. I recognized the miraculous virgin birth of Jesus. I recognized the sinless life Jesus lived so that He could be the sacrificial Lamb of God for the bad things I did. I recognized the substitutionary death of Jesus on the cross, bearing the death that should have been mine. I recognized the resurrection of Jesus and His power to overcome death. I recognized His glorious ascension into Heaven. Most importantly, I recognized He did it for sinners like me. I'm no Biblical scholar by any means, and there's still a ton of stuff I don't understand, but the important part is that I've changed and have accepted Jesus into my heart."

John shot a confused look toward Nathan and asked, "Then, why are you still here?"

"John, it doesn't work that way. Like billions of other people, I had my chance to seek salvation before the Rapture, but I didn't take it. I'm a Christian now, but because of my inaction prior to the Rapture, I and billions of other people–post-Rapture believers and unbelievers–are gonna have to go through the coming Tribulation. In the end, when something or someone kills me, then I'll go to Heaven. This world is, sadly, just a painful stepping stone to get there."

John coughed, then asked, "Nate, have you got anything to drink? I haven't put anything liquid down my throat in hours."

Standing, Nathan said, "I'm a horrible host. I should have offered you something to drink long ago. Water okay?"

"Yeah, that would be great."

John watched as Nathan disappeared around the corner headed toward the kitchen. *If there isn't power, how is Nate keeping his food and drinks cool? Does he have a working refrigerator?* Maybe those were things his friend would talk about later. Nathan quickly returned with a glass of cloudy water, which John took in hand with a look of trepidation.

Hoping to ease fears of drinking the water, Nathan

said, "It's supposed to be okay to drink."

John held the glass up to the sunlight, peered into the murky water and said, "You're not inspiring much confidence here."

"Sorry, that's about all I have. I'm hoping for something better on food day."

Taking baby sips, John noted Nathan's use of the term "food day" and wanted to ask about it, but he felt the time might not be right. They were having a long and informative conversation. He knew, in time, the answers would come. *"Food day"* ...*so odd, though.*

Nathan stepped over to the media player and TV and knelt beside it once again. He pointed to the screen and said, "John, I've got one more video to show you."

"Okay, shoot."

Just as Nathan began pushing buttons on the remote to open the second media file, the engine sound toward the back of the house began to sputter slightly. Nathan moved quicker, sensing that he was about to lose power to the electronics. He opened the second media file and then immediately paused the image on the screen.

"Gotta hurry, John. I think the generator is about to run out of gas."

"I'm watching. Go ahead, Nate."

"Okay, I'm showing this to you so you realize the Rapture was a widespread event and that it wasn't just a local thing. It happened all over the world. What you're gonna see here is at a soccer stadium in England. As best as I can tell, they had a camera rolling in the stadium during a break in play, probably recording the sights and sounds of the crowd. Keep in mind that there are thousands of people at this event. Like before, it's gonna happen quick, so pay attention."

John set the glass of water on the floor next to the couch and leaned closer to the flatscreen. Nathan initiated play of the video with the remote and pointed in silence to the rolling image on the screen. Suddenly, there were intense flashes of light all throughout the stadium, like thousands of camera strobes going off at the same time but much brighter. Then, in unison, the remaining crowd gasped in both surprise and terror, creating a loud and drawn out "oh" sound with intermingling screams.

John and Nathan shared glances, knowing what had just happened. It was Jim "The News" Story but on a large scale. Staring back at John, Nathan broke into a happy and approving smile.

"Now, John, imagine this happening all over the world," said Nathan as the generator finally sputtered to a stop, turning off both the TV and media player.

John tried to imagine the flashes of light occurring around the world. In his mind, he pictured people everywhere vanishing in the twinkling of an eye. People in their houses...gone. People in their cars... gone. People walking the streets...gone. People on the job...gone. People in planes...gone. People everywhere... suddenly gone.

Then, his thoughts turned to Liz. He remembered the nightmare he had in which Liz was pulled away from him. She went to Heaven, while he, sadly, went to Hell. He tried to picture Liz sitting in her rocking chair, possibly singing a hymn or reading her Bible, then zipping out of an earthly existence in a bright flash. He missed Liz so very much.

Nathan returned to his chair in front of John and

said, "This event, the Rapture, was just the beginning. Out of something so wonderful would come the beginning of something awful."

"I'm not following you, Nate. What do you mean?"

"The Rapture was good. Well, it was good for true Christians, anyway. For the rest of the unbelieving world, it was the beginning of a long nightmare that is yet to fully mature."

Nathan squirmed in his seat, realizing he was to be part of the ensuing nightmare. John could see that his friend was uneasy but didn't know what to say to comfort him. Quite frankly, Nathan's inflamed nerves seemed to be infectious, as John also became a bit disturbed. He understood he might also share in the terrifying times to come; the very awfulness Nathan spoke of.

"So, what happened next?" John asked.

Nathan continued, "There was an immediate global panic. Unbelievers all over the world had witnessed something in person that they thought could only happen in movies. Very quickly, they began looking for answers.

"Just days after the Rapture, there was a run on bookstores to find copies of the Bible, but few were found because the government had already secretly started taking them off the shelves. People were even breaking into churches to get copies of the Bible. The number one, all time, searched word on the Internet became 'Rapture'."

"What were the news agencies saying?"

"They were no help at all. Honestly, they and many others had an idea of what it was, but they didn't want to believe it. People don't like to be wrong, John.

Unfortunately, billions of unbelieving people, that day, found out what it was like to be wrong.

"It didn't take long at all for censorship to begin. There was a great effort on the part of many governments to greatly limit the details of the event in news coverage. Within days, new national laws held networks accountable for any information they were putting out concerning the Rapture. Administrations all over the world banned the words 'Rapture' and 'Christian' from any news coverage.

"Of course, the Internet was on fire with all kinds of speculation, most of which was unscriptural. There were videos of proof going out, much like the ones I showed to you. Some believe governments set loose on the Internet a computer virus that killed any file containing the words 'Rapture' and 'Christian.' It didn't take long for people to figure out workarounds, a problem which eventually led to an attempt to shut down the Internet. Control of information became a top priority, especially in nations known to be predominantly unbelieving. They wanted you to hear what they wanted you to hear and nothing more."

"Who's they?" John asked.

"At this point, nobody really knows who 'they' are. Personally, I think it's the unbelieving remnants of organized government here and abroad, consisting of those who were not carried away by the Rapture. Everybody refers to them as 'they,' mainly because nobody knows who they are.

"We're at five months after the event, and there's been no talk of a Federal Government. Supposedly, it's the same in other countries too. John, we don't even know if there's a President or a Vice President. Someone out there is calling the shots, but we don't even know if they're in the country. Rumor has it, whoever is calling these shots is making huge promises to make everything better–to fix things."

"Pardon me, but none of these things seem legal, Nate."

"Law and order went out the window, John. The Rapture created a lawless world. It was already spiritually lawless, but then it became socially lawless too. To this day, it's just plain dangerous to leave your house, that is, if you're lucky enough to still have one. Keep in mind, John, this is only the beginning."

Nathan leaned back in his chair as if mentally preparing to tell the rest of the story, but he was just resting from what he had already told. John could see that his best friend was mentally and physically drained, probably the result of living in the world. John was also feeling exhausted but had only heard a drop in the bucket of bad news.

Leaning forward again, Nathan continued, "There was an immediate and pressing problem in the world following the Rapture."

"I can imagine," replied John.

"I don't think you can. The world was faced with the task of getting rid of all the dead bodies."

With a confused look on his face, John asked, "Why would there be dead bodies if the Christians were taken to Heaven?"

Nathan shook his head as if to brush off John's ignorance. In his own thinking, he had to remember his friend had been missing for several years and lacked any knowledge of world events. He felt some of the things John had missed would be hard for him to hear. However, the reality of the conversation was that Nathan was unaware of his friend's trek through the world's ugliness and that he had already laid eyes on such things. John's hearing of these accounts from Nathan would only enforce what he had already seen.

"John, think about this very carefully. I want you to imagine a carload of people going down the interstate, when suddenly, the Christian driver vanishes. Anybody who happens to be a nonbeliever stays in the car as it careens off the road. The passengers die in the crash."

"Okay."

Annoyed at John's underwhelming lack of understanding, Nathan said, "I don't think you're grasping at what I'm saying here, John."

"Maybe," John casually replied.

"Okay, so picture car crashes like this happening all over the country. Picture them happening all around the world."

Nathan watched John's eyes drop to the floor, a long recognizable sign that he suddenly understood something. With the light bulb now on and shining, Nathan had to drive the idea home. He had to hit one over the fence and bring his friend over the plate.

Nathan continued, "Now, imagine a busload of people going down the road, when suddenly, the Christian driver vanishes in a flash of light. Many of the unbelievers remaining on the bus are swept away by the cold hand of death as the vehicle crashes. The ones fortunate enough to just be injured are taken to rapidly overloaded hospitals. Imagine that happening all around the world."

John lifted his eyes from the floor to look upon Nathan who continued with grim stories of death. He didn't want to hear the morbid tales but needed to.

Nathan said, "I know you're getting it now, but there's more to understand. Imagine a planeload of people flying high, suddenly dropping out of the sky like a bomb because the Christian pilot disappears. Imagine all the unbelievers dying as the plane crashes to the ground, or worse, into an occupied building. Then, John, imagine that happening all around the world."

He didn't have to imagine it because he had seen it. Now he understood why there was a plane in what used to be his living room. Now he understood why a plane had crashed into the school. Still, what he found most disturbing was that events like these local ones had happened all over the world.

"John," Nathan added, "planes were dropping out of the sky all over the place. One crashed into your house, but thankfully, the only occupant was the Christian pilot who obviously wasn't there for the crash. There was another, a military aircraft, an Air National Guard KC-135 refueling tanker that crashed into the school. Thank goodness the jet was already low and wasn't carrying a full load of fuel. Otherwise, the damage and loss of life would have been much worse."

John remembered seeing the tail of the plane sticking up above the roofline of the school. He recalled the vision of teachers and students burning as they ran down the hallway. At that thought, he closed his eyes and buried his face in his hands for a moment, hoping it would all go away.

Nathan, putting a calming hand on his friend's shoulder, said, "John, many people, mostly kids, died in that school when the plane crashed, but many also survived because they were taken to Heaven before the plane ever hit."

John jumped to his feet from the couch and marched to the window. Looking at the sun rising into the sky, he asked, "Were you in the school when the plane hit?"

"No, I took a sick day. I wasn't there, but had I been, I'm not sure I would be alive now. From what I understand, the plane nosed in right on top of my classroom.

"I still have nightmares about what my students and others must have gone through. I also try to remember there were some who weren't there for the crash, that they were taken to Heaven as Christians.

"I remember Sarah's sister coming to me the day before, talking about a project she was working on for her church's food pantry ministry. She started talking about Jesus, and I think she was trying to witness to me. I brushed her off the same way I dismissed Liz on the numerous occasions she tried to talk to me about the Lord and the salvation He offered. I never knew Sarah and her sister were believers until that moment. Honestly, at that time, I probably didn't care. Now, I'm so thankful they had a saving relationship with Jesus Christ."

Turning to face Nathan, with the sun shining warmly across John's body, creating a shadow of metal bars and human form on the opposite wall, John said, "It must have been horrible to live through that day."

"Well, it was an exceptionally bad day, but it would get even worse, John. In the short time following the Rapture, about two weeks, there would be more death and destruction."

Returning to the couch, John asked, "What kind of

death and destruction?"

Nathan sighed and shut his eyes for a moment, as if reliving a painful memory. With disappointing sadness, he said, "Violence erupted everywhere in the panic following the disappearance of so many people. There was rioting and looting like nothing anyone had ever seen before and on a global scale. It was like the world suddenly went crazy. All over the United States, for example, police and fire departments lost key personnel to the Rapture and quickly became bogged down in calls. Even to this day, big cities are like war zones. We're lucky to live here, but death visits every single day, even in this small town.

"There weren't enough police to respond to the massive waves of crime emerging across the country and around the world. Fire departments had to let structures burn down for lack of people and equipment. Even now, the fire and police protective services that are still around are stretched thin, most likely beyond the breaking point. It didn't take long for states to call up their military Guard and Reserve troops to augment the police and fire departments.

"Hospitals were also immediately overtaxed. Thousands died waiting to be seen by a doctor. Thugs raided many of the hospitals looking for meds to support their drug habits or their wallets. Even now, ambulatory services just don't exist. These days, if people need medical attention and are lucky enough to still have an operational hospital near them, they're pretty much on their own getting there."

Nathan watched John settle back into the couch with a flushed face and weakened body. He picked up the glass of water from the floor and handed it to

John, urging him to continue drinking. They both had to be strong, knowing the story wasn't going to get any better.

"John," Nathan continued, "when the Christians disappeared, numerous organizations and their processes no longer had people to perform various jobs. It wasn't that these functions required Christians for proper operation, but instead, the caretakers in these positions just happened to be Christians. It was their job, but they were no longer there to do it. Because of that, processes and procedures began to collapse globally. Imagine a company suddenly losing a tenth or more of their employees. Imagine that happening in government, in the military or anywhere else. Things just aren't going to get done."

"What kinds of things?" John asked, sipping the stale water.

"They ranged from simple things to really important things. For example, stores no longer had a full complement of employees and quickly began to falter, but the looting soon shut them down anyway. Now, months later, the economy hasn't recovered. It's very hard to get anything, including essentials.

"John, there are two very important rules people try to follow closely these days. First, don't miss your food day. Food days are important, and I'm missing mine today to have this conversation with you. No worries, I should be okay until next week. Second, and most important, don't be outside after dark. Being out during daylight hours is bad enough, but night holds increased potential for danger."

John interrupted, knowing he had already broken rule number two. "What about the second rule? What happens if you break that rule?"

"It's really meant to be a safety thing," Nathan replied. "There are bad elements around all the time, day or night, but they really become active under the cover of darkness. The police or guards, whatever you want to call them, have standing orders to shoot anyone out after nightfall. They even have swarms of drones to enforce the second rule. Rumors say many of these drones are armed and can carry missiles and bombs."

John recalled hearing the unusual sound overhead as he trekked through Indian Forest. Now he knew the insect-like hums must have been drones. He also felt fortunate because they failed to detect his presence. If they had discovered him, he might not be having a conversation with Nathan.

John also remembered hiding behind the bushes at his neighbor's house, contemplating whether to show himself to the forces rolling down the street. He now realized, had he done that, he probably would have been shot and killed. He had been in the new world for less than a day and had already broken the most important rule and caused his friend to break the second most important rule. *Not a good track record, John.*

Nathan continued, "Christians in city, county, state and federal governments disappeared, leaving key operations unmanned. Lawmakers were almost useless anyway, but after the Rapture, their power collapsed. When the government fell apart, the services they offered dropped to the wayside. The food days and policing are carried out by the remnants of national leadership, the 'they' we talked about earlier.

"Five months after the Rapture, I'm thankful to be getting food. A lot of people are starving to death.

John, people eventually started eating dogs, cats or any other pets they may have had. I've even heard a rumor that people will eventually be marked somehow to facilitate them getting food and other things they need. Maybe they would be chipped, tattooed or something. I don't know for sure. If a person doesn't have this identification, they're gonna be out of luck."

John remembered the dog he had encountered at the edge of Indian Forest. It was one of the fortunate ones to still be alive, if it was still alive. John couldn't imagine someone eating their family pet to endure, but apparently, the act was widespread.

"Sometimes," Nathan said, "folks can get other needs like lumber, rationed gasoline, clothing or other elements they need to survive. It's very rare that those extras are available, and they don't last long at all. Honestly, the world has turned us all into scroungers and thieves.

"I've about used up all the gasoline I had stored before the Rapture and don't know if I can get more. I've had to chop down my beautiful oak tree, just to have wood to cook what little food I eat.

"A few days after the Rapture," Nathan went on, "power grids all over began to fail. Over the last five months, the power has snapped back on for minutes at a time, but it has never come back on permanently. Numerous people have died because they depended on electricity for something important or life-sustaining. It didn't take long for hospitals to run out of gas for their generators. Worse yet, there was such a high demand for fuel, many of them couldn't get more.

"Other big things have happened too. At the time of the Rapture, heavy rains inundated much of Europe.

I heard that a dam over there burst because there was no one to adjust the gates for engorged waterways. Hundreds died in the flash flooding from the break.

"A nuclear power plant in France nearly had a meltdown and would have if safeguards hadn't kicked in. All over the world, nuclear power plants entered emergency shutdowns. We worry about the safety of these facilities today. If they were to go critical or something, we wouldn't know until it was too late. As you might remember, one of them isn't too far from here. We live in the shadow of a potential radiological disaster.

"These days, it's hard to get news about anything, and we live in a world of rumors and rumor control. Most news is passed by word of mouth. Cell phones haven't worked in at least four months. Some people have landlines that still work, but that's very rare. John, they tell you what they want you to hear and nothing more."

Nathan was becoming visibly irritated, tremoring as he talked. Suddenly, he stood and walked over to the window and began to cry, trying to hide the waterworks from his friend. John watched in silence as Nathan tried to wipe away tears with shaking hands. Understandably, Nathan appeared to be having a nervous breakdown. John considered his buddy might need some time to cool off. He was, after all, telling a terrifying and heartbreaking story.

John awkwardly called from the couch, "Nate, what's wrong? I mean, you seem like you're okay and getting by, maybe. Should we take a break or something?"

Liz could handle this situation like a professional

counselor. She could offer words of comfort and encouragement that could calm even the most saddened or depressed heart. John, on the other hand, could only tell stupid jokes in hopes of relieving the tension of the moment but not now. Nathan was obviously feeling something that was accumulating as the conversation went on. Perhaps it was just too much for him to think about.

Turning back to face John, tears and all, Nathan said, "There's so much to tell you, and I don't know if I can. I feel like I'm gonna leave out something critical or forget something you may need to know just to survive. I feel overwhelmed with an incredible since of urgency to tell you everything I can think of, but I also feel overwhelmed with the detail I need to provide. John, I'm worried I won't tell you what you need to hear. Look at me. I'm afraid I'm not a good Christian. I haven't yet learned how to fully trust."

Standing, then walking over to face Nathan, John said, "Nate, I'm getting a very vivid picture of what the world is like and what happened to get it to that point. You're doing okay, so don't worry about what you've said or haven't said. I'm seeing and hearing everything I need to."

"Still," Nathan replied as he wiped away tears, "there are probably other people who could tell this story better than I could. If it's okay with you, when we finish talking, I'm going to take you across the street to meet the Holladays. They're a nice couple and have been a blessing to my spiritual growth. I think they, especially JoAnn, can better explain the spiritual side of what has happened in the world."

"I'm okay with that, Nate, but don't think for

a minute you're not helping me understand things because you are. I think you're doing exactly what the Lord wants you to do."

Nathan projected a curious stare toward John. *Did John Reidy just speak as if there is a Lord in Heaven?* Nathan knew he, himself, had changed, but maybe both had undergone a transformation. Spiritually altered or not, they were not the same young men from years ago.

Picking up on his friend's curiosity, John continued, "Nate, this is a journey for me, and I'm still not quite sure where the road will end, but I know I was meant to find you and hear these things you're telling me. I'm changing, Nate. My mind and heart, thanks in part to you, are changing spiritually."

Pausing, choosing his words carefully, John looked his friend in the eyes and asked, "Do you remember all the times I played jokes and tricks on you?"

"Yes, I do."

"Well, it was wrong for me to do those things, and I just want to say I'm sorry. After today, I don't know if I'll ever see you again. If I don't, I want you to know that you've been my best friend, and I should have treated you like a best friend. With the Lord's help, I'm gonna try to be a better person."

Nathan was seeing a side of John he had never witnessed before. His pranking, joking best friend was not the same person standing in front of him. Nathan felt like grabbing the changed man by the shoulders, shaking him and asking, "What have you done with my friend?" There was a pleasant weirdness to John that Nathan was finding difficult to grasp. *Only God can make this kind of transformation in a person,* thought Nathan.

John was now fully aware that everything he was

doing was for a God he had not previously recognized. He now understood everything he had seen, heard and done in the last several hours was divinely purposed. He could no longer deny God but also knew there was even more to the journey, possibly a leap of faith not yet taken.

Nathan, putting his hand out to be shaken, said, "Thanks, John. I needed to hear that, and I feel much better now. I'm also sorry for all the jokes and tricks I've played on you, even though you were much better at it than I was."

The two shook hands, exchanged approving smiles and shared a brief laugh in a broken world. Nothing had ever truly brought them together until that moment. Amid the chaos, divine purpose now joined them together in genuine friendship. With peace of mind and determination, Nathan could continue. They returned to their seats, ready to tell and listen.

"All these things," Nathan explained, "were producing dead bodies like the world had never seen before. It got to the point of having to bury people in mass graves. In fact, and unfortunately, they put one of these mass graves in Indian Forest. Nobody cared about landmarks, parks or national treasures anymore. They needed places to bury a lot of people very quickly. They were bringing loads and loads of dead bodies to rural areas like ours for disposal. These mass graves were springing up all over the world."

John remembered the unusual mound he had traversed. His stomach turned inside as he thought about all the dead people he had crawled over, now knowing only mere inches of soil separated him from the heaps of rotting corpses. Had he known what the structure was, he never would have climbed over it like a child going over a pile of dirt.

"Even worse," Nathan added, "was that many bodies were left right where they were to decompose. There were just too many of them to deal with. The rapidly built mass graves and abandoned bodies has created a foul, morbid stench just about everywhere you go, but sadly, many of us have gotten used to it."

John knew this rancid smell. The odor reminded both of them of the death and destruction that surrounded them. Sadly, like the other survivors, he had also begun to get accustomed to it, not giving the repulsive smell much thought as he trudged through the apocalyptic landscape that was once his peaceful home.

Standing once again, with the sun's warm rays behind him, Nathan said, "About two weeks after the Rapture, things got even worse. Middle Eastern terrorist cells were waiting patiently for the opportunity to hit the United States when it was down. Well, the U.S. was down, and those heathen cowards took advantage. With weakened security on all U.S. borders and ports, terrorists were able to sneak weapons of mass destruction into the country."

John sighed deeply and said, "Oh no."

"Yes, John. Terrorists were able to detonate low-yield tactical nuclear weapons in New York City, Atlanta and Los Angeles. They also tried to set off a weapon in Washington, but thankfully, authorities thwarted that attempt.

"America wasn't the only nation targeted. Another cell managed to detonate a similar weapon in London. The world was already suffering from mass death.

To make matters worse, hundreds of thousands more people perished when those bombs went off, and even more died in the radiation aftermath. I can't even begin to imagine how many souls the brutal and uncaring hand of death ushered into Hell that day. Anyway, it was a crushing blow to already battered nations."

John's mind produced images of people's bodies being instantly vaporized, severely burned under the scorching heat of a nuclear blast or dying slowly in the radiation storm that followed. He felt both sadness and anger, even rage.

"Did they get the guys who did it?" asked John through clenched teeth.

"All I know is that it was one or more of a dozen countries supporting terrorism. But yes, John, and it would be the last great military action our country would take to date. Because of the news blackout, all we know is that the U.S. and Great Britain carpet-bombed one nation's three largest cities and turned them into giant piles of rubble. Honestly, Law of Armed Conflict went out the window. They also located the camps in which the terrorist cells were training and operating, then delivered low-yield tactical nuclear weapons to those areas. The camps were obliterated–wiped off the face of the planet.

"America's counterattack came with a big message that basically said, 'We've still got a powerful military! Don't mess with us!' Don't ask me who made the call to retaliate in such an aggressive way because I don't know."

Feeling a wave of national pride, John stood, punched through the air and yelled, "Yeah, take that!"

"Trust me, John, it's nothing to get excited about.

Several hundred thousand people died very quickly, contributing to the world's growing body crisis. The fact that there are clouds of radiation floating all over the world isn't exactly a comforting thought."

"Yeah, but..." started John before Nathan cut him off.

"They chased the cell that bombed Atlanta to our little town. The terrorists were hunkered down in Bradbury's Auto Supply on Broadway. They even had hostages, people we knew."

Nathan walked back to his chair, grabbed John's arm and urged him to sit back down. John knew his friend was preparing him for something shocking.

"Who were the hostages?"

"John, your father was one of them."

Crossing his arms, falling back into the couch, John said, "No. Please, no. Please tell me they didn't hurt him."

Grabbing John's knee to offer comfort, Nathan sadly said, "The terrorists didn't hurt him. The people chasing the terrorists were the ones who put the hurt on."

"What do you mean?"

This was one part of the story Nathan didn't want to tell. Wasn't it bad enough that the Rapture had left John's father in the world as a nonbeliever? Worse yet, Nathan wasn't aware of any kind of conversion in John's father's beliefs. The reality of the situation that might become very clear to John was that his father may have died as an atheist. If that were the case, death would have carried John's father away into Hell. Nathan couldn't be sure about the spiritual status of John's parents.

Nathan continued, "There were no negotiations. City officials were told to evacuate Broadway, but thankfully, because of everything going on, there weren't that many people around anyway. They brought in an Apache attack helicopter from down south and…"

Burying his face in his hands, knowing he had already seen the resulting destruction on his journey to Nathan's house, John finished his friend's words.

"They obliterated Bradbury's, along with much of the west side of Broadway."

"Yes. Your dad was only in there trying to get a battery for your mom's car and was just in the wrong place at the wrong time."

His father was dead, destroyed by the Rapture aftermath. He knew the implications of his father passing as an atheist, that it would mean his dad was in Hell. Oddly, though, he wasn't feeling sad or angry. There were no tears forthcoming, and he didn't know why. He had about him a sense of peace surrounding the knowledge of his father's death. John lifted his face to Nathan, noting a gleam of hope that his mother could still be around.

"What about my mom?"

"John, your mother was killed by looters shortly after the incident at Bradbury's."

John picked up the Bible sitting next to him on the couch. In cold silence, he opened the book and began flipping through pages, observing Nathan's notes and highlights. Maybe John was hoping to find some comforting words, something that applied to his situation. Maybe God would open his eyes to some hidden truth. Still, his mother and father were dead, and he lacked the appropriate emotional response. He struggled to understand why.

"John, in the months following your disappearance, Liz spent quite a bit of time with your parents. I know Liz wasn't afraid to share her Faith with people, so she may have gotten through to your mom and dad. It may be that, after the Rapture, something clicked, and they thought about everything Liz may have shared with them. It's possible Liz's witness and the Rapture made them realize they needed to accept Jesus into their hearts and lives."

"Knowing my dad, that's hard to imagine."

"If anyone could do it," Nathan replied, "Liz could."

"She didn't win me over to Jesus, but then again, I didn't give her much of a chance."

Nathan smiled and asked, "But, now you're thinking about what she said, aren't you?"

"Yes, very much. She was trying to get through to me, but I brushed her off. Nate, do you know how bad that makes me feel?"

"Look," Nathan said, "you can only control what you do. You don't know if Liz got through to your parents. You just don't know. You do, however, know if she's managed to influence you. Take what you know and what you've seen and heard and run with it."

"Believe me, Nate, I'm thinking about it."

"Let's just hope and pray Liz was able to make a spiritual difference in the lives of your parents, right John?"

"Right," he said thoughtfully, "and we need to keep moving through the story of how the world turned into a nightmare."

Prayer was a new concept for John, but he had

already seen it work in his reluctant adventure. Hope was nothing new, and he had spent a short lifetime "hoping" for things. He could tell Nathan's version of hope was intermingled in a spiritual way with the faith he had in a Savior named Jesus. Like never before, John wanted that kind of hope in his life but didn't know how to get it.

Nathan continued, "The Apache helicopter that destroyed a large part of Broadway was from a military under severe strain. When the Christians left the world, the United States Armed Forces suffered a loss to their manpower. Like other organizations, the sudden disappearance of so many personnel caused a huge void in capability.

"Rumor has it that the Air Force had trouble scrounging up enough airmen to get planes in the air for the counterattack following the nuclear terror attacks. I've heard through the grapevine all the armed services had a national recall, pulling people off leaves and other days off. Supposedly, they also initiated a recall of several discharged soldiers, sailors, airman and even retirees.

"After a few weeks, the remnants of the Department of Defense made a decision to recall most of the forces stationed overseas. Many of these service members left everything behind at their overseas locations to come back to the continental United States. Some even had to leave their families abroad under the care of foreign governments."

"Why would they do that, Nate?"

"Well, after the terror attacks on our major cities, it seemed logical to protect the homeland. If they had come up with a new national motto, it would have included the phrase 'look out for number one.' See, as quickly as they could, they had to get as many members of the military back stateside as possible."

John broke in and asked, "What's the worry?"

"John, even to this day, there are persistent rumors of war with either Russia, China or North Korea–maybe all of them. Even before the Rapture had occurred, the Cold War with Russia had already been renewed. On top of that, an even bigger Cold War had been brewing with China and North Korea. Invasion is a real threat these days."

"So, if the military is so weak, why don't they just go ahead and invade?"

Nathan pointed to a back corner of the den, where John directed his attention to a shotgun standing on its buttstock with the barrel leaning against the wall. John wondered if it was the same weapon Nathan had used to scare off the punks who were beating the living daylights out of him. *Is that what he used to save my life?* Another thought crossed his mind. *What if Nate hadn't owned a gun? Would he have had any luck chasing off the thugs with pots and pans? Probably not.*

Pointing to the gun, Nathan said, "John, would you want to invade a country where gun ownership is so prevalent?"

Turning his head back to Nathan, John replied by saying, "I suppose not."

"The fact that the United States had been the only country in the history of the world to use atomic weapons in declared warfare also served as a deterrent. The counterattack on the terrorists also proved our nation was willing to use such weapons to defend itself.

"I will say, John, the rumors of war include full-scale nuclear war. Mutually assured destruction weighs heavily with all nations, but terrorists don't care about it. The fear of war is very real, and there's nothing we can do about it.

"Still, I think there's something else going on that might explain why our country hasn't been invaded or attacked on a larger scale. I think there are dark forces at work here. I think there are agreements being made by people in control who do not have the nation's best interests in mind."

Nathan stood, removed the Bible from John's lap and then gently and reverently returned the precious book to the shelves. For a moment, he stood beside it with his hand resting on its leather cover as if absorbing its spiritual energy. Still standing, he turned to John with a face drawn in sadness.

"John, I believe whatever entity is running the country right now is doing so with evil motives. This person, or group of persons, or whatever, may be the same one promising to make everything better. I believe someone is making evil, behind-closed-doors deals to protect this country. I've seen what they're trying to do. I listen carefully to conversations going on around me, and I've put two and two together. The nation has been, and is still being, destroyed from within."

John stood to face Nathan and said, "I don't understand what you're saying."

Nathan sighed deeply and began a slow pace from one side of the room to the other. He wasn't sure how to best articulate his thoughts in a way that John would understand. Maybe he should just come out with it.

Stopping to face John, Nathan said, "I work for them."

John, with a confused look, replied, "What do you mean?"

Nathan explained, "In the months following the Rapture, people were losing their homes left and right. The economy pretty much tanked with all the stuff going on. For goodness' sake, national and state parks are full of tents, campers and makeshift shanty towns.

"In the panic of Rapture aftermath, there was a run on banks. People wanted their money close, but unfortunately, their efforts to secure close cash had disastrous financial consequences. Combined with rapid unemployment and social collapse, world order turned into a cascading economic mess. There were so many life insurance claims filed in the first month, the insurance industry even went under. I've got over two grand in a safe in the bedroom, and I'm pretty sure it's useless.

"I can't stress how big of an economic mess most of the world is in right now. Anyway, the school, like so many other learning institutions, was closed, and I needed to work."

John crossed his arms, as if unwilling to hear what Nathan was about to say. Surely nothing could be more disappointing or surprising than what they had already discussed that morning.

"Okay," John said suspiciously but with an approving glance.

Nathan continued, "A couple months ago, I was approached by these people who said they were with rehabilitation teams. They came to me because of two things. First, they knew I was a teacher, and second, they believed I was agnostic. They asked me to teach for them in what they were calling Education Centers."

"Did you agree to do it?" John asked.

"I didn't have a choice, John. It was teaching in their facilities or losing my house."

"So, they pay you?" John asked, putting his arms out to imply house payments were secure.

"No, not exactly. They allow me to live in this house, and they provide other things like transportation and additional food days."

"Wait. It's your house, isn't it?"

"All over, anything not already bought and paid for, they laid claims to as leverage to get people to do their bidding. The Holladays across the street are a retired couple who own their house. They saved all their lives to buy that house. Believe me, though, they're still afraid it'll be taken from them."

With sarcasm, John asked, "Have I fallen asleep and awaken in a Communist country?"

"John, you just don't know what a struggle it is to survive in this world."

Nathan knew his best friend was not fully aware of the current realities. How could John be so oblivious to things that had been going on around him? Could he not see how life on Earth had changed in such drastic ways? He had his suspicions about John but didn't want to ask or jump to conclusions. The important thing was that they were together and talking about the events of the last five months.

"Nate, what does this have to do with evil motives and destruction of the country from within?"

"John, you should hear the things they want me to teach. For starters, they want me to teach that Christianity is at the heart of the world's problems. They want me to teach that the Bible is full of lies.

They want me to teach that the United States can rise above belief in God. They want me to teach that a social government is the only true source of religion."

"Do they know you're a Christian? I mean, obviously they don't. Otherwise, you would have been fired by now."

With a trace of nervousness, Nathan said, "They wouldn't fire me. They would kill me."

Waving Nathan off with a swatting hand, John said, "Come on, Nate. Really?"

Nathan stood in front of John, staring at him with a painfully serious face. Why was this so hard for him to believe? Had he not seen how bad his little part of the world had gotten?

John asked, "You're as serious as a heart attack, aren't you?"

"Why in the world do you think I've kept those videos buried in my back yard all these months? John, people who turned to Jesus after the Rapture are an endangered species. These days, everywhere, Christianity is an underground religion."

"Nate, how can you teach the stuff they want you to teach?"

Pulling John back to the couch, then returning to his own chair, Nathan said, "I don't."

"Aren't you afraid of getting caught?"

"Of course, I am, but there's no way I'm gonna teach that junk. I've worked out ways with my class where we can talk about other things. I witness to them, John. Anything I teach them while these rehabilitation teams are watching, I immediately recant once the team leaves. As far as I know, they think I'm teaching exactly what they want me to teach."

"How do you know your students won't turn you in?"

"I don't."

"Nate, isn't that kind of a big risk to take?"

"John, just living in this world is a risk. I've still got a chance to get people into Heaven by telling them about Jesus, and I'm not gonna let the anti-God goon squad ruin that."

"You just be careful that they don't ruin you, okay?"

"It may cost me dearly someday, but if I can help save a few souls from eternal damnation in the fires of Hell, it's totally worth it."

"I get what you're saying, Nate. I just want you to be careful."

"John, one would think, after seeing the Rapture with their own eyes, people would turn to Christianity–to Jesus. That's just not the case. People were angry and grew even more angry as days went by. A hatred, one greater than the time prior to the Rapture, grew to a boiling point.

"Don't get me wrong, though; the Christian population is growing again. People are turning to Jesus in the Rapture aftermath and storm of destruction that's eating the world alive. But, for the most part, people are still chasing desires of the flesh, choosing to live their lives for themselves and not for God."

As Nathan talked, John thought about his own choices. He thought about how he chose to live his own life but now knew he had to make some critical changes. He wasn't sure how, but he believed, somehow, someone would show him.

Nathan continued, "John, in a split second, Islam became the most practiced religion in the world.

Christianity is growing again, but in this time after the Rapture, I don't think it will overtake Islam to become the dominant world religion again."

John put a hand in the air to signal his friend to stop talking and asked, "What do you mean by 'in this time'?"

"Well, I know you've never read the Bible, which means, of course, you haven't read the book of Revelation."

"That's right, I haven't," John replied.

"If you had read Revelation," Nathan said, "then you would know what it says."

"I get it, Nate. I'm not a scriptural juggernaut. What does this boil down to?"

"John, Revelation says Jesus wins. All of this," he said putting his arms out to the world, "will fade away. All evil and rebellion against God and His Savior Son Jesus will be put down and cast into Hell. There will eventually be a new Heaven and a new Earth, one untouched by sin. Right now, though, over the next several years, the world will see evil and peril like it has never seen before."

In an instant, John knew what he needed to do. Somehow, he had to keep people from experiencing this peril Nathan was talking about, but more so, he had to keep them from going to Hell. He had to help change eternal destinations from Hell to Heaven. As of that moment, he wasn't sure how he was going to accomplish that. He certainly couldn't do it from his current place in time, the ugly aftermath of the Rapture.

Sure, he could find salvation for himself first. That would be the easy part. After securing savior and future passage to Heaven, he could go out into the currently hazardous world as a witness, but he knew he wouldn't last long at all. He imagined himself curled up on the ground, under attack by another group of apocalyptic hoodlums. However, this time would be different. He would try to tell them about Jesus while they beat the life out of him. No, the best option would be to go back to his time, before the Rapture. That's where he would do his work.

In these broken times, John felt he couldn't make a positive difference in eternal lives. He couldn't lead people to Jesus in Nathan's hostile world. Maybe the world he was seeing through a visit into the future was too far gone. He had to get back home–not to a home place but to a home time. He had to tell people about Jesus before that instantaneous moment of the Rapture where the Lord ushered Christians away to Heaven. He had to do all he could to ensure more people found their way to God's presence at the Rapture.

He knew there was a way back, a mode of transportation to his own time. The staff! John needed to get back to his house to invoke the miraculous powers behind the old man's staff. He had to use it to get home and start a new Spirit-led life telling people about Jesus Christ.

However, John couldn't let his newfound desires get ahead of his learning. He sensed there was still more for him to see and hear. Nathan mentioned something about talking to the neighbors. Yes, the fallen world had more to contribute to his spiritual education. He would just hold off mentioning his departure to Nathan, at least, until he had the rest of the story.

Nathan continued, "John, this time is a bad place to be, especially for converted Christians. I never knew the world could hate Christians so much, then and now. About a week after the Rapture, the remnants of leadership in our country wanted to try to get an idea of how many people disappeared and why. I think they already knew why but just wanted to know how many.

"All across the nation, people were mobilized to check on their neighbors. If the neighbors were known Christians and were gone, they marked the house with a large, red C. As you can probably guess, that marking identified the home as Christian. The markings were supposed to help officials get an accurate count on how many people vanished, but they turned into something far more sinister."

John knew where this part of the story was going, having seen several of these specially marked houses. God had just imparted another answer to him. *Amazing,* he thought. He wanted to know what the markings meant, and now he knew without asking. The trust aspect of John's spiritual growth was improving rapidly.

"The C's painted on the houses," Nathan said, "served as markers for people who were already enraged by the sudden departure of Christians. People quickly turned their anger on the former Christian homes. Some were vandalized. Some were looted. Some were shot up with bullets. Some were destroyed or burned to the ground. The attacks on these marked homes proved to be symbolic of the world's hatred for Christians and their love for Jesus.

"To make matters worse, displaced people had made their way into many of these houses, thinking they could take advantage of the Christian departure. Numerous homeless people, ones simply seeking shelter, were killed as collateral damage when haters all over the country began attacking the marked homes."

John lowered his head momentarily, thinking back to the first of such Christian markings he had seen on the homes. His neighbors, the Atchleys, were known Christians. Now, their post-Rapture house displayed the truth of their Faith. They were gone now but to a much better place called Heaven. *What if I had listened to them or allowed them to tell me about this Savior named Jesus? Would I be in this situation?* There was no way to know. John had to concentrate on the now.

Looking out the window to see the sun climbing into the sky, Nathan said, "We've been talking for a while, and I think I've just about told you everything I know, except for those things happening to the physical Earth and in space."

"What's going on there?" John asked.

"Our planet is changing too. Beyond the physical damage we've done to it as human caretakers, this big rock we live on now seems to be fighting back with its own brand of pain. Natural disasters like earthquakes, tornados and hurricanes are increasing in frequency. Since the Rapture, we've been having some very freakish weather. People are dying from these things, and it's contributing to the already maxed out body problem.

"Farms are experiencing drought and pestilence like never before. Unfortunately, because of these problems, our food supply has been severely impacted. In just these first five months, a lot of farms around the world have gone under and have stopped producing, which is one of the reasons why we have organized food days. John, I hate to think about what's gonna happen when that food runs out.

"One of the more ominous things happening is that the sun, on occasion, seems to grow dim like it's losing its light. Of course, there's a news blackout about it and everything else, but people notice and are talking about it. Word of mouth spreads quickly when it's bad news. Anyway, this dimming is having disastrous effects on the planet's climate. Strangely, though, the reflective moonlight coming off the sun last night was incredibly bright–much brighter than I can ever remember."

John smiled, wondering if the moonlight really brightened to allow him easier travel in the darkness and help him avoid dangerous obstacles. Earlier in his journey, he had considered the brightening lunar glow weird, but he was now thinking it was more of a miracle.

Perhaps God was helping him during the stresses of travel. A day ago, he would have called it a coincidence, not giving any thought to what the Lord might be doing in his life. However, he now knew it was God's divine leading and providence.

"Did you see any shooting stars while you were out last night?" Nathan asked.

Lifting his eyebrows, thinking about how odd the question was, John replied, "No, I was more concerned about what was happening down here on the ground."

"I have to say, John, it's amazing you didn't see one. They're so common these days. I overheard something from the goon squad that makes me think they're not just shooting stars or meteorites."

"What's that, Nate?"

"A few weeks ago," Nathan explained, "I heard them talking about satellite disruption and collisions. They were saying a satellite, or something else up there, struck another object, maybe another satellite. Supposedly, that set off a chain reaction of impacts, resulting in a growing cloud of debris around the Earth. Some of this space junk falls out of orbit and resembles shooting stars."

"Could that be why stuff isn't working down here?"

"I guess. I'm not sure. If we had power, we might be able to watch over-the-air TV with an antenna, but I think satellite and cable TV are long gone. I don't even know if anything is still broadcasting. Anyway, they blamed it on the Rapture."

"How's that possible, Nate?"

"Well, it goes back to that Christian caretaker thing we talked about earlier. I guess if there's no engineer or technician to make course corrections or to perform other orbital maintenance, then these stellar collisions could happen. Sometimes, these 'shooting stars' come down in masses, which can look very scary, like the stars falling out of the sky."

John had never seen a shooting star in his entire life. He could only imagine how he would have felt if he had seen these masses of burning space machines dropping out of the sky without knowledge of what they were. Yes, he concluded, seeing them would have been incredibly scary. If the debris did fall earthward last night, he was thankful for not seeing it.

"John, I think to say that the world has been shaken and that nations have changed is a vast understatement. In my wildest dreams, I never would have thought I would be a witness to all of this. If I could go back and change the course of events in my life, I would listen to Liz and seek salvation in Jesus before the Rapture. If I had done that, I wouldn't be here in this nightmare."

"You're not the only one thinking that, Nate."

Nathan walked over to the window, then looked at his wristwatch. Time seemed to have flown by. He realized they had been talking for several hours and that lunchtime was at hand. He didn't want the reunion with his best friend to end because realistically, John was the only old friend he had in a world gone apocalyptic.

Turning to face John and realizing he hadn't yet offered him a meal, Nathan asked, "Would you like something to eat? I probably should have already asked by now."

Incredibly, John wasn't feeling too hungry. He was still in quite a bit of physical pain but not from an empty stomach. Though he had never turned down a meal before, John was feeling guilt for even considering partaking of what little sustenance Nathan had. He faced the decision of declining the offer of his friend's meager food stores or strengthening himself by eating.

"I don't really want to put you out, Nate."

"Don't worry about that; the goon squad gave me a little extra last week. I think it was meant for you anyway."

"Sure, I could eat," John said as he rose from the couch.

"No, you sit down and rest. I'll bring it to you."

How nice, John thought, *that my friend is being so service oriented.* There was a time when Nathan would have said, "You've got two functional legs, so go get it yourself." Those days, and the man who lived them, were gone.

John returned to his seat on the couch while his

friend grabbed the water glass from the floor and said, "I'll be right back. Don't go away."

Within a few minutes, Nathan returned to the den carrying a bowl containing a sizable chunk of bread in his right hand and a refreshed glass of cloudy water in the left. Draped over his left shoulder was a pair of blue jeans and what looked like a yellow button-down shirt. Over the other shoulder was a wet wash rag. He gently handed the bread and water to John and then placed the clothing and rag on the couch next to him.

"You take your time eating that," Nathan said sadly. "Sorry it's just bread and water, but believe it or not, bread is kind of a treat to have these days."

Hoping to make his friend feel better, John said, "Nate, old buddy, this is perfect. Thank you."

"I'm gonna run across the street and see if the Holladays would be willing to talk to you, maybe give you a sneak peek into spiritual things. When you finish eating, use the rag to wipe down a little and then throw those jeans and the shirt on. I think we're about the same size. Anyway, I don't want to scare them when I bring you over, so we've got to get you cleaned up a bit. Is that okay?"

"Sure, Nate, whatever you need."

John watched Nathan spin around and head through the spacious living room to the front door. After his friend disappeared behind a wall, John heard the unlatching of multiple door locks. He counted in his head: *one lock, two locks, three locks, a chain and another chain.* Obviously, Nathan was dead serious about security.

Long ago, in the times of their pre-Rapture friendship, there was only one lock and one chain on the front door. Times had certainly changed. He listened as the door opened and then quickly closed again, followed by the sound of the three locks clacking back into secure mode. John couldn't help but to wonder if anything was ever totally safe in that era.

Curious about where Nathan was going, John quickly set the bread and water on the floor, then sprang up off the couch headed toward the window. He watched Nathan sneak down the front porch steps and cross the walk into the high grass of the front yard.

He was carrying a shotgun like the one propped up in the corner of the den. John quickly glanced behind him and noticed the shotgun still nestled in the corner of the room. Apparently, John concluded, Nathan had other weapons, potentially a prerequisite for survival in those days.

Standing in the radiant sunlight spilling through the window, John watched his friend trek through the yard, wielding the shotgun like a soldier going into battle. His head and eyes moved around constantly, scanning for potential threats, tracking targets with the business end of the weapon. It was so odd seeing Nathan acting like that, cautious and ready to kill to protect his own life.

He stopped at the road, made quick glances left and right, then bolted across the pavement directly into the neighbor's yard. He walked through their equally neglected lawn and headed straight for the front door. Upon arriving at the home's entrance, an older man holding a rifle opened the door to greet Nathan. They exchanged a few short words, then both men disappeared behind the closed door.

With curiosity satisfied, John returned to the couch

to quickly scarf down his friend's meager offerings. The bread, he noticed, was slightly stale, but under the circumstances, old bread was better than nothing. He imagined Nathan was probably used to eating stale, maybe even moldy foods. John wanted to go into the kitchen to check out the pantry, but out of respect for his friend, he didn't.

After finishing off the bread and water, John removed his shirt and then used the wet rag to wipe down his seemingly battle-hardened skin. He started with his forehead, gently wiping around painful wounds. His chest and stomach were covered with ugly bruises, all from the fall down the mound and his encounter with the thugs in Nathan's yard. After scrubbing away the night's dirt and grime from his head, neck and torso, he put on the button-down yellow shirt. He felt refreshed with clean fabric against his skin.

Carefully, he removed his pants and saw the source of the incredible pain he had been feeling in his right knee. The joint was swollen and the skin was black and blue from impact on the tree in Indian Forest. His legs were also battered and bruised from the brutal attack in front of Nathan's house. After seeing the damage on his body, he knew he was fortunate to be alive.

While wiping evidence of the night's journey off his legs, John noticed how dirty and bloody the wet cloth had become. He pulled the rag close to his face and stared at it like a forensic scientist examining for evidence of a crime. He knew the world was a hate-filled and painful mass of lost humanity. He saw evidence of that fact penetrating almost every fiber of the cloth.

Unfolding the dirty rag in his hands, he said, "I guess

this is why I hurt so bad."

John slipped into the fresh jeans and then carefully folded his dirty clothing and placed them on the floor at the end of the couch. He felt somewhat cleaner on the outside. However, inwardly, he knew he was not free of the world's filth. He had a physical cleansing, but he knew he needed a spiritual one as well. Perhaps the Holladays, in the conversation to come, would help him achieve, or at least, point him in the direction of the spiritual cleaning he desperately needed.

CHAPTER 9

The Holladays

Nathan returned to find John sitting quietly on the couch, wearing the crisp, clean blue jeans and button-down yellow shirt. Though the cuts and bruises from his worldly clash were still visible, his skin was much cleaner and not bearing the grunge of his travels. John simply sat there on the couch with his hands resting on his knees like a soldier sitting at attention.

"I'll bet," Nathan said, "you were never this quiet in detention."

"Well," John replied, "you should know since you were there with me."

With all the sarcasm he could muster, Nathan shot back with, "Ouch! Your wit hurts right down to the bone!"

To say that the two had been in detention together was an understatement. Truthfully, and to much expectation, they *lived* in detention as brothers in disorder. In fact, those closest to John and Nathan found it truly amazing that they made it to college, that they didn't somehow make detention a profession. Would they become teachers? "Not a chance," people said. Would they become ditch diggers or roustabouts? "More than likely," the skeptics said.

John and Nathan never even dreamed there was potential for such a bizarre future, much less that they would experience it firsthand. They had meandered blindly through the previous world, not giving a thought to the perils that lay ahead. Ignorance of the truth did not protect them. Tribulation was coming, but they lived nonchalantly outside God's will. Unfortunately, in the aftershock of the Rapture, they now knew.

Walking up to John, Nathan said, "I talked with the Holladays, and they're more than willing to talk with you—especially JoAnn. She's really interested in a conversation with you."

"Great, let's go," John replied.

"Listen, John. These are nice, Christian people, and they've been a huge blessing to me. Please lay off the sarcasm while you're talking with them. Okay?"

"Nate, I'm surprised. You know me better than that."

"Yes, I do. That's why I'm asking. Can you promise me?"

With a smirk, John stood and said, "For you, my friend, anything."

The two walked to the front door where Nathan grabbed a shotgun and began the process for exit into the wild beyond. First, he peeked through the curtain covering the window to the left of the door. All clear. Second, he looked through the peep hole in the door. All clear. Third, he unlatched the three deadbolt locks but left the chains in place. Fourth, he made another look through the peep hole. All clear. Last, he removed the chains and began to open the door.

Watching Nathan grab the shotgun caused anxiety to build in John. The door Nathan was about to open served as a barrier between John and the evil world that wanted to eat him alive. He felt more comfortable within the home's walls, barred windows and locked doors. Out there were very scary, very bad things. However, he also knew the wickedness in the world stood between him and getting back to his home and his time.

John felt guilty for leading his best friend on, for not telling him that his time there was limited. He wanted to tell Nathan of his pending departure but couldn't. When the time came to make that declaration, somehow, he would know.

Nathan paused, reset one of the locks and looked back at John and said, "John, I'm really glad you're here."

It was so heartbreaking. *Does Nate think I'm here to stay? Is he counting on our friendship to carry him through these harsh times?* Not waiting for a response, Nathan quickly returned to opening the door. *Maybe he knows. Maybe he doesn't,* thought John.

Unable to bear the burden of truth any longer, John sought his friend's attention by saying, "Nate?"

Leaving the one lock secure, Nathan turned to face his longtime pal and replied, "Yeah?"

They stood there in awkward silence. John knew he needed to tell him. He had to let his dear friend down. Nathan stood there staring back at him with tired, pitifully sad eyes. Suddenly, a voice rang out in John's head saying, "John, not now."

Sensing his friend was at a loss for words, Nathan

asked, "What is it, John? Everything okay?"

Fidgeting, John replied, "Uh, nothing, Nate. I'll tell you later."

"Sure?"

Obeying the voice in his head, John painfully said, "Really, I'll tell you later."

"Okay."

At that, Nathan turned back to the door with shotgun in hand. He inspected the immediate area through the peephole once more and then released the lock. As he opened the door, John instantly took a couple steps backward, throwing his sleeved arm up to his nose. The smell of death rushed into the home through the open doorway. Maybe John wasn't as used to the stench as he thought. Nathan, not skipping a beat, marched on out of the house onto the porch.

Turning to his friend, Nathan asked, "The smell isn't quite as bad in the house, is it?"

Uncovering his nose, John replied, "No, it's way worse out there."

John slowly walked out onto the porch and pulled the door shut behind him. Nathan reached behind John and secured one of the locks on the door. He then headed down the steps toward the jungle he used to call his front yard.

Noticing only one lock was latched, John asked, "Just one lock? Aren't you worried about somebody breaking in?"

Turning once more to look at his weary and worried friend, Nathan stated, "You gotta go with the times. When I'm not in the house, but in the immediate vicinity, I only set one of the locks. That way, if I need to get back in quickly, I don't have a bunch of locks to get through. With the way things are, you've got to think several steps ahead to stay safe."

John guessed something must have happened to Nathan in the past that caused him to develop such a procedure, but he didn't want to ask for fear of dredging up potentially terrifying memories. Instead, he pictured himself, as earlier that day, chased by bad people and not being able to get into the house fast enough. He pictured the up-to-no-good thugs grabbing him as he frantically tried to open all the locks. *Nate, old buddy, I hope you haven't experienced anything like that,* he thought.

"Gotcha, Nate," he replied.

Leaving the security of Nathan's home, John stepped off the porch and into the cruel world that, just hours before, almost killed him. Seeing it again in person renewed his anxieties. Eventually, he hoped he could make his way out of the surrounding mayhem, but for now, he was painfully part of it. Even in the presence of Nathan, a seasoned survivor carrying a shotgun and packing a pistol tucked in the back of his waist band, John felt little reassurance of his safety. *Keep moving and everything will be okay,* he told himself.

John and Nathan eased into the overgrown yard, both highly alert for potential adversaries. How would they deal with any threats to their safety? Incredibly, Nathan, at least in John's eyes, seemed both cautious and confident. Moving slowly, but with dedicated purpose, the two men made their way across the lawn toward the road.

As they marched through the high yard, John looked over to his right to notice a large spot where the grass had been disturbed and was matted down. With reasonable certainty, he knew it was where his attack occurred earlier that day–where he almost died.

Noticing his friend staring hypnotically, Nathan said, "That's where I rescued you this morning. Keep an eye out, John. You've got to keep looking around for threats. Things can change in an instant, even in broad daylight."

He should have known that but replied, "Sorry, bad memories."

"That's okay, but let's not make any more bad ones. Keep your eyes peeled and keep moving."

The two men approached the edge of the road cautiously. It was a hazardous crossing, as that section of Highpoint was relatively straight in both directions. Out in the middle of the pavement, having no cover or concealment, they would be easily visible to predators.

Nathan stopped just short of the road and gave John a hand signal to drop to a knee. They both scanned the way ahead and noticed Tony Holladay was standing in the doorway of his house with a rifle, ready to jump into a fight if needed. John felt like a character in an urban war movie, only the action in his film was all too real.

Nathan looked left and right down the long stretches of Highpoint Road, motioned for John to follow and said, "All clear. Stay low and follow me."

They scurried across the road like frightened animals seeking refuge on the other side. The movements in broad daylight were stressful for John, and all he could think about was that they would have to repeat them to go back. He considered Nathan had to move with army-like tactics all the places he had to go. *This is no way to live.*

They made their way into and through the

Holladay's overgrown lawn, then hurried up the steps and onto the porch to the open front door. *Almost there!* Safety was near, if such a thing were even possible in an evil world.

Tony said, patting each of them on the back as they came through the door, "Come on in, boys."

After they entered, Tony closed the door and began his own elaborate lockdown procedures. One lock, then another, then another and then a chain. As an added measure of security, Tony also placed a large board across the door via two brackets bolted to the wall on either side of the door frame.

The Holladay home was open in design. They stepped into the living room which adjoined a dining room, separated only by a short wall. There was a hallway to the left that led to what John assumed was a bedroom area, and probably, bathrooms.

The furniture and décor appeared old and maybe antique, possibly furnished as a hobby before the collapse of civilization. The house was surprisingly clean and well kept. Light streamed through bar-covered windows to create a soft glow in the home. John's eyes zoomed in on a large wooden cross hanging on the back wall of the living room. The cross itself had three large nails attached to it and displayed an inscription that read, "Three Nails, One Cross and One Savior."

Tony looked at Nathan and said, "It's good to see you again, brother."

Nathan and Tony leaned their weapons against the wall adjacent to the door and embraced one another in a brotherly hug. They exchanged polite words of welcome and thanks, then noticed John was quietly standing next to the door waiting for acknowledgment.

Embarrassed, Nathan said, "I'm sorry, John. I'm so used to coming over here alone. Tony, this is my friend John, the guy I told you about earlier."

Tony was an older man, about retirement age. He was tall, and his frame was thin about the chest and waist. He, just like Nathan, looked worn and beaten down by the world, yet he seemed cheerful.

Tony put his hand out to John to offer a friendly handshake. John reciprocated and joined hands in what was one of the firmest handshakes he had ever felt. Tony, in an unexpected move, pulled John close and engaged him in a hug as well.

"Welcome, friend," Tony said as he squeezed the stuffing out of John.

Nathan was watching the whole salutation play out, observing with a smile from ear to ear. He and John exchanged understanding grins. In his life, a complete stranger had never before hugged John, and it was an odd but pleasing sensation. Instantly, the two old friends knew they were in the presence of the warmth and Christian love of the Holladay home.

An older lady quietly entered the room from the hallway. Noticing her presence, Nathan eased over to her and hugged her as if she were his sister. Hugs all around seemed to be the theme in the Holladay household, and John figured it had something to do with Christian fellowship. He had never seen people act this way before, demonstrating a love that he thought had to be spiritual and not worldly.

"JoAnn," Nathan said, "it's so good to see you again. As promised, I brought my friend."

"Oh, yes," she said, "I see."

"John, this is JoAnn. She and Tony have been a spiritual blessing to me."

John walked toward JoAnn and extended his hand in greeting. She was shorter, thin in appearance and probably not much younger than her husband. She smiled pleasantly and threw her arms out wide in welcome to John.

Flapping her hands, JoAnn said, "John, you put that hand away. I want a hug."

How odd it feels to be embraced by strangers! Maybe the Holladays don't know I've been an atheist my entire life. Would they be showing such love if they knew me? Surely, they knew. Surely, Nate told them. He remembered how Tony referred to Nathan as "brother" and how he referred to him only as "friend." John was touched that they showed so much love for someone who cared so little for their Faith.

John had to bend slightly to hug his new friend. It was the first time he had hugged a woman since Liz. JoAnn's embrace was soft and gentle, like a mother showing love to her child. She smelled of apples, much like the girlfriend he had lost in another time.

He longed for Liz. He so desperately wanted to talk to her and feel her in his arms again. If he just had a chance to change the way things were between them, he would take it in a heartbeat.

As they released from the bonds of a loving hug, JoAnn said, "I have been looking forward to talking to you, John. I think my witness could help you to understand things a bit better."

Stepping back, John replied, "That would mean a lot to me."

JoAnn looked at her husband and said, "Tony, why

don't you and Nathan have a seat here in the living room, and John and I will go have a talk at the dining table."

"That works for me," Tony replied, smiling ear to ear.

JoAnn gently grabbed John's hand and led him to the dining room table. The two of them sat across from each other with only the corner of the dark mahogany table between them. The old wooden chairs moaned in protest as they took on the weight of the newly introduced friends. It was a familiar sound John had heard from his own wooden, but hardly antique, chairs. He saw an opening for conversation, maybe a little ice breaker to get into the groove of whatever she had to say to him.

"I really like your furniture. It looks antique," John commented.

"It's old furniture, but I don't think it qualifies as antique. Tony and I are retired from the Army. With all the station changes we had to go through, it didn't make sense to buy anything old and risk it being broken in the numerous moves we made."

"You were both in the Army?" John asked.

"Well," she said, "Tony was the one wearing the uniform for a little over 24 years, but I might as well have been wearing one too. When you're the spouse of a military member, you're going through all the highs and lows together. He had numerous deployments and two remote, one-year assignments, none of which included my physical presence. While he was alone halfway around the world at all those places, I was alone back home. It can be a rough life."

John felt humbled to be in the presence of people

who had faithfully served their country. Military service, even if his parents had approved, was not something that interested him. It wasn't that he didn't love his country; he did. Honestly, he didn't love it enough to die for it, something that brought shame to him at that moment.

"Well," John said, "I thank you and your husband for your faithfulness to the country. It's just a shame to see the nation like it is now. From what I've seen and heard, it's pretty bad out there."

With a gloomy face, JoAnn stated, as if a matter of fact, "It's only going to get worse, John. What you see and hear out there right now is a cakewalk compared to the wrath that will be brought down on the world in the next few years."

John leaned back in the chair as if recovering from a punch in the face. She was so specific. How did she know about the future? What did she mean by wrath to "be brought down?" If the conversation was supposed to make him feel better, the opposite was happening.

Reeling from her less than encouraging words, John asked, "What do you mean?"

Smiling and reaching across the corner of the table to gently caress John's hand, she said, "Let's not get ahead of ourselves, John. Do you mind if I ask you a question?"

Leaning toward her again, as if preparing himself for the question to come, John said, "Not at all. Ask away."

"Nathan said you're not a Christian. Is that true?"

John wondered if he should take offense to the query. Several times he had seen his father in arguments with Christians. All the confrontations, as he remembered, started with the same question JoAnn had just asked him. He couldn't remember if his dad was ever offended but figured he probably was. He, the son of an atheist and a self-proclaimed atheist himself, might ought to be offended. However, he felt no animosity toward her for asking. Perhaps it was part of the change taking place in him.

"You get right to the point, don't you?" John asked.

"That, my friend, is one of the things I am known for."

"Does it matter right here, right now, if I'm not a Christian?"

"Yes, John, very much," she said as she patted his hand.

"How so?"

"Well, the things of God will sound like foolishness to the unbeliever."

Thinking about her response, John gazed at a small silver cross JoAnn was wearing on a thin chain around her neck. What she said made perfect sense. In all the years he proclaimed himself an atheist, all the "Christian speak" he had heard sounded like foolishness. Even when Liz talked about it, he knew, deep down, it sounded like silly fables. Of course, he never told her that until he implied it on their last date. Goodness knows, that didn't go over well at all.

"So," she asked again, "are you a Christian?"

Continuing to look at the silver cross, he replied, "I'm not a Christian, but things have happened."

Should he tell her about his seemingly incredible journey? Would she understand? No, he had to keep those things to himself.

"What kinds of things, John?"

"Well," he said, returning his eyes to her face, "let's just say spiritual things have happened. I still don't consider myself a Christian, a believer in God, or whatever. However, I'm on a journey of discovery, and things are being made known to me. It's really quite interesting and very terrifying at the same time."

"Okay, John. Just promise me you'll work on it."

"Believe me; I already am," he said smiling.

His eyes were, again, drawn to the cross she was wearing. He knew it was a symbol for Christians all over the world, one he had spent so many years ignoring. Now, though, it seemed to be calling to him, asking him to come closer.

He also thought about the significance of her wearing the cross. If she were really a Christian, why was she still there? They shouldn't even be able to have the conversation they were having. If she were a Christian, her house should be empty with a large, red C painted near the door.

Noticing how John continued to look upon her necklace, she said, "You're wondering why, as a Christian, I'm still here."

"Actually, yes. I can't help but to notice your cross," he said, pointing to her necklace.

Gently touching the cross, she said, "I was wearing this the day of the Rapture."

John's facial expression turned from one of interest to utter confusion. From the intelligence gathered thus far, he knew she shouldn't be there in the after-Rapture world if she really were a Christian. He could see both seriousness and sadness on JoAnn's face.

"But if you're a Christian, you shouldn't be here. I mean, shouldn't you have been called up to the clouds or something?"

Wishing he could take back what he said, John thought his choice of words might seem irreverent to her, something that would offend her, or worse, her God. The conversation was difficult for him because they had no common ground to build on.

"Before the Rapture, I always thought about how horrible it would be to hear the Lord Jesus say, 'I never knew you,' but on that day, I learned all too well what it was like. John, I was a mind believer and not a heart believer."

"What do you mean?"

"I was a false believer. I thought I was a Christian, but I wasn't. Well, I should say, that is, that I thought, in my own mind, I was a Christian. This may be hard for you to understand, John."

Excited, he said, "Maybe, but I need to hear this. Keep going."

"Before the Rapture, I thought, no, I believed I was a Christian. I didn't become a real Christian until after the Rapture. I didn't truly accept Christ until after the Rapture. Tony and I were in the same boat. He thought he was a Christian too, but as you can see, we're both still here."

John looked to his left, toward Tony and Nathan who were sitting in the living room. The two men were facing each other, holding hands, with their heads down in what John assumed was prayer. Tony was speaking, but John couldn't hear the words. He silently wondered what the two Christians were praying about but suspected he was the subject of their calls to God.

JoAnn continued, "John, if you had known me before the Rapture, you wouldn't have called me a

Christian. If I had truly known myself, I wouldn't have called myself a Christian. By the fruits of my life, you would have seen that I lived a life separated from God."

JoAnn paused, and John asked, "How do you figure?"

"Honestly, I wasn't living a life that was glorifying to God. I wasn't living like someone who had been saved by the shed blood of Jesus Christ on the cross. I may have thought I was saved, but the way I lived my life proved otherwise.

"There's no such thing as an unrepentant Christian. As I've so painfully discovered, a person can't live a life of willful sin against God and expect true salvation."

John held up his hand to interrupt and asked, "But, isn't salvation more about what Jesus did than what you did? I mean, I'm just guessing here, but that's what I gather from my limited experience."

"Yes, John, salvation is all about what Jesus did for us on the cross. There's not one thing we can do on our own to earn a place in Heaven. If there were, then there would have been no reason for the Father to send His Son to die on the cross for the sins of the world."

"Okay," John interrupted again, "but if you believed Jesus was your Savior, then why are you still here?"

"Again, I was a mind believer and not a heart believer. My mind said I knew Jesus, so I thought that saved me. However, the truth was not in my heart. Deep down, in my heart, I didn't really believe."

"But, how do you know?"

"By the evidence of my life."

John sat back and crossed his arms, indicating his confusion. He tilted his wrinkled forehead to the side and turned his lips down in an awkward frown, as if pouting. JoAnn could almost see the gears turning in his head as he attempted to calculate the reason behind what she had just said.

"I may look confused," proclaimed John, "but believe me, I'm trying to figure things out. Nate says I'm slow sometimes, and I guess he could be right."

JoAnn smiled in acknowledgment, then said, "Real salvation changes you, John. Yes, it's all about what Jesus did on the cross for us, but there should be change following the acceptance of Christ as Savior. Looking back, there was no change in my life.

"I read my Bible but had no interest in studying it. To be honest, the only time I picked it up was when we went to church. Other than that, it just sat on a shelf collecting dust. Of course, when people saw it in my house, it made me look religious, but I was only vaguely familiar with its contents.

"I went to church but only on Sunday mornings. I've discovered my attendance was out of what I perceived to be necessity. I felt I needed to be at church because God wanted me there, not because *I* wanted to be there. Even then, Tony and I laid out of church quite often to attend some stupid sporting event or to watch the races. Where were our priorities?

"I made no effort to tell people about Jesus, to spread His Gospel Truth. It always seemed to me that telling people about Jesus was the preacher's job, but had I understood His Holy Word, I would have seen it was the responsibility of every believer. But there sits the problem; I wasn't a true believer.

"Do you hear what I'm saying, John? I didn't want to study the Bible. I went to church because I thought I needed to, not because I wanted to. Even though the Bible told me I needed to, I felt spreading the Gospel just wasn't my job.

"Getting to Heaven isn't about what I do. I know that now. If you had seen me, John, you would have seen a woman living her life on extra credit. I did things because I thought it gained me merit toward getting into Heaven. I made donations to charity, and I volunteered my time to all kinds of organizations. Stuff like that means nothing toward getting into Heaven. Yes, it's about what Jesus did and not about what I've done or will do. But, John, I should have done those things anyway, not because I *wanted* salvation but because I *had* salvation."

JoAnn seemed to be on a roll, so John didn't want to interrupt her. He nodded in understanding of the critical things she was telling him. His ears were locked onto every word she spoke—words welling up from deep within her soul.

She was beginning to get emotional about the story she was telling. A passion for Christ was coming out in her, displaying in the way she talked through the highs and lows of her story. She was witnessing her salvation story to him; something, in all his ungodly life, he had never allowed anyone else to do. John very much needed and wanted to hear what she was saying.

JoAnn continued, "I did bad things, John. I lived a life outside of God's will. I kept doing those things with no conviction, or guilt, that what I was doing was wrong and ungodly. I willfully sinned. I sinned and didn't see or feel anything wrong with it. My life demonstrated that I had not been renewed or transformed by the Spirit.

"If I had really found salvation and accepted the Work of Jesus on the cross, I would have felt the Holy

Spirit convicting me every time I did something outside the will of God. The Spirit would have shown me those things were wrong and that I needed to walk away from them. There was no conviction or guilt because there was no Holy Spirit. There was no Holy Spirit because there was no true salvation in Christ."

Forgetting his decision to not interrupt, John said, "Pardon me, but you really don't seem like a bad person. I mean, you're not a murderer or anything, at least, as far as I know."

John had created a moment of awkwardness for himself in the conversation. He suddenly realized living in an evil world might involve killing to survive. What if JoAnn had killed someone to save her own skin? What if Nathan had killed? What if Tony had killed? He supposed, if he had a gun when the thugs from earlier were attacking, he would have tried to shoot them. He could have easily killed one or more of them. Quickly, experience reminded him that death was a harsh reality in this new world.

Seeing John's concern, JoAnn said, "Don't worry, John. I haven't had to kill anyone, but there have been several close calls. I pray when the situation arises where I may have to defend myself, the Lord would help me do the right thing. With the way things are, it's inevitable that I may have to take a life to save my own."

At the conclusion of her last words, the sound of an explosion and the percussion of automatic gunfire rang off in the distance. Frightened, John grabbed the sides of his seat and held on for dear life. He glanced at Nathan and Tony, both unaffected by the sounds, seated quietly and reading through what looked like a Bible. He turned back to JoAnn who sat silently, smiling at him.

Still smiling, she said, "See what I mean? That could have very well been next door or right here in this house. It's a cutthroat, evil world we live in."

Releasing his death grip on the chair, he replied, "I do see. I didn't mean to imply that you were a murderer or anything. I guess I was just using the example to show that you're really not a bad person."

"Bad in whose eyes, John?" JoAnn asked.

"What do you mean? That's how I see it. My eyes, I guess."

Reaching for John's hand again, she said, "Who has the key to the moral standard, John? You? Me? The created beings, we mere humans? Think about it. Each person has their own standard of what is and what is not moral. Different clusters of society have their own standard of what is and is not moral. How can everybody be right? There is only one true moral standard, and it is God's. By the way, this moral standard is in the Bible that I ignored for so many years.

"Each of us sins and falls short of the Lord's Glory. Because of the fall of man way back in Genesis, all are born into sin. Fortunately, there is a sin solution, and His name is Jesus. You probably think you're a good person too, don't you?"

"I like to think I am," said John, nodding his head.

"Tell me, do you think a judge should let a criminal off the hook merely because the criminal says or thinks he is a good person?"

Displaying confusion again, John said, "I suppose not, but I guess it would have to depend on the severity of the crime."

"In God's eyes, sin is sin. God cannot be associated with even the smallest of sins, John. He is holy and righteous. In the same way as the judge must rule against the criminal, so God must rule against the sinner. John, you and I may think we're good people, but in God's eyes, we're a filthy rag."

"So," he asked, "are you saying that I'm doomed to Hell from the get go?"

"You are, and so was I. We're all doomed. But remember, the Lord knows we're sinners, so He provided a sacrificial Lamb to purchase our redemption and our salvation."

"Jesus," John added.

"That's right because we can't redeem ourselves. Jesus came into this world by a miraculous virgin birth. People find that hard to believe because they attempt to put human limits on what an infinite God can do. Do you realize if the Lord wanted to pull this old world through the eye of a needle, then this world would literally go through the eye of a needle?

"Jesus lived a sinless life so that He could be the perfect sacrifice for the sins we commit. See, back in the days of sacrifice, a person couldn't bring an imperfect animal to the Lord to cover their sin. It had to be without blemish. Jesus was sinless, and He was the only person who ever stepped foot on the earth who was.

"He died on the cross and took on the full weight of the world's sins. He endured the pain, suffering and humiliation of crucifixion for each of us. He took the punishment we deserve.

"Yes, He died on the cross, but He didn't stay dead. The Lord Jesus was raised to glorious life to show His power over death. Afterward, He walked the earth for a short time and then ascended to Heaven to be with the Father.

"The best part is that He's coming back for those who truly believe. When He comes back, He will finally put down all evil and rebellion forever. It may seem like evil has a grip on the Earth right now, but it won't last. The book of Revelation says Jesus wins."

JoAnn could see that John might be a little confused, perhaps getting in a little over his head. There was so much she wanted to tell him, but she had to keep it as simple as possible for fear of losing his attention. She tried to comfort him.

"John, I don't want to get too deep into doctrine. All you need to know right now is that, in God's eyes, all people are sinners, and they need a Savior, the Lord Jesus Christ."

"I get what you're saying, but it's hard for me to comprehend because I've never attempted to study the Bible. We don't really have a common frame of reference."

"I know, John. That's why witnessing to people is so hard. The unbeliever doesn't understand something that's unfamiliar. Remember what I said earlier?"

"Yes, to the unsaved, the things of God sound like foolishness."

"See," she said smiling and leaning back into the chair, "you're learning already. You're not slow. Nathan doesn't know what he's talking about."

"I'll be honest with you, JoAnn. I feel spiritually stupid."

"But," she said, "you're making an earnest effort to understand, and you're making progress. A passionate flame for Christ always starts with a tiny spark. It's up to you to fan that spark and turn it into a heart on fire for Jesus. It's up to you to grow in Faith.

"Anyway, John, I couldn't see how bad I was until my eyes were opened spiritually. At the church Tony and I attended, for example, folks used to call me the OMG Lady. See, I had this habit of saying 'oh my God' at things that surprised me. I'll admit there was nothing reverent about my saying it, but I said it often and without giving any thought to the fact that I was using the Lord's name in vain, against His commandment not to.

"I never knew people called me that until after the Rapture when a fellow false believer and I had a discussion about why we were still in the world and not taken up to Heaven. Was it wrong of me to use the Lord's name in such an irreverent manner? Absolutely! I guess nobody cared enough about me to tell me it was wrong. Even if they had, I would have argued with them and tried to justify why I was saying it. We cannot justify sin against God. Today, I wouldn't think of uttering such disrespectful use of the Lord's name."

"To me," John remarked, "you don't seem like the same person you're talking about."

"You're right. I'm not the same person. I still sin, but I feel conviction that tells me to get away from ungodly behavior. When the Lord identifies something to me as bad, I stop doing it and walk away from it. That's what a true child of God does. There's more to the story, though."

"Go ahead," John said as he leaned closer and clasped his hands together in his lap.

"I had what I like to call a 'but' relationship with Jesus. I remember one time posting on social media something that said, 'I love Jesus, but I have a potty mouth.'"

Shooting an odd glance at JoAnn, John said, "Okay."

"It's really simple. The words 'I love Jesus' should never be followed by the words 'but' or 'however.' See, if I really loved Jesus, then I wouldn't have had a foul mouth. I would have felt the conviction for the things I said and stopped saying them. Again, I wasn't really saved. Sadly, this was just one of the ungodly things spewing forth from my life.

"I was a social-minded person. I found more acceptance in the laws of society rather than the laws of God. There were, and still are, things society mistakenly says are okay. Unfortunately, up to the point of the Rapture, I went along with many of these things. However, just because the world says it's okay, that doesn't mean God approves. Now, I realize there is no higher law than God's Law.

"Society was trying to mold God into what they wanted Him to be to justify their ungodly lifestyles. We can't do that. We can't mold God into what we want Him to be. It's the other way around. He molds us into what He wants us to be, that is, if we're obedient to Him. Really, all I had to do was open the Bible, submit to God's will and read for understanding, but the world pulled me away from what I needed to be doing."

"I'll bet you're reading it now, though."

"I spend just about every minute I can in God's Word. In the last 5 months, I've read it several times. I'm not just reading it; I'm studying it in context. I'm soaking in every word and asking God to show me what they mean."

"I guess," John said, "it was just another book to me, and I never really cared to read or learn from it."

"That's got to change, John."

"I know."

John's admission of the need for change wasn't merely lip service. He knew he had to make drastic changes in his life, the greatest of which was his lack of belief in God. Everything happening in the last several hours, or days for all he knew, was pushing him in that direction. Sadly, he also knew such a change would have been unlikely without experiencing the unprecedented peril of that evil time and place.

"John, I wish I could go back and change the way I lived, before the Rapture, so that I didn't have to go through all this terror. It really makes me mad sometimes to think about what a fool I was. Deep down, the Devil had me believing Noah's flood wasn't real. Deep down, that old Devil had me believing the story of Jonah and the great fish was just a fable used to teach a lesson. He had me believing the story of Sodom and Gomorrah was just a story to scare people."

Becoming notably upset with rising tension in her voice, JoAnn said, "The truth is God judged Sodom and Gomorrah for their sin by destroying them with fire, wiping them off the face of the planet. He judged Israel and sent them into captivity for their sins. The Israelites are His chosen people, John, and He punished them. So, how can we, as a nation, expect to get away with sin against God? Our time of wrath and punishment is here and will only get worse. I get so mad at myself sometimes for allowing the Devil's deception to give him a foothold in my life!"

JoAnn was nearly growling through clenched teeth. Her frustration and anger were boiling over into the conversation. Tony, noticing her distress, walked over from the couch, placed a gentle hand on her shoulder and asked her if she was okay. She lovingly patted his hand and said she was fine, that she was just mad at herself.

After Tony returned to the couch, John asked, "Have you ever gotten mad at Jesus for not taking you at the Rapture? Do you ever feel anger toward God for leaving you in the world?"

JoAnn instantly calmed and said, "Why would I be angry with the Lord for something I caused? The fact is that God loves the world so much that He gave His one and only Son that we could live in His eternal presence. Why would I get mad at God because I was disobedient to Him? That's the problem. We think it's never our fault. God didn't walk away from me; I walked away from Him. God didn't walk away from the world, but instead, the world walked away from Him. I'm one of the many who broke *His* rules. John, God doesn't want anyone to perish in Hell, but we all make our own choices."

"I guess everyone here after the Rapture made their choices."

"I'm one of them, John, but let me make one thing perfectly clear. I've changed. I've accepted Jesus into my heart. I'm a heart believer now and not a mind believer. I missed the first calling to Heaven at the Rapture, but you better believe I'm gonna hear the next call. Unfortunately, it's going to be a long, terrifying time before the Lord takes me to my Heavenly home."

John knew there had to be signs of the world's future demise. Liz tried to tell him about some of those things before they parted ways. He should have listened! He knew, now anyway, his lack of concern was because the things of God seemed foolish to him, an unbeliever.

However, he still thought of himself as an

unbeliever, so why were these things of God becoming more meaningful to him? Had the Lord somehow opened his hardened heart that he would begin to understand? Yes, John was trying his best to absorb all the things he had seen and heard.

John was now open to hearing about God and His ways, possibly because he had begun to tear down rigid barriers standing between them. *Maybe Jesus has had His hand on the handle of entry to my heart and life this whole time. He's just waiting for an invitation to come in.*

"I need to know more. Were there signs in the world that this time of peril was coming?" John asked, probing for more information.

JoAnn stood and then walked around to the back of her chair, contemplating her next words. Staring away from John, toward the large wooden cross on the wall in the living room, she fingered the little silver cross hanging around her neck. She closed her eyes in prayer for a moment and then turned to face John who was patiently waiting for fulfillment of his request for information.

Leaning against the back of the chair, she said, "Looking back a few years, I should have seen the world had changed. Terrorism and violence were spreading like wildfire. Ignorant people called for the removal of US troops standing between terrorism, communism and a few other 'isms' that I've probably forgotten.

"Political division was at an all-time high, really to the point of making lawmakers useless. Our elected officials went about their little selfish squabbles, all the while, ignoring the problems of the country and the world. Government became ineffective, while honor and integrity among politicians fell to the wayside.

Worse, our leaders were walking away from God, showing false piety and passing one legislation after another that conflicted with His ways."

John had heard this before. Yes, Liz tried to tell him the same thing not too long ago. The big difference between then and the conversation he was currently having with JoAnn was that, now, he was listening and hanging on every word.

Still propped up behind the back of her chair, JoAnn continued, "Natural and unnatural disasters were on the rise and still are to this day. This created increasing levels of destruction in a world we pathetic humans don't own. We're just stewards of God's creation, and we've done such a horrible job taking care of it. Well, it's groaning back at us now, for sure.

"Our great big mass of humanity was walking away from God in ever increasing numbers to seek earthly pleasure for self. The evil in the United States and abroad grew worse every year. From a moral standpoint, the nation was caving in on itself, self-destructing you might say. God's standards for morality were fading away all around the world, but it was exponentially worse in the United States, a nation supposedly under God. All over, especially among false believers, God's grace was traded for and used as an excuse for immoral behavior.

"The downfall of a nation begins with the people walking away from God, and it continues with the people walking away from the nation.

"You know, John, in Revelation, it says, 'Even so, come, Lord Jesus.' That should have been my battle cry. Instead, I and the rest of the unrepentant world went about our sinful ways, caring little or nothing about the truths and warnings in God's Holy Bible."

Returning to sit in the chair, with a deep sigh, JoAnn continued, "The signs were there. Everything began falling apart. National unity faded away with an entire generation that cared little for their nation and even less for God. More and more, it was about what the country could do for them and not what they could do for the country."

John stood and walked to the barred window behind him. He gazed upon Nathan's overgrown yard across the street, concentrating on the disturbed, flattened grass where he had been attacked just hours before. The world was indeed painful, but even before the Rapture, it was revealing itself in the form of a wayward mankind.

John turned back to JoAnn and said, "I see it now. I see it as clear as day. I was blind to the things happening in the world, all of which were warnings of even worse things to come. I was so worried about myself and where my next pleasant feeling would come from that I ignored what was happening all around me."

"You're not the only one, John. We all ignored it. Right now, today, only four kinds of people live in the world. First, we have the unbelievers. They are the ones who refuse to believe, even after the Rapture exposed their folly. We also have those who thought they were good. They're like you and me before we heard the truth. Sadly, some of them continue, even to this day, to believe their so-called goodness will still earn them passage to Heaven. They were wrong before, and they'll be wrong again. Obviously, as you've so painfully learned, we also have multitudes of bad people, godless before and after the Rapture. They are heathens, serving their only commander, Satan. Finally, John, we have people whose spiritual eyes have been opened in the storm after the Rapture, people who have accepted Jesus in faith."

Turning back to the window, John muttered, "She tried to tell me. She tried to keep me from this."

JoAnn left her seat at the table and walked up to John as he looked out the window. Standing behind him, she lightly placed her hands on his shoulders. She was playing the part of a comforting mother.

She said, "You can't fix the past, John. You can only make the best of what comes next. Which of these four kinds of people are you going to be?"

Turning around to face JoAnn, John said, "So much for love in the world. I just don't see it. Maybe I never have."

With a frown, she replied, "John, the world doesn't know real love. The love the world knows is an evil and fleshly love. Spiritual love is different from worldly love. Spiritual love is supernatural and divine. It seeks out God's will, and it comes from the Holy Spirit. Worldly love is physical, emotional and from a tainted human heart and mind. Worldly love seeks to satisfy worldly needs, even at the cost of sin and eternity in Hell. It used to be said that love always wins. No, John, worldly love destroys.

"A person without Christ cannot know true spiritual love. More importantly, the basis for spiritual love is that there is no greater love than the love of the Father in Heaven who gave His Son to die for us."

JoAnn could see John's eyes were tearing up but that he was also fighting it. She knew exactly that feeling. Forces were at work in his heart and mind telling him to ignore what she was saying, to go his own way.

Sniffling, holding back the urge to cry, John asked, "How can you love something you can't see? How can you know it's real?"

She smiled, framed John's cheeks with her hands and said softly, "My dear John, blessed are those who believe but have not seen. When the Holy Spirit resides in you after accepting salvation, you'll feel it. You'll feel the Lord's leading and presence through conviction. Your very life will change right in front of your eyes. The way you see the world will change, and the way the world sees you will also change. It's a feeling like no other in your life."

He was holding back the tears. No, he didn't want to cry again. This time was different. Something was dragging the tears out of him, perhaps pulling them from his very soul. *Is it possible,* John thought, *that the tears might have words attached to them?* Maybe the Spirit JoAnn lovingly mentioned was saying, "What are you waiting for? You need Him. Go to Him."

Suddenly, John's mind was a jumbled mess, thinking about all the things that had happened in the last several hours. The images from his experiences played over and over in his head, always ending with the dream of Liz fading away into the clouds. He couldn't stop the replay, and he began to feel faint, as if part of his life was being drained from him. His eyes blurred, and JoAnn's motherly face began to fade away.

John heard her yell to Tony, "Tony, get in here, please. I think John's about to pass out!"

As JoAnn held him steady, Tony and Nathan came running into the room and strategically placed themselves at each of John's shoulders. John was barely aware of their presence but felt them grab his arms and drag him back to the chair. They were all talking but with faded and muffled voices, indistinguishable to his ears. He could see them moving around, like shapes and figures behind a fogged lens.

Once John was firmly planted in the chair, Nathan slid around to face his distressed friend and then began lightly slapping him on the cheek. Tony and JoAnn held him up in the chair, while Nathan rendered whatever aid he knew how.

"John," Nathan asked frantically, "are you okay? You've got me worried, buddy. Come back."

"Nathan, has he ever done this before?" asked Tony.

"I've never seen him do this before. I don't know what's going on."

JoAnn jumped into the conversation and said, "I think he just needs some time to decompress. I think everything's hitting him all at once. Maybe he's mentally overloaded."

Nathan continued to lightly slap John's cheeks and shake his friend by the shoulders. All of them shouted through John's weariness for his attention. He only mumbled unintelligibly, almost as if in a trance-like state.

"Is he trying to talk to us?" Tony asked.

"No," Nathan suggested without certainty, "I think he's talking to himself."

John's friends were only guessing, but they were right. He was talking to himself, verbally limping through the images flowing through his mind like a torrential river. He was aware of their attempts to bring him back to a state of coherence, but their efforts were futile.

Suddenly, John heard a familiar voice, very clearly, above the calls of Nathan, JoAnn and Tony. The voice of the old man rang in his head like thunder and said, "John, you must go and tell them of the things to come."

John heard the man in white speaking, but as quickly as he boomed in, he was gone. Immediately, the memories playing in his mind went away, and he precisely heard the calls of all three of his friends. Clear vision returned, and John could see Nathan, Tony and JoAnn standing around him with concern on their faces.

They all noticed John's sudden return to cognizance as he scanned each of them with equal concern. All three of them halted their calls, removed supporting hands and then backed away. From their point of view, John seemed to be coming back.

Nathan was the first to speak. "John, are you okay?"

Slightly confused, speaking as if he had just come out of sleep, John replied, "I'm fine."

"Are you sure? You don't look fine."

"Really, I'm okay. Nate, we need to go."

JoAnn placed her hand on John's shoulder and said, "I don't understand, John. We were having such a good conversation. Did I say something to offend you?"

"Not at all, JoAnn. In fact, you've been more helpful than you can know. The things you've said have been and will continue to be a blessing. I can't explain it, but Nathan and I just need to go."

She looked deeply into John's eyes trying to figure out why he so abruptly wanted to end their conversation. She and Tony exchanged sad glances and curious shrugs. On Earth, she would never know the true impact she had on John's life.

"Okay, but do you mind if I pray for you before you go?" she asked.

With full acceptance, and to Nathan's surprise, John said, "That would be great. I'm going to need it."

JoAnn pulled her chair around the corner of the table and seated herself directly in front of John. She gently took hold of his hands, dropped her head and began to speak. Unexperienced with such procedures, John did likewise and began listening to the words she spoke to God. In that moment, John felt a light hand on his right shoulder and then another hand on his left shoulder. He knew it had to be Nathan and Tony putting their hands on him, joining in silent prayer.

JoAnn prayed, "Heavenly Father, thank you for all you do for us. Thank you for each breath of life you breathe into these earthbound bodies. Dear Lord, thank you most of all for the salvation you've given in your Son, that we who believe, shall have everlasting life in your presence."

As she prayed, a warming sensation began to spread throughout John's body. His spine tingled as his nerve endings spiked in sensations he could only call love. JoAnn lightly squeezed his hands as she spoke and emphasized her grip when she mentioned salvation. *I understand,* he thought. He could almost feel a spiritual-like power flowing into him from all his friend's touches.

JoAnn continued, "Lord, I know you've led John into our lives this day. Knowing you have purpose in everything you do, Lord, I pray your perfect will to be done in John's life. I pray, Lord, that you would guide, lead and direct his actions in the days to come. I pray, Dear God, you would bring conviction to John's heart, that he would seek the salvation you offer in your Son Jesus."

John couldn't hold back the tears any longer. Sobbing, his heart ached for the salvation Liz had tried to introduce to him. His heart yearned for the love of God to surround him and make him a better person. Pride, however, welled up from deep inside, preventing him from asking how to achieve such saving grace.

Gripping his hands even harder, JoAnn continued to pray. She spoke softly and reverently, saying, "Lord, you know the thoughts of his mind and the condition of his heart. I pray, Dear God, you would bring to John the knowledge of his sinful nature. Please lead him to ask for your forgiveness, that he would change and walk away from sin. Help him, Lord, to understand the miraculous virgin birth of the Son Jesus. Lord, please help him to understand the Savior's sinless nature, His atoning death on the cross and His life-giving resurrection."

As she spoke in prayer, JoAnn also began to cry. John knew her tears were for him, that she was crying out of love for his lost soul. *Why would anyone care about, no, love me enough to pray for my salvation? How could God love me enough to save my eternal soul? How could Jesus love me enough to die for me?*

Talking through sniffles and drops of love flowing down her cheeks, JoAnn pleaded with God, "Heavenly Father, I pray John would become acutely aware that salvation is of the Son and not of himself. Please, Lord, open his heart to the knowledge that there isn't anything he can do to earn salvation and a place in your Heavenly Realm. Please, Lord, let him come to realize his need of you, that he can be spared the wrath to come. I pray these things in the name of Jesus Christ, Lord and Savior. Amen."

JoAnn and John both raised their heads, released their handholds and wiped away tears. Without any further words, John lifted out of his chair and hugged the woman who had just done the most meaningful thing anyone had ever done for him. Nathan and Tony stood by and exchanged happy smiles. After hugging JoAnn, John turned his embrace to the two men who had laid strong, spiritual hands of support on him during the prayer.

"Come on now, you guys are gonna make me cry too," bellowed Tony in a deep, tough-guy voice.

"Yeah, John," added Nathan, "cut it out."

Jokes aside, Nathan, Tony and JoAnn all knew what had just happened. John was one step closer to finding salvation in a God-man named Jesus. In their hearts, they knew it was just a matter of time before he took the final step toward the Savior.

"John," said JoAnn, shedding her final tears, "Jesus has His hand on the doorknob of your heart, and He's just waiting on an invitation to come in. Don't walk away from Him."

"I won't. You've got my word on that."

John turned to Nathan, planted a firm hand on his shoulder and said, "It's getting late. We need to go, Nate."

"Sure, John, whatever you need to do."

Nathan also questioned why his friend was cutting this most important meeting so short. He could see determination in John's eyes. The man had something on his mind. Maybe he just wanted to get back across the street well before darkness descended on the world.

Considering John's brutal attack had occurred while dark, Nathan knew his friend probably didn't want to risk gang exposure again. That made perfect sense. *But it's just midafternoon,* he thought. However, he understood why John might be a little skittish.

The four of them walked away from the table where JoAnn and John had their critical talk. They meandered across the living room and around the couch to the front door where Tony started his preopening security checks.

Before Tony released the last lock and removed the chain, John turned back to JoAnn with a final question. "Oh, I almost forgot. Earlier, you said something about the wrath to come, about how this is only going to get worse. You were specific about the timeline too, saying that it would be in the next few years. How do you know?"

She pointed to a well-used Bible sitting on the coffee table where Nathan and Tony had been talking. John followed her eyes and finger to the precious book and noted how similar it was to the Bible he had seen at his best friend's house. *Obviously,* he thought, *they're serious about their studies in Scripture. Maybe one day,* he pondered, *I could be just like them.*

Pointing to the Bible, JoAnn proudly stated, "Prophesy, John."

"What do you mean?"

"Bible prophesy, John. Up to this point, most of it has come true. There's only a handful of it that remains unfulfilled, but God will fulfill the remaining ones in the next few years. It's just a matter of time as stated in Daniel and Revelation. Unfortunately, for the lost in the world, disbelief of it isn't going to make it go away. Don't be one of those people, John."

With one final hug from her, John said, "I won't."

Tony checked the peep hole and window one more time before opening the last lock and releasing the security chain. With rifle in hand, he carefully opened the door to allow Nathan, armed with a shotgun, to slip out onto the porch first and take point. John started to follow but again turned to JoAnn in curiosity.

"One last thing, JoAnn. Does the Way, Truth and Life sound familiar to you?"

Smiling, she proclaimed, "Absolutely! In John 14:6, that's how Jesus referred to Himself. Jesus is the Way, the Truth and the Life."

Remembering back to the time he and the man in white first met in the living room, John clearly recalled the old man's, then confusing, words. He had said, "You must warn those who deny the Way, the Truth and the Life."

Everything about the adventure was coming together. The pieces of the puzzle were now starting to fit together perfectly. Questions were answered, and marching orders had already been given, even before John realized exactly what those orders were. He had to go tell people about Jesus before it was too late, before the Rapture passed them over.

The four of them exchanged final goodbyes and parted ways. Just like before, Nathan and John traveled with stealth precision, like soldiers in an urban warzone carefully returning to their headquarters.

As they trudged through the high grass of Nathan's yard, a new burden weighed heavily on John. He knew he had to leave Nathan and felt awful for having to do so. How was he going to tell his best friend their time together was over? As they approached the house, an overwhelming sense of dread as the bearer of bad news swept over him.

CHAPTER 10

The Return

Nathan unlatched the single lock on his door, carefully pushed the door open with the barrel of his shotgun and then slowly entered. After quickly ushering John across the threshold, he closed the door and engaged, once again, a single lock. John watched him with curiosity as he directed the barrel of the shotgun to the rest of the house.

Nathan put a shushing finger to his lips and whispered, "John, stay here. I've got to make sure someone didn't break in while we were out."

John nodded in acknowledgment and watched his hypervigilant best friend move about the house scanning for intruders. He glided silently from room to room with intension to shoot anything or anyone that wasn't supposed to be there.

With sadness, John wondered to himself if a mandatory survival course existed for people of this age. Had his friend been through such training? Regardless, Nathan seemed to know exactly what he needed to do to outlast the terrors of the world. Still,

Nathan shouldn't have to endure. He should be able to enjoy life, but his behavior was light years from enjoyment.

In just over a minute, Nathan returned from his security sweep, set the shotgun in the corner next to the door and finished his lockdown procedures. John moved forward into the room, listening to the clicks and clacks of the locks and the jingle of the chains.

"Why," John asked as he turned to face Nathan, "didn't you secure all the locks before you went searching through the house?"

"Remember what I said earlier about thinking ahead?"

"Sure."

"Well, let's suppose there was someone in the house when we got back. Would you want to mess with all those locks and the chains to get out if you had to?"

"I see what you mean. You're making your escape route a little easier."

"You got it."

As intricate as his security procedures were, they seemed to come naturally to Nathan–normal operations. He had become accustomed to living constantly on guard. *I don't know if I could live like this,* thought John. Remembering how carefree his friend used to be, John felt great sorrow for him. Sadly, still to come, John had to inflict more grief with the news of his exit.

Nathan whizzed past John, headed for the back of the house. John started to put his hand up to get his friend's attention but only managed to watch Nathan disappear behind a wall into the kitchen. He had to tell him now!

From the living room, John hollered for Nathan's attention, "Nate?"

Within seconds, with his face drawn in sorrow, Nathan reappeared. He walked up to face John and said, "I know. You've got to leave."

Somehow, he already knew. *Maybe I'm giving off vibes of imminent departure.* More likely, knowing Nathan's spiritual turn around, he had come to the knowledge prayerfully. Regardless, the news clearly saddened his friend. If an artist needed a model for dejection, Nathan was the perfect example.

"I wanted to tell you earlier, but..."

Interrupting John, Nathan said, "No worries. I know this isn't your time, and I know the Lord has laid an extraordinary task on you. When He tells you to do something, you've got to do it."

"Nate, I really don't know what to say. You've been a better friend to me in these last few hours than you've been the whole time I've known you."

"Well, John, we've both done things in the past we're not proud of, but I think you and I both know Who can fix that."

Nodding in agreement, John replied, "It's not me. That's for sure."

Nathan's downcast expression turned into a broad smile. His friend had learned a valuable lesson and was, quite possibly, on his way to accepting the salvation offered by Jesus Christ. Often, Nathan had wished for the ability to go back in time to tell John about the post-Rapture world. In doing so, he hoped to convince him that the Christians really did know what they were talking about. John's appearance was an answered prayer and a miracle.

John reached out for a handshake and said, "Thanks. Thanks for everything, Nate."

Still smiling, Nathan grabbed John's hand, pulled him into a tight hug and said, "You're much too important to me for just a handshake. I love you, brother."

"I love you too, man. I wish there were something I could do for you. I wish I didn't have to leave you in this mess."

For whatever macho reason the two of them may have had in the past, they had never exchanged the words "I love you." Honestly, they wouldn't have even thought about saying it. However, there in the middle of that evil and tragic world, was the beginning of a brotherly, spiritual love and bonds in Christ that could never be broken.

Stepping back from the hug, Nathan said, "John, I could die today a happy man because I can see you're now going in the direction of Promise."

For a moment, the long-time friends stood facing each other, looking at one another in awkward silence. Each was dreading the next steps. Neither of them wanted to initiate departure, but necessity required it.

Nathan spoke up and asked, "What do you need me to do?"

Raising his eyebrows in embarrassment, John said, "This may sound crazy, but I need you to take me back to my house on Liberty."

Without expressing even a hint of judgement, Nathan replied, "Okay, you've got it, my friend. We do need to get going. It's gonna start getting dark soon."

"Do you have a way of getting me there?"

"Let me worry about that. Just do whatever you

need to do to get ready."

Nathan went back to the door and retrieved the shotgun from its customary place. He then walked past John and disappeared down the short hallway leading to the kitchen and back door. John listened intently to the clacks and pops as Nathan went through his exit procedures at the rear of the house. While Nathan was doing what he needed to do, John had to get ready to go home–so to speak.

John went back into the den where he and his best friend had renewed their lost relationship. He took one last look around the room, walking its perimeter walls until coming to Nathan's Bible on the shelf. Pausing his walkaround, John placed a shaking hand on the worn leather cover of the sacred words of God. He then looked up, closed his eyes and sighed deeply, as if seeking comfort from the Creator in whom he was becoming increasingly familiar. It was time to move on.

John made a beeline to the corner of the couch where his soiled and torn clothing was neatly folded on the floor. Quickly and painfully, he removed Nathan's borrowed jeans and shirt, then replaced them with his own filthy rags. The strikingly vast difference between the borrowed, clean clothing and his own well-used garments was a testament to all he had been through the previous night. Just as he thoughtfully finished folding and placing the lent shirt and pants, Nathan walked into the room.

Surprised, but understanding, Nathan asked, "What? My duds not good enough for you?"

Knowing his friend was joking, John responded, "They're not really my style. But seriously, Nate, I'm not gonna take your clothes. I know how hard things are to come by these days. Besides, my dirt-laden clothes are perfect camouflage against the evil that's waiting for me out there."

Nathan grinned ear to ear and said, "You always were smarter than me, John. I never would have thought of that."

"Well," John replied, "I guess I'm learning."

"Right. Are you ready to go?"

"As ready as I'll ever be."

"Okay then, let's go. Daylight is gonna start fading soon."

Nathan led John out of the den, through the living room and down the short hallway ahead of the kitchen. As John walked by the kitchen on his right, he saw opened cabinets containing sparse supplies of canned foods. The refrigerator door stood open, showing it had no power and no contents. There were piles of empty cans on the counters and floor. Dirty footprints ran back and forth from the kitchen to the back door they were about to use to exit the house.

Looking back to notice John staring at the clutter and bleakness of the kitchen, Nathan said, "Sorry about the mess. It's the cleaning staff's day off."

Unsure how to respond, John said, "Whatever you say."

Nathan halted at the back door leading onto the enclosed porch and motioned for John to step behind him. With shotgun in hand, Nathan began his security check. He looked out the windows to make sure there was nothing or nobody on the porch. He then removed a heavy board placed across the door and then released all but one of three locks. He quickly peeked out the windows again, then unlatched the remaining lock.

Before opening the door, Nathan ordered, "Stay close to me, okay?"

"Sure," John replied.

Nathan opened the door, pulled his friend through, then closed the door behind them. However, this time, he left all the locks released. John assumed Nathan had a good reason for not securing the locks for the door leading back into the house. He saw that the porch was enclosed with boarded up windows and that it had a door with its own locks and crossbar. He knew the porch could be secured, leaving quick, unhindered access to the rest of the house. John was quickly catching on to this security thing.

As Nathan removed the crossbar and began to disengage the locks on the porch door, John looked around to notice a small wood-burning stove in the corner. It was dirty, well-used and had a fire-stained exhaust pipe running through what appeared to be a homemade hole in the roof. A small stack of split wood, which John assumed was from the tree in Nathan's front yard, stood against the back wall.

"Nate," asked John, pointing to the stove, "is that where you cook your meals?"

Without turning back to look, Nathan said, "Yeah, when I have stuff to cook."

John imagined his friend huddled near the stove, heating a small pot of soup. He also imagined him crouching on the floor in the kitchen like a starved man, slurping a rare meal out of a rusty bowl. On the inside, John was shaking the images out of his head, trying not to think about how his friend's fight to survive would continue after he was gone.

With all but one lock unlatched, Nathan lifted a

small leather flap attached to the boarded window adjacent to the door leading off the porch. He scanned the surrounding area for dangers. All clear. He then lifted another leather flap on the porch's rear-facing covered window to examine the back yard for anything or anyone. All clear.

After one final look through the makeshift leather peepholes, Nathan released the bolt of the remaining lock. Carefully, in readiness and deterrence, he opened the door and eased the barrel of the shotgun through the doorway. He then walked down the steps and motioned for John to follow.

Pulling the door shut behind him, John hobbled down the high steps leading off the porch. Nathan quickly returned to the door and secured all three of the deadbolts. For John, it was a bit unnerving to see his friend so alert to protect life and limb. But, at the same time, he was also impressed that his friend had become such an expert in personal security.

Nathan grabbed John by the arm and forcefully moved him across the overgrown, trash-infested yard. *He's throwing his garbage out the back door,* thought John. They made their way to a detached garage standing behind the house. It was a small two-car garage, or shed really, probably original to the home. In days past, John had noticed the structure standing at the end of the driveway but had never actually seen inside it. Of course, he realized this was no time for a tour.

Standing in front of the short, metal-reinforced wooden doors, Nathan handed the shotgun to John and said, "Here, keep an eye on things while I get the door unlocked."

Wow, thought John, *Nate trusts me with our lives.*

Yep, I'm in control now, wielding this shotgun like a pro. His eyes scanned the area for intruders while his hands guided the business end of the weapon. *Yes, sir! I'm in charge of security now!*

After removing two rusty chains and two heavy locks, Nathan reached for the shotgun and sarcastically said, "Okay, soldier, I got it now. Help me open the doors."

Each of them grabbed a door handle, one on the left and the other on the right. Slowly, they pulled the doors outward until they could be secured to two small cleats planted in the ground next to the driveway. Nathan, John noticed, never kept his back turned to any one direction for very long. He was always moving and scanning.

With the doors open, the shed revealed its secrets. The moment wasn't exactly thrilling. John only saw two automobiles covered with tarps, sitting in a ratty old shack collecting dust. He assumed this had to be where Nathan kept his car. However, he didn't recall there ever being a second vehicle among the possessions of his friend. Perhaps he had been holding out on John all these years. *You sly dog! You've got two cars,* he thought.

Walking back over to John after securing the door in place, Nathan, once again, handed the shotgun back to John and said, "Keep watch again while I get this cover off."

John turned away from the shed and assumed watchful attention of the area, probing for danger like a radar searches for planes. Behind him, he heard the crackles and pops of Nathan ripping a tarp off one of the covered vehicles. Wisps of dust from the tarp permeated the air around him, nearly making him choke.

Nathan walked out of the dust-trap garage, retrieved the weapon, then grabbed John's arm to spin him around so that he was facing the newly uncovered vehicle. Upon seeing the secret his friend had just unveiled, John's mouth dropped open in complete surprise.

Before him, in all its automotive glory, was Little Red, his beloved truck. Near stunned, John approached the little truck with the awe and wonder of a child walking up to a beautifully decorated tree on Christmas morning. Little Red had survived all these years and was right in front of him in Nathan's garage.

With cautious eyes scanning the area but occasionally stealing a glance at John as he walked around the truck, Nathan said, "About a year after you disappeared, your parents asked me if I wanted your old truck. I think, in part, it was their way of letting go. I told them I didn't want to own it, but I would watch over it until you came back."

With childlike excitement in his voice, John asked, "Does it still run?"

"Oh yeah, like a champ. I've tried to come out and start it occasionally to keep the engine working and the battery charged. Before the Rapture, I drove it all the time because it made me feel closer to you."

John considered Nathan's emotional statement and saw an opportunity to create some levity. He shot back by saying, "Whatever! You just wanted to drive a spiffy set of wheels!"

"Yeah, that probably had something to do with it too. Anyway, I figured we could use it to get you back to your house, kind of a trip down memory lane, so to speak."

John headed for the driver side door, forgetting their circumstances. He badly wanted to drive the truck again, to feel the power behind all eight cylinders. He wanted to scream down the road like a madman, leaving burnt rubber in his wake.

Before John could open the door, Nathan said, "Hold on, Sport. You've never driven in this mess. I think it would be a good idea for you to ride shotgun this time around."

After calling John "Sport," Nathan wished he could retract his words, like a produce manager recalling a batch of bad apples. Without thinking, he may have inadvertently reminded his friend of Liz and her absence. John only looked up in acknowledgment of Nathan's demand to drive.

Nathan apologized by saying, "I shouldn't have called you that, John. I'm sorry. I didn't mean anything by it."

"I know you didn't, Nate. I would much rather Liz be where she is than here with us. That's very comforting to me. No worries."

"Shortly after you went missing, Liz told me why she called you Sport."

"Really?" replied John with an excited smile.

"She said when she saw you at the airport for the first time, she thought you looked like an athlete. She said that word was the first thing that came to mind during your awkward attempt to hit on her. It stuck. She called you Sport because she liked you from the very beginning."

"I really love her, Nate."

"I know you do," said Nathan smiling.

John slid around the front of the truck, pausing briefly at the hood in remembrance of the wall of rain he had experienced the night before. Looking back, he knew that event, along with all the others, were prepping him for what he was now going through. At that time, he was being softened for a gigantic spiritual storm in a post-Rapture world.

As Nathan stepped to the driver side of Little Red, John walked on around the truck and opened the passenger door. He expected loud squeaking and squealing but heard only the gentle rattle of the door pulling away from the frame. *Incredible,* he thought, *my baby is no longer crying out for attention.*

"The door doesn't squeak!" he exclaimed.

Nathan opened his door, jumped into the truck and said sarcastically, "Yeah, John, there's this great invention out there called oil. It works wonders. You should try it sometime."

As Nathan settled behind the steering wheel, John slid into the passenger seat and flashed a grin of acknowledgment. Nathan placed the shotgun on the passenger side of the cab so that they could use it in an emergency. Before closing the door and starting the truck, he leaned forward and pulled a semiautomatic pistol from his waistband. He then slid the weapon under his right thigh between his leg and the seat.

With concern, John asked, "Do you think we'll need the guns?"

"You never know. I'm gonna try to take the back way and avoid urban areas, but there are evil people out there with working cars and trucks. It's better to be safe than sorry. There's another pistol under your seat, by the way."

Nathan pulled the door to the truck's frame but didn't shut it all the way. Then, he reached behind the steering wheel and turned the key to bring Little Red to life. The engine roared within the confines of the garage, creating a louder than normal echo that listening ears could surely hear several hundred feet away. In the silence of a dead mechanical world, Nathan knew the sound could potentially carry much further, maybe even up to a mile or more.

Quickly, he put the truck in gear and drove it out of the garage, almost immediately lessoning the deafening sound of the engine. Once clear of the building, Nathan jiggled the gear stick to find neutral, set the parking brake and then got out of the truck to close the doors on the garage.

Putting the pistol back in his waistband, Nathan said, "Keep an eye out while I lock up the garage. Okay?"

John slid a hand over to the shotgun and said, "Sure."

As he watched for trouble, John thought about the actions needed to live in his friend's broken world. *Unlock, hurry and then lock up again. Grab a gun, go out, be careful, use the gun if necessary and then come back to do it all over again later. Fight to survive if necessary. Be ready to take a life to save your own. Be ready to die! Kill or be killed!*

Soon, Nathan came back and slipped into the truck. Again, he placed the pistol between his leg and the seat. He pulled the door shut, locked it and then reached across John to lock the other door. Then, for a moment, he sat with his hands resting on the top of the steering wheel, eyes closed, head bowed, mouthing a silent prayer.

After prayer, Nathan clutched the truck, put the shifter in first gear and said, "Here we go. Keep an eye out, John."

Nathan slowly advanced the truck down the driveway past his house on the left. He scanned the surrounding property for bad elements. He knew the Holladays across the street would keep a watchful eye on things, just as he did on the rare occasion they left their own home. Pausing at the end of the driveway, like a hyperalert child crossing the street, Nathan carefully inspected both ends of the road. He looked, looked again and then looked another time for good measure.

There were two options for traveling to John's house on Liberty. First, they could go right out of the driveway, a choice which would get them there quickly but at the risk of going back through town. Second, they could turn left to go the long way around and avoid the dangers of town completely. Even though the latter route was significantly further, it was much safer. The extended drive had no urban areas and was mostly open road with a few sparse residential areas. Nathan knew this meant there were fewer places for bad people to hide or congregate.

With a gentle roar from Little Red's engine, they slowly pulled out of the driveway and headed left. The road was eerily empty and devoid of any kind of traffic. John saw plenty of dead cars and trucks along the way, some just burnt out shells in driveways and yards, but they sat harmlessly where their automotive lives ended.

John looked through the back glass of the truck to see the soft glow of a setting sun. *Maybe we should have waited until tomorrow.* He didn't want to force Nathan to break one of the cardinal rules of survival–don't be out after dark. He didn't want to be responsible for his friend's injury, or worse, his death. It was too late; they were speeding down Highpoint.

Soon after leaving Nathan's place, they drove by the apartments Liz once called home. Half of the Hidden Reserve Apartments were burned to the ground, and the other half appeared to have been trampled and beaten, as if they were byproducts of war. Between the buildings, several ragged people stood around a fire in a barrel, perhaps cooking whatever meal they could scrounge up.

"People still live there, Nate?"

"People live wherever they can get out of the elements, wherever they can find safety," Nathan replied as John watched the ravaged apartment complex fade away behind them.

Remembering he was riding shotgun, John quickly brought his attention back to the road ahead, a straight stretch of pavement with very few houses. However, off in the distance, coming around a curve, was another vehicle. It approached them slowly, as if setting up for an intercept.

John watched as Nathan let up on his own accelerator to reduce their speed and rate of closure. Nathan reached between his leg and the seat, pulled the pistol out and held it in his lap, readying himself for combat. John's mind raced. *Does he suspect something? Does he see something? What's going on?* In a similar action of readiness, but with undertones of nervousness, he placed his shaking hand around the barrel of the shotgun, ready to jump into the fight if needed. John's eyes bounced frantically back and forth between his friend and the potential enemy coming down the road toward them.

As the car approached, Nathan increased his speed. *What's he doing? Maybe the danger has subsided. No, he's still holding the pistol in his lap.* The car was getting closer by the second. It was an older vehicle, well-used and badly damaged but still operational. Nathan moved the truck over to the right edge of the road as much as he could without getting off the asphalt. He gripped the pistol tighter and slightly lifted it off his lap. John's eyes continued to dart between his friend and the swiftly closing beater coming down the road. Terror reigned as he feared the situation was about to get rapidly violent.

Just before reaching Little Red, the driver of the oncoming car also moved to their right, inching as close to the edge of the road as possible. Nathan lowered the pistol back down to his lap but kept it ready until the danger was out of sight behind them. John watched the clunker through the rear facing window until it disappeared down the road.

Calming, John asked, "What was all that about, Nate?"

"Did you see what they did?"

"What do you mean?"

"When we moved over, they moved over. They were just as afraid of us as we were of them. Typically, if they mean harm, they're not gonna move over. Instead, they'll take some kind of action toward you, not away from you."

Once again, John was both impressed and saddened with his friend's survival skills. Nathan could never be the happy-go-lucky person he used to be. The world demanded his constant attention and caution.

Suddenly, John's eyes became very tired, as all the

action of the last several hours was finally starting to impact his ability to remain alert and awake. His head bobbed back and forth, and his movements became sluggish. Noticing John was beginning to fall asleep, Nathan talked to him, hoping to keep him conscious.

"John," Nathan said, snapping his friend back from a doze, "I can't tell you enough how much it's meant to me to be able to see you again. Honestly, when you disappeared and all the searching stopped, I started to think I would never see you again. Even after that old guy appeared, I had doubts.

"I'm not gonna lie and tell you I haven't asked myself where you've been all these years. Maybe I don't want to know. I'm confused. I know there's divine purpose here, and I think you can see that too. I guess the 'why' and 'how' things aren't as important as the 'is' and 'are' things.

"Still, where did you come from? Why am I taking you back to your house? Where are you gonna go from there? Will I ever see you again? As crazy as this sounds, I suspect this isn't your time.

"I should know by now not to question divine purpose, but there's a weak human being in me that still wants to cling to self-trust rather than God-trust. I guess, as long as I'm in this earthly body, I'll tend to want to trust myself more than God. That's not right, and I know it. I guess I should pray for strength, right? Right, John?"

Nathan peeked over to John and noticed he was leaning against the door sleeping. His efforts to keep his friend from slumber had failed. Nathan considered waking him to have another set of eyes on the road. However, if the eyes were groggy and tired, they wouldn't be helpful anyway. Besides, he had already made numerous trips without the benefit of someone riding shotgun. Surely this trip to John's house wouldn't be any different. He knew this reckoning was an attitude of complacency, but he would let him sleep. He needed the snooze time.

John had a peaceful look about him as he slept. Nathan had no way of knowing the dreams running through his friend's mind during the blissful doze. He didn't know John was dreaming of talking to Liz about Jesus, soaking in every bit of information he could get. He couldn't guess John was dreaming about having a conversation with his parents, trying to convince them of their need of Jesus. Sadly, he couldn't imagine John was dreaming about persuading the pre-Rapture, agnostic Nathan that he could know God through His Son Jesus Christ. John would continue to sleep and dream until Little Red pulled up in front of his former home.

Someone was softly calling his name. "John."

John was still sleeping when Nathan pulled up in front of the house on Liberty. He could hear someone attempting to break into his dreams, trying to end his peaceful state of sleep and wonderful visions of friends and family. He grunted at the displeasure of trading a nap for consciousness. *Come on, just five more minutes.*

"John," Nathan said, poking his drowsy passenger in the shoulder, "we're here."

John slowly opened his eyes and peered through Little Red's fogged window to see his house. The last time he saw the long-ago shattered dwelling, it was illuminated only by the moonlight. The sun's rays revealed the true condition of the structure. A plane was still sticking out of the roof, and from the outside, his home looked no better than it did in the dark. Instead, it was much worse. To be honest, the place looked like a shanty in an advanced stage of dilapidation. He never would have willingly lived anywhere like it. Even in the light of the sun, it was still no longer his home.

This place in the middle of a global apocalypse was where his adventure started, and surely, it would end there as well. The time had come to part ways with Nathan, to leave him to survive among the evil remnants of a broken civilization. Oh, what John had gone through to get to his friend, only to painfully leave him now. He was hurting inside but not about to shed a single tear. He knew he would see Nathan again but not in that world.

Without speaking, John unlocked and opened the passenger door, then slid out of the truck with his feet landing firmly on the pavement. He mentally agonized over what he was going to say to Nathan. He searched the recesses of his tired mind for parting words to share with his friend. *Is this gonna get any easier?* he thought. Sadly, he didn't have any big words of encouragement or speeches about hanging in there. He simply stood next to the open truck door in awkward silence, scanning the high grass of his forgotten yard.

"I see," said Nathan, "you've had some work done on the old homestead. The plane really adds to that funhouse vibe you're going for."

John chuckled to himself. He knew Nathan was trying to ease the tension of the moment by using humor to let him know everything was okay. He seemed to be very good at taking painful moments and easing the hurt away, even if it was just a temporary reprieve.

John turned around to face Nathan who was sitting behind the wheel smiling. He replied, "Yeah, it does add to the overall appearance of the house. I'm thinking of getting another one for the front yard."

Nathan winked in acknowledgment, but his smile quickly slid away to reveal the true sadness hiding behind the humor. This was the part of the journey neither one of them wanted to experience. John could see tears forming in Nathan's eyes, ready to give way at any moment to gushing cries of sorrow. His lips trembled, perhaps as a defense mechanism against the tears. John knew he couldn't drag the moment out any longer. He had to break away rapidly, like snatching off a bandage to avoid extended pain.

"Nate, thank you, for everything. Do me a favor, though."

Choking back tears, Nathan asked, "Sure. What favor is that?"

Leaning on the door and side of the truck, John said, "Take care of Little Red for me. More importantly, take care of yourself."

"I can do that, but I need you to do me a favor as well."

"Sure, Nate, anything."

Taking a deep breath, Nathan said, "Please remember everything that's happened. Don't walk away from Jesus. Walk toward Him. Seek His presence in your life while you still can. Okay?"

John extended a hand into the cab of the truck. Nathan quickly received the handshake as John said firmly, "You got it!"

John locked and closed the passenger door, then backed away from the truck. Almost immediately, Nathan revved Little Red's engine and took off down the street without looking back to his friend. If he had taken one last look at John, the situation probably would have become unbearable. Nathan was making a clean break as best as he knew how, looking to the future and not to the past.

For a few seconds, John watched as Nathan drove down Liberty, dragging dead, brown leaves in his wake. The sound of the decaying foliage sliding and crackling on the pavement was almost hypnotic and nearly as loud as the truck. *Enough,* thought John as he about-faced, *it's time to go.*

As he trudged through the high grass of the yard toward the front door of his forgotten home, a gust of wind blew in from ahead. The sudden rush of air caused the overgrowth around him to dance and sway like millions of ballerinas moving in rhythm. The cool squall rushed past his ears, speaking nearly intelligible murmurs.

John stopped halfway through the yard, felt the chilled breeze across his skin and then closed his eyes to concentrate on what seemed like breath sounds. As Little Red's engine faded in the distance, a familiar voice suddenly rode in on the wind that was now circling him like a cyclone.

"John, run!" the man in white firmly ordered.

At that moment, John heard the squealing and screeching of tires on pavement down Liberty where Nathan was now driving. Curious, John tore away from the wind and zipped back to the street to see Little Red's brake lights shining brightly. The truck was stopped in the middle of the road, blocked by a large, black SUV. Smoke from the big vehicle's agitated tires drifted away from the scene like a fluttering ghost.

Looking through the rear glass of the truck, John could see Nathan sitting still with his hands atop of the steering wheel. He didn't move at all, but instead, just stared at the SUV blocking his way. Nathan remained motionless and calm, even when the rear passenger door of the mysterious vehicle opened to reveal a man in a black uniform, armed with an automatic weapon. The equally mysterious masked man quickly jumped out of the SUV to stand in front of Little Red.

"Nate, why aren't you doing anything?" John mumbled to himself.

Was there about to be a fight? Should he run to Nathan's aid? Fight or flight? John didn't know what to do. He was unarmed, but clearly, the aggressors down the street were heavily weaponized.

Then, in another breeze, he clearly heard, "John, run!"

Just then, the man standing outside the SUV raised his automatic rifle and aimed it directly at Nathan who was still sitting quietly in the cab of Little Red. To John's utter horror, the masked man fired a stream of bullets into the windshield in front of Nathan. Clack! Clack! Clack! Clack! Clack! The sound of the rifle reverberated down the street as shards of glass from bullet impacts blasted into the air.

The scene was playing out like a movie. John's best friend was being murdered while he watched helplessly from afar. Nathan's body bounced around in the cab of the truck as the bullets penetrated his soft flesh and shattered bone. The gunman lacked mercy as he continued to fire away, piercing Nathan's delicate skin and entrails with a multitude of life-destroying projectiles.

Nathan was at death's doorstep. Like a coward, John just stood there watching the event from a position of safety down the street. In that moment, sadness and intensifying anger grew within him, seemingly building from the very tip of his toes to the top of his head. He couldn't stand it.

Finally, with dying echoes of gun blasts chiming off in the distance, the shooting stopped. The sound of the death shots faded away, as if their memory lived on to kill again somewhere else. Nathan's lifeless body fell forward and left to rest between the door glass and the steering wheel. *It didn't happen! It's not real! He can't be dead! Nate wasn't just snuffed out of the world like a candle's flame! He can't be gone!*

Running forward, John angrily yelled, "Nate!"

The only response was from the masked gunman. He saw John down the street and brought his weapon's sights directly to bear on him. John stopped in his tracks, nearly skidding on the pavement. *I'm the target now!*

To his surprise, the man wasn't shooting at him. For a moment, John stood there on the dark asphalt, terrified of what was to come. Still, the gunman just stood there with his evil eyes blazing back toward him. He aimed and seemed ready but didn't fire. The shooter lowered his rifle in frustration, feverishly slapping the magazine and lower receiver. *Thank God! He can't shoot!*

Again, the familiar voice rang out all around him like a booming loudspeaker, "Run, John!"

Motivated by the thought of imminent death, John managed to unglue his feet from the pavement of Liberty Street, quickly turn around and run toward the house. He knew it was survival time and that he couldn't possibly win a fight with the assassins who would undoubtedly come after him. As he ran toward the house, he questioned the notion of being safe inside its dilapidated walls. However, he knew he wasn't seeking shelter in that world. Like the gunman, John had a target too; he just had to get to it before the guy with a gun got to him.

As he ran through the high grass, he heard a vehicle door slam shut down the street, followed by squealing tires. John looked back over his left shoulder to see the black SUV whipping around Little Red to get on an intercept course with him. *They're coming! I've got to get to the staff!* He guessed the pursuers, whoever they were, probably didn't want to take him alive. They wanted to kill him as a witness to the heinous murder of his friend. No, there wasn't time to mourn for Nate. *Gotta run faster!*

As John ran up the steps, the SUV roared to a stop in the street less than a hundred feet away. Surely, being that close, they could shoot and not miss. As he ran for dear life, he tried to calculate how long it would take a bullet to travel from the street to his back. He ran across the porch to the front door, trying not to dwell on being shot down like a wild animal. With his heart pounding and lungs choking for air, he flung himself through the partially closed front door, causing it to slam loudly into the wall behind. His momentum carried him across the threshold but caused him to stumble to his hands and knees. *Man, that hurt! Who cares! Just keep moving!*

The masked man jumped out of the SUV, leaving the door open behind him. He zipped through the overgrown lawn headed for the house in pursuit of his prize. The dark soldier was locked in on John, rapidly closing on him like an eagle swooping down on its prey.

Getting closer and closer, John could hear the rattle of his assailant's body-mounted equipment. Even though he had fallen, his legs and arms continued to pump furiously, propelling him into what used to be his living room. The man with the gun was gaining on him every split second. John halted his frantic run in the center of the room, crouching under the plane. He looked around, eyes darting about like those of a madman. *Where did I leave it? Where is it? How could I misplace something so important?*

Just as the masked gunman entered the house behind him, John saw it! It wasn't lost! It was right there in front of him just a few feet away. The staff was resting against the baseboard at the bottom of a rotting wall, near the overturned recliner. *Thank God! It's still there!* The soldier was now just feet away, stretching his arm out, preparing to take John by force.

No, thought John, *he's right behind me! It can't end this way!* He hated the idea of his mission ending with Nathan's murder and his own capture. Would his sentence be death or life imprisonment in this ugly world? Maybe death would be better than an existence in a place growing in evil every day. The staff had gotten him there, so it had to take him away. Surely, he had been a witness to what the Lord wanted him to see. It had to be time to go. What was left for him to do? *Please work!* he hoped. Unlike any other time, his hope wasn't just a mere thought for something better; it was a prayer to the mighty God who brought him there. He was praying and not giving the act a second thought.

John lunged for the staff in a less than graceful dive to the baseboard, barely avoiding the plane protruding through the living room ceiling. His torso landed on the soggy floor, quickly knocking the breath from his overexerted lungs. At the same time, his right hand landed on the middle of the staff and automatically locked around its carved surface. Immediately, his environment changed. Thankfully, the ugly, broken and evil world that had been his home for the last several hours was gone in an instant.

After darting around the plane, John's attacker stood dumbfounded, having just seen his prey disappear right before his eyes. Thinking his target may have just slipped away somehow, the gunman quickly scanned the room, but the search yielded nothing. The witness of his murderous act had simply vanished. He knew the man he was chasing didn't just slip away. He had seen this before, or at least, something similar. Several months back, he was an onlooker to the disappearance of millions of Christians. His worldly mind couldn't begin to understand what had just happened.

Thinking there was nobody to see his true identity, the armed man removed his mask. Little did he realize, God knew every pore of his face, even when covered by the mask. Without fail, the murderer's time would come.

Frustrated with his intended victim's disappearance, he slung his weapon over his shoulder and walked back to the front door. What was he going to tell his comrades; the enemy just disappeared? No, he couldn't tell them that for fear of enforcing the idea that there may be a God after all. Walking out onto the porch, he looked to the waiting SUV, put his palms up and shrugged his shoulders in defiance to what had just happened.

Meanwhile, darkness and cold surrounded John as he floated through an invisible dimension. His ears were tuned into thousands of voices speaking and singing all at once, resembling the percussive flow of a great, rhythmic flood. The voices were different this time; all speaking out in what sounded like acclamations and tributes. He knew he was hearing the prayers and praises of thousands of believers. He hoped Nathan was among them.

A great calm and peace filled John's mind and body as he drifted through the darkness. He listened to the sounds of voices ringing out in unison. His immediate thoughts, though not stressful, were of his friend Nathan, murdered by the evil that penetrated the hearts of man. John wanted the comfort of knowing his friend was in Heaven, the place where he said he would be should death find him.

As John moved through time and space, the voices faded away to silence, and a beautifully soft light began to appear above him. It was just a glimmer at first, but it began to expand across what he could only describe as the sky. As rays of light broke through the blackened firmament, a great wind began to push away darkened clouds hiding the brightness. Storm-like clouds gave way to fluffy white ones which rolled, twisted and flowed across an incredibly clear blue sky. It was the most pristine view of the heavens he had ever seen. It was unmatched by any beauty anywhere on Earth.

The clouds slowly drifted out of the scene to reveal an intense sphere of light, possibly the sun. Suddenly, wings emerged from the outside edges of the bright orb. They flapped gently and seemed to spread across the whole sky. Soon after, a beautifully perfect, pure white dove, backlit by rays of light, flew toward John in a slow-motion glide. The animal's graceful flight captured his complete attention. It maneuvered close to him, but as he reached out, he was unable to touch the angel-like bird. The creature turned and fluttered away to disappear into a white, cotton-like cloud.

As John gazed intently toward the cloud, a light from its fluffy interior flashed with an intensity that forced him to close his eyes in protest. The heat from the light radiated across his body as if he were sunbathing, quickly eating away the chill from the previous darkness. As the penetrating brilliance began to fade away, John slowly reopened his eyes. Standing on the pristine cloud, in a bright white, almost glowing robe, was Nathan.

John studied the vision of his friend with the awe and wonder of a child. Nathan was happily smiling, as though he had finally reached his Forever Home. Gone from his gleaming presence were the worries, struggles and harsh realities of an earthbound life. A look of healthy youth replaced the worn and haggard appearance of Nathan's previous, worldly face.

He was renewed and restored to life, a life unlike anything found on Earth. He stood firmly within the cloud with his hands clasped at his waist, void of movement but full of eternal energy that seemed to radiate outward like heat from the sun. With absolute certainty, John knew Nathan's new and full life was from the Son of God.

John was unable to form words to speak and simply gazed upon his friend, wondering if he would say anything at all. He had assurance of his well-being but still wanted to hear his voice. Finally, Nathan mouthed a single word. "Go," he appeared to say. His word was not audible, but John knew Nathan was pushing him along, telling him to end his incredible journey.

Nathan soon faded away and was replaced by a divine, Heavenly light. *It's so beautiful,* thought John. He dared to guess that maybe he was seeing the Glory of God. *It's true! God is real!* He was certain of it now.

As John began to slip away from the glorious scene, tingling sensations of motion surged throughout his body. Invisible hands, forces he didn't yet completely understand, began to pull him away. He hoped and prayed to be on his way home. *Please, Lord, take me home.*

Once again, he slid through the archives of time. All around him, scenes of life rolled like film, but this time, in reverse. The images became so fast they turned to mere pulses of light that nearly brought about convulsions to his fatigued mind and body. The sounds of so many voices, unlike the chants of acclamation in Glory, invaded his ears, playing in a loud backward garble. *Here we go again! Please, God, take me home!*

A great chill broke out across the tender skin of his already aching body. The kaleidoscope of backward images began to spin around him, and the voices began to fade away. Then, he considered, it wasn't the life images that were spinning; it was him, whirling around like a leaf caught in the wind. He felt as though he were in a funhouse, only he was tumbling out of control and there was no floor to break his fall. *Am I falling?* he asked himself.

His body twisted and turned while his shaking hands tried to grab hold of anything to stabilize his movements. *It's no use!* He could only hope his landing would be on solid ground but softly and not catastrophically violent. There was no sense of direction–up, down, left and right meant nothing. Something or someone was moving him against his will and desire for gentle flight.

Finally, the film-like images began to fade away until darkness surrounded John again. He was still in motion and could now feel and hear the cold rush of air whistling past his ears. He felt like a skydiver falling through the air but without the security of a parachute. *Yeah, I think I'm falling!*

Below him, in the bowels of the blackness, a pinhole of light appeared. He was headed toward the far away beacon, watching it expand outward beneath him. His head and eyes darted about, looking for anything familiar, anything he could claim from memories past. Nothing! The light below grew until it was piercing white, seemingly able to penetrate through skin and bone. Absolutely everything turned bright white, overpowering his vision's ability to adjust. *Here it comes!*

Situational awareness was now impossible. John continued to fall as the intensity of the moment grew. He slipped into unconsciousness as his mind finally gave way to sensory overload. In his near-comatose state, he could hear again the voices of people he knew, now clearer than ever. He very much wanted to acknowledge them but couldn't. He could listen but not talk. As quickly as the voices entered, they faded away–

except for one. Liz was calling his name.

CHAPTER 11

Salvation

"John!" Liz yelled.

Am I hearing things? Am I really hearing her voice? Maybe this is another part of the quest. Maybe this isn't over. He couldn't talk, but he could plainly hear her calling his name. Her sweet voice was soaking into his ears like a love song. *Why don't you answer her?* he thought. *Maybe I'm hearing the voice of an angel. Is Liz an angel? Oh no! That would mean I'm…*

This time, accompanied by a shake to his left shoulder, Liz yelled, "John!"

Wait a minute. Dreams can't touch me. They can't physically move me either. I felt a push, a shove and a hand on my shoulder. This is no dream! John, open your eyes!

He very much wanted to set eyes on her but was afraid of what he would see. His mind was still reeling from his witness of apocalyptic torment. His heart cringed at the idea that he had gone back to that ugly place to discover Liz was there. *No, it can't be! It doesn't work that way. There's no way she's there.*

"John, wake up!"

Something was different this time. Through closed eyelids, John could see the glow of artificial light from a bulb powered by electricity. The smell of a decaying world was notably absent. Best of all, he could feel her hand on his shoulder, though it wasn't the gentle touch he had once known. It was a frantic, scared hand screaming for attention. *Open your eyes, John! Look at her! It's got to be Liz!*

For the first time in what seemed like an eternity, John's eyes fluttered open, fighting against the light from the table lamp directly behind his head. To help his tired eyes adjust, he pulled his hand to his face as a shield to the blinding light. He waited a moment and then slowly removed his hand, allowing for the gradual restoration of his visual acuity.

He looked upward with fragile and blurred eyes and saw his ceiling–his wonderful ceiling, minus an airplane. With drearily tired eyes, he saw his walls, his furniture and his beloved couch, on which he was apparently now resting. Its plump cushions felt so good underneath him. Before his horror-ravaged eyes was his completely intact home. *I'm back! Thank God,* he thought, *the nightmare's over.* However, he had just enough doubt left in his life to think that his journey might not have been real. *Did I experience all those things?*

"John, are you okay?"

Wait, I can smell her! He could smell the perfume Liz was wearing the night they parted ways. He knew she had to be close. Her fragrance replaced the sour odor of death that previously permeated the air. Present now, were just the familiar aromas of his living room and yes, of course, Liz. His olfactory receptors were well pleased and on fire for her.

Dropping his hand to his chest, John slowly rolled his head to the left. There she was, wearing the same beautiful dress she had worn to Grover's Roost the night they broke up. Her pale skin and red hair seemed to glow from the light that radiated from the lamp behind his head. She was on her knees by the couch, leaning toward him, gently rubbing the shoulder she had been shaking moments earlier.

Liz was clearly in a concerned, mother-like state. Lacking was her usual happy face; instead, she exuded a dire, almost frantic, expression of worry. It was so unlike her to be fearful of anything and seeing her like this wasn't pleasant. John's eyes scanned the area around Liz, darting from her to objects in the room, then back to her. He wanted to talk to her but was still unable to formulate words.

She gently caressed his cheek with the backs of her fingers and asked, "John, are you okay?"

John thought how he should talk to her. *Should I speak to her like she's a girlfriend or maybe like we're just friends?* For a moment, he even considered if they had actually parted ways. *Could it be that the entire incident at Grover's was just a figment of my imagination?* The way she touched his cheek led him to believe things between them were still hunky dory.

Sometimes, in the past, with Liz, it was hard to distinguish between mere friendship and romance. John had seen times where she had cried loving tears for people she had never physically met. She expressed love for people who, in John's eyes, weren't deserving of love at all. Now, however, John knew her love for others was a Christian love, an unbreakable bond given by God

Himself.

He looked at her with the confusion of a child and then asked, "Liz? Is it really you?"

She gently took his hand into her own and replied, "Of course, John, who else would I be?"

He scooted up on the couch until he managed to prop himself up on his elbows. Still in a daze, he continued to scan his surroundings in disbelief of where he was and who was with him. Liz continued to show concern for him, having never seen him in such utter confusion. She looked him up and down from head to toe and shook her head.

"What's wrong, Liz?" he asked.

Pulling away from him to stand, she pointedly said, "John, are you serious? I felt so bad about the way things went down tonight and the way we parted, so I called. You didn't answer! I kept calling you, but you never answered, John!"

Okay, so we did break up. Why was she there, though? Perhaps she wanted to try to mend broken fences and get back together. Maybe she was mad at him and wanted to give him a piece of her mind. No, Liz couldn't be mad. She may be concerned but not mad.

"Tonight? Our date, tonight?" asked John, trying to shake the cobwebs out of his head.

"John, you're really scaring me. Of course, tonight. Well, last night anyway. It's just past midnight."

He was confused. Apparently, Liz's time stood still while he warped away to see mankind's awful future. He tried to make sense of everything and wondered if any of it really happened. Slim were the chances he could calm her and make her understand something he didn't quite grasp himself.

"There's no reason to be scared, Liz. I must have left my phone in Little Red or something. I'm sorry."

Like a worried mother confronting a wayward child, she barked, "No reason to be scared? Are you kidding me, John? Have you seen yourself?"

He remembered Nathan asking the same question and rightly so. Afterall, John had been trudging through the forest, climbing graves, walking through destruction and running for his very life. Well, maybe he had done those things. He wasn't sure.

In fact, he hadn't taken the time to look himself over. John painfully pushed himself up to a sitting position. Doing so made his head and knee hurt, but why? He had sustained injury somehow. Yes, he remembered falling down the mound of the mass grave in Indian Forest, and he remembered being beaten. He could feel a multitude of bruises and scratches on tender skin underneath his clothing. After recognizing the sum of all his pains, his eyes were immediately drawn to his dirty and torn jeans. He rubbed the dirt encrusted fabric of his pants and then noticed his shirt was in equally bad shape. *Maybe it was real. I don't think it was just a bad dream.*

"Uh, I don't, uh…" he awkwardly babbled, unable to put his thoughts to words.

"John, what's going on? Have you been rolling around in your back yard or something? First, I can't get in touch with you. Then, I come over here and find you passed out on the couch, looking like you just went ten rounds with a gorilla."

Liz was notably upset and not her usual calm, collected self. John sat there on the couch looking deep into her mesmerizing blue eyes, waiting for some off-the-wall explanation or way to rationalize why he looked the way he did. However, only memories leapt to mind.

Little did John realize that Liz didn't know what was going on and was even more confused than he was. *Was it all real?* He couldn't stop repeating the question in his mind. John's eyes fell upon her beautiful face and the cute, little freckles he loved so much. She was real, very real; she was right there with him.

By his actions, he could see he was hurting her again. He had broken her heart that night (yes, that night) by denying her Faith, and now he was tearing at her heart strings again. Her eyes began to flood with emotion, preparing drops of sadness to rain down her cheeks. No, he couldn't do it to her again!

Then, suddenly, the memories and sheer reality of what he had gone through came crashing in. He remembered the heavy rains, the storm-like weather, the wall of water and the man in white. He recollected the heartbreak of his date with Liz and the dream he had lying there on the couch. He could clearly see her slipping away to the heavens above and feel himself falling into a crevasse in the earth. He recalled so clearly the horrible act of wading in a lake of fire, tormented forever by agonizing pain.

It was all painfully rushing back into his mind. He remembered seeing himself on the baseball field as a kid, a sweet memory but just preparation for a bigger trip through time. He remembered travelling with the man in white, the mysterious old man who forced himself into John's life. He remembered going into the future, that ugly future where he nearly lost his life, where death and evil reigned and where Nathan was murdered. The images were burned into his brain cells like a brand on a cowhide.

John began to shake as chills of fear swept over his body. His own eyes were filling with uncontrollable tears. Trembling, he looked to Liz, hoping for the warm comfort of her Faith. She only stood there crying, cupping her hands over her mouth, unsure what to say.

John, ignoring the pain surging through his body, rolled off the couch onto his knees and immediately threw his arms around her thin waist. As he rested his head just above her stomach, she returned his affection by gently cradling his bruised head in her hands.

Through a torrent of tears and emotional overload, John begged, "I'm sorry, Liz. I am so sorry."

She dropped down to her knees, framed John's face within her hands and said through her own tears, "John, you just don't know how much I love you. I'm hurting and I can see you are too."

"I don't want you to hurt, Liz."

"I know, John."

He moved closer to her and engaged her thin frame in a firm hug, forgetting the tribulations of the last several hours. He was in her arms again, feeling her compassionate warmth and drawing on her spiritual energy. His eyes blurred with the flood of weeping overflowing from the depths of his soul.

As they held each other in a comforting embrace, John's blurred eyes tracked behind Liz to the decorative arch leading into the dining room. He saw something. The tears obscured his vision, but he saw something familiar. Releasing his right hand from their mutual engagement, he frantically wiped the sadness from his draining eyes. Yes, it was there.

John's mouth dropped open in amazement. He couldn't believe what he was seeing. Leaning against the wall, next to the arch, was the very staff the man in white had introduced into his life. Harsh reality flooded in, and he suddenly knew his adventure had been all too real. His experiences weren't just memories embedded with a purpose; they were cold, hard facts of his life.

He had seen exactly what the Lord wanted him to see, a Godless world ahead, struggling to survive in the aftermath of Rapture. He had seen the things to come, the horrible truth of the world that would soon arrive. Now his mission in life was clear–he had to keep people from seeing any of it. He had to win souls to Christ.

With the realization that he had to seek salvation for himself first, he began bawling like a lost child, one desperately seeking the love, comfort and security of his parents. Everything Nathan and JoAnn had preached to him was now bringing life to his lost soul. God was working in his life in ways that were beyond his meager comprehension. John knew now, more than ever, that Jesus Christ was the answer and that he had to find Him.

Squeezing Liz tighter, clinging to her for spiritual nourishment, John choked back tears and pled, "Liz, tell me about Jesus."

Stunned, but thankful, she lifted her tear-blurred eyes skyward and mouthed the words, "Thank you, dear Lord. Thank you."

For most of the night, John and Liz sat at the dining room table under the sparkling glow of its mini chandelier, talking about a Savior named Jesus.

Hours passed as the two gave up the night's sleep to discuss the most important person in the history of the world. Time faded away outside as the hours of darkness retreated, now just a memory, giving way to the morning sun.

John clung to every syllable as Liz told the greatest story in the history of mankind–the life, death, burial and resurrection of Jesus Christ, the Son of God. John listened to every word, permanently committing them to his mind, soaking them in like a dry sponge drawing in water.

Of course, he had questions, and Liz had most of the answers. His thirst for knowledge had never been greater. Even in college, studying for a critical test, his sense of urgency in learning was nothing compared to his heartfelt desire to learn about Jesus right then. Never had Liz's witness to the saving grace of Christ been more critical than it was with John. She knew he was on a journey of discovery, one that had to start with the simple truth.

She carefully discussed the sinless life of the Savior she had known since she was a little girl. Pulling from her knowledge of the Bible, God's Word, she talked about how Jesus knew no sin and lived a completely blameless life. She stressed to John that it was this innocence that allowed Him to be the sacrificial Lamb of God for all mankind. John eagerly acknowledged understanding.

She meticulously covered her Savior's death on the cross for the sins of the world. She gave great detail about the excruciating pain and shame the Savior endured at the hands of a rebellious world born in sin. Liz, with tears in her eyes, helped John explore the significance of the shed blood of the cross, a cleansing flow of blood for those who accept Jesus in heartfelt faith.

She delicately talked John through the eternal, life-giving gift of His resurrection. With praise and acclamation, Liz detailed the glorious resurrection of Christ three days after His placement in the tomb. She expounded on Jesus' predictions of His own death and His glorious return to life. She stressed how Jesus proved who He claimed to be. She imparted to John the critical fact that because Jesus overcame death, He had power over death and could, therefore, raise all who accept Him in faith.

Showing great hope, she talked about the ascension of her Savior Jesus and His promise to remove His Church from the world. She told how He would later return to destroy wickedness and rebellion once and for all. At that time, Liz didn't know John had seen the aftermath of the exit of the Church. She didn't realize John had already seen the post-Church era, as well as the escalating depravity that Jesus would one day crush at the end of the Great Tribulation.

The morning light beamed through the glass of John's home. Looking through the window, he could see Liberty Street was normal again. Homes were intact, lawns were neatly trimmed, and neighbors were walking carefree on their properties. The Atchleys sat on their front porch sipping some morning orange juice. The world, at least John's little part of it, was back to the way he left it.

However, there was a part of it that needed to change. Liz and John had talked all night about Jesus Christ, the Savior, but they knew their discussion wasn't enough. He had to make his change of life's direction more concrete. He had to take the next step, beyond mere knowledge of the salvation offered in Christ.

John's heart now yearned for the Faith Liz had most of her life. His heart ached for true salvation and the Christian life to follow. He could feel the Lord knocking on his heart's door and knew he only needed to let Him in, but how?

Knowing his redemption had to be greater than just familiarity with Jesus or even a secret handshake, John asked Liz, "What do I do now? What do I have to do to be saved?"

She lightly grasped his hands in hers and softly replied, "John, if your heart is really in this, if your heart is true, you need only to pray."

"All I gotta do is pray?"

"Yes, about the things we've discussed. You've got to mean it, John. The Lord knows when your heart isn't in it. He knows when someone is making a false profession."

"I've never been more serious about anything in my entire life."

"Then your time is now, John. Let's pray."

Liz stood and pushed the chair away behind her. She motioned for John to stand, then pushed his chair back as well. As she dropped to her knees on the dining room floor, she pulled John down by the shoulders into a similar kneeling position. For a moment, with heads reverently bowed, they knelt next to each other in awkward silence, perhaps the Devil's last tug on John's life.

Liz grasped John's right hand with her left and

placed her right hand on his left shoulder and said, "It's okay. Go ahead; the Lord is listening."

With heartfelt confidence, John prayed, "Dear Lord, thank you for bringing me to this point. Thank you for the people you've put in my life, especially Liz, the woman I love."

He paused because he could feel the tears forming in his eyes. He could feel the spiritual energy surging around him, waiting for the invitation to enter. Liz gave encouragement and affirmation with a soft squeeze to his shoulder and hand.

"Thank you, Lord, for bringing John into my life," she added.

Fighting tear-soaked words, John continued, "I'm a sinner and always have been. Lord, please forgive me for the sins I've committed against you."

"Yes, Lord, please forgive him," Liz whispered.

"I can't do this on my own," John said, now crying. "I need you in my life to help me fight sin and to be a better person. I need Jesus to be the Lord of my life. I need Him to cleanse me of my sin because I know nothing I can ever do on my own would be good enough in your eyes."

"Yes, Lord, he needs you," Liz added.

"Yes, Lord, I accept your gift of eternal life in Jesus. I believe in my heart Jesus was born of a miraculous virgin birth."

"Yes, Lord," Liz confirmed quietly.

"I believe in my heart Jesus was sinless so that He could be the Sacrificial Lamb to take the punishment I deserve."

"Yes, Lord," whispered Liz.

"I believe in my heart Jesus died that sacrificial death for a sinner like me."

"Yes, Lord," said Liz as she rubbed John's shoulder.

"I believe in my heart Jesus was raised from the dead three days after His death on the cross to prove His power over death."

"Yes, Lord, you did," Liz softly agreed.

"Lord, I believe Jesus ascended to heaven to the right hand of the Father but will one day call me to my Heavenly home," said John as tears rolled down his cheeks.

"Yes, Lord, we'll wait for you," affirmed Liz as John choked back tears to finish.

"Dear Lord, please lead, guide and direct all the days of my life from now on, and help me to be forever pleasing in your sight. It is in the name of Jesus I pray. Amen."

Liz concluded with a firm, "Amen."

In that sacred moment, John felt as if a large weight was lifted off his shoulders—from his very soul. He could feel the spiritual energy surging through his body like a whirlwind, a sensation he had never felt before. An immense calm settled in his mind, body and spirit, causing him to instantly stop crying and peer skyward. He knew life would never be the same again, that his old self was gone, and in him, a new man with a passion for God was born.

As he looked upward, he said, "Thank you. I am so unworthy. Thank you."

Liz, excited for John's transformation, quickly jumped to her feet and pulled him up by the hands until he was standing in front of her. His body was still hurting from his encounter with an evil world, but the pain no longer mattered. Despite his dirty jeans and shirt, she rushed him with a giant hug. He returned the gesture by wrapping his arms around her, squeezing her tightly and showing the love he had always had for her.

"I'm so happy for you, John. I've prayed for this day since I first met you in the airport. I love you so much."

Holding her tightly, he said, "I love you too, Liz. I want to spend the rest of my life with you."

Pushing away from him, she smiled and asked, "Are you proposing to me, Sport?"

Also smiling, John replied, "I guess I am, Liz. I want to go on this new journey with you."

After hopping on her toes with excitement, she nearly tackled John with another hug. Everything she had prayed for was suddenly coming to fruition right there in the moment. All her hopes, dreams and prayers were standing right in front of her in a man she so dearly loved.

Liz was barely able to contain her thankfulness to God. She had prayed all her life for a man who would share her Faith. She had pleaded with God every day for John's salvation and a change in his life. She had hoped and prayed John Reidy would be the man the Lord brought to her for marriage. Without a doubt, she knew God faithfully answered all those prayers. Praise the Lord!

Fourteen months later, John and Liz stood in the concrete and steel bowels of an arena, listening to the chants and praises of Christian worshippers enjoying live praise music. The rhythmic beat of the music reverberated throughout the arena and its skeletal underneath like echoes bouncing around in a deep valley. Liz and John, standing hand in hand, were swaying to the music that seemed to penetrate their very souls.

An enthusiastic young man in a dark blue t-shirt displaying the word "STAFF" in bold yellow letters marched up to John, covered his microphone and verified, "Sir, you'll be up right after this song. Are you ready?"

Calmly, John replied, "You bet."

"Great. When I get the call, I'll escort you to the end of the tunnel. After you're introduced, you'll take the stairs up on stage. From there, you're on your own."

"I'm ready," John confidently said.

"Okay. You've got about two minutes."

As the young man faded away down the tunnel, John turned to face Liz. She was standing there in front of him with glowing red hair, cute freckles, pale skin and all. As always, she wore one of her trademark floral-pattern dresses, something that never grew old for John. She was beautiful inside and out–in John's eyes, absolutely perfect.

As they held hands, Liz asked, "Are you nervous?"

"No," he replied, "the Lord is with me, and I feel energized."

John released her hands and then gently rubbed the sides of Liz's swelled, eight-month-pregnant belly. As he smiled like the soon-to-be proud father he was, Liz placed her hands on his shoulders. Her gold wedding band, glistening like a star on her hand, reflected the fluorescent lights of the arena's staging area. They were literally a match made in Heaven.

"Go make some evangelists, Sport," she directed.

"You've got it," he replied.

As he leaned in to kiss her on the forehead, a familiar voice behind him broke through the music and said, "Okay, that's enough of the public display of affection. You've got work to do."

John turned around to see Nathan standing with his hands on his hips, posing like a father scolding his child. His serious expression cracked into a grin as he put his hand out for John to shake, but he was immediately wrapped up in a hug instead. Nathan and Liz exchanged approving smiles during the embrace.

"Brothers in Christ don't shake hands; they hug. Nate, I'm so glad you're here," said John as he squeezed the stuffing out of his best friend.

Nathan released himself from John's grasp and stepped back to look him over from head to toe. John knew there was a safe bet that Nathan, acting as his self-proclaimed publicist, was about to give him some fashion advice.

"Really, John? You're about to talk to thousands of people, and you're wearing slacks and a polo. Please tell me you've got a jacket out in the truck."

"Nope! The way you see me is the way you get me."

Liz chuckled behind John, knowing the moment was just a humorous exchange between two of the closest friends in the world. Now that both were brothers in Christ, they were even closer, sharing an unbreakable bond in the love of their Savior.

The young stage manager returned and said to John, "Sir, you're on in 30 seconds."

He gave one final hug to Liz and said, "Love you, Liz. To God be the glory."

"To God be the glory," she repeated. "Go get 'em, Sport!"

John right faced to follow the young man into the tunnel and toward the stairs leading up to the stage. Just before he entered the passageway, a familiar face appeared among the many people crowded around the entrance to the tunnel. Standing among the exuberant onlookers was the man in white, obviously unseen by those around him. He smiled John's way and gave him a reassuring nod.

As he walked, John glanced back to Liz and Nathan to see if they had also noticed the mysterious man. There were no indications they saw him. Instead, they both waved to John, and he lovingly waved back. Just before proceeding up the stairs, John glanced back to where the old man was standing, but like times before, he had vanished. John smiled and began ascending the steps, prepared to make evangelists to the world, to fulfill his God-given purpose of winning souls to Christ.

John Reidy was a very happy man. He found salvation in Jesus Christ, married Liz and had a baby on the way. However, inside, his heart ached and was deeply burdened for those in the world who didn't know Christ as their Savior. He hurt for those who denied the Lord Jesus, those who would one day enter the apocalyptic, post-Rapture world looming on the horizon.

If, through his actions, he could win just one soul to Christ, everything he had went through would all be worth it. For just one saved, the aches, injuries and mental battering he had taken as souvenirs of an unrepentant world would be well worth it. For even just one saved person, the countless hours of study in God's Word would be worth it. For just one gain in Heaven, the newfound persecution by those ignorant of his Faith would not only be worth it but would also be a blessing.

However, he couldn't stop with just one, two, ten or even a million. He had to press on, to fight, to win the race, as Paul the Apostle said. In the not-so-distant future, he knew there was a place where both the finish line and start line occupied the same space.

In the not-so-distant future, the physical Christian life on earth would end with the Rapture. Then a new time of unequalled peril and evil would commence for those remaining on Earth. Yes, John's heart hurt for those who wouldn't finish the race, those who would skip over the finish line to the start of a time of awful tribulation never seen before.

John's mission was simple; he had to win souls to Christ. He had to do all he could to prevent the lost from seeing that future world. With tears forming in his eyes, he paused at the top of the stairs and listened to the applause and shouts of thousands ringing in his ears. *Glory to you, God,* he thought. One last time, he looked back to Liz and Nathan.

As Liz waved on beside him, Nathan silently said, "Go," reinforcing John's need to go forth and tell the world–to spread the Good News of Jesus Christ!

EPILOGUE

The Approaching Peril

With two heavy bags of groceries in her arms, Liz struggled through the door of the Reidy home, doing her best not to drop her precious cargo. As she pushed the door closed behind her using her foot, she could see the top of John's head over the back of the recliner. She also saw his Bible spread open across his legs with his right hand resting on its sacred pages. She knew he spent nearly every conscious moment in God's Word, and she admired him for his spiritual zeal.

She started to blurt out greetings to her husband but saw her daughter sleeping in a bassinet set up along side John's chair. She could see John had his left hand resting on the pink-sleeper-covered belly of his snoozing infant. For just a moment, she thought about the peace and tranquility of her child's sleep.

"That is just so adorable," she softly said, hoping not to wake the napping baby.

Liz quietly walked through the decorative arch, through the dining area and into the kitchen where she delicately set the bags on the counter and started to pull out her purchases. Because she didn't want to wake her daughter, she decided to put the refrigerated food away and leave the nonperishable items on the counter.

As she unpacked the provisions, she spoke softly to John. "I talked to the Atchleys on the way in, and they said they were still fine with dinner tomorrow. They sent their hellos and asked if your studies were going okay. I told them you were hard at it. Roaming around the store, I wasn't sure we would have anything to serve them tomorrow. I was starting to think you might have to go to the lake and catch some fish. It's getting harder and harder to find stuff. The store didn't have any chicken, and I'm pretty sure I grabbed the last pack of hamburger. You should have seen the empty shelves, John. I couldn't find a quarter of the things we had on the list. Oh well, I'll try again later."

Once the bags were empty, she turned around and gently placed the sacks on the dining room table. With a giant smile splashed across her face, she headed to the bassinet. She knelt at her daughter's feet and gently touched the baby's puffy, soft cheeks.

"Charlotte Caroline Reidy," she asked quietly, "why is it you never fall asleep for me like you do for your daddy?"

She expected a smart comment from John, giving an answer Charlotte was not yet able to provide. Perhaps he would say, "I've just got the touch." Instead, he remained oddly silent.

Liz rubbed Charlotte's little hands and said, "I can look after her for a bit, if you and Nathan want to hang out. You've been hitting the books quite a bit lately. You could probably use a break."

No response. She noticed John's hand was twitching slightly, and she thought she heard him grunt in displeasure. It wasn't like John to not answer her. As she thought about his silence, she remembered how he normally greeted her with a hardy "Hi, Honey" or how he would immediately jump up and give her a hug and kiss. Most of the time it was all three, but on that particular day, she received nothing.

"John?" she said, trying to get his attention. Still, no response.

She patted his hand and asked, "John, are you okay?" Again, no response.

Liz stood and then walked around the bassinet to the front of John's chair. As she approached, she could see tiny beads of sweat on his forehead and could see his eyes darting about behind their lids. Occasionally, his face would convulse and contort into a most painful expression. Without a doubt, he was sleeping through an unpleasant dream. She wondered if she should wake him or let him go, hoping he would settle into a more restful state. After about a minute of concerned overwatch, she decided to carefully wake him.

Liz rubbed John's right hand as it rested on his Bible and softly called to him. "John? John, can you hear me?"

His eyes popped open almost instantly, and he gulped in a deep breath as if he had been under water. Liz stepped back as John stared at her with one of the most pale, frightened faces she had ever seen on a person. He seemed to be paralyzed with fear.

She rubbed his hand again and asked, "John, are you okay?"

Gazing, as if looking straight through her, he clearly stated, "It was so scary, but I didn't get to see the world at its most evil. I didn't get to see the peril in the world at its peak. I only saw the beginning. To me, that's terrifying. We've got to work harder and faster, Liz. I don't know how much time we have left."

She knelt in front of the recliner and reached forward to caress her husband's moist cheek. With understanding, she replied, "Okay, John. Let's pray."